DEADFALL

Lyndon Stacey is the bestselling author of *Cut Throat*, *Blindfold* and *Deadfall*. She lives in the Blackmore Vale.

Praise for Lyndon Stacey's previous novels:

'Entertaining . . . fast-paced . . . absorbing, enlivened by witty dialogue' *Publishers Weekly*

'Great characters both human and equine. The climax of the story makes it a real page-turner and offers the reader plenty of surprises' *Horse Magazine*

'This horsy English debut clears its fences neatly . . . Wonderful' *Kirkus Reviews*

'Few thrillers have such an arresting opening section as this one' *Amazon.co.uk*

'This highly adroit piece has a more sophisticated level of characterisation than even Dick Francis himself ever attempted . . . stirring and entertaining' *Crime Time*

D0724275

By the same author

Cut Throat
Blindfold

LYNDON STACEY

DEADFALL

arrow books

Published by Arrow Books in 2005

1 3 5 7 9 10 8 6 4 2

First published in the United Kingdom by Hutchinson in 2004

Arrow Books
The Random House Group Limited
20 Vauxhall Bridge Road, London SW1V 2SA

Random House Australia (Pty) Limited
20 Alfred Street, Milsons Point, Sydney
New South Wales 2061, Australia

Random House New Zealand Limited
18 Poland Road, Glenfield
Auckland 10, New Zealand

Random House (Pty) Limited
Endulini, 5a Jubilee Road, Parktown 2193, South Africa

The Random House Group Limited Reg. No. 954009

www.randomhouse.co.uk

A CIP catalogue record for this book is available from the
British Library

Papers used by Random House are natural, recyclable products
made from wood grown in sustainable forests. The
manufacturing processes conform to the environmental
regulations of the country of origin

Typeset by SX Composing DTP, Rayleigh, Essex
Printed and bound in the United Kingdom by
Bookmarque Ltd, Croydon, Surrey

ISBN 0 09 946338 5

This book is dedicated, with thanks, to Maggie, Hettie and Pat, my test readers, for their enthusiastic support.

Acknowledgements

My thanks go to international three-day event rider, Mary King; Emma Johns at the British Greyhound Racing Board; Jo Aitchison at Debretts Peerage; Alison and Brian Shingler at Gants Mill, Bruton, and Richard Harte at Alderholt Mill, Fordingbridge, all of whom have willingly and patiently answered my questions over the past year. Thanks too, to Kim Bevan and Mark Randle of the Wiltshire Police, both of whom were extremely helpful.

And last but not least, I'd like to thank my brother, Peter, for taking the time to set me up with a new computer system at a critical point in the proceedings.

1

If Lincoln Tremayne's reactions had been even a fraction slower the speeding vehicle would have hit his car head on.

There was no warning; just blinding headlights, a dark bulk careering past and a jolting, metal-tearing impact as the side of his car hit the wall.

Braking to a screeching halt, Linc knew he was lucky not to have been killed. The vehicle had come round the corner on the wrong side of the narrow lane, leaving him no option but to run into the brickwork. If it hadn't been for the buttress he might still have made it relatively unscathed but that extra ten inches or so proved decisive. When the Morgan finally came to rest, he was alone in the lane. One headlight was clearly no more, and there was the depressing sound of loose metal vibrating to the pulse of the powerful engine.

Linc swore. Repairs to a Morgan Plus Eight were a specialist job and consequently cost the earth.

He shifted into first gear and straightened the car up. There was nothing to be gained by staying. The maniac in the other vehicle wasn't likely to return – and frankly he'd rather they didn't. It was too dark to inspect the damage to the Morgan or the wall, and they would both have to be settled through his insurance company. Not much hope of the premium coming down next year then.

He wondered briefly where the vehicle had been going to in such a hurry. The lane was merely a loop coming from, and leading back to, the main village street of Farthing St Anne. It wasn't a busy road at any time, and at ten-past eleven on a Friday night he hadn't really expected to meet anything.

Linc remembered the time guiltily. He was on his way to plait up Noddy, his intermediate event horse, ready for an early start the next morning, and he'd told the Hathaways, whose stable he rented, that he'd be over about half-past nine. It wasn't his fault that work commitments had kept him far longer than he'd foreseen, but young Abby Hathaway had offered to help him plait and she was at that tricky age where such relatively unimportant things seemed to matter a lot.

The truth of it was that Abigail had a king-sized crush on him. Linc had discussed it with her mother just a couple of weeks before, and they had agreed that in the absence of adult opposition the fifteen year old would soon grow out of her infatuation and doubtless look back on it with acute embarrassment in due course.

Something on the front of the car was rubbing on the wheel and Linc was glad when he pulled into the Vicarage's driveway. Immediately, thoughts of the damaged sports car were banished. Underneath the welcoming lanterns the double wooden entrance gates were open and swinging in the breeze. On the rare occasions when they *were* left open, they were invariably fastened back. With a frown, Linc edged the Morgan through and into the stableyard beyond.

It was a small, L-shaped yard with five loose boxes, a feedstore and a tackroom bordering concrete and pea-shingle, and shaded by several majestic copper beeches. When Linc drove in the area was in darkness, the only light coming from the open tackroom door. The car lights swept briefly across the wooden half-doors as he swung round to park but the expected motion-sensing security light failed to operate. In that brief moment of illumination, he could see that all three of the stabled horses were alert and staring out over their half-doors.

Seriously alarmed, Linc was out of the Morgan almost before it stopped rolling and heading for the tackroom, hoping against hope that his fears were unfounded.

They weren't.

He stopped short on the threshold, his hand on the splintered edge of the door where the padlock had been wrenched away. On the walls of the familiar cosy, cluttered room five metal saddle racks stood empty. The hooks where seven or eight bridles normally hung were bare, as was another larger rack that Linc knew had held the two sets of harness belonging to Abby's driving ponies, Syrup and Treacle.

His mind registered the stripped walls even as his eyes were drawn to a greater tragedy. On the thin rug that adorned the concrete floor, half in the shadow of a ransacked chest of drawers, a girl in hipster jeans and a grey, hooded tracksuit top lay sprawled on her side. Her eyes were closed and blood oozed from her dark hair to run in a thin trickle down her white face and drip slowly off her jaw.

Abby Hathaway, who should by now have been in bed; and who, Linc thought with a stab of guilt, had probably been waiting the best part of two hours for him to arrive.

'Oh, dear God!' he muttered, stepping forward and dropping to his knees beside the motionless figure. 'Abby? Abby, can you hear me?'

There was no sign of life from the unconscious girl but Linc's shaking fingers searched for and located a regular, if weak, pulse below the jawline. Shallow breaths warmed the back of the hand he held to her slightly parted lips, and he forced himself to calm down and think rationally.

Remembered lessons in first aid reassured him that her position on her side was as close to the ideal as could be hoped for, and that his most immediate priority was to keep her warm. To this end he pulled a thick horse blanket from one of the opened drawers to spread over her body and legs, and a thinner one to fold and ease beneath her head. The grey top and jeans may have met when she was upright but now they gaped about six inches apart and, feeling irrationally like a Peeping Tom, Linc noticed a small jewelled ring sparkling in her navel and wondered if her mother knew it was there. He covered her with the blanket, tucking the edges round her, and reached into the inner pocket of his leather jacket for his mobile phone.

He made two calls: one to request an ambulance and the police, and the second to the Vicarage, just a hundred yards away up the drive.

4

Abby's older sister, Ruth, answered the phone and barely two minutes later was running across the gravel of the yard, breathlessly calling her sister's name.

'Whoa, whoa, whoa! Steady! She can't hear you,' Linc said, slowing her down in the doorway. Ruth, at nineteen, was a slim and very attractive five foot eight, with long wavy red-gold hair and large hazel eyes that were at this moment wide with panic.

'What happened?' she demanded in bewilderment, side-stepping him to go to Abby. 'Oh, my God, is she going to be all right?'

'The ambulance is on its way. Were you able to reach your parents?' He knew they'd been dining with friends.

Ruth was on her knees, smoothing Abby's dark fringe away from her brow. 'Yes. They were already on their way home. Dad said twenty minutes at the most. But I don't understand . . . What's she doing here? She should have been in bed.'

'You've had your tack stolen. I imagine Abby disturbed the thieves. I passed a van or something, going like a bat out of hell. They ran me into the wall just up the lane there.'

'Oh, my God!' she said again, noticing the empty walls for the first time. 'But why would she come down here on her own? Why didn't she tell me?'

'I'm afraid she might've seen the light down here and thought it was me,' Linc admitted. 'She was going to help me plait up.'

Ruth frowned. 'But I assumed you'd been and gone ages ago. I've been in the studio all evening.'

'Yeah, I'm sorry about that. I didn't intend to be

this late but I got held up. I'd have rung ahead to let you know, but I knew your parents were out and the gate would still be open.'

Ruth looked down at her sister's ashen face with its cruel streak of crimson, and her lips quivered. 'Abby, hold on, d'you hear me? *Please* be all right!'

Several long minutes passed, during which Linc silently cursed the circumstances which had led to his lateness and fought the temptation to tidy up the mess left by the thieves. No doubt the police would want everything left strictly alone.

Ruth knelt on the rug, stroking her sister's hand and murmuring a stream of desperate entreaties. After a while she looked up at Linc, eyes swimming. 'We were quarrelling earlier. I said some horrible things. I wish I hadn't!'

'She'll be all right,' Linc soothed her, with a confidence he was far from feeling.

The sound of an approaching ambulance fore-stalled any further self-recriminations on either side and he moved thankfully out into the yard to meet it.

It was barely five minutes later, while the paramedics were still in the tackroom with Abby, that her parents, David and Rebecca Hathaway, arrived, parking their ageing Mercedes a little way up the drive so as not to block the ambulance in.

Rebecca hurried down to the lighted doorway to be met with a tearful hug by Ruth. Following, her husband cast a glance at the already overcrowded tackroom and paused beside Linc, worry creasing his brow and fear in his eyes.

'How is she?' he asked urgently. 'Will she be all

right? Ruth was incoherent on the phone. What happened?'

Linc repeated what he'd told Ruth, adding that so far the ambulance crew hadn't said a lot.

The Reverend David Hathaway listened gravely. At fifty he was four years older than his wife, a big-built, imposing man, six foot two in his socks, with grey hair and a neatly trimmed beard.

'And you think you saw their getaway vehicle?'

'I think it must have been, but other than saying it was a large one, maybe a van, I can't tell you a lot. I was too busy trying to avoid being creamed on the wall. They were travelling pretty fast. I guess they panicked.'

'Bastards!' Abby's father said with sudden explosive fury. 'She's only a kid! Why couldn't they leave her alone?'

Linc shook his head and, without waiting for an answer, David Hathaway turned to follow his wife, only to be brought up short by the arrival of a police car, adding its blue light to that of the ambulance. Two officers – one uniformed, one not – spilled out on to the gravel at the same time as the paramedics emerged from the tackroom with Abby on a stretcher. They intercepted the procession, questioned the ambulancemen briefly and then the uniformed one headed back to the car.

Rebecca, following her daughter's stretcher across to the waiting vehicle, turned to look at her husband. 'David, are you coming? Ruth's going to stay with the children.'

He hesitated, looking at the approaching plain-clothes officer. 'Linc, could you . . .?'

'Sure. You go.'

7

There was a general re-shuffling as the police car backed to let the ambulance and the Mercedes out before joining the convoy to the hospital. As the blue lights flashed their way out of sight the sense of urgency was suddenly extinguished, leaving a flat depression in its stead.

A middle-aged, grey-haired man in a tired grey suit came over to where Linc waited by Noddy's box. He'd switched all the stable lights on while he was waiting, partly to check on the inhabitants and partly to relieve the gloom of the yard. Ruth had disappeared, presumably to resume her babysitting duties.

The grey man held out a hand, shaking his head sadly. 'It's a bad business, this. Very bad. Young lass like that, at home . . . Detective Inspector Rockley, CID. And you are . . .?'

'Lincoln Tremayne – Linc. I stable my horse here.' Linc shook the hand.

'Isn't there an outside light in this yard?'

'It's been smashed.'

'*Tremayne*, you say. As in the Tremaynes of Farthingscourt?'

'Viscount Tremayne is my father.'

'Yes, I know your father quite well. So you're the missing heir?'

A muscle tightened in Linc's jaw. 'Hardly missing. I've been working away, that's all. Is this part of your investigation?'

'Mind my own business, eh?' Rockley said unabashed. 'Fair enough.' He regarded Linc from under bushy brows. 'Take after the old man, I see. Could do worse.'

Linc returned his gaze, silently.

8

'Okay. Now tell me what happened here. David Hathaway I know. The injured girl is one of his daughters, I take it?'

Once again Linc related what little he knew; from his narrow escape in the lane, to finding Abby unconscious in the tackroom.

'And is it your normal practice to call here at this time of night?'

'No, but I'm due to ride at Andover tomorrow in a one-day event and I'd come over to plait up my horse. I intended to get here about nine but I was running late. Estate business. Why? Am I a suspect?'

For a moment Linc thought Rockley wasn't going to answer him; he was gazing at the open doorway of the tackroom, seemingly absorbed in thought.

'Until I have the complete picture, I can't see which pieces don't fit,' he said after a moment. 'It's important to ask. One should never assume. It would seem to be a bit of a security risk, having the stables so far from the house.'

'Yes – well, the gate would normally be bolted at this time of night but David and Rebecca were out this evening so I knew I'd be able to get in.'

'Are there no stables at Farthingscourt?'

'If you know my father as well as you seem to think, you'll know why I don't keep my horse there,' Linc said.

'Hmm. So the older girl . . . Ruth, isn't it? . . . she was unaware that her sister had come down here?'

'Yes, until I called her on my mobile. She said she was in the studio. Pottery,' he added, seeing the question forming on Rockley's lips. 'She's got a workshop next to the house.'

'I'll have to have a word with her later. I must ask you not to touch anything here until forensics have had a chance to go over it. The CSI team are on their way now.'

'Okay. Well, if you've done with me for now, I'll just go up to the house and see if Ruth's okay. She's had a nasty shock.' He began to move away, then paused. 'By the way, that's my car over there, if you need to inspect the damage.'

Rockley nodded. 'We'll do that. And tell Miss Hathaway I'll be along to see her in due course.'

Linc trudged up the slight incline of the Vicarage drive reflecting on the fragile balance of life. By the light of the lantern halfway to the house, his watch read ten to midnight. Less than an hour ago his most immediate concerns were a petty disagreement he'd had with a colleague, and what bit he should use on Noddy in the dressage the next day. Now a young girl was on her way to hospital, possibly gravely injured, and he had neither bridle nor saddle left to worry about. It kicked things sharply into perspective.

Ruth opened the back door to his knock and invited him into the kitchen, the hub of Vicarage life. The family's two springer spaniels, Dorcas and Sukey, looked up from their beds in the corner and sleepily wagged their tails, comfortably unaware of the night's events.

'I'm just making coffee, would you like some?' Ruth looked pale and worn out.

'That'd be great. Er, the Inspector said to tell you he'll want a word later,' Linc warned her, sitting down at the table.

'*Me?* What about? *I* didn't see anything.'

'So he can get the complete picture.'

'Come again?' Ruth spooned coffee, frowning.

'He's very thorough. He'll probably want to know your life history,' Linc told her wearily. 'I suppose he's just doing his job.'

'He'll probably think it's my fault for not keeping a better eye on Abby,' she said, passing him a mug. 'I don't know how you can drink that without sugar, it makes me shudder.'

'Ruth, she's fifteen. You can't control her every move.'

'But it wouldn't have happened if Mum and Dad had been here. I was in the studio all evening. I didn't have a clue where she was.'

'You might as well say it's my fault for being late,' Linc pointed out. 'As far as I can see, the only person to blame is whoever did this to her.'

'I still can't believe it's happened,' Ruth said, shaking her head. 'I just can't take it in. Why? Why us?'

The hall door opened a few inches and a rather plain face with a mop of short brown curls peered round it.

Hannah, at thirteen, was the youngest of the three Hathaway sisters still living at home, and as the only one of them not interested in horses, was the one Linc knew the least. Toby, the baby of the tribe, was presumably still sound asleep. The eldest sister, Josie, whom he'd never met, was a model and worked away from home for the most part.

'Is Abby going to be all right?' Hannah padded in on bare feet, a grey fleece dressing gown wrapped loosely over striped pyjamas. Lace and frills she regarded with tomboyish scorn.

'I expect so,' Ruth said, almost visibly pulling herself together. 'We'll know more in the morning. The kettle's just boiled, d'you want a drink? She heard me phoning Dad about Abby,' she added to Linc.

'I told Abby not to go down there. She'd been watching the yard for ages, waiting for you to come,' Hannah told Linc, sliding into a seat opposite him.

'But you can't see the yard from here,' Ruth protested.

'You can from Mummy's room, if you stand on the windowsill. You can just see the light come on.'

'And she was standing there all that time? Why on earth didn't you tell me?' Ruth handed her sister a mug of hot chocolate with the spoon still in.

'None of my business if she wants to make a fool of herself,' Hannah observed with a touch of smugness. 'Besides, she'd kill me if I ratted on her.'

That was the crux of the matter, Linc thought, sipping his coffee. Caught somewhere between a child and a woman, Abby's erupting hormones had not improved an already volatile temper and Hannah, with her sometimes debatable tact, came in for more than her fair share of her sister's flare-ups.

A tentative knock sounded at the back door and the dogs, apparently sensing a stranger, sat up and growled.

'It's all right, girls.' Ruth went to answer it and reappeared with Rockley close behind.

'Coffee, Inspector?' she asked over her shoulder.

'Thank you. White, two sugars.' Rockley's keen grey eyes scanned the room and he nodded at Linc before turning his attention to Hannah. 'And who's this young lady?'

'My sister Hannah. She was with Abby this evening before . . .'

'Only until half-past ten. Then I went to bed,' Hannah put in. 'There's no school tomorrow, so I'm allowed.'

'So you can't tell me what time she actually went down to the yard?' Rockley said, settling himself at the table. The dogs sniffed him suspiciously, accepted his friendly advances, then went back to their beds and curled up, sighing deeply.

'I heard her go downstairs just before eleven,' Hannah said, thinking hard. 'I thought perhaps Mum and Dad had come home.'

'Are you sure that was the time?'

'Yes, because the grandfather clock in the hall had just struck and it's five minutes fast,' she said with characteristic accuracy.

'And did she say she was going to go down to the stables?'

'Yes. She wanted to see Linc. She thinks she's in love with him,' Hannah told the inspector, in a voice loaded with scorn.

'And you don't think she is?' he queried, taking the mug that Ruth held out.

''Course not! It's only a crush. Mum says she's just at that age.'

Rockley's lips twitched but Ruth wasn't amused.

'Ooh, you little horror! You've been listening at doors,' she exclaimed. 'Mum was talking to me when she said that.'

'I was behind the curtain, reading,' Hannah countered. 'It's not my fault!'

'Well, thank you, young lady. You've been very helpful,' the inspector said. 'But I'd like a little word with your sister now, if I may.'

'It's time you got back to bed anyway,' Ruth told her.

As the door closed behind Hannah, Rockley sighed. 'Nice kid. What is she – twelve? Thirteen?'

'Thirteen,' Ruth confirmed. 'Going on thirty. She's a monster at times!'

'No, she's a nice, ordinary kid. It makes a refreshing change after some of the kids I come across in my line of work. You should be thankful, believe me.' Rockley shook his head, and then switched abruptly back to the business at hand, looking thoughtfully from Linc to Ruth. 'I hear you're a potter, Miss Hathaway. I'd be interested to see your studio.'

'Now?' She was surprised. 'Okay. It's through here.'

The two went out, Rockley asking questions in his deceptively soft voice and Ruth answering without hesitation.

Left alone in the kitchen, Linc sipped his coffee. He had to admire the policeman's skill in getting the girls to relax and open up. He'd probably learned as much about the family in those few minutes as Linc himself had in the five months he'd known them. And now, unless he was very much mistaken, Rockley was trying to learn a little more about Linc Tremayne.

The night ticked slowly on, rhythmically counted by the old grandfather clock in the hall. Ruth came back after ten minutes or so, carrying two empty mugs and saying that the inspector had gone back down to the yard.

'He was nice, wasn't he?' she said. 'Not like a policeman at all. I couldn't tell him much but it was odd, he seemed more interested in you than anything.'

Linc hid a smile.

'He wanted to know what your relationship with Abby was. I said you didn't have one. Honestly, does the man know nothing about teenagers?'

On the huge Welsh dresser the telephone trilled and Ruth went to answer it, picking up the receiver with a hand that shook visibly.

'Mum! How is she?'

Linc could just hear Rebecca's voice on the other end but could make out no words. He watched Ruth's face, trying to read her expression; dreading seeing the shock of bad news.

'When will they know?' she asked, and the indistinct tones answered.

'Yes . . . Yes, I'm okay. Linc's still here . . . Yes, I will . . . 'Bye, Mum.' She replaced the handset and turned back to the table.

'How is she?' Linc asked, softly.

'Still unconscious but stable, apparently. Whatever that means,' Ruth replied, her voice trembling on the brink of tears.

'I should think it means she's out of immediate danger.'

'I hope so.' She sniffed, fumbling in her pocket for a handkerchief. 'They're going to do more tests in the morning. Mum says try not to worry. Yeah, right . . .'

They made more drinks, after which Ruth was

nodding over the kitchen table in spite of the double dose of caffeine, and Linc suggested she go to bed.

'I'll be here if Rockley wants anything,' he said. 'You ought to get some sleep or you'll be a zombie tomorrow.'

'But what about you? What'll you do about riding at Andover tomorrow?'

Linc shrugged. 'Not much I *can* do with no tack.'

'But weren't you supposed to be riding Nina Barclay's horse as well?'

'Oh, hell! Yeah, I'd forgotten about that. Look, I don't s'pose they'll be much longer down there. When they go, I'll doss down on the sofa, if that's all right?'

The Vicarage kitchen was home not only to the usual range of cupboards and appliances, but also, in addition to the table and chairs, one of the biggest settees Linc had ever seen. He heartily approved of it as an item of kitchen furniture.

'Of course. I'll get you a blanket. But are you sure? Haven't you got to get home?'

'Not much point now. I won't be missed. Besides, I'm not sure the Morgan's fit for the road.'

'I'm sorry. Oh, God, what a mess!'

'Bed!' Linc said firmly.

Rockley knocked quietly on the back door just after one o'clock to say that he was leaving but forensics would be an hour or so longer. He gave Linc a card with his number on, saying he'd probably need to speak to him again and telling him not to hesitate if he thought of anything further.

Linc had fallen asleep over a crossword puzzle by the time another officer came up to the house at something past two, with the information that the

CSI unit had now finished and were heading off, if he wanted to bolt the gates.

Linc followed him down and locked up, then returned wearily to the kitchen and crashed out on his makeshift bed.

He tossed and turned for all of fifteen seconds.

2

Half-past eight that morning found Linc turning the Morgan between wrought-iron gates into the long gravel drive of Farthingscourt. He passed the pretty South Lodge where Geoff Sykes, the deputy estate manager, lived, and drove through a band of ancient beech woodland before coming out into the rolling parkland that surrounded the house.

In spite of the horror of the previous night's events, the first sight of Farthingscourt on the far side of the valley gave him the buzz it always did. The drive curved to the right and ran down an avenue of stately copper beeches to the stone bridge spanning the river, and then climbed steadily all the way up to the house's impressive raised portico.

Built of Bath stone in the Palladian style, it was not so large as some stately homes and perhaps a little austere, but with the April morning sunlight glinting on the dozens of rectangular panes of glass in the huge sash windows, and bathing the masonry in a warm golden glow, Linc thought it beautiful.

He drove along past the front of the house and

round into the courtyard at the rear, trying not to cast his usual, wistful glance at the empty stables as he let himself in at the side door to the old kitchens. Although the Vicarage at Farthing St Anne was no more than fifteen minutes' drive from Farthingscourt, to an outsider it would probably seem absurd that someone with a stableyard and several hundred acres of park and farmland on his doorstep should keep his horse somewhere else, but Linc had to respect his father's wishes. When Sylvester, Eighth Viscount Tremayne, had lost his wife in a three-day-eventing accident seventeen years before, he had had all her horses destroyed and made it clear that no other horse would be tolerated on the Farthingscourt Estate from that point forward.

As he ran up the narrow back stairs to his apartment on the top floor, Linc remembered his father's words when, just five months ago, he had come back to live at the family home and announced that he now owned a horse.

'Well, I can't stop you keeping the bloody animal, I suppose, but you'll not keep it here as long as I'm alive!'

The declaration was made with a quiet vehemence that brooked no argument and Linc knew better than to offer any. His riding had been a bone of contention between his father and himself ever since he'd been caught secretly riding a friend's pony, just ten months after his mother's death. He had never ridden just for the sake of rebellion, though he suspected his father thought he did. Even as a twelve year old, Linc could not fail to be acutely aware of the depth of the Viscount's grief and would not willingly have added to it, but he was his mother's son where horses were concerned and, unlike his father, he didn't blame *them* for the tragedy. In a way, riding had been his way of dealing with the loss of his mother. He'd felt closer to her when on the back of a horse, and was sure she would have been pleased and proud that he was following in her footsteps.

The rooms Linc now occupied, right up in the attics of the building, had recently been converted from the long-empty servants' dormitories and comprised a sitting room, galley kitchen, bedroom and bathroom. He had furnished and decorated them himself and was very content in his self-contained isolation, far from the sumptuous grandeur of the public areas of the house.

Three low sash windows offered panoramic views over Dorset's Cranborne Chase, in which the Farthingscourt Estate sat, but Linc hadn't time on this occasion to stop and enjoy them. Nina Barclay, a friend of the Hathaways', had recently broken her wrist and was desperate for someone to keep her promising novice going for her until she was able to ride again. Her groom was keeping the horse fit but didn't have the confidence to compete on him, so as Noddy was entered in many of the same events, Linc had happily stepped into the breech. Today was to be his first outing with Hobo's Dream and though fate had decreed that Noddy should miss the competition, he didn't want to disappoint Nina if he could help it.

He'd eaten a hurried breakfast at the Vicarage after helping Ruth with the horses, and all he had to do now was change into his riding clothes, touch base with his father and head for Hampshire.

In search of Sylvester Tremayne, he let himself into the main part of the house on the first floor and made his way along the Long Gallery towards the wide central flight of stairs. From either side of the corridor, oil-painted images of previous Tremaynes looked down with varying degrees of hauteur from their gilded frames. A runner of hardwearing carpet protected the polished boards from the thousands of visiting feet, whilst stanchions bearing heavy ropes kept sticky fingers away from the priceless portraits.

Linc gave a mock salute to one of these as he passed. St John, Third Viscount Tremayne, had been, according to tradition, the closest the family had had to a black sheep, frittering away much of its quite substantial wealth, killing a love rival in a duel, and finally meeting his own death racing his curricle from London to Brighton. He had died in the reign of George III, aged just twenty-nine, without producing an heir, and the title had passed to his younger brother, Sebastian.

Now the same age as his ill-fated ancestor, it was said by many that Linc was extraordinarily like him to look at, a comparison which didn't displease him. St John was pictured here dressed in riding clothes and leaning against a stone balustrade, whilst in the background a groom hung on to a spirited grey stallion. In keeping with his rebellious reputation he wore his hair unpowdered and tied back with a black ribbon, and if not exactly handsome his features were at least regular and strong enough to be considered good-looking. On one hand he wore a beautifully chased gold ring with a sizeable emerald at its centre, and another gold ring adorned his left ear. What had always drawn Linc to the Third Viscount was the suggestion of a sardonic smile that curved his lips; he looked like a man who was nobody's fool but who found much amusement in life.

At the far end of the gallery, near the top of the stairs, hung the portrait of the current Viscount, Linc's father. It had been painted thirty years ago, when Sylvester Tremayne was first married and in a break with tradition also portrayed his new wife, Marianne. The style was informal; the Viscount wearing his usual camel-coloured corduroys and tweed jacket, and Marianne seated by his side, dark-eyed and lovely, laughing up at him in amber cashmere and pearls. The artist had captured their mutual love and the portrait always inspired a tinge of sadness in Linc. Both his parents had effectively been lost to him on the day Marianne Tremayne had suffered her fatal fall.

A quick search of the first floor proved fruitless and he eventually ran his father to ground downstairs in the library, one of the many rooms that were off limits to visitors.

Aside from the desk, at which he was seated, several red leather-covered reading chairs stood about, each with its attendant table and lamp, and towering bookshelves exhibited row upon row of gold-embossed leather spines; volumes that Linc could not recall ever having seen anybody read. The library was, as always, poorly lit, heavy velvet curtains and north-facing windows combining to protect the treasures within.

As Linc went in, his father's two wolfhounds, Saxon and Viking, got to their feet and padded across to see him, flattening their ears and wagging their long feathery tails with pleasure.

Viscount Tremayne, on the other hand, greeted his son with an unencouraging grunt.

'Thought you were off playing with your bloody horses today,' he remarked.

'I am. I just thought I'd check everything was okay with you before I went,' Linc said evenly.

'Well, you only just caught me. Sykes wants me to look at the roof of the summerhouse – something about loose ridge tiles, I gather – and I've got Bennett coming out about the forestry grant at half-past ten. Some of us have work to do, you know.'

'I was up 'til almost eleven o'clock last night going over the farm accounts with Geoff,' Linc retorted, goaded in spite of himself.

'Well, you wanted the job,' his father observed, looking over the rim of his spectacles. His hair and beard were grey, and seventeen years of grieving had left their mark, but at sixty-four he was still an imposing figure, and one who'd been known to reduce junior staff to mumbling confusion with just such a look.

Linc was made of sterner stuff.

'I did, and I do, but I'm entitled to some free time, and how I choose to spend it is my affair,' he replied. 'I'll be back in plenty of time for the sponsors' meeting tonight, don't worry.'

The Viscount regarded Linc for a long thoughtful moment before returning his attention to the papers on his desk. 'Suit yourself,' he said. 'It's all the same to me. Just don't expect me to hold your job open for you if you end up in hospital with a broken neck!

There'd be no shortage of takers. Reagan, for one, would jump at the chance.'

'I'm sure he would, but you know as well as I do that he's not the right man for the job,' Linc pointed out. 'Sykes is worth ten of him.'

'Sykes doesn't want the job, Reagan does. You put his nose severely out of joint turning up when you did.'

'You had no intention of giving him the position,' Linc protested. Reagan was Farthingscourt's head forester, and a very able one at that, but there was something indefinable in his manner that meant that as far as the Viscount was concerned, he had risen as far as he was going to. 'Anyway, I don't intend ending up in hospital, if I can help it,' he added cheerfully.

'Your mother didn't intend ending up in a coffin!'

Linc knew the futility of further discussion.

'I'll see you later, then. Oh, and by the way, I met a friend of yours last night.' He gave his father a brief account of the raid on the Vicarage and the ensuing investigation.

'I'm sorry to hear about the Hathaway girl,' his father said. 'Rockley's a good man. If there's anything to find, he'll find it. Is the girl going to be all right?'

'Her father rang from the hospital this morning but there's no real news. She's still unconscious and they're going to do a brain scan. Apparently they think she may have been struck from behind and then hit her head again when she fell.'

'Bloody thugs!' the Viscount growled.

'Yeah. I just wish I'd got there ten minutes

earlier . . .' Linc walked over to the door. 'Well, I'd better get going before the stampede starts.'

The 'stampede' was the family name for the hordes of visitors who tramped round Farthingscourt on Saturdays, Sundays and Wednesdays. In reality it started with little more than a trickle at Easter, but in the high season numbers stepped up considerably, to the point where a limit had to be set to safeguard the antiquities they came to see, and even the very fabric of the building itself.

His father raised a hand but not his eyes, and with a sigh, Linc let himself out.

He left the damaged Morgan in the open-fronted barn that did duty as a garage, heading for Andover in the Land-Rover Discovery instead. His competition start-time was half-past ten and although Nina and her groom would already be there with Hobo, and could warm him up, Linc wanted to leave himself a little time in hand to renew his brief acquaintance with the horse before competing.

Once clear of the back roads and doing a steady sixty-five in light traffic, he tried to concentrate on mentally rehearsing his impending dressage. Dressage is basically the horse's version of a dog's obedience test: a succession of linked moves combining changes of pace and direction which is marked on precision and style. But whereas a ring steward calls the instructions to the dog handler, the dressage rider must memorise his test in advance. With around half a dozen different novice tests and a similar number of intermediate ones, concentration was vital.

Today's test was one Linc had ridden on Noddy

only a few weeks ago and knew fairly well. Before long he found thoughts of Abby and his own troubled relationship with his father increasingly intruding.

Guilt about his own, unwitting contribution to Abby's plight had passed, and what he felt now, aside from anxiety, was chiefly anger. In the short time he'd known them the Hathaways had become very dear to him, in a way representing the kind of ideal family life he'd missed out on. In attacking Abby the thieves had dealt a devastating blow to the whole unit.

Linc remembered the stricken look in her father's eyes last night. Given time, the Reverend David Hathaway, currently a university lecturer in theology, would no doubt find comfort in his faith but that first outburst of fear and anger had been the instinctive reaction of any distressed parent.

Linc wondered if his own father would have coped better with his wife's death if he had had such a strong faith to fall back on. While Marianne had been alive the local vicar had held a service every Sunday in Farthingscourt's private chapel for the benefit of the Tremayne family and their estate workers. These days the vicar visited just once a month, and the family usually only attended in force at the traditional times of the year, and then more through duty than conviction. Indeed the Viscount had been heard to say that in his opinion the Sunday regulars were merely hedging their bets.

Notwithstanding this, the chapel services were well supported by members of the Farthingscourt staff, among them Viscount Tremayne's secretary and PA, Mary Poe, who was at present on holiday.

Mary was probably, Linc thought, both the most valued *and* undervalued worker on the estate. She had taken up her position at around the same time as Marianne had come to Farthingscourt as a young bride, and, although she was a few years younger than the Viscountess, they had soon become great friends.

After Marianne's death, Mary was the one who had stepped in to look after Linc and his younger brother Crispin, while their father shut himself away with his grief. Without her, the family would quite possibly have fallen apart.

Aside from the loss of his mother, Linc's childhood had been a fairly happy one, but looking back, he recognised that running through it there had always been a thread of conflict between his inherited passion for horses and his desire to live up to his father's expectations.

It wasn't something that had left him emotionally scarred for life. After all, a sizeable portion of his teenage years had been spent away at school, and there it had been fairly easy to arrange to ride in his spare time. But his relationship with his father had never been all that Linc would have wished.

It had not been solely in an attempt to please *him* that Linc had studied business management, marketing and commerce at university. He had known from an early age that Farthingscourt would one day be his and had always embraced the prospect with enthusiasm. He loved the house and land, and wanted to be involved in the running of them, so it seemed as though fate was taking a hand when the estate manager gave in his notice a month before Linc was due to graduate. As soon as he'd completed his course he hurried home to plead his case.

Lord Tremayne ignored his pleas and gave the job to an outsider.

Twenty-two years old, his newly gained qualifications spurned, as he saw it, Linc packed his bags and left.

He walked out with no clear idea of where he was going or what he was going to do. He wasn't ready to acknowledge the truth of his father's argument that he lacked the necessary practical experience for the top job; all he wanted was to put some distance between them and find a way of showing that he could get on, with or without his father's help. In defiant mood, his first spell of employment was in a top eventing yard where he quickly rose to the status of stable manager. The job gave him a chance to further his competition experience and it was during his second year there that he bought Noddy, the first horse he had ever owned.

Linc was almost completely happy working with the eventers.

Almost, but not quite. Farthingscourt was inextricably a part of his life and, no matter where he found himself, the urge to return was always tugging at his subconscious. However strong the pull, though, he was not about to go back, cap in hand; the Tremayne pride wouldn't allow that. He was prepared to admit that his father had been right, but not until he'd made up the deficit. With that in mind, Linc reluctantly left the stables and trawled a succession of large country estates for work.

He finally found a position as an assistant estate

manager and settled down to learn everything he possibly could about the job. Over the next four and a half years he returned home infrequently, saying little of what he'd been doing, and it wasn't until his younger brother Crispin wrote to tell him of the impending retirement of the Farthingscourt estate manager that he handed in his notice and returned to Dorset with Noddy still in tow.

The fatted calf could rest easy.

If Sylvester Tremayne was overjoyed to see his son and heir return, he hid it well. It took weeks of stubborn persistence by Linc to bring his father to the point of offering him a trial period as estate manager. Mary, desperate to see them settle their differences, added her subtle persuasion to the cause, and Linc even produced references for his father's perusal, with an ironic deference which almost provoked a total falling-out.

So far, even the Viscount could find no fault with his work, though he fought every suggestion for change that his son made. One notable exception to this was Linc's plan to restore Farthingscourt Mill to working order. It was his aim to utilise the old building for its original purpose, that of milling grain from the estate's organic farms, and then to sell the resulting flour under their own label.

He'd expected to have to fight for his idea but surprisingly his father had been quite prepared to listen; in fact, he'd yielded so swiftly that Linc suspected he was being given rope with which to hang himself. If he hadn't been completely confident in his research this prospect might have unnerved him but he'd been working on the idea for some time and was convinced of its viability. A grant had been secured and work was already under way.

Management experience wasn't all Linc had brought back with him to Farthingscourt. On one of his fleeting trips home he had also brought his girlfriend of the time, Nikki, and when he finally succeeded in detaching himself from her overeager clutches two or three months later, she had returned of her own accord, unbeknownst to him, and struck up a relationship with Crispin. A year before Linc came back for good, he was best man at his little brother's wedding. To his relief, and in spite of his private misgivings, the union seemed to have been an unmitigated success.

Traffic around Salisbury brought him back abruptly to the present and he looked at his watch. Forty minutes to go. With a wary eye open for lurking traffic police, he made a reassuring call to Nina Barclay on his mobile and, twenty minutes later, arrived at the venue in person.

One-day events differ from their three-day cousins in more ways than the obvious; one of the main ones being that the cross-country phase often comes last, after the showjumping, instead of halfway through the competition, and another being that the horses are not asked to complete a steeplechase course or miles of roads and tracks before tackling the jumps across country. The aim of both competitions is to find the horse and rider combination which is truly versatile. A bit like a human decathlon event, contestants are tested on their suppleness, speed and endurance, obedience and accuracy. What is also tested, in consequence, is their temperament. A faint heart or lack of mental stamina will be laid bare as surely as any deficiency in the physical department.

Hobo's Dream at home had not inspired Linc with any great excitement but he was clearly a horse who came alive on the big day. At eight years old he was just beginning his third year in horse trials and was on the brink of grading up to intermediate. When Nina Barclay's groom led the brown gelding across to meet him, Linc could see that he was fit and raring to go.

'He's warmed up nicely. You just need to hop up and get the feel of him before we head for the arena.' Nina was walking beside Linc, dark-haired and fortyish with a lean angular figure that would probably stay the same into her seventies and beyond.

'Yes, I'm sorry I'm so late. You must be cursing me!'

Nina shook her head. 'Not at all, it's not your fault. I'm just glad you could still ride him. How is poor Abby?'

Ruth had promised to update him as and when there was any news, so he had to assume she was still unconscious. He explained to Nina as he mounted Hobo and let the stirrups down to a comfortable length.

'I can hardly believe it! Attacked in her own yard. You're not safe anywhere these days, it seems, and they've lost all their tack, too.'

'Yeah. I said I'd look up Sandy Wilkes and see if he'll bring some out to tide us over. Is he here today?'

'Third stall up, second row. Right next to the

Land-Rover stand,' Nina confirmed. 'I've been over there already for a new saddlecloth, mine was somewhat less than white.'

Hobo sidled impatiently as Nina's groom tightened his girth and then Linc was riding away at a swinging walk to put him through his paces. All around them competitors and their helpers were hurrying about their business; horses of all shapes and sizes were being warmed up, walked round or were waiting their turn to compete. Few independent spectators were in attendance, most being the friends, family and grooms of the competitors, and these were catered for by the provision of straw bales to sit on and numerous vans selling anything from jacket potatoes and hot dogs to crêpes Suzette and frozen yoghurt. The showjumping ring was bounded by metal posts and nylon tape, and the air resounded with commentary, via the PA system, which was repeated in a series of overlapping echoes across the acres of the cross-country course, in a way that was somehow peculiar to such events.

In spite of the last-minute nature of things, or maybe because of it, the dressage test went surprisingly well. It was the phase of the competition which Linc was least confident about and this usually set off a vicious circle of nerves and tension which in turn disturbed the horse's own composure. On this occasion he'd hardly had time for nerves to take a hold, and what Hobo's performance may have lacked in accuracy, it more than made up for in flair and impulsion.

'Well done!' Nina exclaimed as he rode out of the arena and dismounted. 'That's as good a test as he's ever done.'

'Thanks. It's all down to him, though. I can never get Noddy to take that much interest. He usually slops round looking half-asleep and swishing his tail every time I ask him to do anything. My score sheet always reads "Lack of impulsion. Tail swishing" all the way down.'

Things were apparently running late in the showjumping ring and with time on his hands Linc went in search of Sandy Wilkes, the saddler.

Sandy's lorry was parked, as Nina had said, next to the Land-Rover stand. It was a horsebox which had been fitted out with racks, shelves and drawers to hold saddles, bridles and every kind of equine accessory that one could imagine, and then some. It was his proud boast that he had the largest collection of bits of anyone in England. Snaffles, pelhams, bridoons and kimblewicks; in fact anything that had ever been devised to go in a horse's mouth, he had in stock. He had a workshop and extra storage in a business unit near his home in Shaftesbury but most of his business was conducted out of the back of the lorry, in which he could visit his customers on their own premises.

Linc hadn't seen much of Sandy over the last few years but had known him quite well way back, when as a teenager he'd spent happy hours in other people's stableyards. Seven or eight years older than Linc, Sandy had just been starting out in business at that time and had made frequent calls to all the horsy premises that he could find, in order to drum up business. These days the riding fraternity called *him* and he was a popular figure at shows and events, a fact borne out by the numbers crowding under the awning at the side of his lorry.

As Linc progressed through the queue of prospective customers waiting for a word with the saddler, he was impressed anew by Sandy's unrivalled service and generosity. One harassed competitor, obviously finding himself short of the necessary, was told to drop a cheque in the post, and to another he said, 'Well, look. You take the vulcanite pelham and try it for a week or two, then if he isn't happy, bring it back and we'll try something else. We'll worry about the money later when we've got you settled. How about that?'

His pretty, female customer apparently thought it very acceptable, including a kiss in her expressions of gratitude. At five foot nine Sandy was a couple of inches shorter than Linc but thick, wavy fair hair and boyish smile ensured he was never short of female company.

'You're a pushover, you are!' Linc declared as he reached the front of the queue.

'Linc! Nice to see you, mate!' Sandy's attractive, lightly freckled face lit up as he punched Linc lightly on the arm. 'Where've you been hiding yourself lately?'

'Oh, I've been working away. But seriously, how many times do people take up your kind offers and disappear without trace?'

Sandy lowered his voice. 'Very rarely, actually. You see, I know where most of them live and I know who their friends are. A word dropped here and there can be very damaging to someone's credit rating. Yeah, sure, I've lost the odd snaffle or stirrup leather but my open-handed reputation is my biggest draw.'

Linc laughed. 'You're a fraud! I should have

known it. Underneath that warm, friendly public face you're just a cold, calculating businessman.'

'Shhh, think of my sales!' Sandy warned in mock alarm. 'Well, what can I do for you anyway?'

Soberly, Linc told him what had happened to Abby. 'So they're left with no tack at all until the insurance comes through, and of course, whatever else happens, the horses still have to be exercised,' he finished.

'So they'd like me to pop over and drop off a couple of saddles and bridles in the meantime?'

'That'd be brilliant, if you could.'

'Sure. It won't be till Monday, though. I'll still be here tomorrow, it's the Open Intermediate.'

'Monday's fine,' Linc assured him.

'That's rough about Abby. Poor kid. Will she be okay?'

Linc pursed his lips. 'Too soon to say.'

'And do they have any idea who did it? The police, I mean.'

'If they do, they're not telling. I was first on the scene and *I* didn't see anything. But maybe forensics will turn something up.'

'Let's hope so.'

Several other customers were hovering hopefully and Sandy made an apologetic face at Linc. 'Look, I'll have to get on, sorry. I'll ring about Monday.'

'Thanks. Oh, and Noddy goes in a five-and-a-half-inch, half-cheeked snaffle, if you've got one.'

'Right you are. See you later, then.' With a smile, Sandy turned to his next customer.

It was with a degree of relief that Linc made it out into the fresh air again. He was heading for Nina

Barclay's horsebox when a voice spoke hesitantly behind him.

'Excuse me . . .'

He turned to see a middle-aged strawberry blonde in jodhpurs and a Puffa jacket.

'Yes?'

'I'm sorry. I don't know whether you're interested but the thing is, I couldn't help overhearing about your tack being stolen, and the same thing happened to us just a week ago. My name's Tricia Johnston, by the way.'

'Linc Tremayne.'

'Yes, I know. I saw you at Radstock. Abby was grooming for you, wasn't she? Poor girl, I hope she'll be all right.'

'Me too. Er, look, I'm due to ride in a minute . . .' He'd told Nina he'd be back in twenty minutes and he was cutting it fine.

'Sorry. Actually, there's not much more to tell because no one saw anything. They just forced the padlock on the tackroom door and cleared us out. All the new stuff anyway. We reckon it was between half-ten when my daughter gives the horses their last lot of hay and half-twelve when my husband and I got back from a party.'

'You were out then?' Linc asked with interest.

'Yes, a fund-raising do for the local hunt. It was a dreary affair as well. I wish we'd never gone.'

'Do you think you'd have noticed if you had been at home? Can you see the stables from the house?'

Tricia shook her head. 'No, not easily. But you always wonder, don't you?'

Linc nodded. 'Still, if it was the same person or

people, perhaps it was a good thing nobody did see. Look what happened to Abby.'

Tricia was much struck by this but had no more information to offer so Linc excused himself to go in search of Nina and Hobo and, twenty minutes later, after warming up once more, jumped a competent round to add just four more penalty points to his dressage score.

In due course, having replaced his black jacket with a body protector and a sky-blue polo-necked jumper provided by Nina, Linc was waiting at the start of the cross-country section. Sky-blue was the colour she usually rode in and although event riders don't have registered colours such as jockeys wear, many make a point of always wearing the same colour or combination of colours on all their horses.

Hobo had undergone a transformation too. Gone were the neat plaits of the dressage arena; his mane now hung free in a wavy black mass on his neck. A jumping saddle was fitted, and rubber grip reins, and his hard, black legs were protected by bandages, overreach boots and quantities of thick white grease to help him slide over any rails he might hit. He was ready to go.

Linc rode into the roped-off starting box, leather-gloved hands surreptitiously sliding up the reins one at a time in preparation for the horse's leap forward. As the official began the countdown Linc started the stopwatch on his right wrist.

'Three ... two ... one ... good luck!' the steward called, and in a flash was left behind and forgotten as Hobo forged out of the box and into a gallop in three powerful strides.

Linc eased into a balanced position, weight out of

the saddle and off the horse's back, hands amongst the flying mane, moving in time with the nodding head, maintaining a steady contact. As always, the nervous tension of waiting was blown away in the wind and he gave himself up to the thrill and enjoyment of five or six minutes of galloping and jumping.

Due to his late arrival that morning, he hadn't had time to walk the course before the competition started, doing it after his showjumping round instead. This meant that the first riders were already out on the course and he had to choose his moments to pace out the combination fences. On the other hand, he did have a chance to see how well the course was riding and it had seemed as though bold, forward-going animals were finding little problem with it.

So it proved.

Nina had warned him that Hobo could sometimes balk at drop fences; those where the ground was substantially lower on the landing side than the take off. Sometimes, as was the case on this occasion with fence twelve, these had no upright obstacle, merely a platform faced with railway sleepers followed by a drop of several feet on to a downward slope. For a horse, with its limited forward vision, this manoeuvre requires a good deal of faith in its rider. The ideal situation is to slow up sufficiently for the horse to lower its head and land reasonably close to the sleeper wall, but not to slow up so much as to allow it time for second thoughts.

The worst scenario is for the horse to approach too boldly or even fighting for its head, and to launch itself out into space without a thought for the landing. This had only once happened to Linc, with the almost inevitable result. Both he and his equine partner, another borrowed ride, had collapsed in a heap on landing and rolled a good few yards further down the hill. He'd walked away that time with nothing worse than a sprained wrist and some bruising, but it could easily have been a broken neck, and he'd learned caution.

Hobo was bold but sensible, an event rider's dream. As they landed neatly on the slope and galloped on, Linc wondered fleetingly if it was Nina who didn't like drop fences rather than the horse, then pushed the thought away and concentrated on the challenges ahead.

The course was biggish but fair. Cross-country and horse trials fences are nowhere near as high as those facing a showjumping rider of a similar standard; the difference being that cross-country obstacles are not built to be knocked down by careless hooves. Stone walls, tree trunks and wired-on rails of easily twelve inches in diameter have to be jumped uphill, downhill and into water. Hedges, banks, chicken coops and picnic tables, singly or in combination, have to be negotiated in the open or amongst trees. The variation is immense, limited only by the imagination of each course designer. The only constant is the inescapable fact that mistakes are potentially dangerous. It is not a sport for the faint-hearted.

Linc had a super round. Hobo lacked experience but made up for it with a willingness to be guided, and although he took a strong hold, Linc was able to steady him at the appropriate moments and they crossed the finishing line with a clear round inside the time. At the end of the day it was good enough for second place. Nina was euphoric.

'Second? You're kidding!'

Ruth turned from making coffee in the Vicarage kitchen. Linc had called in on his way home for news and to see if he could help with the horses.

He shook his head.

'No one was more surprised than me, I can tell you!' he said. 'And Nina was so excited I thought she'd never stop hugging me.'

'It's brilliant! What was your dressage score?'

'Forty-two,' he announced with a certain amount of pride.

'Well, good old Hobo!' she exclaimed.

'Thanks!' he said dryly, and they both laughed.

The door swung open and a young woman stepped inside.

Tall and slender with long dark brown hair and an unseasonable golden tan, Linc recognised Ruth's older sister Josie from family photographs and a couple of professional portfolio shots her mother had proudly showed him. He'd privately thought then, as he did now, that Ruth, with her sunny smile, was the prettier sister.

'Well, I'm glad someone's had an enjoyable day,' Josie remarked, her displeasure aimed squarely at Linc. 'If that's your Land-Rover outside, you're going to have to move it. You're blocking me in.'

'Sure. Sorry.' He stood up and made for the door straight away. He had noticed the sleek, white E-type on his way in and Ruth had told him it belonged to her sister. She had apparently driven back from London that afternoon to see Abby, in whom there had been no change. Both their parents were still at the hospital, and although Ruth would never have admitted it, Linc could see that she was immensely relieved to have some of the responsibility for home and siblings lifted off her shoulders. He guessed that just the presence of someone older was a comfort to her.

'I'm not sure what time I'll be back, Roo,' Josie said as Linc passed. 'I'll see how Mum's holding up, but I don't suppose I'll be long. Okay?'

Outside, Linc gave the car a second appreciative glance as he strolled towards the Farthingscourt vehicle. Josie was evidently doing well for herself in the modelling world. He slid behind the wheel of the Land-Rover, started it and backed out of the yard into the drive.

As he walked back, Josie emerged from the house and got into her car without a word to him. Wearing very little make-up and a long leather coat over jeans and a jumper, she didn't look much like a model. He shrugged off her rudeness and headed for the back door.

The Jaguar wouldn't start.

Linc paused in the doorway listening to Josie's efforts for a moment or two, then retraced his steps.

'You'll flood it,' he warned her, putting a hand on the hardtop and leaning down to look inside.

'I know that, dammit!' she said through gritted teeth. 'I haven't got the choke out.'

'D'you want me to have a look?' he offered.

'No, it's always a bugger when it's hot. I'll have to let it cool down. Mind out!' She thrust the door open briskly and Linc had to skip back smartly to preserve his kneecaps.

Following her into the house, he caught Ruth's reply to her query.

'I'm sorry Josie, you can't. It's loaded up with my gear for the exhibition tomorrow. I daren't let you take it to the hospital. I've packed it up as best I can but I'm going to have to drive at about ten miles an hour. I'm really sorry.'

'Damn! I'll have to call a taxi.'

In the doorway, Linc cleared his throat.

'I could give you a lift, if you like?' He didn't know why he'd said it. He certainly didn't relish the idea of driving twenty miles or so back the way he'd just come with an antagonistic female in the passenger seat. On top of which, Farthingscourt was entertaining the sponsors of his watermill project that evening and he was a fair way to being late already.

Josie looked at him in surprise. 'Why? Are you going that way?'

'I can do, if it'd be any help. I *was* going to give Ruth a hand with the horses but I expect she'll forgive me . . .'

Ruth nodded vigorously.

'If you're sure . . .' Josie wavered, looking all of a sudden very tired.

''Course. No problem at all.'

After a mile or so, Linc could see that it was going to be up to him to break the silence.

'You've been working in London, then?'

'I got back half an hour or so ago,' Josie confirmed. 'Mum phoned me from the hospital this morning.'

Her tone signalled no significant unbending and

Linc wondered what he'd done to upset her. It surely couldn't all be down to his blocking her in. The silence stretched on again, fairly buzzing with unspoken thoughts.

'Ruth says Abby went down to the stables to meet you,' Josie said at last, voice unmistakably accusing.

'Ah,' Linc said, realisation dawning.

'What d'you mean, *ah*?'

He ignored the question. 'Yes, she did. She was going to help me plait.'

'But you were late.'

'Unfortunately, yes.'

A pause, then, 'If you'd been there on time, none of this would have happened.'

'Probably not,' he agreed. 'I guess it's all my fault.'

Another pause.

'Haven't you got stables at Farthingscourt?'

'Yes, but there aren't any teenage girls there to fetch and carry for me.'

Linc felt rather than saw the contemptuous look directed at him but it seemed Josie had exhausted her bitterness for the moment and the remainder of the journey passed in hostile silence. He dropped her off at Odstock Hospital, where she thanked him with icy politeness, and turned wearily for home. The spark of neighbourly kindness that had prompted his offer had been effectively extinguished.

3

Sunday at Farthingscourt was always a busy day and Linc spent most of it doing the rounds with Geoff Sykes, his second in command, whom he valued both as a colleague and a friend.

Stocky and bespectacled, with a weathered face and not much gingerish hair under a flat cap, Geoff was a born under-manager, confident enough to make decisions when the need arose but unwilling to take on the ultimate buck-stops-here responsibility of the top job. His father had been the gamekeeper until he retired to live in one of the estate cottages and Geoff had lived and worked on the estate all his forty-eight years. His experience was worth a mint to the Tremayne family, and his unambitious dedication made him the best deputy Linc could have hoped for.

'How'd the dinner go last night?' Geoff asked.

They were on their way to the mill in the Land-Rover to cast an eye over the progress made by the contractors.

'Very well,' Linc replied. 'The guys from Water

Heritage seemed very pleased with the work so far and they've agreed to extend the loan to cover the new budget.'

The meal had indeed gone well. Since coming to Farthingscourt, Crispin's wife Nikki had taken on the role of hostess there. It was one that she relished and, it had to be said, carried out with flair. Blonde and pretty, she dressed elegantly and used just the right degree of flirtatious charm to ensure that her male guests enjoyed their evening, without upsetting any wives who might be present.

Linc took his hat off to her. The daughter of a wealthy London night-club owner, he had met her at a party and introduced her to his family after only half a dozen dates almost as an act of rebellion, knowing she wasn't the type of girl his father had in mind as the future Lady Tremayne. However, she had neatly turned the tables on him, enslaving both Sylvester and Linc's brother Crispin with her big blue eyes and pretty ways, and never once giving a hint of the hard edge Linc knew her to have.

Now, nearly eighteen months after her marriage, he was prepared to admit he might have been mistaken in her. Their own brief relationship had been a stormy affair, initiated in an unguarded moment and governed by Nikki's clingy possessiveness. Unsurprisingly, she hadn't taken the break-up well. He supposed he couldn't altogether blame her, for although he'd never led her to believe he was in any way serious, taking her to visit Farthingscourt had perhaps raised her hopes unfairly high and it wasn't something he was proud of. In the end, through her marriage to Crispin, she had made Farthingscourt her home anyway, albeit in one of the cottages on the estate, rather than the main house.

She had, over the months, immersed herself in the preparations for the many functions and events that the house played host to, showing a natural flair for creating exactly the right mood with music and decoration, and had recently taken over the twice-weekly flower arranging in the show rooms. Linc knew his father thought her a major asset, and Nikki showed by the looks she occasionally cast in Linc's direction that she was well aware of her triumph.

Farthingscourt Mill stood higher up the river from the house and its lake, at the point where the valley narrowed and the water became much faster-flowing. When the mill was built, some two hundred years before, the river had been dammed and a millpond excavated to provide the fall of water necessary to turn the breastshot wheel.

A private lane ran from the east of the house, about a mile and a half along the side of the valley, past the mill and on to join the public road that linked the two villages of Farthing St Anne and Farthing St Thomas. The mill car park, just off the lane, was currently a cleared area spread with hard-core and awaiting a top-dressing of asphalt when the heavy machinery no longer visited the site.

Linc and Geoff Sykes climbed out of the Land-Rover, accompanied by Geoff's two bouncing black Labradors who immediately made for the water and plunged in. The mill house was a beautiful stone building from which the accumulated ivy growth of the last fifty years had recently been cleared, allowing light to flood through its mullioned windows and spill on to the dusty wooden floors once more.

In spite of the years of neglect, the three-storey building was found to be surprisingly sound, the biggest repair project being the roof where many of the timbers needed replacing but which had, thankfully, not leaked to any great extent.

Linc and his deputy-manager walked along the front of the building to the narrow footbridge that spanned the tail race, just below the wheel. Crossing this and turning left, they passed the wheel itself, newly refurbished and re-hung on its massive hexagonal axle-tree made of seasoned oak which, alone, had cost the project some two thousand pounds of its budget.

The channel, or head race, that fed the wheel was at present nearly empty, as was the pond itself, both in the course of being drained in order to remove the silt, shore up the banks and retaining walls, and repair the weir. The millstream was currently being diverted away from the pond by way of a temporary dam and a huge pipe, and only three or four feet of murky water remained, some of which would have to be pumped out before work could commence. About twenty feet away from the head race the curving steps of the weir were dry and already under restoration, as was the bridge which crossed above it. Thirty feet or so downstream, the diverted flow poured back into the river and away down the valley.

The projected timescale for finishing the main stage of the project was just over a month, but Linc found it hard to believe that it would be achieved. He said as much to Geoff as they returned to the car park.

'It's mostly only man-hours. You get behind, you

just have to throw a few more men at it,' he said placidly, whistling up the soggy Labradors.

'I guess so. But we're at the mercy of the weather, too, and I really want to get this right.'

'His Lordship can't hold you responsible for the weather,' Sykes said, well aware of the peppery relationship between the Viscount and his eldest son.

'Don't you believe it!' Linc responded.

The afternoon brought two police officers to Farthingscourt to take a statement from Linc regarding the theft at the Vicarage. He took them through to the library and, having read and signed the resulting document, asked them if any other stables in the area had been targeted.

'Unfortunately it's all too common,' he was told. 'There's been a number of similar thefts over the last few months. There was another one later on Friday night, as a matter of fact. A riding school north of Shaftesbury lost most of their tack for the second time in a few weeks. We don't know for sure that it was the same gang, but it tends to go in waves and, as I told the Hathaways, the thieves will often hit the same area again in a couple of months' time. That's just long enough for people to use the insurance money to replace their old tack with new. In fact, it's not unknown for the old tack to be found dumped somewhere.'

'Really? And when the thieves have got the new tack, where do they sell it on?' Linc wanted to know. 'Presumably not locally?'

'We think some of it's sold at auction, and we suspect a fair amount finds its way to Ireland.' The police constable stood up and moved towards the door. 'Anyway, as I told Miss Hathaway this morning, it would be wise to install some security at the Vicarage. I've left some leaflets with them. Normally, our Horse Liaison Officer would visit to advise but she's on maternity leave at the moment.' His radio crackled with news of another call-out and he paused to listen before saying, 'Well, if that's all, sir, we must be on our way. Rest assured that everything possible is being done to track these thieves down. Robbery with violence is a particularly nasty business.'

Linc showed them out, ignoring the curious gazes of the paying visitors and reflecting that in attacking Abby the thieves had made a big mistake. From being the subjects of a routine ongoing investigation, however thorough, their violent raid on the Vicarage had made their apprehension a matter of priority. Thinking about what the constable had told him, Linc experienced a sudden wave of anger. It would have been naïve to suppose that what had happened at the Vicarage would have given such organised criminals much pause for thought, but to find out that they'd quite possibly gone on to make another hit that very same night seemed to put them in a different league altogether.

After a morning spent on estate business, Linc arrived at the Vicarage Monday lunchtime to find that Sandy, the saddler, had already been there an hour or so and had been invited into the kitchen for soup and sandwiches.

Abby's mother Rebecca was also there, having come home from the hospital for an hour or two to have a bath and change her clothes. She looked up from the table as Linc came in, and he was shocked by the change the stress of her hospital vigil had wrought in her face. She wore her light brown hair short and normally carried her forty-six years so lightly that she had on more than one occasion been taken for Ruth and Josie's elder sister, but today she looked grey and exhausted, her eyes shadowed and red-rimmed. Hannah and Toby sat either side of her, six-year-old Toby snuggling against her with only the top of his golden-brown head showing by her elbow, and Ruth sat across the table, next to Sandy.

'Hello. Hi, Sandy,' Linc said. Then to Rebecca, 'Any news?'

She shook her head. 'Not really. She's still unconscious. There's no more bleeding and no sign of a fracture but nobody seems to be able to tell us when she might come out of it or even . . .' Her voice trailed off and she ruffled Toby's hair, summoning a bright smile. 'And I've been neglecting the rest of my family shamefully, haven't I, little Toby Tobias?'

Toby looked up at her, his misleadingly angelic face adoring.

'Never mind,' she continued. 'When this is over and Abby's on the mend, I'll make it up to you all.'

'Ruth's been doing a great job,' Linc told her. '*And* looking after the horses.'

'I know she has,' her mother said warmly. 'I expected to find chaos when I got back but it seems my family can manage just fine without me. The place is spotless.'

'That was mostly Josie,' Ruth admitted. 'She had

a blitz yesterday whilst I was at the exhibition.'

'*I* had to hoover *all* the bedrooms,' Hannah put in. '*And* I've been looking after Abby's chickens without being asked.'

'You've all been marvellous,' Rebecca acknowledged. 'I'm proud of the lot of you.'

'Will I get the money for the next lot of eggs?' Hannah wasn't one to allow sentiment to get in the way of advancement.

'Lord, child, you're mercenary!' Ruth exclaimed. 'What would your father say? No one would ever take you for a vicar's daughter.'

'Well, Abby gets the money when *she* does them,' Hannah pointed out unabashed. 'It's only fair.'

'Of course it is,' her mother said soothingly. 'And I'm sure Abby will be very grateful to you when she's better. Now I really think I ought to be getting back to the hospital. Daddy will come home this evening for a while, I expect.'

Faced with the prospect of losing her again so soon, Toby clung even tighter and she had to prise his arms from around her waist as she stood up.

'You're going to have to be a brave little man,' she told him gently.

'I don't want to be a brave little man,' Toby sobbed. 'I want you back. And Daddy, and Abby. I want things to be right again.'

'I know, darling. We all do.'

Sandy cleared his throat and fidgeted, looking a little uncomfortable amidst this show of familial affection, then got to his feet.

'I ought to be moving, too. We've got these horses to sort out yet. Thanks for the soup and everything.'

'I'll go down with him, if you like?' Linc offered, looking at Ruth. 'We need to sort out some stuff for Noddy, too.'

'Thanks. I'll be down in a minute, and if you've got time to ride, I'll be taking our two out later.'

'That'd be good, yes. 'Bye, Rebecca. Say a few words to Abby for me, just in case she can hear.'

'Thank you, Linc. I will.'

Ruth's chestnut mare, Magic, had been fitted with a saddle and bridle before lunch but finding anything suitable for the remaining two took the best part of an hour. Sandy's lorry was parked in the yard and he went in and out of it countless times with bits and pieces of tack, followed by a chunky brindle-and-white dog of mixed parentage which went by the name of Tiger.

Fitting a horse with a saddle is rather like fitting a person with new shoes. Horses' backs come in all shapes and sizes: short or long, wide or narrow, bony or round. Using a saddle that doesn't fit can produce much the same results as wearing the wrong pair of shoes: discomfort, lameness and bad temper. A surprising number of behavioural problems in horses can be traced back to ill-fitting tack.

Both Noddy and Cromwell, the horse shared by Josie and Rebecca, had problem backs. Noddy had higher than average withers and needed a saddle with good clearance at the front, and the grey's back was unusually broad.

Sandy was endlessly patient, and at the end of the session would accept no money, saying they could reckon up when the insurance payment came through and they had decided what they wanted to keep, and what to replace. He'd come up trumps with Noddy's half-cheeked snaffle, which earned Linc's immense gratitude, and departed with a cheery wave and a special wink for Ruth, who seemed rather pleased.

'He fancies you.' Hannah had come down to watch the proceedings.

'And what would you know?' Ruth demanded, colouring significantly.

'He couldn't take his eyes off you at lunchtime,' her sister observed. 'I'm not stupid.'

'I thought you were supposed to be looking after Toby,' Ruth remarked, trying a change of subject. 'Where is he?'

'He's playing with his rabbits in the haybarn. I reckon you fancy Sandy, too,' she persisted.

'Well, I reckon you should mind your own business,' Ruth told her, resorting to pulling rank. 'Go and help Toby catch the rabbits and then take him up to the house. Josie should be back in a minute. What are you laughing at?' she asked Linc severely as Hannah departed.

'Nothing. Nothing at all,' he assured her, taking the coward's way out. 'Has Josie been at the hospital today?'

'This afternoon she has. This morning she had to go back to London to sweet-talk her agent. Apparently she skipped out on a job to come home at the weekend and he wasn't happy.'

'That's a bit hard,' Linc said. 'It *is* her sister, after all.'

'Mmm, that's what *I* said.'

In due course, Josie's E-type swept in through the gates and off towards the house, and Ruth and Linc took the three horses out for much-needed exercise, sharing the chore of leading Cromwell. Thankfully, living out in the field, Syrup and Treacle could be left largely to their own devices.

When they got back and Linc was rubbing the saddle stains off Noddy with a piece of sacking, Josie came down to the yard. A brown horse with a pink and white muzzle, Noddy was standing with his long lop-ears drooping and an expression of bliss on his honest face.

She leaned on the half-door, watching Linc work, and after a moment or two he looked up questioningly.

'Hi. Is there something I can do for you?'

'No, not really. Well, yes. I . . . er . . . came to apologise for the way I behaved the other day. I was being a cow. I shouldn't have said those things.' She'd scooped her hair up, fixing it in a loose knot at the back, and now looked uncertainly at him through the resulting wisps.

'No problem,' Linc told her, turning back to rubbing Noddy's coat. 'We all need someone to blame. It makes it easier – saves dealing with the real issues.'

'That's awfully cynical,' she protested.

'It's true, though.'

There was silence for a couple of minutes and Linc looked round, wondering if she'd gone.

She was still there, looking thoughtful.

'The thing is, I'd had a bloody awful day,' she explained. 'Mum rang me first thing but I was already on a shoot. I came as soon as I could but I had to break an afternoon appointment and the client wasn't happy. My agent was livid and it all got very messy. That's why I had to go back this morning – to make peace.'

'Yeah, I wound up in trouble with my boss, too.'

'Oh, you work . . . ?'

'For my father. Estate manager – probationary.'

'I'm sorry,' she said in confusion. 'I didn't mean . . . That is, I never thought . . .'

'You thought I was a rich playboy with nothing better to do than amuse myself flirting with teenagers.'

Josie coloured. 'I'm sorry about that. Mum explained this afternoon, and about why you keep Noddy here. It's just that every time anyone opened their mouth, it was Linc this and Linc that – I felt like you'd taken over my family!'

'Preconceptions are grossly unfair . . .'

'I know. It's not how I am, normally.'

'Take myself,' Linc went on, ignoring her. 'I assumed that a model was going to be spoilt, egotistical, self-centred . . .'

'And that's how I behaved,' Josie said unhappily.

'Shallow and . . . and bimboistic!' he finished with a flourish.

She giggled. 'Now that's not a real word! Even with a model's limited vocabulary, I know that much!'

'Well, it ought to be,' Linc declared, slapping his horse's brown rump affectionately. 'That's your lot, Noddy, old boy.'

'Who gave him that ridiculous name?' Josie asked as Linc set him loose and came out of the stable.

'I did. But it's not what it seems. His full name is Noddy's Friend.'

'Big Ears!' Josie exclaimed with a dawning smile. 'You're crazy, you know?'

'Certifiable,' he agreed. 'But quite harmless. Ask anyone.'

Josie followed him as he took saddle, bridle and grooming kit along to the tackroom. Ruth had cleaned her tack and left a bucket of warmish water for Linc, who used a damp sponge to wipe the leather over, paying closer attention to the dried slobber and hay mixture that had stuck to the edges of the bit. Left to harden, it could well result in a sore mouth, something Noddy, with his pink-skinned muzzle, was especially prone to. He had to wear sunblock, too.

'So what's Linc short for? I've never heard the name before,' Josie remarked.

'Lincoln,' he told her with a grimace. 'Outlandish names are a sort of tradition in my family. In the past we've had St John, Gabriel, Ludovic and Emmanuel. On the whole I think I was quite lucky.'

He was rubbing the stainless steel with a dry cloth now, and suddenly his brows drew together in a puzzled frown.

'I don't believe it,' he murmured. 'Good God!'

'What?' Josie leaned closer to look.

'Well, see here, on the cheekpiece,' Linc said, pointing to the spatulate metal protrusion above the bit rings on each side. 'It's been filed down – you can see the scratch marks.'

'Yeah, I see . . .'

'I did that,' he stated. 'This is my bit. The one that was stolen on Friday night!'

'But it can't be, surely!'

'It is, you know. These snaffles aren't all that

common. I filed it down because when I bought it, it had a kind of blip in the metal. Lots of people wouldn't have bothered but Noddy's skin rubs very easily. The chances of there being two with these marks on in one area must be pretty slim.'

'But what if someone else had the same problem you did and filed theirs too? It could have happened, if they were from the same lot,' Josie said. 'I mean, otherwise . . .'

'It's possible but it would be a sizeable coincidence,' Linc said, unconvinced. 'I think I should have a word with Sandy.'

'But you're not saying that Sandy . . .? We've known him forever.'

'No, not Sandy himself, but he buys in stuff all the time. It might be worth asking him if he remembers where and when he got the bit. If it was months ago then we'd have to think again.'

'I suppose so. But if you really think it's yours, shouldn't you tell the police?'

'I will, but as you said, Sandy's a friend. I don't want to throw him to the wolves without giving him a chance to explain how he came by it. And after all, as you said yourself, there's still a slim possibility it's a coincidence. I'll maybe swing out that way before I head for home.'

Shaftesbury was only five or six miles from Farthing St Anne, and Sandy's base was a unit on a small industrial estate, not much more than a large storeroom with a tiny cluttered office attached.

Linc parked the Discovery between Sandy's lorry and a gleaming white BMW, and let himself into the building via a personnel door set into the larger,

steel sliding one. The building was mainly con-
structed of painted corrugated panels, lined with
what looked like chipboard, although this was
almost completely covered by the multitude of
shelves and hooks carrying Sandy's massive collection of stock. A second level was reached by way of
a steel staircase, and to Linc's right, as he entered,
was the small office made of breeze-blocks.

He hadn't telephoned ahead, for even though he
didn't suspect Sandy himself, he could imagine DI
Rockley's scorn if he learned that Linc had given the
saddler prior notice of his visit.

Another man, presumably the owner of the
BMW, was in the office with Sandy when Linc
knocked and went in, and they both looked up,
frowning slightly.

'Sorry. Am I interrupting something? I can wait
out here,' he offered. As he paused, Tiger appeared
from somewhere and pushed his way into the room.

'Linc! No, that's okay, come in,' Sandy said with
his ready smile. 'Did we forget something earlier?'

'Er . . . No, not really. I'd just like a word, if I
could.'

The other man tossed back the last of something
in a tumbler and stood up; a tall, well-built, dark-
haired figure probably in his late-thirties or early-
forties, prosperously dressed in a brown leather coat
and twill trousers. When he moved, Tiger gave vent
to a low-voiced growl and he favoured the dog with
a look of dislike.

'Right. Well, I was just leaving anyway. I'll see
you later.'

Linc stood sideways on to let him pass, which he
did with a brief smile and a whiff of aftershave.

'So, take a seat. What can I do for you?' Sandy gestured to the chair his visitor had just vacated.

Linc sat down and Tiger immediately pattered across and put his front paws up on his knees, wagging happily.

'I wondered if you could remember where and when you got this bit?' Linc asked, taking the snaffle out of his coat pocket. 'Presumably it *is* second-hand?'

Sandy's eyes narrowed. 'Er, yes, it is. Why? Is there a problem with it?'

'Not precisely,' Linc said, hedging. 'Can you remember where it came from?'

Sandy appeared to rack his brains, then shook his head slightly.

'Oh, Christ! I buy stuff in all the time. Wait a minute . . . yes! I bought that one at the weekend, I think. It was in a box of odds and ends some guy brought to Andover on Saturday. Said he didn't have a horse any more and was clearing out. Only wanted a tenner. There wasn't anything very remarkable amongst it – a couple of pairs of reins, some stirrup leathers and irons, a pelham and that snaffle.'

'So you've still got the rest?'

'Well, yes. But not together. I brought it home and cleaned it up – sterilised the bits, as I always do – then put it all into stock. I couldn't say for sure which ones they were now because I did a couple of part-exchanges over the weekend. Sorry. Why d'you ask?'

'I don't suppose you could describe this guy?'

'To be honest, no. I see so many people at an event, they all blur into one another. Let me see . . .'

He rocked his chair back on to two legs, balancing with one toe against the desk. 'It was towards the end of the day. Yes, hang on, he was fairly old – retired, I should think. Grey hair, corduroy trousers, waxed jacket and glasses . . . yeah, he was wearing some of those wire-rimmed glasses you see advertised on TV. You know, the bendy ones. Now, are you going to tell me why you want to know?'

'Yeah, sorry about that. The thing is, wildly improbable as it may seem, I'm pretty sure this is the same bit that was stolen from the Vicarage on Friday night.'

'You're kidding!' The front legs of Sandy's chair hit the floor with a bump. 'Are you sure? How can you tell?'

Linc explained, showing him the abrasions.

'I shall have to let the police know, of course,' he said. 'But I thought it was only fair to warn you before they landed on you like a ton of bricks.'

'Thanks, I appreciate that.' Sandy pushed the telephone towards him. 'Why don't you ring them now? I've got nothing to hide and we don't want them saying I got rid of the gear after you left, do we?'

Linc had been intending to call Rockley on his mobile as soon as he left the building, and was grateful to Sandy for making it so easy. The call was made, using the number Rockley had given him for the purpose, and as luck would have it, Linc reached the detective inspector at the first attempt. He received the news with interest but also a good measure of annoyance that Linc had already approached the saddler.

'Well, now you're there, be so good as to stay

until we get there,' he growled. 'Or we'll find he's ditched all the evidence. I'll be twenty minutes or so, I expect. I really wish you'd left it to us. We've lost the advantage of surprise, thanks to you.'

DI Rockley's mood hadn't noticeably improved when he arrived not more than fifteen minutes later. Followed by a younger, uniformed officer, he entered Sandy's office, rapping on the door as he did so, and favoured Linc with a sour look.

'If you could wait outside, please, sir,' he said shortly.

'Sure.' Linc obediently got to his feet and wandered out into the gathering dusk where, after some ten minutes or so, Rockley found him sitting in the Land-Rover.

'Do you have the stolen article with you, sir?'

'I do.' Linc picked it off the seat beside him and offered it to the policeman.

Rockley produced a polythene bag from about his person and held the open top towards Linc who regarded it with some amusement.

'I don't suppose there's much evidence left to contaminate,' he remarked. 'It's been sterilised, polished, in a horse's mouth and then washed again. The only fingerprints are likely to be Sandy's and mine.'

'Nevertheless,' Rockley prompted.

Shrugging, Linc dropped the bit into the bag.

'Will I get it back?' Noddy could be ridden in another bit at home but he liked the half-cheek for competition.

'Eventually. Now, if you don't mind, we have work to do. If there's nothing more you can tell us, you may as well be on your way. With all the stock in there, it looks like being a long night.'

'How do you know what to look for?' Linc was curious.

'We have a list of items stolen recently, some of which had identifying marks. Some were even postcoded. We just have to go through it all, one piece at a time.'

'But Sandy's not a suspect, is he?'

'With respect, I'm not about to release that sort of information, sir. We have searched Mr Wilkes's premises before, with his permission. As a dealer in second-hand saddlery, he'd be ideally placed to receive stolen goods – either knowingly or otherwise – but he's by no means the only one.'

'Oh, well.' Linc reached for his seatbelt. 'Will you let us know if you find anything?'

'As soon as there's anything concrete, you'll be told,' Rockley assured him. 'I'll say goodnight now. And, remember, crime is our business; best leave it to us.'

Linc started the Discovery's engine. 'You're probably right,' he acknowledged. 'But the Hathaways are friends of mine.' Then reversed out of his space leaving the DI looking after him with a thoughtful frown.

Heading for home, Linc was in contemplative mood himself. Until Rockley's polite warning off, he hadn't really considered doing any investigation of his own but the need to bring someone to account for the brutality of Friday night had been growing ever stronger in him over the past couple of days.

By the time he reached Farthingscourt he had

decided on a plan of action and, accordingly, spent a couple of hours the next afternoon ringing or visiting a number of local saddlers and horse-feed merchants. In each case he asked if the proprietors knew of any other victims of tack theft and left a postcard advertisement asking any such persons who were willing to be interviewed to contact him by letter, care of a Post Office box number. He also placed similar advertisements in three local papers.

In the event, it wasn't the adverts that produced the first useful lead but a friend who rang the Hathaways to ask after Abby. Linc had gone to the Vicarage a couple of days later to exercise Noddy before breakfast and had returned from his ride to find Josie mucking out the stables.

'Good ride?' she called, coming out of Cromwell's box with a pitchfork and broom.

'Lovely. It's a beautiful morning. I didn't know you were back.' She had been in London on Tuesday, working.

'Yeah, well, I've taken a week or two off now to help out here.'

'Will you miss much?'

'Bits and pieces, but to be honest I was glad to get away. I seem to have been working solidly for months.'

'Do you enjoy it?'

Josie wrinkled her nose. 'Not much. It's pretty much of a cattle market, being poked and prodded and having your attributes discussed as if you weren't there.'

'Sounds dire,' Linc agreed, stripping Noddy's saddle off. 'But I suppose the money's good.'

'It is. I wouldn't do it otherwise. I'm saving to go back to uni and do an archaeology degree, but you can't go on being a student forever, it's too expensive. Especially when you come from a large family like mine.'

'Any news from the hospital?' Linc asked, throwing a sweat sheet over the horse.

'Nothing new. We heard from some friends of Abby's last night, though. They also had a visit from the thieves a couple of weeks ago and lost everything.'

'Oh. Do you think they'd mind me asking them a few questions?'

Josie stopped sweeping and looked at him. 'I don't suppose so, but what for? They've already spoken to the police.'

'I don't know, really. I just feel so frustrated that nothing seems to be happening. It doesn't look as though the police have turned anything up yet, or if they have, they're keeping it very quiet. Anyway, it can't do any harm, and it might just do some good, you never know.'

'Mmm, I suppose. I'll pop up to the house and get the number for you.'

When Linc visited Abby's friends in his lunch break they were happy to help but had little of any significance to tell him. The thieves had broken into their tackroom from the back, in the early hours of the morning. Out of sight of the house they had levered and broken several planks and then made off with three complete sets of tack and a number of fairly new winter rugs, including two straight off the horses' backs, leaving them unprotected and shivering in the cold night air.

'They hit the Jenkinses' place, just down the road, the same night,' Linc was told. 'They didn't get much there, though, 'cause Mrs Jenkins and two of the girls were away on a course – horses, tack and all.'

Given directions, Linc decided to call on the Jenkinses straight away and walked into their expensive-looking yard just as the farrier was leaving. The stables were built in a C-shape, separated from the house by a small turnout paddock, and had obviously been positioned so the horses were visible from the Jenkinses' home. Unfortunately this meant the tackroom door faced away from it, as did the open-fronted haystore next to it.

A slim, thirty-something woman in jeans and a guernsey, with blonde hair scraped back in a loose ponytail, was helping a teenage edition of herself saddle a breedy pony. Linc introduced himself and explained his mission.

'I see. Well, I'm afraid we can't be a lot of help,' the woman said, frowning slightly as she squinted into the April sunshine. 'Although we were broken into, there wasn't much to take. My two older daughters and myself were on a dressage course at Stockbridge and Cara had Dandy's tack in the house to clean while watching telly. She's not normally allowed to do that when I'm here but as luck would have it, it was fortunate that she did.'

'Do you know what time you were broken into? Did anyone see anything at all? Even the littlest detail might turn out to be important.'

'No, I'm sorry. The police were very thorough but they couldn't find anything. We think it was about one o'clock in the morning. Our neighbour heard a vehicle start up when she got up to let her dog out but didn't think anything of it until she heard what had happened. My husband was here with Cara and her brother but their bedrooms are at the front of the house and, as you see, it's a fair way off. We've actually got an alarm but *somebody* forgot to turn it on, it seems.'

Cara squirmed under her mother's accusing gaze and muttered something sulkily. It was obviously a sore point between them.

'Ah well, it was worth asking,' Linc said regretfully. 'It seems to be the same story everywhere.'

'Have you been robbed too?' Mrs Jenkins asked.

Linc told her about the Hathaways and Abby's plight, and her reaction was the usual mixture of shock and pity. She didn't know Abby well, she said, but as a mother she could imagine how Mrs Hathaway must feel.

Absent-mindedly, Linc promised to pass on her best wishes and took his leave, but instead of turning for home, he drove the Discovery a few yards down the road and pulled into a field gateway. He'd been watching Cara Jenkins as he was speaking to her mother, and could have sworn he'd surprised a flash of guilt in her eyes. It was so fleeting that he might have thought he'd imagined it, except that when she'd realised he was looking she'd flushed pink and ducked hastily down to tighten her pony's girth.

He hadn't long to wait. Barely five minutes after he'd left the yard the gate opened and Cara rode out. For once, luck was on his side; she was alone.

As she approached the Land-Rover he got out and stood waiting.

After the slightest of hesitations she walked the pony all the way up to him and pulled up, looking a little defiant and very unsure of herself.

'Have you got something you want to tell me, Cara?' Linc asked gently. 'You know something, don't you?'

'No! I can't tell you . . . Mother would kill me if she found out.'

'Is there something you didn't tell the police? Please, Cara. It's important.'

She fidgeted with her reins, unwilling to meet his eyes.

'I can't tell you,' she said again. 'It's not just me who'd get into trouble.'

'Do you know who did it?'

'No! It's not that . . .'

'Think of Abby Hathaway,' he said persuasively. 'She's about your age. She's in hospital now, in a coma. If you know something that could help catch these people, you must tell.'

Cara nudged her pony forward and Linc fell in alongside, half expecting her to push it into a trot and leave him behind. She didn't. Her face was twisted with the difficulty of her dilemma but finally she made up her mind.

'If I tell you, you can't tell anyone. Not a soul. Promise!'

'Cara, I can't promise. Not if it's important. The police should know.'

She shook her head vehemently. 'No! Promise or I won't tell you.' She shortened her reins with the obvious intention of kicking the pony on.

Linc put out a hand and caught the rein.

'All right. I promise. Nobody will ever know you told me.' He hoped the qualification would escape her notice and it seemed to, for after a short pause she began to talk.

'I'm seeing this boy, see. I can't tell you his name,' she stated with another defiant look at Linc. 'Only Mum doesn't like him 'cause he comes from the council estate down the road. She says they're a rough lot, but Ricky's different, honestly he is.'

'So he came round while she was away?' Linc hazarded. 'Did your dad know?'

'Of course not,' Cara said scornfully. 'He'd have told Mum, wouldn't he?'

Linc agreed that he probably would.

'Well, I met him down at the stables that night and we were sitting in the hayshed on top of the hay, talking and stuff. Only it was cold and wet, so I fetched a couple of blankets from the tackroom.'

'And turned the alarm off,' Linc put in.

'Yeah, well, I would have turned it on again after, only these men came and I forgot.'

'The men who broke in? Did you see them?'

Cara shook her head. 'We were up on the hay – right at the top – when we heard them and we kept really quiet. I'd locked the door again and they forced it open, that's what we heard, and then they started arguing when they found there wasn't much tack in there. We couldn't hear it all but it sounded like one of them said, "What the fuck are we going to tell old Barnaby?" That's the word he used,' she said defensively, colouring a little. 'You want to know exactly, right?'

Linc hid a smile. 'Yes, please.'

'Well, and the other one mumbled something and then the first one says, "Well, he'll have to know, won't he?" And the second one says, "Are you gonna ring him then? He was running a dog tonight, so he'll either be out celebrating or in a shitty mood."'

'Running a dog?' Linc asked quickly. 'Are you sure that's what he said?'

'Yeah, 'cause they'd come out of the tackroom by then and were standing down in front of where we were. We were terrified they'd shine a torch round or something but they didn't.'

'And he called him Barnaby?'

'Barnaby . . . Barney . . . something like that.' Cara frowned, trying to remember.

'Did they say anything else?'

'No. They moved away. One of them looked in all the stables and then they disappeared. We didn't see them go, it all just went quiet. But we waited quite a long while after, just in case. Then Ricky went home, so we didn't do anything, honest!'

'It's all the same to me, kid. It's none of my business, is it?'

'But you won't tell anyone – you promised!' she pleaded.

Linc shook his head. 'No, I won't tell.'

Casual enquiries amongst people he came into contact with during the rest of the day turned up no useful information concerning local greyhound racing venues until Geoff Sykes remembered that Reagan, the head forester, had spoken once or twice of having a bet on 'the dogs'.

'He's working on the other side of Home Wood

today, isn't he?' Linc said. 'I might drive out that way later and have a word with him.'

It was nearly knocking-off time when he drove down the track beside Home Wood in search of Reagan, but the forester was still there, clearing ditches with the aid of an ageing JCB. He switched the machine off when he saw Linc and jumped down from the cab as it rattled to blessed silence.

'Evening, sir.' He wiped his broad hands on bottle-green estate overalls and waited for Linc to state his business. Six foot or so tall and stockily built, Reagan had black, tightly curling hair above weather-beaten features, and a fuzz of the same on all the visible parts of his body. He lived in a cottage on the estate with his wife and a new baby girl.

'Evening, Jack. How's it going?' After five months, Linc knew most of the estate workers by their first names and preferred to address them that way even though his father frowned upon the practice.

'All right, I think, sir. Should be finished tomorrow, I reckon.'

'And then you'll do Piecroft Copse?'

'That's right.'

As usual, Reagan was civil but unforthcoming and, as usual, he inspired in Linc an irritation far greater than his words merited. There was something about the manner of the man; a kind of barely stifled cockiness that suggested resentment of their relative positions.

After a brief discussion about the schedule for the next few days, Linc asked the forester where the nearest greyhound track was and if he knew of any local trainers.

Reagan looked surprised. 'Don't know about trainers, but I go to Ledworth or Poole. Poole's bigger of course but Ledworth's nearer. There's one at Swindon, too.'

'When's the next meeting, do you know?'

'Ledworth, tomorrow night.' Reagan was practically bristling with curiosity but apparently couldn't bring himself to ask a direct question.

Linc enjoyed not telling him.

'Thanks for that. By the way, how's the baby doing?'

'She's well.'

'And your wife – Lynne, isn't it?'

'Mrs Reagan's fine, thank you.'

His tone clearly said that his private life was his own, so Linc left it at that.

When he visited the greyhound track at Ledworth it was just waking up in preparation for the evening's sport. The stadium was located on the edge of an out-of-town business park, and from the approach road the sloping roof of the stands looked like another warehouse or workshop unit. There was a vast, unfinished car parking area, as yet sparsely occupied, in which Linc left the Discovery, trudging across the puddled gravel to the turnstiles.

In the ticket office a fifty-something woman with improbably red hair and even redder nails was counting change into a cash tray. She looked up with a measure of suspicion as Linc approached, dropping the remainder of the bagged change into the till and closing the drawer with a snap.

'We're not open yet.'

'I know,' Linc told her, with what he hoped was

a reassuring smile. 'I wanted to come before it got too busy because I'm looking for someone and I wondered if anyone here could help me.'

The heavily mascara'd eyes looked him up and down a time or two and apparently saw nothing threatening.

'Who'd you want?'

'Chap named Barnaby. I'm not sure if he's an owner or a trainer but the fella I was talking to at Poole the other night said to ask for him.'

'Barnaby who? Or is it Mr Barnaby?'

'I'm not sure. He just said Barnaby. I should have got more details but we'd just had a big win and I wasn't really thinking straight.' He fervently hoped she wouldn't press him for more information on his fictitious good fortune. In future, he would make a point of doing more thorough groundwork.

'And he's running dogs here tonight?'

Linc made a face. 'That's just it, I don't know. Pretty hopeless, isn't it?'

The woman's expression agreed with him. 'What d'you want him for?'

'I was told he might have a dog for sale.' He'd anticipated that question.

'Plenty of dogs for sale, luv,' the red-head told him. 'A dozen or so in here, for that matter.' She held up a glossy booklet depicting a running dog and bearing the title *Ledworth Greyhound Stadium*. She slipped a slimmer, typed section out of the centre to show him. 'Tonight's races. Gives the names of the owners and trainers, too.'

'Oh. Could I have a copy?'

'Two pounds fifty,' she stated uncompromisingly. 'You know, I'm not the best one to ask really.

I get to know the punters doing this job; don't see much of the racing.'

Linc fished in his trouser pocket for loose change. 'Is there anyone else I could talk to, d'you think?'

'You can come back later, when we're open, but I can't let you in now, luv – sorry.'

Linc turned as footsteps sounded behind him. A leather-jacketed man was coming across from the car park. He looked hard at Linc then turned to the woman.

'Everything all right, Lily?' From his accent he was a Londoner.

'Yeah, I'm all right, luv. This gentleman is looking for someone, that's all. Here,' she said to Linc, 'Marty's the fella you want to ask. Works on the traps and knows everyone, don'tcha, luv?'

'That's right. Who you looking for?' Around forty, Marty had short dark hair, an earring and a hard, uncompromising expression.

'Someone called Barnaby. Friend of mine told me to look him up. Said he was well-known around the dog tracks . . .'

Without appearing to give the matter any thought, Marty pursed his lips and shook his head. 'Not this one. Who wants to know anyway?'

'I do,' Linc said equally unhelpfully.

Marty's face hardened still further. 'So what d'you want him for – this Barnaby chap?'

'If you don't know him, it won't interest you, will it?' Linc replied. He waved the schedule at Lily. 'Thanks for your help. I might try some of these numbers.'

As he walked back to the Land-Rover he fancied he could feel Marty's eyes boring into his back and a surreptitious glance as he turned to get in showed the man was indeed still watching him. Linc supposed the race card with its list of owners and trainers might be of some use but aside from that, his visit had patently been a waste of time. He hadn't time on this occasion to wait and attend the meeting itself, and even if he had, he couldn't see that he'd have a hope in hell of finding the elusive Barnaby in a sea of owners, trainers and spectators. He would just have to try another approach.

Between riding Noddy and estate work, Linc hadn't yet had a chance to look at the day's mail and a depressing mound of it awaited his attention when he returned to Farthingscourt. Rapidly sorting it into three piles for business, personal and bin, he found a brown manilla envelope from the Post Office and opened that first. Inside, two further envelopes were addressed to his box number: one a reply from another victim of the thieves, and the second a folded sheet of newspaper.

Puzzled, Linc spread it out on his desk. It was a complete page from the *Sun* and he saw immediately that a number of words had been picked out with a neon-yellow highlighter pen. From top left, working across and down, they spelt out a message.

People who mind their own business live longer.

4

Linc read the words twice before their meaning really hit him, then it took his breath away.

It was strange but in spite of what had happened to Abby, he hadn't really considered how dangerous it could be for him personally to tangle with whoever was behind the tack thefts. The truth was, of course, that the men who had raided the Vicarage that night must be well aware, from newspaper reports if nothing else, that Abby's condition was serious and should she not recover they would face a charge of manslaughter at the very least. It was not so surprising that they should be prepared to use threats of violence to discourage Linc from prying too closely.

When the first shock had worn off, though, he was able to think more clearly. The very fact that the warning had come by way of the Post Office box number was proof enough that the sender had no idea of his identity. Rather than panic, he told himself, he should regard this in the light of a wake-up call and be more vigilant in future. All the same, there was nothing like receiving a death threat to alter one's outlook on life.

Calling at the Vicarage for his early-morning ride the next day, Linc found the mood there had become even more sombre. Ruth was mucking out the stables in slightly tearful silence, and he learned that after a day of increased brain activity that had raised the hopes of doctors and family alike, Abby had apparently succumbed to an infection and taken a turn for the worse.

'I *was* going to offer to groom for you at Talham tomorrow,' Ruth told him. 'But Josie's staying at the hospital with Mum and Dad so I'll have to stick around. Besides, I don't want to be away from home in case . . .' Her voice broke, and with a sob she said, 'We thought she was getting better. Why did this have to happen?'

Linc gently took the broom out of her hands and pulled her into a hug. 'Hey, don't give up on her. You have to keep believing she'll be okay. She's a tough cookie, your sister.'

Ruth sniffed into the front of his fleece. 'I know. But I wish I could be at the hospital with Mum. It's hard to be cheerful for Hannah and Toby when you know everything's going wrong.'

'Would it help if I stayed here with the kids tomorrow to let you go with Josie?'

Ruth pulled back, tears shining on her lashes. 'Oh, no! You must ride Hobo again, and Noddy – you didn't take him last week. You know Abby would want you to go. You'll never get to the Olympics if you keep missing competitions.'

Linc smiled. His mother had been short-listed to

ride in the Olympic team later in the year she'd had her fatal accident and it was his stated ambition to fulfil that dream on her behalf.

'I don't think missing Talham would make much difference, one way or the other. It's hardly Badminton, is it?'

'Nevertheless, you should go,' Ruth said firmly. 'We all want you to. Go and win, for Abby!'

Talham Hunter Trials was a relatively new event but was already attracting riders from well outside its Wiltshire location. They were drawn by its growing reputation as being a well-built course that offered a good variety of challenging fences. It was only cross-country, rather than a one-day event, and included no dressage or showjumping in the day's competition, although a clear-round jumping ring was provided for those who wished to use it.

Linc drove Noddy to the venue in the Hathaways' two-horse lorry and was met on the field by his sister-in-law Nikki, who had volunteered to be his groom for the day. Because of the potential hazards of the sport, it's sensible for riders competing in cross-country events to provide themselves with back-up drivers, or failing that, to notify the secretary on arrival that they are attending alone.

'Well, this is just like the old days, isn't it?' Nikki exclaimed as Linc jumped down from the cab and stretched the kinks of the journey out of his back and legs.

During their brief relationship she had accompanied Linc and Noddy to several events, proving herself to be a competent groom. Now she was dressed in jeans and a thick fleece, with a cotton headscarf tying her blonde curls into a ponytail. Her china-doll face was, as always, perfectly made-up and with nail varnish, earrings and a bead choker, she managed to look both workmanlike and glamorous at the same time. Linc was struck by the comparison between her and Josie's 'off-duty' casualness.

'Yeah, thanks for stepping in at the last moment like this.'

'No problem at all!' she assured him with a smile. 'I love doing it. And now of course Cris has decided that a few horsy action shots are just what he needs for this exhibition he's planning.'

'So where is he?' Linc asked, looking round for his brother. A talented photographer, Crispin made quite a good living doing portrait work and supplying material for picture libraries but his dream was to have a full-scale exhibition in one of the well-known galleries.

'Oh, he's gone off to scout for good vantage points. We probably won't see him again for ages.'

Another lorry was easing into position beside them and the field was abuzz with horses and people. Leaving Noddy in Nikki's capable hands, Linc departed in search of Nina and Hobo, finding them at the other end of the lorry park, conveniently near the secretary's tent. After completing the formalities, they left the horse with his groom and set off to walk the cross-country course together, pacing out the combinations and discussing the best way to ride each fence.

Returning some forty minutes later, Linc found Noddy tacked up and ready and being walked round with a blanket over his quarters. All he had to do was put on his body protector, number and crash cap, before mounting and riding away to warm up.

'You're a star,' he told Nikki as he took the reins from her. 'Did you put the Vaseline on his mouth?' When he got excited Noddy tended to generate a fair amount of frothy saliva and on occasion the tender pink skin around his mouth became chapped and sore.

'Yep. Done his lip gloss,' she joked. 'And his mascara.'

'Poor fella! Don't tease him. Oh, and by the way, if you want Crispin, he was last seen over by Lovers Leap, looking for the most dramatic angle on the drop fence. A formidable female in tweed was trying to keep him at a safe distance but every time she turned her back he moved in a couple of feet.'

'Sounds like him,' she agreed, laughing. 'I think I'll leave him to it and go hunt for bargains around the trade stands.'

Noddy felt fresh and eager for the challenge when Linc rode him over to the start area. Nikki had returned by then and given him a final tidy up, greasing his legs and sponging his eyes and nostrils. Linc had taken his windproof jacket off to reveal a polo-necked sweater in dark jade green; the same colour his mother used to ride in.

The starter counted him down, Nikki called encouragement, and then they were away and the rest of the world ceased to exist.

Noddy settled into his usual, ground-eating gallop and took the first three relatively easy fences without a check. The fourth was actually a combination of three parts, requiring control and accuracy. Noddy steadied obediently and jumped through it neatly, flicking his long lop-ears back to receive Linc's spoken praise as they accelerated away on the other side. Linc settled down happily to ride the rest of the course.

Ten minutes later, after a fast and faultless round, they flew the two tiers of strawbales that made up the last obstacle on the course and galloped up the run-in to the finish. Linc patted his horse delightedly. At moments like these he could really believe his Olympic dream might come true.

Nina appeared as he led Noddy back to the lorry with Nikki.

'Well done, Linc! That was a smashing round! Hobo'll be ready when you are. Listen, I don't know whether you're interested but a woman approached me a minute ago wanting to speak to you. Apparently she's got a horse here, entered in the bigger class, but her rider's let her down and she wondered if you'd be interested in an extra ride. Someone had told her that you'd ridden Hobo for me last week. It's entirely up to you what you do about it. I've never met the woman before and I've absolutely no idea what the horse is like. *Her* name is Dee Ellis.'

Linc shrugged. 'I can talk to her, I guess. Where is she now?'

Nina gave him directions, and after he'd helped Nikki settle Noddy he searched the owner out, finding a petite, fiftyish, peroxide blonde disconsolately stroking a huge steel-grey gelding. She brightened visibly when Linc introduced himself and he learned that the horse, registered as Night

Train but affectionately known as Steamer, had been bought for the woman's daughter to ride but she'd gone off to university and transferred her interest to boys instead.

'Steamer came from Ireland,' Dee Ellis told him. 'He was doing quite well over there. Susie had such big plans for him but all of a sudden she seemed to lose interest. I couldn't bear to sell him, though. He's my baby. He's such a big pussycat.'

While she was talking, Linc looked the horse over and liked what he saw. Steamer had hard, clean-boned legs, cool to the touch, powerful quarters, a deep chest and a bold, honest eye.

'Tell you what,' he said. 'All being well, when I've ridden Hobo for Nina, I'll pop this lad round the clear-round course and if we get on okay, I'll ride him cross-country.'

'That's great. I'll have him ready for you,' she promised. 'And I'll sort it out with the secretary. See you later.'

The course at Talham was a little bigger than the one Hobo had jumped the previous week, but he set off undaunted, jumping boldly but carefully once more. There were two drop fences on the course. One was a straightforward leap down off a platform; the other – known as Lovers Leap – involved jumping up a step, taking one short stride, then launching out over a rail and ditch to land some six feet below. Nina had expressed doubts about both of these when Linc had walked the course with her, reinforcing his belief that such fences were her bugbear rather than Hobo's, and sure enough the horse took the first drop in his stride. Several more obstacles passed by uneventfully under his capable hooves, including a watersplash and a lane crossing of low hedges taken on the bounce, before horse and rider swung round a bend in the course and began the approach to Lovers Leap.

Noddy had coped easily with the fence and Linc had no qualms about Hobo's ability but as the obstacle came into sight, so too did a steward, standing directly in their path and frantically waving a red flag. Disappointed, Linc recognised the signal for a stoppage, sat back in the saddle and slowly eased Hobo back to a trot and finally a walk.

'Sorry, sir,' the steward called. 'We've got a faller up ahead. I'm afraid you may be held up for several minutes.'

'Okay.' Linc nodded and held up his hand. Beneath him, Hobo sidled and tossed his head impatiently. Linc rode him in a circle, trying to get him settled so as not to use up too much energy while he waited. Being held up on a course was always a frustrating experience but could, depending upon the horse, have either a negative or a positive effect. If your mount is slightly lacking in fitness or finding the course hard work, then a rest part way round can prove beneficial. Other, more excitable animals are liable to work themselves up into a lather if forced to wait, and for any horse and rider, a prolonged stoppage is unfortunate, resulting in muscles cooling and a loss of impetus.

Linc continued to circle, occasionally letting Hobo trot, while further up the course people were swarming round Lovers Leap like flies on a carcass. He couldn't see precisely what was happening but a little further off someone was leading a brown horse in slow circles, so he guessed it was the rider who was in trouble. Sure enough, after a few moments an ambulance could be seen approaching over the bumpy ground and soon, two fluorescent jackets joined the swarm.

The steward's radio crackled and he spoke into it briefly.

'Nasty incident,' he said, coming towards Linc. 'Young girl, only seventeen. Looks like back trouble. Be a while yet. Sorry.'

'No problem.' Linc knew he wouldn't be the only one held up on the course. With competitors sent out every two or three minutes there would probably be at least two more stopped at various points behind him.

It was in fact nearly fifteen minutes more before he was given the all clear, by which time Hobo had switched off completely. Linc rode him in three big circles, gradually increasing speed, and then sent him forward down the eighty metres or so to the next fence, wishing he didn't have to restart over the most daunting obstacle on the course.

Hobo apparently had no such worries. He just seemed delighted to be moving again. Linc steadied him three strides out and he sprang lightly up on to the mound, put in the requisite short stride on top and leaped out over the rail to land with barely a check on the lower ground beyond the ditch. The watching crowd clapped appreciatively.

'Good boy!' Linc patted Hobo's neck as he galloped on. Halfway up the following stretch they passed the riderless brown horse being led back and Linc mentally crossed himself. Within moments he'd put the incident out of his mind, lost to the rhythm of Hobo's bobbing head and pounding hooves. It looked like being another faultless round until they suffered a communication breakdown over Linc's intended route through the last combination and almost hit a tree. The mix up left Hobo unbalanced and unable to attempt the final rail, and circling to take it again meant they finished with twenty penalties.

Nina, waiting at the end of the course, brushed his apologies aside.

'No, don't worry, Linc. I'm just glad you're both all right! We heard over the Tannoy that someone had fallen but it was ages before we could find out who. When you didn't come back, we weren't sure whether *you'd* fallen or whether there was someone else ahead of you.'

'It was the girl in front of me,' Linc told her, dismounting and running his stirrups up. 'Quite nasty, according to the steward. But Hobo wasn't fazed by the wait. He was brilliant!'

Noddy and Hobo's class was a big one, so after relinquishing Nina's horse to the groom Linc had plenty of time to return to his own lorry for some lunch. He went by way of the trade stands, looking to buy a new pair of riding gloves as his were fast becoming more hole than glove. He was pleased to find Sandy Wilkes's stand, and went in under the canopy to see him. Sandy himself was taking advantage of a quiet moment to drink a cup of soup but stood up with every appearance of pleasure when he saw Linc, apparently not bearing a grudge for Monday night's events.

'Hi, mate,' he said. 'How are you doing today?'

'Thanks. Not bad at all. But I could do with a

new pair of gloves.' He held his hands up to illustrate his point.

'You certainly could,' Sandy agreed. 'Though I'm not sure I should serve you after the other night. Those nosy policemen kept me up till two o'clock in the morning and left one hell of a mess for me to clear up!'

'Ouch! Sorry about that.'

'Nah, it wasn't your fault.' Sandy reached down a tray full of a variety of gloves. 'Have a look through that lot. By the way, I put your advert up.' He had been out when Linc had called and put the postcard through the door with an explanatory note. 'So, have you had any luck with it so far?'

Linc shook his head. 'Not a lot. I've spoken to a few other people, though, and got a couple of things to check up on.'

'You have?'

'Mmm. Nothing to tell yet, though.' Linc didn't mention the warning message. He had passed it on to Rockley, in spite of the inevitable 'I told you so', in the hope that something might be gleaned forensically but the DI had held out little hope.

When Linc returned to the horsebox, Noddy was tied up outside, warmly rugged up and munching on a net of hay, whilst Nikki was happily chatting to the owners of a neighbouring lorry. She broke off as Linc walked up, and came to meet him.

'That was bad luck,' she commiserated. 'Getting held up like that must have affected him.'

'Actually, he was very good about it. The run-out was my fault.'

'At first, we weren't sure who'd fallen. Then I remembered that Cris was somewhere out there

85

and I called him on his mobile. He said you were okay. The girl didn't look too good though. Apparently the horse rolled on her.'

Linc took over guard duty at the lorry while Nikki went to buy a hot dog and see if she could locate Crispin. In this she failed, and by the time she returned and Linc set off in search of Dee Ellis and Steamer, word had begun to filter round the venue that the girl who'd been taken to hospital had in fact died on the way. The atmosphere became sombre as the shock set in and people huddled in groups, talking in hushed voices. One or two who had known her well scratched from the competition and went home early, and for Linc it took the edge off the news, presently, that Noddy had come second in his class.

Steamer was tacked up ready, wearing protective boots and a breast girth to stop his saddle slipping back.

'Are you still okay to ride?' Dee Ellis asked anxiously. 'After . . . you know . . .?'

'Sure.'

Linc fastened his crash cap and mounted, making the big grey stand while he adjusted the length of his stirrups before riding away to warm up. Steamer felt broad and powerful beneath him.

The clear-round course consisted of twelve colourful show jumps standing at around three feet in height. Riders could attempt the course as many times as they liked, paying a small entry fee each time and collecting a rosette for a faultless round.

Dee paid and Linc rode Steamer in. He was the perfect gentleman, taking a strong but manageable hold and jumping high and wide. Linc was impressed and told Dee he'd be glad to ride him in the main class.

With a few minutes to go, he was riding the grey round near to the start with a couple of other riders who were waiting their turn, when one of them drew alongside.

'That Dotty Dee's grey?' he asked.

'That's right,' Linc said cautiously, and the other rider raised an eyebrow.

'Hmm. Well, good luck, mate.'

There was something odd in his tone but Linc was called to the start line before he could follow it up.

'Ready?' the starter asked. 'Five, four, three, two, one. Good luck!'

As the words left the steward's lips Dee Ellis's 'pussycat' ripped the rubber-coated reins through Linc's fingers and set off as if all hell was after him. Caught napping like a novice, Linc swore, desperately trying to regain his balance and some semblance of control. The first fence was looming, a low, inviting hedge and rail – but even so not designed to be taken at full tilt. All the fences on a cross-country course need to be treated with respect.

By the time Linc had gathered his looping reins, the hedge and rail were upon them and it was far too late to try and steady the grey. Steamer took off a full stride early and landed a similar distance out the other side.

'Steady, you mad bastard!' Linc shouted at him, alternately pulling and releasing as they approached the oil barrels that formed fence two.

Steamer wasn't about to relinquish his advantage

without a fight. He skipped over the barrels with scornful ease and thrust his nose earthwards, almost pulling Linc from the saddle. As the reins slipped again, he set off with renewed vigour, and the best that Linc could do was steer him towards the third and pray.

As in Noddy and Hobo's class, the fourth was a combination fence, and as they landed over the third Linc knew he had to get a hold of the grey before they reached it. There was no way any horse could jump three solid fences in quick succession going at that speed.

As a general rule of thumb, to achieve the right trajectory a horse needs to take off the same distance away as the height of the fence. Too close and he risks hitting it with his front legs and tipping over. Too far away and he is liable to catch it with his hind legs. Combination fences compound any error. If the first element is met wrong, the problem tends to be magnified by each successive part. Steamer was showing every likelihood of meeting the first element very wrong indeed.

Clamping his legs as tightly as he could to the horse's sides, Linc sat down hard and physically forced Steamer to change his rhythm, driving him on to his bridle with all the strength he could muster. The grey's gait became ragged for a few strides, then his neck and back rounded and his pace dropped. By the time they reached the first rail he was still going far faster than Linc would have liked but at least he felt they had a chance of clearing it.

Steamer was as clever as a cat. He skimmed through without touching a rail, and in a crazy, irresponsible kind of way, Linc began to enjoy himself. The course flashed by in a blur, speed nearly proving to be their undoing at the water-splash where the dragging effect of the stream unbalanced the grey and caused him to miss the log jump out. He then jumped so fast and wide at the lane crossing that he took both hedges in one leap, landing with his quarters in the second and kicking himself free. Linc did take an extra pull on the approach to Lovers Leap but Steamer had other ideas and he could do little more than console himself with the thought that to have qualified for the bigger class, the grey must surely have safely negotiated obstacles such as these before.

One leap up, a brief touch on the top of the mound and a sky launch over the rail and drop. Linc sat back and Steamer landed running.

Somewhere nearby, a loudspeaker was updating people in other parts of the venue. 'Lincoln Tremayne and Night Train have just landed safely over fence number eighteen, Lovers Leap,' it announced in unemotional tones, 'and are gaining on the pair in front.'

Sure enough, rounding the next bend Linc could see a chestnut rump ahead, and almost immediately the course stewards began to signal to the slower pair to give way to Linc and Steamer. Linc shouted thanks as he swept by and sent the grey on up the last hill. Three more fences were taken without incident and suddenly the whirlwind ride was over.

Once across the finish line Steamer allowed Linc to pull him up with very little fuss and, as he slowed to a trot, Dee flew across the trampled turf, threw her arms round the horse's sweaty neck and hugged him, half-sobbing with joy.

'Bloody hell!' Linc exclaimed as Steamer finally halted, grey flanks heaving. 'Does he always go like that?'

Dee looked up at him, her eyes shining. 'Oh, yes, always.'

'You know, you really should have warned me!' Linc was almost as short of breath as his mount.

'But Nina said you could ride anything,' she replied, surprised.

'Oh, she did, did she?' he said, making a mental note to have a word with Miss Barclay. 'Well, I'm sorry about the run-out at the watersplash. I just couldn't get him to listen.'

'Oh, that's nothing! At least you got round! That's the first time he's finished a course since we've had him! And it just proves that I was right. He *is* a good horse, it's the *riders* that weren't up to it!'

Linc could have said a thing or two about that but he kept his tongue between his teeth. He dismounted on to legs that were suspiciously shaky and stretched his aching arms. On the whole, he thought, it was probably a good thing that the Eighth Viscount wasn't in the habit of watching his son and heir compete.

'I've a bone to pick with you, my girl!' Linc announced, as Nina joined him on the way back to his lorry. Dee had disappeared with Steamer in tow, promising Linc many rides in future should he want them, to which he returned a carefully non-committal answer.

'I didn't know he was a maniac!' she protested, laughing.

'And *she's* not much better. It seems she's known as Dotty Dee. That ought to have told you something.'

'Well, it probably would've, if I'd known,' she countered. 'Anyway, you coped, so what's all the fuss about?'

'Mr Tremayne? Lincoln?'

A new voice hailed him from behind and he turned to see a wiry woman with greying blonde hair hurrying to catch him up. She looked vaguely familiar but he couldn't think why.

'Yes. I'm Linc,' he confirmed.

'Can I have a word?'

'Well, I'm on my way home, but . . .'

Nina touched his arm. 'I'll phone you, Linc,' she said, peeling off in the direction of her own lorry.

'My name is Hilary Lang,' the newcomer said. 'And I've been watching you over the last few weeks. I have to say, I'm impressed.'

Hilary Lang. No wonder he'd felt he should know her. She had been a very successful international three-day event rider at around the time his mother had been riding and was still closely involved with the sport.

'Pleased to meet you,' he said warmly, putting out his hand.

'I just wanted to sound you out about possibly coming on one of our training courses,' she continued as they shook hands. 'It wouldn't be until July or August but I need to start sorting out a list. I'd very much like to see you there.'

Linc battled a feeling of unreality. Hilary Lang

did a lot of the coaching for the British international team.

'Where would it be?' he asked. As if it mattered! He would travel to Timbuktu for the chance to be included on one of her courses.

'Possibly Stoneleigh. It'll probably be a long weekend. Do I take it you're interested?'

'Extremely,' Linc confirmed.

'Good. I'll be in touch,' she said briskly. 'And by the way, well done for riding that grey. Sean O'Connor used to ride him in Ireland and had some success but I don't think even *he* was too sad to see him go. Night Train needs a hell of a lot of work but you did brilliantly. Your mum would have been proud of you.'

Back at the lorry Linc saw Crispin for the first time that day. Boyishly handsome with brown eyes, a wide infectious grin and short brown hair that he'd recently taken to wearing softly spiky, he was enough like Linc for them to be recognisable as brothers, but took after his mother more than the paternal line.

'I've got some incredible shots!' he exclaimed with enthusiasm. 'I kept moving between the water-splash and that Lovers Leap fence and absolutely *everything* happened at those two jumps!'

'What happened with that poor girl?' Linc asked.

'I don't know.' Crispin hadn't ridden since their mother had died and wasn't in the least bit horsy. 'The animal seemed to hesitate and then slip off the edge. Its front legs went down in the ditch and it somersaulted on top of her. It was gruesome! Nikki says she died on the way to hospital. I'm not surprised. Honestly, Linc, I don't know why you do it. You must be mad! Especially with our family history.'

'Oh, come on, Crispin. You're beginning to sound like Dad. You know as well as I do that accidents like that are pretty rare. By the way, you'll never guess who I've been talking to . . .' He told his brother about Hilary Lang and her exciting proposition.

'So what does this mean? Are you chucking in the job to become a full-time eventer?' Crispin joked.

'No. Even supposing I could afford to. Actually, I've been thinking about the money thing; it's not cheap, this eventing business, and I could really do with a lorry of my own. I can't keep borrowing the Hathaways'.'

'Well, what about a sponsor?'

'Mmm. Unfortunately it's not all that easy to drum up much interest in eventing. It's not exactly a sport that gets massive exposure.'

It was something he'd thought about quite a lot lately. Eventing was an extremely expensive sport, with relatively poor prize money – even at the very top – and offers of sponsorship were like gold dust. For a rider aiming for the national teams, it was impractical to have to rely on one horse, even if that horse was a dazzling talent, which Linc had to admit Noddy wasn't. Two horses, however, meant double the bills. Double the feed bill, two sets of shoes each time, more tack, more vet bills, entry fees, and livery fees. If only he could keep them at home that would be one less expense. Ah, well.

Linc didn't visit the Vicarage the following day.

Ruth and Josie had offered to see that Noddy had some gentle exercise to ease any stiffness in his muscles and Linc was able to give all his attention to estate business. When he'd got back from Talham the news on Abby had been indeterminate. Her condition was no worse but neither was it improving. The determined cheerfulness amongst the adult members of her family was heartbreaking. They had been thrilled with Noddy's blue rosette and Hilary Lang's interest, and pressed Linc to stay for a meal to give them the complete story of the day's events, which he did, skipping over the fatality at the drop fence. They didn't need any more bad news.

The whole atmosphere couldn't have been more different than on his return to Farthingscourt, where the subject was taboo and his father never asked how his day had been.

Sunday was largely uneventful, except for reports in the late afternoon of two men being seen taking too close an interest in the JCB that was parked out at Piecroft Copse. Linc went over to look but saw nothing suspicious. As a precaution he notified the police who promised to drive out that way a couple of times during the evening.

Routine work on the Sunday had given Linc a chance to rethink his strategy re the tack thieves, and in the evening he found the Jenkinses' telephone number in the directory and called to ask if they could remember the exact date the attempted robbery had taken place.

Because of having been away on the riding course, Mrs Jenkins was able to tell him straight away and, after ringing off, Linc called Jack Reagan.

'Jack, can you remember where the greyhound racing was on April the second?'

'Second of April?' the forester repeated. 'Swindon, I think.'

'Did you go that night?'

'Yeah. Lousy weather it was. Why?'

'I don't suppose you'd still have the racecard, would you?' Linc asked, mentally crossing his fingers.

'Probably,' Jack said slowly. 'I make a note of the placings to study the form. What do you want it for?'

'I'm looking for someone who was running a dog that night. Look, could I borrow it? I'll let you have it back.'

'It doesn't give details, you know. Only names, and some of those are syndicates.'

'Yeah, well, it's a start. If you could take it to work, I'll drop by and pick it up.'

Linc drove to the Vicarage just as the sun was rising the following morning, and found that even so Josie was at the stables before him.

Wearing jeans and a hooded fleece jacket, she had her long dark hair in a loose plait and wore no discernible make-up but still managed to look good. She greeted him with a friendly smile that was a million miles away from the coldness of their initial meeting.

'I'm on stable duty today. Roo's having a lie-in.'

'Hi. You haven't fed him, have you?' Linc asked.

'No. Ruth said you'd be wanting to ride early. I – um, thought I might come with you, if that's okay?'

'Yeah, fine. That'd be nice.' Linc was surprised how much the idea appealed to him.

Cromwell, the cobby grey that Josie and her mother shared, was a stout gentleman approaching middle age and, according to his rider, reminded her of a portly country squire in tweed and a yellow waistcoat.

'And a pipe,' Linc suggested, joining in. 'Don't forget his pipe.'

Josie laughed. 'What about Noddy?'

Linc shrugged. 'To be honest, I've never really thought about it. What do you think?'

'Well, I see him as handsome but slightly foppish and indecisive, like the sort of character Hugh Grant plays.'

'Oh, no!' Linc protested. 'He's quite a strong character when you get to know him. More of a James Bond type.'

'Roger Moore, then. Definitely upper-class. Not like Syrup and Treacle. Abby used to say they're like Punch and Judy, loud and vulgar.'

Her voice trailed away, and Linc guessed that she'd recognised her own accidental use of the past tense.

'How is she this morning?' He knew their mother telephoned first thing every day.

'No change,' Josie said. 'It's like we're all in some sort of limbo; not knowing whether to be sad that there's no improvement or happy that she's no worse. She just lies there, day in and day out, with those machines bleeping and hissing, and sometimes the noise drives you mad and you just long for silence, but then you remember what silence would mean . . .' She paused, clearly distressed, and Linc wished there were something he could say that would help. Realistically, there wasn't.

'So, what about your advert, Sherlock?' she asked then, brightly. 'Did you get much feedback?'

'Very little,' he admitted. 'One woman who doesn't answer her phone and a warning to mind my own business.'

Josie looked at him, sharply. 'Seriously? Someone warned you off?'

Linc nodded. 'It doesn't help, though. They didn't give anything away.'

'And you're going to leave it now, I hope?'

'Well, I might have to, I'm not making a lot of progress. But there are a couple of things I want to look into first.'

'I thought you'd got over that guilt trip thing. Remember what you said to me?'

'Yeah, I am over it. But I can't just leave it if there's a chance I can uncover something.'

Josie looked doubtful. 'Well, for goodness' sake, don't get yourself into trouble. One in hospital is bad enough.'

Linc looked at his watch.

'I think we'd better be turning back now. I've got a meeting with my father at half-past nine.'

Josie was successfully diverted. 'You have to have an appointment to see your own father? That's archaic!'

'He's a busy man,' Linc pointed out. 'And he's my boss – sort of. Anyway, it's not really an appointment. It's just the regular Monday morning briefing on the business of the week. This week we're de-sludging the millpond.'

As they rode back he found himself telling her

all about his plans for the mill and its produce.

'How wonderful! I find watermills fascinating, and windmills too. They're so – well – elemental, I suppose. No electricity and you can see exactly how they work. I'd love to come and see it when it's up and going. Is it going to be open to the public?'

Linc was amused. 'That's the plan, but you don't have to wait till then. Come and see it any time. It's a bit sad at the moment, of course, because we're in the middle of everything. But you're welcome if you want to see the transformation. Just give me a call.'

Mill business took up all the morning and Linc was finishing a late sandwich lunch in his office in the old stables when his phone rang.

It was the forester.

'Sir, one of the new lads thinks he saw someone nosing around by the machine store. I'm on my way over there. Do you want me to call the police?'

'No, that's all right, Jack. I was coming out to see you so I'll swing by there myself and meet you.'

He rang off and, leaving Geoff Sykes to go and oversee operations at the mill, drove out of the yard, round the back of the house and out towards Home Farm, on the edge of which the machine store was situated. Jack Reagan, coming from Piecroft Copse, had only half the distance to travel and his four-wheel drive was already parked outside. Linc drove on and drew up in the yard alongside the huge corrugated-iron building that housed most of the estate's larger machinery, but Reagan was nowhere to be seen.

At first it looked as though whoever had been seen there had gone. Linc walked right round the store, then selecting a key from a bunch that hung from his belt, he unlocked and opened the sliding door to check inside. All appeared to be quiet and nothing was obviously disturbed. He came out and refastened the padlock, turning round just in time to see two rough-looking men taking a close look at a digger that was parked on the other side of the yard. One, in his late-teens or early-twenties, wore torn denim jeans and a checked shirt, and was on the step of the machine, peering into the cab. The other was an older man, wearing a grubby blue boiler suit. Both had dark, greasy hair and stubble.

'Good afternoon,' Linc called out, going towards them. 'Can I do something for you?'

The older man looked him up and down and shook his head, apparently finding nothing threatening in Linc's lean five foot eleven, dressed as it was in jeans and an Aran sweater.

'Nah, I don't think so,' he replied.

'Then I think you'd better leave,' Linc told him. 'This is private property.'

'We gotta right to roam,' the elder man retorted. 'It's the law.'

'Not with one of our JCBs, you haven't.'

'We wasn't gonna touch it. You can't prove we were.'

'Probably not,' Linc agreed. 'But nevertheless, I think you should leave.'

'Says who?'

With a sinking heart Linc realised that the man was spoiling for a quarrel no matter what he said. He wondered where the hell Reagan had got to.

'Come on, Dad,' the younger man said, tugging at the sleeve of the other man's boiler suit. 'Leave it.'

Dad shook off the hand.

'Says who?' he repeated coming closer.

Linc could smell drink on his breath and guessed he'd spent lunchtime tanking up at the local pub.

'*I* say so,' he observed. 'This is private land and, regardless of rights of way, when you interfere with estate property it becomes an offence.'

'So, you're one of the la-di-dah Viscount's busy little drones? Scurrying round to do his bidding, earning yourself brownie points and a pat on the back, and making his fat purse even fatter.'

'And what if I am?'

'You make me sick! Tugging your forelock to that rich bastard in his palace!'

'Dad, come on. You're not doing no good.' The son was beginning to get agitated. He put his hand out again but his father lashed out, catching him in the chest and sending him staggering backwards. This time he stayed back, plainly giving up.

The older man advanced to within a foot or so of Linc, who restrained an impulse to look round for Reagan.

'You can tell the la-di-dah Viscount,' the man said, wagging a stumpy finger under Linc's nose. 'You can tell him I didn't need his fucking job!'

'In fact you're doing just fine without it,' Linc said, but his irony was lost on the man.

'Too bloody right!'

'I expect there's a good living to be had by stealing farm machinery.'

'Dad! We should go!'

The older man's eyes narrowed. 'Who *are* you?' he asked, suspicious at last.

'I'm the la-di-dah Viscount's son,' Linc told him.

'And, by the way, our machines are all fitted with tracking devices. So if they go walkabout, we know exactly where they've gone.'

For a moment he thought the man was going to take a swing at him but then he stepped back a pace or two, hatred twisting his features. 'You fucking bastard! You're scum, the lot of you!'

'You all right, sir?' Suddenly, far too late, Reagan was walking towards him. 'What's going on here?'

The boiler-suited man turned and stomped away from Linc, saying as he passed the forester, 'Go lick his boots, why don't you?' His son hurried after him.

Reagan came right up. 'Sir?'

Linc heaved a sigh of relief.

'I could have done with you earlier. Where were you?'

'Sorry, Mr Tremayne. There didn't seem to be anyone about when I got here, so I went and had a look round the fields over the back.'

He didn't sound particularly concerned and it occurred to Linc that he might not have been too devastated if 'Dad' *had* socked him one.

'Okay. No harm done. Better give a description of those two to the police. I'm not sure we've seen the last of them. And I want a man with a dog patrolling this area for at least a week. I don't want this place going up in smoke one night!'

'No need for a description. That's Jim Pepper and his son. The old man used to work here but he was unreliable. Your father sacked him last year.'

'I see. Can't say I blame him.'

'Yeah, but you want to watch Pepper, he's mean,' Reagan warned him, somewhat unnecessarily. 'I'll get on to the police then. Oh, here's the racecard you wanted.'

Linc thanked him, taking the slim booklet and glancing briefly at it. There were twelve races listed, each contested by six dogs, but there didn't appear to be anyone with the surname Barnaby. There were, however, one or two initial Bs and a couple of the dogs seemed to be owned by syndicates.

'Do you know any of these owners or trainers?' he asked Reagan. 'I'm looking for someone who had a dog running that night, name of Barnaby or Barney.'

Reagan pursed his lips. 'Doesn't ring any bells but then I don't know many of them. There's a bloke who might know, though. Local trainer called Sam Menzies. He's got dozens of dogs and goes all over the place. Might be worth asking him.'

'Yes, he's listed here,' Linc said, looking through the names. 'Thanks. I'll try him.'

After checking on progress at the mill, via mobile phone to Geoff Sykes, Linc returned to the office and the unending paperwork, but somehow, before long, found himself searching the internet for Sam Menzies, greyhound trainer.

He was in luck. Sam Menzies had his own website, extolling the virtues of his Warminster-based training kennels. Linc printed off the details, wondering if he had time to pay the man a visit in what remained of that afternoon. He could always catch up on the paperwork in the evening . . .

A telephone call took the decision away from him. It was Rebecca Hathaway.

'Hi,' Linc said, his casual tone hiding the cold

dread that had instantly gripped his heart.

Rebecca obviously anticipated his reaction for she quickly said, 'It's all right. Nothing's happened. There's no change in Abby's condition. In fact, that's why I'm calling. The doctors can't say if she can hear us at all, but then they can't say she doesn't either. One of the nurses suggested we play her some of her favourite music or maybe a video of a movie or pop star she likes. Then I – *we* – thought perhaps if *you* were to come and talk to her . . . knowing how she feels about you. We wondered if something like that might give her the incentive to try and come back to us . . .' Her voice tailed off uncertainly. 'I'd understand if you didn't feel comfortable with that, though.'

'No. I don't have a problem with it, if you think it might do some good, but is it okay with everyone your end? I mean . . .'

'You mean Josie? She's fine with it. She knows you now. Well enough to know that seducing impressionable teenagers isn't your style, anyway.'

'I'll give it a go then,' Linc told her. 'Seven o'clock okay?'

The hospital that Abby had been transferred to from Odstock was unlike any hospital Linc had ever been in. Coming from a blessedly healthy family, none of whom had ever had to endure a lengthy stay in a hospital of any kind, his limited experience of them had been of visiting the busy casualty departments of general hospitals. This private one was in a converted stately home and its reception area, where David Hathaway was waiting for Linc, made the hall at Farthingscourt look decidedly shabby.

Suddenly his own health insurance premium seemed better value.

It was the first time Linc had seen Abby's father since the night of the attack and he looked years older and immeasurably weary. In olive corduroys and a shirt that had obviously been slept in, he led the way to his daughter's room, explaining that although she seemed to have fought off the infection she showed no signs of returning consciousness.

'The doctors have done all they can,' he said. 'They've made her as comfortable as they can and all her vital signs are stable. It's as if it's down to Abby to decide to come back to us now.'

'Can the doctors tell if there's any permanent damage?' Linc asked.

David shook his head. 'Before she caught the infection there was a fair amount of brain activity, but since . . .' He sighed heavily. 'I've spent hours in the hospital chapel begging God to bring her back to us, but to no avail. Then Becky had the idea of asking you to come. I wasn't sure at first, but I think it's worth a try. If the love of her family can't do it then perhaps Abby's hormones can. Maybe this is the answer I've been praying for. After all, I believe Our Lord is an infinitely practical being.'

They had stopped outside a brass-handled, panelled door that bore Abby's name and the number eleven. Her father turned to Linc and managed half a smile.

'See what you can do, Linc. But, please, don't feel bad if nothing comes of it.'

'Okay.' He nodded, hesitating with his hand on the doorknob. The Reverend David Hathaway was one of the non-riding members of the family and, as such, Linc had had little opportunity to get to know him. 'I never encouraged her, you know,' he said quietly.

'I know,' the older man replied. Then as Linc opened the door, 'But encourage her now, will you?'

Rebecca got up from the bedside as Linc went in and came forward to greet him warmly. 'Thank you for coming, Linc. I'll leave you alone with her. David and I will be downstairs having a cup of coffee.'

Linc spent a good half an hour beside the still, pale figure in the bed. At first it was hard to see beyond the myriad of tubes and wires that connected her to monitors, drips and other equipment at her side, but then as he sat down and took Abby's thin hand in his, he found the regular mechanical sounds faded into the background.

Someone had brushed her dark hair but it lay looking lank and lifeless on the pillow around her head, and her long lashes provided a stark contrast to the pallor of her skin. It was frightening to think that she had neither woken nor moved since Linc had found her in the tackroom ten days before.

He started talking, as much to comfort himself as for her sake. He told her all about the Andover and Talham events, detailing the rounds of each horse he had ridden, dwelling especially long on his experience with Dee Ellis's crazy horse, Steamer. He told the silent girl how much he was missing having her grooming for him and ended by telling her about Hilary Lang's exciting invitation and asking her if she might possibly find time to be his groom on the coaching weekend.

As he finally wound to a close, he sat back and watched her for a few moments. There was no discernible change in her face and when he gently squeezed her hand there was no answering squeeze of her fingers. He hadn't really expected that there would be, but now and again you did hear of such things happening.

With something bordering on guilt he wondered if his own negative expectations had prevented the message getting through, but didn't know what he could have done about it. It was a bit like religion; you either believed or you didn't. No amount of wanting to could provide a substitute.

'Come on, Abby,' he said suddenly. 'What's happened to the stubborn little wretch we know and love? You're not going to let this beat you, are you?'

She didn't stir. Only the monotonous bleep of the heart monitor and the slight rise and fall of her chest showed that life remained.

With a heavy sigh Linc got to his feet and, after kissing her lightly on the forehead, turned and left the room.

5

'She moved! Abby's moved her fingers!'

It was half-past seven and Linc had just arrived to ride Noddy before work. Ruth yelled the wonderful news at him as soon as he opened the Discovery's door.

'She has? That's great! When?'

'Mum phoned a couple of minutes ago. She'd been sitting with her most of the night and was just getting up to go and have some breakfast. She says she squeezed Abby's hand and said, "Back soon, darling," and her fingers twitched!' Ruth's face was radiant. 'It wasn't much but the doctors say it's a very good sign. Mum could hardly talk for crying and we've all been laughing and crying, too. Even Hannah!'

'Oh, Ruth, that's wonderful!' Linc stepped out on to the gravel.

'Mum says she's going to give you a big hug when she sees you!'

'Me?' Linc was startled. 'It's got nothing to do

with me! There wasn't even a whisper of movement when I was there.'

'Maybe it was something you said that started her thinking,' Ruth suggested, reluctant to relinquish the romantic idea.

Linc shook his head firmly. 'Much as I would love to think I'd helped, I really can't take any credit. I'm sure it was just a coincidence. Let's just hope she goes on from here.'

'Oh, she will now, I'm sure of it,' Ruth declared happily, and Linc hadn't the heart to point out that there was still an awfully long way to go.

That afternoon Linc travelled to the north of the county to meet the owners of a working watermill. His architect and builder were waiting in the car park when he arrived and together they were taken on a fascinating guided tour of the mill house and adjacent bakery and tearooms.

The mill was magnificent, and Linc was fired with even greater enthusiasm for the Farthingscourt project. He stood for several long minutes watching the water slide from the smooth surface of the millpond, gathering speed down the head race to fall in a silver stream into the metal buckets of the huge overshot wheel.

In contrast, with the stream diverted away from the wheel and the pond empty, the mill at Farthingscourt was at the moment a sad, lifeless affair, awkward and inelegant, like a ship in dry dock, and he longed for the day when it would start milling once again.

After spending a couple of informative hours discussing marketing and ways of maximising efficiency, he left the mill, and with no set appointments or meetings for the rest of the day, turned the Discovery towards Warminster and Sam Menzies' greyhound training kennels.

The map he had printed from the website proved relatively simple to follow and in twenty minutes or so, Linc saw the glossy, white-painted sign that announced *Redshaw Training Kennels* to the passing world. Mindful of the warning-off he'd received, he drove past slowly and stopped about fifty yards further on, in the car park of a pine furniture showroom. In common with all the estate vehicles, the Discovery bore the Farthingscourt name and logo in yellow on its dark green paintwork, and although he had no intention of allowing himself to become paranoid, it seemed sensible not to advertise his investigation unnecessarily. Having had a quick look round the pine shop and bought a letter rack he didn't really want, he left the Land-Rover in the car park and walked back along the road to the kennels.

These were reached via a long gravel track with trees on one side and an open field on the other. An unimaginative square bungalow sat at the end with a cluster of outbuildings and wire-netted pens to one side. The doorbell beside the blue front door summoned a dark-haired, middle-aged individual who probably hadn't seen his feet for many years, and three snuffling pug dogs that yapped at Linc from the safety of the doorway.

'Sam Menzies?'

'Yes.' The trainer scratched his ample stomach through a cotton shirt whose seams and buttons defied all the known laws of physics. He looked his visitor up and down through rather puffy eyes and waited.

'Good afternoon, Mr Menzies. My name's Lincoln. I'm interested in buying a greyhound, and I'm told you're the man to ask.'

'I might be.' Menzies looked marginally more animated, and the pugs, evidently deciding that Linc didn't constitute a threat, waddled down the step and began to sniff round his feet. 'How much do you want to spend?'

'I've no idea,' Linc said honestly. 'But I want a decent animal. One with a good pedigree and a realistic chance of winning.'

'Puppy or in training?'

'You tell me.'

'Well, I know of a lovely Green Baize litter just born a week or two ago,' the trainer told him, looking all at once much more enthusiastic. 'Green Baize was a champion in his day and the bitch was the top money-winning bitch of her age group last year. You could look a lot longer and do a lot worse.'

'That sounds interesting.' Originally conceived as a cover story, the idea was quickly taking root in his mind. 'How much would I have to pay?'

Menzies wasn't sure, but the sum he guessed at was an eye opener for Linc.

'Come and have a look at my dogs, Mr Lincoln,' the trainer suggested quickly, perhaps sensing that his prospective customer was having second thoughts. Pulling the door shut behind him, he hitched his flannel trousers up a reluctant inch or two, came down the steps and set off for the kennels with Linc and the three pugs in his wake.

'Fellow I was talking to at Ledworth a few weeks ago suggested I look up a chap called Barnaby,' Linc said as they reached the outbuildings. 'Not sure if he's an owner or a trainer but I was told he might have a dog for sale.'

They had halted in front of a metal door, for which Menzies produced a key from one of his pockets.

'Don't think I know anyone called Barnaby,' he said, shaking his head. 'I know a Barney. Barney Weston. But I wouldn't go to him for a dog. He's small fry. Wouldn't know a good running dog from a mongrel if he didn't see its papers!'

'It could have been Barney, I suppose. Is he local?'

'Wincanton way, I think. But I wouldn't go to him,' the trainer reiterated. 'He's not been training long. You want someone with experience, being new to it yourself.'

Happily unaware that his determined running down of the opposition was doing him no good in the eyes of his visitor, Menzies took Linc on an extensive tour of his facilities, missing no opportunity of comparing his kennels with those of his smaller rival. The dogs were wide-awake and expectant; Menzies explaining that they were due to be fed in twenty minutes or so. They all looked well cared for and happy, and Linc had no doubt that the trainer knew what he was about; he just couldn't like the man.

He took his leave a quarter of an hour or so later, promising to let Menzies know what he decided but already sure in his own mind that Redshaw Kennels wouldn't be receiving his custom.

Halfway down the drive he was forced to step on to the verge as a pick-up truck with oversized wheels and darkened windows swept by. Two horns and a row of lights decorated the roof of the cab and Linc took an instant dislike to its unseen driver.

Partly because Menzies had tried so hard to put him off, and partly because of the chance that the name Cara Jenkins had overheard might have been 'Barney' instead of 'Barnaby', Linc thrust the thought of waiting estate business to the back of his mind and drove as fast as he dared to Wincanton. His borrowed racecard had helpfully furnished him with the telephone number of *Weston's Greyhounds*, in the form of a small advertisement, and a call had ascertained that its owner would be in and happy to see him.

Barney Weston couldn't have been more different from Sam Menzies. A neat, softly spoken thirty-something, he greeted Linc and showed him round his kennels, welcoming his interest but never once trying to push him into a decision. Linc had once again posed as a prospective owner and was impressed that Weston made it clear that greyhound ownership should not be undertaken lightly.

'You have to remember that your puppy won't race until fifteen months at the earliest and, even barring injury, will retire at four or five,' he warned, before showing Linc a litter of puppies in what he called his maternity wing. 'Therefore he'll probably have six or seven years or more in retirement. Rescue centres are full of unwanted, retired or injured greyhounds.'

Linc assured him that *his* dog, should he get one, would be cared for to the end of its natural.

The maternity wing, housing the nursing bitch and her five leggy, lean pups, was a cosy room well away from the main kennel area, where mother and babies could enjoy a little peace. Linc was fascinated by them. They were like nothing he'd seen before. Even his father's wolfhounds had been more conventionally puppy-looking than these were.

Leaving the puppies behind Barney took Linc to see the food preparation room.

'What do you feed your dogs?' Linc asked with interest, looking round at the clinically clean, stainless steel bowls and a gas cooker with what looked like a huge jam-making saucepan on top. He sniffed appreciatively. 'It smells good.'

Barney grinned. 'Beef chunks, natural gluten-free biscuit, seaweed and a vitamin supplement. I buy frozen beef and cook it up every day.'

'Do they have anything special when they're racing?'

'Pasta,' the trainer said. 'Chock full of carbohydrates for energy.'

He completed the tour, speaking to each dog as he passed its kennel, his fondness for all of them showing on his face. He told his visitor of his plans for a room with heat lamps, and, further in the future, a swimming pool to assist with fitness and recuperation. As they left the kennel area, Linc found the idea of greyhound ownership had well and truly taken root.

'So if I were to buy a dog, would you be willing to train it for me?' he asked, as Barney made him a much-needed cup of tea in the cramped kitchen of his cottage. It seemed the animals' accommodation had priority in this household. There had been no mention of a Mrs Weston, and the house had all the hallmarks of a bachelor pad.

'I'd love to.'

'I spoke to Sam Menzies earlier and he mentioned a litter by a dog called Green Baize – if I have that right.'

'Green Baize is a super dog,' Weston agreed. 'His first season's pups are starting to win already. They won't be cheap but then it costs just as much to keep a slow dog in training as it does a champion. It's worth making that initial outlay.'

Linc nodded. It was the same with horses.

'But actually, I can offer you an even better deal. I've got a couple of saplings – young, unraced dogs – that you might be interested in. They're also by Green Baize, out of my own bitch. I was going to keep them for myself but if you'd let me train it I might be prepared to sell you one. To be honest, I could do with the cash.'

'That sounds very interesting. I'll bear that in mind.'

'So you weren't tempted to go with Sam then?' Weston asked after a moment. 'He's very successful.'

'Yes. So he told me,' Linc said.

Weston laughed. 'I take it you didn't tell him you were coming here.'

'You *were* mentioned.'

'I can imagine what was said. No, it's all right,' he said, shaking his head. 'Sam and I will never see eye to eye. We're on different planets. You see, he's in it for the money, and I'm in it for the dogs. I'll probably never be as successful as the Sam Menzies of this world but I'll be content, and you can't ask for more than that, can you?'

By the time Linc left the Weston establishment, ten minutes later, he was a fair way towards deciding to invest in one of the Green Baize saplings Barney Weston had offered. The possibility of his being the mastermind behind the tack thefts hadn't survived beyond two minutes of Linc's meeting him.

When Linc arrived to ride Noddy just after eight on Thursday morning, he was surprised to find Ruth chatting to Sandy, who was sitting on the bonnet of a battered MG. Noddy was already saddled and waiting, as was Ruth's own horse, Magic; each with a blanket thrown over to keep their backs warm in the chill of the spring morning.

'Hi there,' Linc said, sliding out of the Discovery. 'What brings you here?'

'Sandy's found you another half-cheek snaffle,' Ruth said, her creamy complexion tinged with a pink that indicated that this wasn't the only reason for his visit.

'Good of you to bring it over,' Linc told the saddler.

'Made a good excuse to come and chat up a beautiful lady,' Sandy told him frankly. 'And you know me – I'm not one to miss an opportunity like that!'

'I thought that might be it,' Linc said, laughing. 'Well, I'm on a tight schedule, so I shall have to get going. Are you coming, Ruth? Or have you had second thoughts?'

'Oh, no. Magic comes first,' she said. 'Itinerant tradesmen are two a penny!'

*

Mounted and clattering down the road, Linc enquired after Abby, in whom there had apparently been no further change, and they chatted about everyday matters for a few minutes before he voiced a query that had been on his mind for a day or two.

'Do you think, if I asked your sister out, that she would accept or slap my face?'

'Aha!' Ruth said, smiling. 'I wondered how long it would be before you overcame your preconceptions about models.'

'I don't think I was the only one with preconceptions, but was it that obvious?' Linc asked ruefully.

'In a word, yes! But I don't blame either of you, really.'

'Thank you. That said, do I take it that I've got a chance?'

'Better than evens, I'd say.'

'Great. My next problem will be where to take her. I've not done much socialising since I've been back. Got any ideas?'

'Well, Sandy was telling me about a pub in Shaftesbury that has live music on Friday and Saturday nights. In fact, he's taking me there tomorrow night,' she added, the pinkness again in evidence. 'If you can wait till Saturday, I'll scout it out for you. Josie loves live bands.'

Linc's workload at Farthingscourt was eased a little by the return from holiday of his father's secretary, Mary Poe. She sought Linc out, shortly after, with the information that, for a trial period, she was to split her services between the Viscount, in the morning, and Linc in the afternoon. Within a couple of days, he was wondering how he had ever managed without her.

'Clive – your predecessor – had his own secretary,' Mary informed Linc as she returned his filing system to some sort of order. Fiftyish and invariably attired in the kind of tweed skirt and twin-set that first came to fashion around the time of her birth, she had a neat figure and wore her honey-blonde hair short. Living in the cosy stable cottage, as she had for the last twenty-five years, she had been heard to comment that Farthingscourt had been more faithful to her than any man. She steadfastly refused to discuss her private life and it was generally held that she had been badly let down in her youth and had never trusted again.

'Well, I didn't want to admit defeat, but it was rapidly getting to the point where I was going to have to ask for help,' he confessed.

Mary shook her head and tutted in exasperation.

'You're just as stubborn as your father,' she said. 'You've taken on far more duties than Clive ever did, and he's let you get on with it. I think he was waiting for you to buckle under the strain, but you didn't, so I guess Round One goes to you. That should please you,' she added.

Linc found that it did, immensely.

'Oh, by the way,' Mary said, after a moment. 'Your father wants to know what's been going on between you and Jim Pepper. Apparently he's been heard making threats against you when he's had a few too many of an evening.'

'I found him sizing up the JCB over in the machine yard, the other day. He shot his mouth off before he realised who I was,' Linc told her. 'I think he's more mouth than trousers, but I tipped off the police all the same.'

'Sylvest— that is, your father had trouble with him a year ago,' Mary said. 'He got quite nasty. I wouldn't take Pepper too lightly, if I were you.'

Asking Josie out had, in the event, proved easy.

On Friday Abby moved her fingers again and Linc arrived at the Vicarage on the Saturday morning to find the mood there light-hearted. Rebecca Hathaway was home and invited him into the kitchen where Ruth was giving a glowing report of her evening out with Sandy.

Linc walked in just in time to hear Josie exclaim, 'Ooh, you jammy cow! That sounds brilliant!'

'What does?' he asked.

'Sandy took Roo to a pub in Shaftesbury last night to hear a live band,' Josie told him. 'Sort of Irish folk slash rock, if there is such a thing.'

'Sounds dire!' Hannah put in, but apart·from earning a frown from her mother, she was ignored.

'They're playing there again tonight,' Ruth said casually.

'Why don't you go then?' Linc suggested to Josie, as if the idea had only just occurred to him. 'I'll take you, if you like? I love live music. I'll even treat you to a meal.'

Josie had thanked him and accepted, and the only hitch in the arrangement had been that, due to the venue's popularity, the dining facilities were completely booked up. They decided to eat nearby and relocate to the pub later.

In the continued absence of the Morgan, Linc picked Josie up in the Discovery and they got to

Shaftesbury just before sunset that evening, twenty minutes or so early for their booking at the restaurant. The weather was unseasonably warm and although a light breeze rippled the silky fabric of Josie's hipster skirt, in the golden glow of the late sun she needed no more than a cardigan, and Linc carried his jacket over his arm. They filled the intervening time with a stroll along Park Walk; a broad paved area at the top end of the town, beside the abbey walls. The view from this point was magnificent, the ground falling away sharply toward the meadows in the bottom of the valley.

Just out of sight to their left, as they stood looking across to the Dorset hills in the distance, was the famous Gold Hill, a steep cobbled roadway that had once been used in a memorable bread commercial. Flanked on one side by a variety of tiny cottages, each half-a-door or more lower than its neighbour, and on the other by twenty feet or so of buttressed stone wall, holding back the hill, it was a glimpse of Old England and tourists flocked to see it in their droves.

Their chosen restaurant was family-run and unpretentious, and the food was wonderful. Linc and Josie swapped potted versions of their life stories over the meal, and the wine seemed to have a mellowing effect on Josie. She relaxed and her body language became less wary and defensive. Candles burned in wall-sconces, the soft light gleaming on her loosely knotted hair and accentuating the size and darkness of her eyes. Her combination of flawless skin, regular features and a certain unconscious grace left Linc in no doubt as to why she had become so sought after in the modelling world. He couldn't believe he had ever thought Ruth the more attractive.

'I don't think I'd better have any more wine tonight,' she confided as they left for the short walk to the pub, 'or you might have to carry me back to the Land-Rover.'

'No, I'd just prop you against a wall and leave you to sober up,' he joked.

'You beast!' she exclaimed, punching his arm. 'I believe you would too!'

'Well, I'm a sportsman. I have to look after my back. Can't just go lugging drunken damsels all over the place.'

Josie laughed and made no complaint when he tucked her hand under his arm.

They could hear the music long before they reached the pub, and several other latecomers were making their way toward the sound. As they joined the short queue to go in, Linc heard someone call out, and turned to scan the road they had just crossed.

'What's the matter?' Josie was watching him.

'I could have sworn I heard someone call my name,' he said. 'Silly really, because I can't imagine who would.'

'Sign of a guilty conscience, perhaps,' Josie suggested as they moved slowly forward into the pub doorway.

The venue was packed and the landlord had fastened back folding doors that led from the lounge bar to the function area, making one big room. The five-member band was playing on a raised dais at the far end, surrounded twenty or more deep by their enthusiastic audience.

'I don't think we're going to get very close,' Linc said apologetically.

'It doesn't matter. They're great, aren't they?'

He agreed readily, though in truth Irish jigs had never really been his thing. In the event, he enjoyed the music more than he'd expected and, even had this not been the case, Josie's shining eyes were reward enough.

The band were well into their second set of the evening, and Linc was wishing that the plump female directly in front of him had a slightly less piercing whistle of appreciation, when Josie turned and looked up at him with unmistakable distress in her eyes.

'What's the matter?' he asked, concerned, leaning close to make himself heard.

She forced a smile and shook her head, but Linc wasn't accepting that. He took her hand and gently but firmly led her back through the crowd in the lounge bar and into the foyer beyond.

'Now,' he said turning to look at her, 'tell me what's wrong.'

They were much of a height but she bowed her head to avoid meeting his eyes.

'Would you like to go home?' he asked.

'No . . . yes . . . I don't know,' she said, glancing up at him helplessly. 'Sorry, I'm not making much sense, am I?'

'Come on. Let's go.' He held the door open and she went through, swinging her cardigan about her shoulders as she did so. Together, they moved round to the side of the building where it was blessedly cool and, to Linc's mind, just as blessedly quiet.

'I'm sorry,' Josie said. 'I didn't mean to spoil it for you.'

'That's okay. I'm about jigged out anyway,' he reassured her. 'Is it Abby?'

'Yes. I know it's stupid but it suddenly seemed awful that I was having such a good time, and with . . .'

'With me,' he supplied, understanding.

'Yes. I know there wasn't anything going on between you and Abby but it felt almost as though I was betraying her trust.'

'Come on. Let's walk a bit,' Linc suggested, putting his jacket on. 'Unless you'd rather I took you home?'

'No. I'd like to walk.' In spite of her confused loyalties, Josie tucked her hand through his arm again as they set off.

At the upper end of the High Street, where the road curved, they turned in unspoken agreement down one of the two narrow, cobbled-stone alleys that led, between the buildings, to the top of Gold Hill. Linc and Josie emerged beside the unlit window of a daytime café to stand looking down the lovely old street, which was softly lit by three or four orange wall-lights. The night was essentially quiet; even the chatter and laughter from the beer garden of an unseen pub didn't unduly disturb the sense of peace. A couple of distant lights twinkled on the other side of the darkened valley and as a gentle breeze blew his hair, Linc felt deeply content.

He moved his arm so it squeezed Josie's hand. 'Feeling better?'

She nodded. 'Thanks.'

They stood for a few moments longer, then

turned to make their way back. As they did so, a group of nine or ten youths came towards them down the narrow alley, chattering amongst themselves. They were all dressed in the current teenage uniform of baggy jeans or combat trousers, with tracksuit tops and a variety of headgear.

Linc instinctively stepped to one side a little to give the youngsters room to pass but as they did, one of them, a tall beefy lad in khaki combats, a hooded sweatshirt and a knitted beanie hat, swung his shoulder and bumped into him.

'Sorry,' Linc said, out of habit.

The youth rounded on him.

'Why don'tcha watch where you're fuckin' going?'

The others had turned back now and began to gather round enquiringly.

'What's up, Bro?' one of them asked.

'He fuckin' pushed me!'

'I didn't, you know,' Linc said quietly. The youngsters had formed a semi-circle, effectively blocking any retreat, and at his side he could feel Josie's tension. He found her hand and squeezed it reassuringly.

In the poor light it was difficult to tell the age of the kids; all were probably teenagers but they could have been anywhere within that bracket, and regardless of age, two of them were easily as tall as Linc, and quite possibly heavier. A couple of them, he realised on closer inspection, were girls.

The lad with the beanie leaned closer, an ugly expression on his face. A ring gleamed in his eyebrow.

'You callin' me a liar?'

'No. I'm saying you're mistaken.'

'Nobody calls me a fuckin' liar!' It was as if he'd rehearsed his lines and wouldn't be put off.

'Nobody has,' Linc pointed out reasonably.

The lad obviously wasn't in the market for reason.

'Think you're fuckin' tough, don'tcha? I'll show you tough!'

He accompanied the words with a sudden, powerful push, and Linc stepped back involuntarily. As he regained his balance he caught sight of Josie's face. She looked pale and frightened, and he felt a rush of anger.

'Come on, guys,' he said, trying to keep a rein on his temper. 'You've had your fun, but enough's enough, don't you think?' He was glad his voice sounded steady; he could by no means say the same for his pulse rate. The other youths were crowding round now, almost jostling them, and he sensed that the situation was on the verge of turning very nasty.

This couldn't just be dismissed as a bit of posturing bravado. Teenagers these days, empowered by too complete a knowledge of their rights, were a force to be reckoned with. They were clued up, often tooled up, and the possibility of some of them being drugged up couldn't be discounted, either.

He tried again. 'Look, whoever's fault it was, I said sorry so just let it go, will you? You're frightening the lady.'

'Oh, boo-hoo!' Beanie sneered. 'Somebody bring me my violin . . . Anyway, there's no need for the pretty lady to be afraid. My boys'll take care of her, won't you, lads? My quarrel's with you.'

Taking their cue, three of the other youths moved

behind Linc and Josie, and two of them took hold of her arms, pulling her away from his side.

'Linc!' she cried, struggling to free herself.

'Leave her alone!' he said sharply, following and pushing one of them roughly aside.

'Or what?' came Beanie's sneering voice and someone grabbed Linc's shoulder, spinning him around and sending him stumbling away. As he straightened up, he found himself facing seven of the youngsters spread out in a ragged line across the walkway, with Beanie striking a belligerent pose slightly ahead of them. They looked like nothing so much as the cast of a pop video, but they obviously had something a deal more serious than singing on their minds.

Then one of them produced a flick knife from his pocket and activated the blade.

Linc felt a spasm of fear.

'Put that away!' the ringleader hissed, looking sideways. 'I don't want him cut.'

For the first time that night, Linc found himself in complete agreement with the lad. He looked over his left shoulder to where Josie stood, flanked by two boys, one of whom had put his hand over her mouth to keep her quiet. She was standing still now, her eyes wide with fright.

'Don't worry about her. You're the one in deep shit,' Beanie observed.

Linc knew it. He looked desperately around but it was still half an hour until last orders and Gold Hill, so popular during the day, was deserted save for the kids. Even the cottages were for the most part in darkness; a few of the windows glowed but the only real illumination came from the rising moon and the sodium wall-lights, which were spaced at unhelpfully long intervals.

He supposed he should shout for help but something – maybe pride – held him back. If Josie were being attacked, he wouldn't have hesitated, but it seemed that *he* was the object of their spite, and he couldn't bring himself to let them see his fear.

The ringleader approached, his eyes locked menacingly on to Linc's, and as if by prior arrangement his gang closed in on either side. Linc tried to memorise the lad's features but it was difficult to concentrate and in the poor light he looked like hundreds of others. It was as if they were turned out, en masse, from a mould. Even the pierced eyebrow couldn't be considered a distinguishing feature in this day and age.

Determined not to back off, Linc waited until Beanie was about two feet away, then launched himself at the lad's waist with his head down and arms spread, rugby-style. He had the satisfaction of hearing a grunt of pain and shock as his shoulder drove the breath from the boy's body and they landed, with Linc on top, on the cobbled slope.

Unfortunately, the incline caused Linc to fall sideways as soon as they hit the ground, and it took a moment for him to regain his feet. The rest of the gang seemed temporarily stunned by this unexpected attack but Beanie unfortunately still had his wits about him.

'Shit!' he exclaimed, lying on the cobbles, clutching at his midriff. 'Get the bastard!'

Linc started towards Josie and her captors, but before he reached them he was surrounded once more. The group was closer now and he was aware of a strong smell of cigarette smoke. A foot hooked behind his knee and someone shoved him hard, and suddenly he was down on the stones again at their feet. Hands pressed down on him, keeping him there, and one or two experimental kicks were tried.

'Let me through!' The ringleader was back in business once more, and from the tone of his voice, his temper had not been improved by Linc's stunt.

The gang separated to let him through and Linc tried to get up. The attempt was doomed to failure. Beanie let him get one foot under him before putting his boot against Linc's shoulder and giving a powerful push.

Combined with the degree of slope, the action was enough to send him somersaulting backward, cracking his head painfully on the stones. He would have continued to roll if something narrow and hard had not caught him across the shoulders, halting his downward progress. Muzzily he remembered a row of wooden posts that ran down the right-hand side of the hill, about two feet from the wall, supporting a metal rail to aid less agile members of the public.

It seemed that the gang hadn't finished with him as the light was suddenly all but blocked out by their crowding forms. It felt bizarre but somehow all the more unpleasant that the assault was being carried out by what was, to all intents and purposes, a bunch of kids. It reminded him of a camp 1960s film he'd once seen. He couldn't remember what it had been about, but in it somebody had been attacked by a horde of dolls with vicious metal teeth. At the time he'd found it funny, but the grotesque image came back vividly now. Most of these kids were still school age, for God's sake, and at least two of them were girls! Where did their parents think they were? Or didn't they care?

A fist closed on a handful of his shirt and another on the neck of his jacket, pulling him away from the support of the post and pitching him down the slope once more.

This time, with no post to break his fall, Linc rolled and slid several yards before friction slowed his descent. By the time he was sure which way was up, the gang was already following in his wake. He managed to get his feet and hands under him and was halfway to his feet before they attacked again, pushing and tripping him so that the cobbles came up to meet him bruisingly for the fifth time in quick succession.

This time he rolled over one shoulder and was able, by some fluke, to find his feet almost straight away, albeit wildly off-balance. He was obliged to hop and skip several yards further before he could stop but it was a definite improvement.

The group came warily on, and Linc decided the time had come to shelve pride and involve a third party. He headed, in a stumbling run, for the nearest cottage that showed lights behind the curtains, and thumped heavily on the door.

The youths, some of whom had rushed, unsuccessfully, to head him off, now halted uncertainly, looking to their leader.

Linc thumped again, urgently, and a movement of the curtain showed that he'd been heard, but nobody came to the door and after a moment the light went out.

'Damn you!' he shouted in frustration, hitting the

door with his fist for a third time. Even so, as the gang moved forward with renewed confidence, he couldn't find it in himself to blame the unseen watcher, and could only hope that he or she would at least call the police.

'Looks like you're on your own, lover boy,' Beanie observed. 'Well, come on, then. Whatcha gonna do now?'

Linc had absolutely no idea. He felt bruised, battered and defeated. There had been a judo club at university but he'd done orienteering instead; somehow, map-reading skills weren't much of a comfort just at the moment. Breathing heavily, he turned his palms up, shrugged and waited for the first of the youths to come within reach.

Possibly taking this for a sign that Linc had abandoned any thought of self-defence, one of the smaller, cockier youngsters approached unwarily, ahead of his mates. Trying not to let consideration of the lad's size stay his hand, Linc grabbed him and flung him back at the others with enough force to floor two of them. Amidst the confusion he slipped through the gap in their ranks and set off in a limping run, back up the hill to where Josie was being held.

This simple plan was frustrated, firstly by the distance he had to cover, and secondly by the better physical shape of Beanie, who had obviously read his intention immediately.

Coming at him from an angle, the lad caught hold of the back of Linc's jacket and pulled hard, swinging him round, off balance. He stumbled sideways once more, feeling weak and tired, and without allowing him to recover, Beanie hit him hard across the face with the back of his hand.

Linc went down and what followed was a blur of cobblestones, feet and sky, as the rest of the gang joined in once more. It seemed his manhandling of one of their number had done him no favours, for there was a certain vicious enjoyment in their efforts now, and their faces, when he caught a brief glimpse of them, were not pretty.

When movement eventually stopped, Linc found himself lying face down on tarmac. A strong smell of engine oil caught in his throat and made him cough. The very fact that it *was* tarmac beneath him meant that, in all, he'd been pushed and kicked almost three-quarters of the way down the hill to where the residents' cars were parked.

Something moved close to his head and he opened his eyes to the unwelcome sight of what looked like a pair of Doc Marten boots not six inches from his face. In spite of himself, he groaned. Even though he'd suffered no single serious injury he felt battered beyond belief, and if Beanie and his gang wanted any more sport, they'd have to look elsewhere. He was all through with getting up.

There came the sound of a scuffle and his focus shifted past the boots to where two figures were struggling with a third.

Josie! He was aware of a sudden overwhelming sense of failure. Whatever they chose to do with her now, there wasn't a damn' thing he could do about it. Coming so soon after what had happened to Abby, how could he ever face her parents?

Suddenly the night air was rent by a horribly strident, electronic whooping noise, and somebody swore. It took Linc several long moments to realise that the racket was the result of a car alarm being activated, and over the din he heard someone shout, 'Leave her! Go on, scarper!'

There came the sound of footsteps running both up and down the hill, and then Beanie bent down and rolled Linc on to his side.

'Compliments of the boss!' he said, stuffing something scratchy down the front of Linc's tee-shirt, and while he was still struggling to make sense of the remark, Beanie too had loped off into the darkness.

6

'Oh, my God, Linc! Are you all right?'

With the departure of Beanie, Josie had lost no time in running across to Linc.

For his part, he found that 'all right' was a relative term. The car alarm was still enthusiastically doing its thing, and each pulse of sound seemed to touch a nerve deep inside his skull; every bone in his body felt bruised, and he could taste blood. On the other hand, he was ten times better than he'd been just a few moments ago. It was bliss just to lie still and know that the ordeal was over.

'Linc?'

'Give me a minute,' he told Josie. 'I'm working on it.'

Somewhere nearby a door opened, and someone emerged, grumbling, into the street.

'Please?' Josie called, standing up. 'My friend needs help . . .'

'Call him a taxi,' a man's voice replied. 'And stay away from my car.'

The alarm cut off suddenly, mid-whoop, leaving a

shocking silence in its place.

'No, you don't understand,' she said, trying again. 'He was attacked. He's hurt and I haven't got my mobile . . .'

'Won't get a signal here anyway.' The man came halfway across the tarmac and stopped, peering at Linc as if bruises were contagious.

'Do you want me to call the police?' he asked then, reluctantly.

'Yes, please. And an amb—'

'Thanks, but no,' Linc cut in.

'Linc!' Josie exclaimed, crouching down again. 'We *must* report it.'

'Yeah, we will,' he promised, pushing himself up on to one elbow and finding out the hard way that he'd been lying partially under the front bumper of another parked car. 'Just not now, okay? The kids have gone – scattered. I shouldn't think there's a hope in hell of finding them. The last thing I feel like just now is spending hours talking to the police.'

Although he couldn't have heard much of what Linc said, the man from the cottage had evidently heard enough. He backed off a pace or two, patently relieved that his involvement wasn't required. 'All right then, I'll leave you to it,' he said, and seconds later the front door shut on his rapid retreat.

'But, an ambulance?'

'No, honestly,' he said, easing himself into a sitting position and retrieving a crumpled fold of paper from inside his tee-shirt. 'I'll be okay in a minute. If you are?' he added hastily, scanning Josie's face in the poor light. 'They didn't hurt you, did they?'

She shook her head. 'No, I'm fine,' she said, then

her eyes filled with a sudden rush of tears. 'Oh, Linc! How can you be so bloody calm? I thought they were going to kill you! How *can* you be okay?'

'Hey! Shhh!' Linc put one arm round her and drew her towards him. Her hair was silky and fragrant. 'Well, perhaps okay was the wrong word. But it's really just bumps and bruises; like coming off a horse. I'm feeling better all the time.' If he said it often enough, he might even start to believe it himself, he reflected with grim amusement. With his free hand he slipped the paper into his pocket and withdrew a handkerchief, which he silently offered.

'Thanks,' Josie said, gently pulling out of his grasp and blowing her nose. 'I'm sorry. It was just so frightening! I mean, I had my bag snatched once, in London, and you kind of expect that sort of thing there, but here? And what for? Just because you bumped into him.'

'That's just it – I didn't,' he told her. 'He made that up.' He decided against mentioning Beanie's note until he'd had time to read it. If she had any idea the attack had been anything other than random, his chances of persuading her not to call the police would be non-existent.

Josie shook her head again, in disbelief. 'So what now? Can you get up?'

'With a little help from my friends,' Linc suggested.

Actually, he made it first time, and began the climb back up the famous hill with a creditable show of fitness. He sensed Josie relaxing a little, at his side, but it had to be said that by the time they reached the top, having paused for a rest halfway, he was blessing whoever it was who had had the idea of providing a rail for the elderly and infirm.

Any hope he had that the degree of effort had gone unnoticed was banished when they reached the Discovery. Josie stood between him and the driver's door and held out her hand for the keys. Music could be heard on the night air and it was with a shock that Linc realised the band was still playing. Looking at his watch he found that it was not yet eleven o'clock. Incredibly, the whole nightmarish episode had taken only a few minutes from start to finish.

He was quite content to let Josie drive. Somewhere between Gold Hill and the car park the shakes had set in, and he felt weak and decidedly unwell.

'Are you all right? You look a bit green,' she observed as they left the lighted outskirts of Shaftesbury behind. 'I'm still not convinced that I shouldn't be taking you to hospital.'

'I feel a bit green,' Linc admitted, trying not to let his teeth chatter. 'I think perhaps we should stop if you come to a convenient gateway . . .'

'Sorry,' he said, minutes later, sliding back into the passenger seat.

'Don't be daft. I shared a flat with a bulimic for most of last year, so I'm quite used to it. But are you sure you're not concussed? You must have hit your head at least once.'

'No. Actually, I feel much better now.' Then he groaned. 'Oh, God! That was one hell of a first date. I'm so sorry. I wish I could have done something . . .'

Josie had just put the Land-Rover into gear but now she took it back out and turned to face him in the gloom of the interior.

'Well, of all the stupid things to say! You're not serious? There wasn't anything you could have done, nothing *anyone* could have done, so don't be daft!'

Linc frowned at the dashboard. 'But they were just kids, Josie! Two of them were girls . . .'

'They were thugs!' she stated firmly. 'And there were ten of them. This isn't the movies – it's real life, and if you weren't so caught up in macho pride you'd remember that!'

'I'm sorry,' Linc said, managing a wistful smile. 'I should be comforting you, and here I am feeling sorry for myself.'

'You did comfort me,' Josie said, engaging first gear and steering back on to the road. 'And I'm fine now. We're tough, us Hathaway women! Only, I think perhaps it would be better if we don't mention this to Mum and Dad. It's all over now and they've got enough to worry about.'

Linc agreed, leaning back against the headrest as the Discovery sped through the darkness.

'I don't really see myself as macho, you know,' he commented thoughtfully, after a moment. 'It's just – I suppose I've always thought I could handle most situations . . . It's a bit of a shock, I guess. Like being reminded of one's own mortality.'

'You did handle it,' Josie told him. 'You stood up to them.'

'Mmm. Didn't do me much good. You know, it was lucky that car alarm went off when it did . . . I hate the bloody things but tonight it was the sweetest sound.'

136

'Lucky?' Josie queried. 'Give me some credit! I bounced on the bonnet.'

'Oh, no! The final blow to my self-esteem!' Linc moaned. 'Rescued by the distressed damsel!'

By the time they reached Farthing St Anne, Linc felt sufficiently recovered to drop Josie off and drive himself home.

The mysterious note had been burning a hole in his pocket all the way back from Shaftesbury and he waited only long enough to see Josie safely into the Vicarage before switching on the Land-Rover's interior light and reading it. It was a torn sheet of newspaper with a number of words highlighted, and its contents confirmed the suspicion Beanie's last words had aroused.

This is the second warning.
Three strikes and you're out.

'Linc? Are you all right?'

He struggled up through layers of sleep and blearily focussed first on his father and then on his bedside clock.

Twenty-five-past nine! He'd forgotten to set the alarm, but that didn't explain his father's unexpected arrival in his bedroom.

'I'm sorry. I'm just getting up,' he said, wishing the pile driver inside his skull would take a break.

'I've just had a female by the name of Josie on the telephone,' his father told him. 'Said she'd being trying to reach you.'

'Oh, sorry. My mobile was turned off.' Being a

flip-top, it had survived the skirmish unscathed, secure in a zipped inner pocket of his jacket.

'Apparently she was worried that you hadn't turned up to exercise your animal this morning. Said you'd had a spot of bother last night. She would appear to be right,' he added, regarding Linc with a judicial eye.

'Yeah, we did. A street gang looking for kicks.' Literally, he thought with thin humour.

'Where? Bournemouth?'

'No. Shaftesbury.'

'Good Lord! What did the police have to say?'

Linc avoided his gaze.

'Ah, I see. Well, I told the female that I'd get you to ring her back when I found you. It's high time you had an extension put in up here, then I wouldn't have to keep running after you with messages.'

As this was the first time in five months or so that he'd had to this was a little unfair, but Linc knew better than to argue the point. 'I'll get on to it,' he promised, swinging his legs over the side of his bed and gingerly sitting up.

His father stood watching him for a long, frowning moment, then turned away without a word and left the flat.

Linc sighed and shook his head sadly, left with the feeling that even by getting himself roughed up he had somehow earned paternal disapproval.

Moving stiffly, he made his way to the bathroom and had a shower, wishing he had time for a long soak in the bath instead. As he dried himself, the half-length mirror showed him a rather pale face with a grazed cheekbone and a developing bruise over one eye, and a lean, hard-muscled torso decorated with mottled patches of red and purple.

'Oh, *lovely*,' he told his reflection. No wonder his father had frowned. Linc customarily slept in shorts so his visitor would have been treated to the full display.

He put the radio on, took painkillers and made toast and coffee, thinking that, on the whole, things would have been easier if Josie hadn't rung to check up on him, but nevertheless feeling rather pleased that she had. He was finding that she occupied quite a large part of his thoughts nowadays. Using his mobile, he tried to reach her but the Vicarage telephone was answered by Ruth, who told him that Josie had gone out.

'How did it go last night?' she asked. 'Did you like the band? Josie did.'

Linc returned an affirmative, said they'd had a lovely meal too, and finished by saying that he'd try Josie on her mobile.

'You can try, but you won't have much luck, I'm afraid. It's here on the kitchen table,' Ruth told him.

In his office, when Linc made it down there some twenty minutes later, Mary was coping admirably in his absence; prioritising the reported crises of the day – of which there were invariably several by mid-morning – and fielding his calls. She had sorted his post into urgent, non-urgent, personal and begging, the last of which she had filed in the shredder.

'I don't think there's anything desperately important to tell you,' she said, scanning the notes she had made. 'Geoff is taking care of most things.'

Linc eased himself into the chair behind his desk,

and sat looking without enthusiasm at the piles of correspondence.

'You look rough, if I may say so,' Mary observed with the informality of long service. 'Your father said you had some trouble last night. What happened?'

'Oh, just some kids looking for trouble. I was in the wrong place at the wrong time.'

'What did the police say? You did report it . . .' She let the question hang in the air and so did Linc.

'Okay,' she continued evenly. 'Well, can I get you a cup of coffee or something?'

The telephone trilled, its display indicating an internal line, and Mary picked up the receiver.

'It's your father,' she said, after a brief interval. 'He wants to see you in the library.'

Linc groaned and stood up. 'Okay. Tell him I'm on my way.'

Lord Tremayne wasn't alone in the library when Linc let himself in. As he closed the heavy, panelled door behind him, the first person he saw, seated in one of the leather chairs, was DI Rockley.

'Ah,' Linc said, going forward with a certain resignation. 'I take it you're not here to see my father?'

Rockley stood up to shake hands. 'No. Lord Tremayne was worried about you. And I can see why,' he added, looking critically at Linc's face. 'He said you'd been attacked. What's the story?'

Linc hesitated, looking across at his father who was sitting on the edge of his desk.

His father stood up. 'All right. It's your business. I'll leave you to it.'

As the door closed behind him, Linc sighed and sat down, inviting Rockley to do the same.

'So. Tell me that this has nothing to do with your misguided attempts to do my job for me, and you'll take a weight off my mind,' Rockley informed him.

Linc returned his look steadily for a moment or two, then reached into his back pocket for the folded newspaper and handed it over.

Rockley read it through a couple of times.

'The same style as last time,' he observed. 'But delivered with a taster. The thing is, what have you been doing to make them so nervous? What have you found out?'

'Sod all!' Linc said ruefully. 'It wouldn't be so bad if I had.'

Rockley shook his head. 'Oh, no, you're wrong there, young man. Judging by this note, it might have been ten times worse! Now, tell me exactly what happened last night.'

It took the best part of twenty minutes before Rockley was satisfied that he'd got the whole story, and even then Linc managed to gloss over some of the more unpleasant detail.

The detective scribbled something in his pocket book, then stopped and looked speculatively at him. 'You say one of the boys had his hand over Josie's mouth? Nobody could have stopped *you* from shouting for help so why didn't you? Did they threaten to hurt her?'

'No. They didn't. It was just . . .' Linc shrugged. He didn't know what to say. From anyone else's point of view – even from his own, now he looked back on it – it seemed daft that he hadn't.

Rockley watched him thoughtfully for a long moment then nodded, seeming to understand. But he still hadn't finished.

'Can you show me the damage?' he asked. 'Please?'

Linc stared hard at him for the space of several heartbeats, then looked away towards the window, stood up and pulled his shirt clear of his waistband and off over his head.

'Turn round.'

Still not looking at the policeman, he obediently turned through one slow revolution.

'Okay, thanks.'

Linc put the shirt back on, tucked it in, sat down and stared at his hands, feeling a quite irrational degree of humiliation.

Rockley made a few more notes, then looked up and regarded him with some compassion.

'You know, it's quite common for victims of assault to feel the way you do,' he said.

'And how *do* I feel?'

'I'd say you feel you're somehow to blame for what happened; that you think you should have been able to do more to defend yourself, or even to prevent it happening in the first place. And for you it's worse because Josie was there and you couldn't do anything to protect her either.'

He'd hit the nail right on the head.

Linc looked up at him. 'And?'

Rockley shook his head. 'I can only say to you what I'd say to anyone else – even one of my officers: there was nothing you could have done; nothing any *one man* could have done in that situation. You said yourself there were a couple of big lads there. There's no shame for you in what happened. The shame is all on them.' He paused. 'Having said that, your reaction is natural. In time you'll see it differently.'

Linc sighed. 'I guess.'

'You know, when I first joined up I had a crusty old sergeant who was only a year or two off retirement. He could be a bugger to work with but he'd seen a hell of a lot in his time and he had a few pet sayings. One of his favourites was, "*They can only win if you let them.*" Think about it.' Rockley laughed then, almost self-consciously. 'Here endeth today's sermon. But you still haven't told me what you did to provoke last night's attack.'

'I really don't know,' Linc reiterated. 'I thought I'd hit a dead end.'

He gave Rockley the short and unproductive story of his investigative efforts so far.

'So, all you can tell me is that the thieves apparently report to someone called Barnaby or Barney, who has some connection to greyhound racing?'

'That's about it,' Linc admitted. 'Nobody I've spoken to seems to know anyone locally in the greyhound world who answers to that name.'

'Except this Barney Weston.'

'Yes. Except him. But as I said, if he's a master criminal then I shall lose all faith in my ability to judge character.'

He watched while Rockley scribbled something.

'I guess you don't go much on faith in your line of business, do you?'

'Actually, more than you might think,' the policeman said with a half-smile. 'But we do like to back it up with fact. Helps us sleep at night. Now, given that you've never seen the lad in the Beanie or his mates before, how do you think he knew who to deliver his message to last night? Have you given it any thought? Do you often go to Shaftesbury on a Saturday night?'

'No. That was the first time in years, but it's not too hard to find me when I'm driving one of the Estate vehicles. And also – I've just remembered – when we were queuing to get into the pub, I could have sworn I heard someone call my name. I actually turned round and looked back across the road. I guess they were checking me out then, so they'd know what I looked like for later.'

'Mmm, but I should imagine your friend in the hat was probably just meant to bump into you and deliver the message. It's all he *could* have done if you'd come out with the crowd.'

'And then we made it easy for them by coming out early and wandering around the town,' Linc put in.

'Unfortunately, yes,' Rockley agreed.

'Do you think there's any hope at all of catching the lad in the beanie?'

'To be honest, not much,' Rockley admitted. 'We can have a word with one or two of the usual suspects – to coin a phrase – but Shaftesbury is, by and large, a fairly quiet place. We normally only have a single unit there even on a Saturday night, and though there are one or two troublesome youngsters, they're strictly minor league. You know – graffiti, under-age drinking and the odd joy ride. I'm afraid all the signs point towards the ring-leader being imported muscle. I should imagine it wouldn't be difficult for him to recruit a few extra bodies locally. Teenagers are all too easily led.' He closed his pocket book. 'Well, now you've had first-hand experience of the dangers of going it alone, I hope you'll leave the detective work to us in future.'

'It's certainly made me think twice,' Linc replied.

Rockley looked hard at him, as if unsure whether this was deliberately ambiguous, but Linc's face gave nothing away.

'And you still won't tell me where you got your information from?'

'I gave my word.'

'But in the circumstances . . . .?'

Linc shook his head. 'Sorry.'

They could hear voices in the hall, not unusual on a Sunday when Farthingscourt was open to the public, but in this case followed by three sharp raps on the door.

Linc raised his eyebrows at Rockley, who nodded.

'Okay. Come in,' he called, and his father entered, ushering Josie ahead of him.

'Ah, Miss Hathaway.' Rockley had plainly been expecting her.

'Josie!' Linc hadn't.

'I called Miss Hathaway earlier this morning after speaking to Lord Tremayne,' the DI explained. 'I needed to speak to her and as she didn't want to worry her parents, we decided it would be easiest if she came here. Now, if we could perhaps just have a few words alone . . .?'

Josie emerged from the library twenty minutes later

to find Linc waiting for her in the hall. She greeted him with a trace of anxiety in her eyes.

'Linc, I'm really sorry about all this, but when you didn't turn up this morning I didn't know what to think. I tried your mobile and then I rang the number you gave Mum for emergencies.'

'My office number,' Linc put in, leading the way out of the huge front doors. It was a lovely bright day and sunlight slanted under the pedimented façade and spilled across the stone paving at the top of the twin flights of steps, casting shadows from the ornamental balustrade and pillars.

'I didn't expect to get your father,' Josie continued, determined to explain. 'And when I did, I had to say something. He kind of took the whole thing out of my hands . . .'

'He would,' Linc agreed. 'Don't worry about it.'

'But I knew you didn't want a fuss.'

'I expect I would have had to tell Rockley sooner or later. Might just as well get it over with.'

'Because of the note?'

'Ah, he told you about that.' Linc strolled forward to lean on the stone balustrade. The view down the valley from here was breathtaking.

'Wow!' Josie said in quiet awe, momentarily distracted from the business of the morning. 'This is to die for!'

'Mmm.'

'I suppose you're used to it. I can't imagine seeing this every morning.'

'It's a privilege. I never grow tired of looking at it.'

Several small groups of visitors were wandering across the drive from the ticket office and two elderly ladies had just mounted the steps.

'Do you mind having to open to the public?' Josie asked.

Linc shook his head. 'No, not really. It's only three days a week, and somehow it would be a shame not to share it. Most people are very appreciative and respect the fact that it's a home. You just get the odd family group where the kids seem to think it's another theme park and run round shrieking and touching things with their sticky little fingers.'

'Oh, dear,' Josie observed with amusement. 'Don't you like children?'

'Children, yes. Undisciplined monsters, no,' Linc said firmly. 'When they skid on the carpets and duck under the security ropes, I honestly don't know how the house guides keep their tempers. I find myself wishing you could buy a can of anti-brat spray and zap them like you do mosquitoes!'

He broke off to exchange pleasantries with the two ladies who had finally completed the climb. Remembering the way he'd felt the previous night after struggling back up Gold Hill, he could sympathise with them.

Josie had been laughing at his remarks about the unruly children but as the elderly visitors disappeared into the cool interior of the house she returned to their previous conversation.

'Why didn't you tell me about the note?'

'I thought you had enough to worry about.'

'That's patronising,' she observed.

'Yes, I'm sorry.'

'So it wasn't a random attack after all? It was because you've been asking about the tack thieves.'

'Yes. Rockley doesn't think it was ever meant to go that far, though.'

'But when I asked, you told me you weren't getting anywhere,' Josie persisted, faintly accusing.

'I wasn't. And I still don't know why they reacted like that.'

'I told you to be careful.'

'So you did.'

'You'll stop now, though? You'll leave it to the police?'

'Has Rockley been priming you?' Linc asked, squinting into the sunlight.

'He said if I had any influence, I should try to make you see sense,' she admitted, a faint blush staining her clear skin. 'I said I didn't think I had.'

'I just can't bear to think that anyone can do what they've done to your family and get away with it,' Linc said, avoiding the issue. He didn't think now was the time to explore the depth of his attraction to Josie.

'Well, it won't help us if you end up in hospital with Abby,' Josie pointed out sensibly.

Back in the hall a door opened and Linc could hear the voices of his father and the DI. Moments later Rockley came out of the doorway behind them.

'I'll be going now,' he said. 'Goodbye, Josie. Give my regards to your parents. As for you, young man,' he said sternly to Linc, 'next time I ask for a detailed description of events, I'll expect just that. Not edited highlights! That said, I sincerely hope there won't be a next time. Having put Abby in hospital, they're in a position where they may feel they've nothing to lose. I'm sure I don't have to spell it out for you.'

'I think I've got the message,' Linc confirmed.

'Well, I'll say goodbye then.'

As Rockley trudged down the steps to his car, Linc turned to Josie.

'Just what *did* you tell him?' he enquired.

'The truth,' she said. 'How was I to know you'd glossed over half of it? Does it hurt very much today?'

'Enough,' Linc hedged. As a matter of fact his whole body was one big grinding ache.

'All right, I won't go there. Did you know your father's invited me to dinner on Wednesday?'

This time she did succeed in shaking his composure.

'He has? Oh, Lord!'

Josie laughed. 'I'm not sure how to take that.'

'What did you say to him?'

'I accepted. You don't mind, do you?'

'Not at all, but I don't want you to feel you have to come. He can be very autocratic sometimes.'

'As a matter of fact, he was very sweet to me.'

'Sweet? Hmm.' Linc bit his tongue.

Sometime after Josie had departed, the Viscount sought Linc out in his office and informed him that he'd made an appointment for him with his own GP.

'Or rather Mary has,' he amended.

'I don't need an appointment,' Linc protested. 'If I did, I'd have made one myself.'

'As my employee, you'll do as you're told,' his father asserted.

'And, while we're on the subject,' Linc went on, ignoring him, 'I'll thank you to stay out of my love life! What on earth made you invite Josie here for a meal?'

'Nikki's mother is visiting and I thought it would even up the numbers,' his father said, blithely disregarding the fact that such considerations had never troubled him before. 'Why? Are you ashamed of her?'

'No, of course not! But we've only been out once – which by anyone's standards wasn't a roaring success – and a family dinner in full Farthingscourt style would be testing even for a long-term relationship.'

'I thought you'd be pleased. *She* was. She's obviously a sensible girl. Now, don't forget your appointment. Twelve o'clock, Dr Small. He's fitted you in as a favour to me, so don't be late.'

He swept out of the office without waiting for a reply, and behind him Linc glared at the pencil he was holding and found momentary release in snapping it in two.

Seconds later Mary came in carrying a file, took a look at his face and the pencil and said astutely, 'Don't let him wind you up. Take a deep breath and put it out of your mind.' She put the file down. 'By the way, you had two calls while the detective was here. One was from a Barney Weston, and the other a rather strange woman called Dee. Something about a horse, I gather. The numbers are on the pad.'

Linc called Dee Ellis straight away and found her in. She had phoned to tell him that Steamer was entered in a one-day event the following weekend and to offer him the ride. Hoping that his bruised muscles would be on the mend by then, Linc said he'd be delighted to ride the horse, and replaced the receiver wondering if he'd had one blow to the head too many the previous night.

He hesitated a moment before returning Barney's call. He was still feeling too fragile to reach an objective conclusion on whether or not to call a halt to his amateur sleuthing efforts, but he stood by what he'd told Rockley; he really couldn't believe that Barney was a ruthless criminal. The problem was that he didn't know which of the contacts he'd made had got him into trouble. Surely it couldn't hurt just to see what the man wanted. Who was to know, anyway?

'Barney? Hi, Linc Tremayne here,' he said when the greyhound trainer answered the phone.

'Ah, hello, Linc. Yes, I was just calling to follow up your visit the other day, and to see if you were interested in coming to Ledworth on Thursday night. You know, to see what goes on from an insider's point of view.'

'Thursday?' Linc repeated, stalling for time. It seemed the decision about his further involvement couldn't be postponed after all. To be seen at the dog track with Barney, albeit in all innocence, could easily be misconstrued as continued snooping, if the greyhound connection was indeed the right one.

Damn!

'Yes, I'd love to,' he heard himself saying.

'Great.' Barney sounded really enthusiastic. 'I've got two dogs running and they're both in with a chance. Should be a good night.'

He arranged to meet Barney at his kennels and travel with him rather than trying to find each other amidst the hustle and bustle of a busy meet, then put the phone down and sat, deep in thought. He had a strong suspicion that Detective Inspector Rockley would give him a severe raking down if he ever found out and, looking at it from his side, Linc couldn't blame the man at all.

'Sorry to interrupt,' Mary ventured diffidently, 'but don't forget you've got an appointment with Dr Small in less than half an hour.'

'Oh, bugger!' Linc muttered.

Mary looked at him with a certain wistfulness. 'He didn't do it to annoy you, you know. He worries about you.'

'Got to look after the succession.'

'That's a bit hard,' she responded.

'Yeah, I know. I'm sorry, I'm not feeling my best this morning.'

Dr Small turned out to be not some doddery white-haired, ex-Harley Street GP, as Linc had feared, but a young man not much older than himself who was, he confided to Linc, off to play rugby when he'd seen his last Sunday patient off the premises.

Linc apologised for his own presence, but Dr Small assured him that the surgery usually had to open for an hour or so every Sunday morning.

'There are always a handful of people who are convinced they won't see the weekend out if they don't get their symptoms checked straight away,' he said, cheerfully inspecting Linc's multi-coloured person. 'You, on the other hand, have some really quite interesting bruising.'

'It might be interesting to you, it's a bloody nuisance to me!' Linc said with feeling.

'Mmm. I expect it is. Still, there's no concussion

and no broken bones – but no miracle cure either, I'm afraid. I can only advise rest, and paracetamol if you want it, and time will do the rest. Oh, and I wouldn't go picking on any teenage thugs for a day or two.'

Almost opposite the entrance to the surgery car park was the Silver Pine health and fitness club. As Linc was waiting to pull out into the traffic, the smoked glass front doors opened and his sister-in-law Nikki came out dressed in a pink and silver tracksuit. She was carrying a sports hold-all and wore her blonde curls in a ponytail under a pink baseball cap.

Linc was idly wondering whether she was a member and how much the subscription was costing Crispin when a large, tanned, bald-headed man in a tracksuit joined Nikki on the steps. As Linc looked on, momentarily forgetting to watch for a gap in the traffic, Nikki turned to the newcomer and, standing on tiptoe to reach, put her arms round his neck and kissed him. Laughing, the man extricated himself from her grasp and stepped back, glancing around as he did so. Then he looked down at his watch, showed Nikki, and after dropping a kiss on the top of her head, disappeared back through the smoky doors.

The toot of a car horn behind him recalled Linc sharply to attention. Out on the road, a man in a sports saloon was flashing his headlights urgently, and he realised that a space had been left for him to move into. With a grateful wave he put his foot down, pulled out and drove back to Farthingscourt in a very thoughtful frame of mind.

★

Nikki's mother, Beverley Pike, was a forceful and ambitious woman.

She arrived on Monday evening, leaving behind her spacious detached house in Surrey where she lived for the most part separately from her wealthy, night-club-owning husband, to stay in Farthingscourt's North Lodge with Crispin and her daughter.

She had visited her daughter and son-in-law the previous summer but at that time Linc was still working away from home and so it was the first time he had met her, apart from briefly at the wedding. Brief though it had been, that one meeting had been enough to make it perfectly clear to him that theirs would be a relationship built on mutual antipathy.

Coming from a well-connected but not so well-to-do family, Beverley had married Eddy Pike for his money, as Nikki had unashamedly told Linc when they were dating. Having sacrificed her own position – as she saw it – for financial comfort, she was a determined social climber on her daughter's behalf, and although on the one hand she was patently delighted that Nikki had married into a titled family, she was just as obviously disappointed that her daughter had missed out on the prospect of the actual title. She held Linc entirely to blame for this, even though Nikki had apparently put their stormy break-up well behind her.

Any hope that time would have resigned the woman to the unalterable was banished by the coolness of the reception she gave Linc when he came down from his rooms to dinner on the Wednesday evening.

The first thing that he noticed, on entering the drawing room, was the presence of Mary, whose inclusion in the party, though not unprecedented, gave the lie to his father's attempt to even up the numbers. Wearing a simple but classic tan jersey dress, she appeared perfectly at ease chatting to Crispin, and Linc had an unworthy suspicion that his father had invited her solely to put Beverley's nose out of joint. He was well aware that the fondness his father had developed for Crispin's wife did not in any degree extend to her mother.

Crispin himself was looking devastatingly handsome, as he always did when he made the effort. Linc had long accepted, without a shred of rancour, that his younger brother would invariably cast his own less flamboyant looks into the shade.

Nikki, standing next to her mother, was sparklingly pretty in an evening dress of pale, shimmering blue that accentuated the colour of her eyes and clung invitingly to her curves. Beverley, in her late-forties, was still well able to attract the opposite sex in her own right but made the mistake of trying to hang on to her youth. The 'little black dress' she wore was just a few inches too short to be flattering, and her hair just a little too improbably golden.

The bell at the front door jangled, and Linc went to answer it, waving away the family's part-time butler who appeared on the same errand. He had offered to pick Josie up from the Vicarage but she'd assured him that it wasn't necessary, her only concern about the evening being what to wear. His efforts to describe the fairly liberal dress code that applied to such family gatherings at Farthingscourt had obviously been reasonably successful because as he kissed her cheek and took her coat he could see that, in a long slim dress of amber silk, Josie had got it just right.

'Wow! You look stunning!' he said, and she smiled and thanked him.

His opinion was clearly echoed by each of the occupants of the drawing room as he showed Josie in, but while Mary and Crispin looked warmly appreciative, Nikki looked pensive and her mother, for one unguarded moment, downright venomous. It was the expression of deep satisfaction on the Viscount's aristocratic features, however, that struck Linc. He guessed then that Josie too was being used as a pawn in a little game his father had orchestrated to amuse himself.

Linc was silently furious.

The conversation round the dinner table drifted from one subject to another as it does on such occasions, but it wasn't long before it got round to the attack on Linc and Josie. Nikki had exhibited a certain ghoulish interest in Linc's battle scars when she first ran into him on Monday morning, but the bruises had, after four days, faded to not much more than dark shadows and he'd somewhat naïvely hoped that the matter would be forgotten.

It was in fact Beverley who started the ball rolling. Perhaps sensing that Linc was uncomfortable talking about it, she took advantage of a pause during the discussion of an entirely different topic to say loudly, 'You must have been terrified the other night, Josie.'

Josie appeared momentarily startled by this completely unheralded comment, and after darting a look at Linc replied, 'Er, yes . . . I was. But it was much worse for Linc. They didn't really threaten me at all, just wouldn't let me go.'

'So, what exactly happened?' Nikki's mother asked. 'How did it all start? I know Linc won't tell me anything.'

'Well, I don't think . . .' Josie shot another unhappy glance at him.

'Surely we've got better things to talk about,' he interjected in bored tones. 'It was just a bunch of young thugs looking for trouble. All in the past now, and hardly a pleasant subject for a mealtime.'

'Did he take them all on single-handed?' Nikki had plainly had a little too much wine. Eyes shining, she looked from Josie to Linc, and back again. 'Did he fight for your honour?'

'Oh, for goodness' sake.' Linc was exasperated. 'I didn't fight anyone. *They* attacked *me* and, if anything, Josie was the heroine. She set a car alarm off and frightened them away.'

'Oh, well done, my dear,' Mary said warmly. 'It always annoys me when the women in films are portrayed as helpless creatures who can do nothing except stand and scream in a crisis. Most of us are just as resourceful as men, given the chance.'

'I know what you mean,' Josie agreed, grateful to have the spotlight taken off her. 'In a film, if they're being chased, the girl always has to fall and twist her ankle at the crucial moment and slow the hero up.'

'I wonder how far they'd have gone if Josie hadn't set the alarm off.' Beverley was like a terrier at a rat hole. 'You could have been badly hurt, you know. Even killed.'

The prospect didn't appear to disturb her unduly, as far as Linc could see.

'Shall we change the subject?' Sylvester suggested from the head of the table.

'Presumably they wouldn't have done any serious harm if they were just trying to warn you off, though,' Crispin remarked, looking thoughtfully across at his brother.

Linc frowned and shook his head slightly but the damage had been done.

'Warn you off? What do you mean?' Beverley demanded.

'Oh, Lord, Linc. Sorry!' Crispin said. 'But surely it doesn't matter? I mean, family . . .'

While explaining his bruises, Linc had given Crispin the gist of recent events, requesting that he keep the knowledge to himself. He should have known better, he reflected with hindsight. Part of his brother's charm had always been his openness. He was a very adept practical joker, but in serious matters was the sort who would blush if he told a lie.

'No, it doesn't really matter,' Linc told him. And hesitated, wondering how to close the subject without seeming rude.

His father had no such scruples.

'Linc has foolishly been dabbling in such matters as would be infinitely better left to the police,' he stated from the head of the table. 'I trust he's now learned his lesson, and I think the matter is best left there. We will talk about something else.' He bent one of his most quelling looks on Nikki's mother, who flushed and pursed her lips.

'I was only concerned for his safety,' she protested in injured tones.

'Yes, I'm sure you were,' Sylvester replied.

The ever-reliable Mary cleared her throat and

diffidently introduced a non-contentious topic of conversation and, apart from a slight sulkiness on Beverley's part, the uncomfortable interlude appeared forgotten.

Much as he often deplored his father's high-handedness, Linc had to concede that it came in useful at times.

When the meal was over the younger members of the party left the dining room on a mission to acquaint Josie with the rest of the house. Linc would have preferred to show her around on his own but when Nikki declared, 'We'll come too, won't we, Cris?' there was little he could do about it, save for resorting to the kind of rudeness his father employed.

Crispin, indolent by nature, looked as though he would just as soon drink coffee with the others in the drawing room but obligingly got to his feet and followed his wife instead.

'I can't wait to see Josie's face when she sees the chandelier in the ballroom,' Nikki said excitedly as they made their way across the hall, and Linc suppressed his uncharitable feelings towards her. After all, *he* still enjoyed the reactions of visitors to the house, and it was all much more of a novelty to Nikki.

Josie's exclamations of delight were enough to satisfy any guide; she took great interest in everything she was shown, especially the Long Gallery with its ranks of past Tremaynes gazing down from the walls.

'Wow!' she breathed. 'This beats the normal family photo album into a cocked hat! Doesn't it feel weird, having all your relations looking down at you? They all look so stern, too. Except your mother, of course, she looks a sweetie! And your father looks . . . Well, you can see they were very much in love.'

'My father was very different in those days,' Linc told her, divining her thoughts. 'My mother's death shattered him. He's never really got over it.'

'Oh, poor man!' Josie said with quick and very genuine sympathy, and watching the play of emotions across her face, Linc wished more than ever that Crispin and Nikki had stayed downstairs.

'This is my favourite,' Nikki called from a little further along. 'The Third Viscount, St John Tremayne. The black sheep of the family.'

Josie moved along and Linc smiled at her shock as she registered the strong likeness.

'Oh! For a moment I thought . . . Obviously it isn't, because of the costume, but doesn't he look like you?' she exclaimed, turning to him. 'Why is he the black sheep? What did he do?'

'He nearly gambled the family fortunes away,' Nikki answered, gazing up at the portrait. 'He's very handsome, don't you think?'

'Hey, no! That's not fair!' Linc protested. 'You're putting her in an impossible position. Don't answer, Josie.'

Josie turned a little pink but looked up critically at the devil-may-care face on the canvas. 'Yes, he is handsome,' she admitted after a moment. 'But I'm not sure he'd be an easy man to know.'

Crispin gave a shout of laughter. 'Take that as you will!' he told his brother.

'Well, *I* think he's gorgeous,' Nikki reiterated. She stepped over the ropes and reached up to caress the frame of the picture.

Crispin went after her, gently removing her hands. 'And *I* think you've had too much to drink.'

'Maybe I have,' she agreed with a sigh, allowing herself to be guided back on to the central runner.

'So, what happened to the black sheep?' Josie enquired. 'Did he see the error of his ways and settle down to raise a huge family?'

'Not exactly,' Linc said. 'He was wild to the end and – according to the records – died when a wheel came off his curricle during a race from London to Brighton.'

'I've often wondered whether someone loosened that wheel,' Crispin remarked thoughtfully. 'Before old St John gambled the house out from under them.'

Linc shook his head. 'Oh, no, you don't! I don't mind admitting to a ne'er-do-well, or even a womaniser – like the Fifth Viscount – but I won't have it said that we Tremaynes ever stooped so low as to bump off one of our own!'

'When are you going to sit for *your* portrait?' Josie asked.

'Cris and I had one done together as kids but the official one's not usually done until the title is handed on.'

The tour of the house continued, finishing with a look at the servants' quarters, part of which had been restored to their original state for the benefit of the paying visitors, and ending back in the main hall where it had started. Here Josie demurely expressed a wish to powder her nose and was directed to the cloakroom, and Crispin went ahead to the drawing room saying that he would bespeak more coffee.

Left alone with Linc, Nikki drifted round the half-panelled hall, humming and running her fingers over the furniture like a child. She stopped and looked in the mirror above the fireplace, then moving on, picked up an umbrella from the stand in the corner and, apparently inspecting it closely, said suddenly, 'She's a nice girl, your Josie. I like her.'

'Good,' Linc said, slightly surprised.

Nikki put the umbrella down and wandered up behind him.

'But I'm nice too, aren't I, Linc?'

'Of course you are. Cris is a lucky chap.' He could hear the wine talking and knew from experience that it would be best to humour her.

'But you had your chance, Linc, and you didn't take it. I would have been good for you. Your father likes me too.' Nikki came round to stand in front of him, gazing soulfully into his eyes from about six inches away.

'It wouldn't have worked, though,' he said gently. 'We'd have been at each other's throats all the time!'

She smiled at him, dreamily. 'Yes, but think of the fun we'd have had making up,' she murmured, and before he could stop her, she slid her arms round his neck and reached up to kiss him full on the lips.

Startled, Linc tried to draw back, but for a moment she clung tightly. She was surprisingly strong and even when he turned his head away she remained draped against him, forcing him to take her weight.

'Nikki, please!' he protested, trying to extricate himself from her grasp.

162

Across the hall a door opened and Josie came through, half-checking in embarrassment as she took in the scene. Almost simultaneously, Crispin reappeared from the drawing room.

Trying to shake off the feeling of being part of a staged farce, Linc said lightly, 'Come and collect your wife, Cris. She's come over all emotional.'

'I had a feeling this might happen,' Crispin sighed, coming forward. 'She and Beverley opened a bottle before they came out. Sorry, Bro.'

'Don't worry about it.' Linc prised Nikki's arms away from his person one at a time and transferred them to Crispin. 'I'll tell you something – she's a lot stronger than she looks!'

'She's been going to the gym, haven't you, Niks? Got a personal trainer.'

'I love Linc,' Nikki told her husband earnestly. 'And he loves me too.'

'We all love you,' Crispin said tolerantly. 'But just at the moment I'd love you more if you weren't standing on my foot. Those heels are lethal! I think perhaps I'll take her home now,' he added over her head to Linc.

At this, Nikki seemed to regain the strength in her legs and stood up very straight. 'I am home. *This* is my home,' she stated.

'I'll tell Beverley,' Linc said, moving towards the drawing-room door. 'Come in and make yourself comfortable, Josie.'

'Er, actually, I think I'll call it a night, too,' she told him, hanging back. 'It's been lovely but . . .'

'Oh, please. At least stay and have a cup of coffee.'

'No, really. I ought to go. It's getting late and I

have to be in London tomorrow at ten o'clock. I'll just come and say thank you to your father.'

She looked resolute, and Linc didn't try any further persuasion.

After all the usual politenesses had been exchanged, and Crispin had departed for the Lodge with his two ladies, Linc helped Josie into her coat and she accepted his escort to her car.

It was a lovely starlit night but as they descended the steps Linc's mind was on other matters. Although Josie had said nothing to indicate that she was upset, she seemed a little reserved and had hardly made eye contact with him in the last ten minutes.

'Have you got a job on in London?' he asked as they reached the gravel.

'Yes. Something I was booked for ages ago. A car launch.'

Her E-type was parked not ten paces from the bottom step and they stopped beside it, both fidgeting awkwardly.

'I'm sorry about tonight . . .' Linc spoke first.

'Why? I enjoyed it,' Josie sounded sincere. 'It was quite an experience. And the house is wonderful. Thank you for showing me round.'

'Yes, but Beverley was a pain, and Nikki isn't normally like that, you know.'

'Oh, well. Dad always says you can't choose your relatives. But they were okay, really. I didn't mind.'

'Are you sure? I thought you seemed a bit quiet at the end there.'

'I'm a bit tired, and I've got a long day tomorrow,' she said, fishing her car keys out of her bag and jingling them in her hand.

'Okay, I'll let you go,' Linc said. Her body language was uncertain, so he reined himself in and had to be content with kissing her lightly on the cheek.

As he stepped back she bowed her head, opened the door of the low-slung Jaguar and slid into the driver's seat. Winding the window down, she smiled and thanked him again before gunning the engine and driving smoothly away.

Linc was left very thoughtful. Although she'd said it hadn't bothered her, Nikki's untimely display had definitely been the turning point in Josie's attitude. He was almost sure she'd been intending to stay for coffee until she'd walked in on that little scene.

He wandered back into the house and made his way to the drawing room where he found his father and Mary seated at either end of the sofa. There was nothing remarkable in this, but something about the relaxed way Mary was sitting, with her shoes off and her stockinged feet drawn up beside her, suddenly struck him.

'I'll say goodnight, then. And thank you.'

'I like your Josie,' Mary said warmly. 'She's a lovely girl.'

Linc thanked her, reflecting that it was the second time that evening that Josie had been described as his girl. He found he didn't mind at all, but judging by her demeanour, Josie herself wasn't so sure.

'You must bring her again,' his father suggested.

'I will, if she'll come. But it wasn't the most harmonious of atmospheres.'

'You say she comes from a big family. I should think she'd be used to it. All the same, Beverley was a confounded nuisance, as usual. Don't worry about it. I'm sure Josie won't.'

He seemed more mellow than usual and Linc looked speculatively at Mary. Lay the wind in that quarter? It was food for thought. Nevertheless, he couldn't help wondering if his father would have been so genial if he had known where Linc had arranged to spend the following evening.

7

Linc thoroughly enjoyed his evening at Ledworth greyhound track. Barney was a pleasant companion, and Linc found the charged atmosphere of the stadium on race night exciting. Absorbed in the preparation of the dogs and learning the order of things, he easily forgot his original reason for getting involved and it was with a sense of shock that he rounded a corner and came face to face with Marty Lucas, the unhelpful stadium worker he had met on his previous visit.

The man was wearing an official jacket and badge, and had his hands full of cardboard cartons which he nearly dropped as he collided with Linc in the narrow space behind the stands.

'Shit! Look where you're fucking going!'

'Sorry.' Linc made a swift decision to duck his head and carry on past but he couldn't resist looking back when he was well clear and Lucas was still standing there, staring after him with a slightly puzzled expression.

So much for keeping a low profile, Linc thought

as he went on his way. He had no reason to suspect that Lucas was involved in anything illegal but it was quite possible that he'd passed on news of Linc's interest to those who were. *Somebody* must have said *something* to provoke the attack in Shaftesbury. And might well report this second appearance at the track, he supposed gloomily. If he ever found out, Rockley would not be pleased.

Later in the evening, after he and Barney had cheered his first runner to a close second place, Linc spotted Marty Lucas again, apparently having a beer with Sam Menzies at the trackside. He pointed him out to Barney, asking what he knew about him.

'Marty Lucas? He's Sam's son-in-law, or at least he was until he got divorced last year. He's a lorry driver and does odd jobs here and there. He's a bit of a chancer, but okay so long as you keep on the right side of him.'

It was a bit late for that, Linc reflected ruefully.

A little later, when he was walking back to the van with Barney and his second dog, they met Lucas and Menzies together. The trainer acknowledged Barney with a brief nod and scowled at Linc as he passed. Lucas ignored them both.

'Oh, dear. I'm afraid you've put our friend's nose out of joint, taking up with the opposition,' Barney said, shaking his head gravely but with a twinkle in his eye.

'I guess so,' Linc agreed, thinking that, in fact, being seen with Barney Weston might just save his bacon. His original story had been one of trying to track down someone called Barney or Barnaby to buy a dog; to any suspicious onlooker it would appear that he had done just that. Coming to the track might just have been a good thing after all.

Early the next morning, Linc rode out with Ruth, giving Noddy and Magic a steady hack with a short, pipe-opening gallop as they were both travelling to the one-day event the following day. Josie was still in London, having stayed on for a couple of days to look up some friends, according to Ruth. She apparently saw nothing unusual in this, and neither would Linc have done if it hadn't been for Josie's reserve when they parted on Wednesday night.

He gave himself a mental shake. He was almost certainly reading too much into it; after all, there was no formal understanding between them. Certainly their friendship had seemed to be flourishing but maybe that was all it was destined to be. Nothing had been said between them to the contrary. Deciding that dwelling on the matter was unproductive, he returned to Farthingscourt and immersed himself in the business of the day, refusing to acknowledge the faint depression that was dogging him.

The cross-country course for the following day was open to be walked from two o'clock on the Friday and, as it was fairly local, it had been Linc's intention to walk it that evening before going on to the Vicarage to plait Noddy. But, as on the night of the burglary, work commitments kept him longer than he'd anticipated. The delay on this occasion was caused by his father requesting an update on the restoration work at the mill, and suggesting halfway through Linc's report that he would rather like to see the progress for himself.

At any other time Linc would have welcomed the chance to show off his pet project, but just now he wanted to get away. It was unfair to leave all the preparatory work to Ruth, even though he knew she'd cheerfully do it. He'd not mentioned his plans for the weekend, but as he turned the Discovery into Mill Lane, he tried to rid himself of the suspicion that his father was aware of both his desire to get away in good time that evening, and the reason for it.

With what he felt was commendable strength of character, he managed to hide his frustration, reflecting that if his father were being deliberately obstructive, then any show of impatience would only gratify him.

In the event, they never made it to the mill. Halfway along the lane, at the edge of the wood known as Millersholt, Linc's mobile trilled and he fished it out of his jacket and flipped it open.

'Sir?' It was Reagan, sounding flustered.

'Jack. What can I do for you?'

'It's South Lodge Farm, sir! The barn's on fire!'

'Christ! Okay. Calm down, Jack.' Linc stood on the brakes and swung the Land-Rover one-handed into a convenient gateway. 'Has anyone called the fire brigade?'

'Yes, sir. They've just come. But—'

'Okay, I'll be right there.' Linc snapped the phone shut and dropped it in his lap so as to use both hands on the wheel. With regret he was forced to relinquish any hope of walking tomorrow's course this evening.

South Lodge and its accompanying farm were at the diametrically opposite corner of the estate from the mill, and much further away from the house itself. It took Linc the best part of ten minutes to get to it, even driving at a pace that had his father wincing and reaching for his seatbelt – a precaution often neglected within the confines of the estate. Retracing their tracks, they shot past the house and raced down the drive, over the bridge and up the other side through the avenue of beeches, before turning right along what was generally known as the top road. This led away from Geoff Sykes's home at the East Lodge and the turning to Farthing St Anne and, after a mile or so, took them past Jack Reagan's cottage and through the nearby copse.

Due to the wooded nature of the surrounding land, Linc and his father saw no sign of the fire until they were almost upon it. They burst out of South Lodge Wood doing close on fifty and Linc had to slam the brakes on hard to avoid a collision with a police car that was parked across the lane. Beyond it, two red-and-silver fire engines stood, their wheels spanning the width of the tarmac, and four men manned the hoses that were pouring water in silvery streams on to the burning wreck of the barn. A southerly wind was blowing the smoke away from the lane, and in the farmyard several other helmeted individuals could be seen going about their business.

One of the two uniformed police officers who had presumably arrived in the car swung round with startled anger on his face at the speed of Linc's approach, but bit any intended reprimand off short as he recognised the occupants of the vehicle.

Linc leapt out of the Land-Rover, hardly noticing the policeman; his attention immediately caught by the sight of an unkempt figure in blue overalls who was talking to another officer, a little further off. He couldn't see Reagan.

'What the hell's *he* doing here?' Linc demanded, marching round the back of the police car and glaring at Jim Pepper.

'Ah, Mr . . . er . . .?' the PC began. He was a young man, thickset and blond; Linc didn't recognise *him* either.

'Tremayne,' he supplied. 'What's this man doing on our land?'

'It was Mr Pepper who discovered the fire and called the fire brigade,' the policeman stated.

'Well, what a coincidence!' Linc exclaimed with heavy irony.

'Sir, I don't think this is the time . . .'

'You should be grateful to me,' Jim Pepper put in unctuously. 'I saved two of your tractors.' He pointed a grimy finger to where the machines stood in the lane.

'Yes, he did,' the policeman said, nodding and turning a little pink under the pressure.

'And I suppose you *had* to drive them *through* the new farm gate?' Linc observed.

'You should be thanking me,' Pepper said again.

'You shouldn't have been on my land in the first place.' The Viscount had caught up with them. 'You've been warned off more than once.'

'Mr Pepper thinks he saw some children running away from the barn just before the fire started,' the policeman interposed. 'I was just—'

'How very convenient,' the Viscount cut in. 'And then, seeing the smoke, I imagine he rushed to fetch the farm's own fire hose and put the fire out . . .'

Pepper shifted uncomfortably.

'Perhaps Mr Pepper wasn't aware of the fire hose?' the officer suggested reasonably.

'Oh, I think he was. After all, he used to work here three days a week.'

The policeman dried up, looking unhappily from the Viscount to Pepper and back again. His colleague passed behind the group, heading for the fire engines.

Linc had been scanning the area. There was no sign of Phil Sutton, who managed South Lodge Farm, but he could see Reagan now, watching the proceedings from a safe distance.

'Where's Phil?'

'He's took his wife to the hospital,' Jim Pepper replied, sulkily.

'Ah,' the Viscount said on a note of dawning understanding. 'So there was no one here except you? Oh, and the kids with the matches, of course, we mustn't forget them. No doubt, knowing Sutton was out, you felt you ought to come and see that everything was all right? Very neighbourly of you.'

'Now, sir!' the officer protested. 'You really have no grounds for those kinds of allegations . . .'

'Everything all right?' His older colleague had returned.

'Yes. Well, no. Lord Tremayne is suggesting . . .'

'I'm saying I think it's very unlikely that Pepper's presence here has anything whatsoever to do with coincidence,' the Viscount said bluntly. 'The man is known to bear a grudge against me and it's quite obvious you need look no further for your arsonist.'

Jim Pepper spluttered indignantly and the young policeman tried once more. 'But, the children . . .'

'Oh, spare me that cock and bull story, I'm not interested!'

'I think if you've finished with Mr Pepper and have his contact details, we should send him on his way now,' the newcomer advised. 'Lord Tremayne, Constable Diller. Could I have a word?'

He moved away a little and, with a sour look at Pepper, the Viscount followed.

'You heard the constable. Go,' Linc told the former estate worker. 'And from now on, stay off Farthingscourt land or there'll be trouble.'

'You can't talk to me like that! Can he?' he appealed to the young PC.

'I think you'd better go, sir,' the officer said, apparently deciding to fall in with the majority.

Jim Pepper gave both of them a dirty look, hissed a number of expletives and something that sounded suspiciously like a threat at Linc, and stomped off.

Linc sighed and turned his attention to the burning barn. Edging between the fire engines and the hedge he made his way into the farmyard, nodding to Reagan as he passed.

The air was heavy with the acrid tang of smoke and Linc's eyes began to sting a little but there wasn't much to see. What was left of the barn was no longer burning but it would clearly be a long time before the three or four hundred bales of hay it had sheltered would stop smouldering. One of the two hoses still poured gallons of water through the beams that had once held the roof and, down below, half a dozen men in fluorescent-striped jackets raked hay out into the yard to be soused by the other hose. None of it could be salvaged. It was all such a waste.

'There wasn't anything I could do,' Reagan stated, coming to stand beside him. 'I didn't get here till after the fire engines did.'

Linc shook his head. 'Once it gets a hold on a haystack, there's nothing much anyone can do. I suppose you know it was Pepper who called them? Have you seen him around the place since that business the other day?'

'No, sir. I would have told you if I had,' Reagan said a touch defensively.

'Mr Tremayne, sir?'

Linc turned to find Phil Sutton, the farmer, standing at his elbow. Stocky and bespectacled, he wore a permanently anxious expression, especially marked now.

'I'm sorry, sir. I've only just got back. I had to take Cindy to the hospital for her scan, and I told the boys they could go when they'd finished. I didn't know how long we'd be but, honest to God, I thought the yard would be all right for half an hour with the dog here. He usually keeps folk out.'

'Unless he knows them,' Linc agreed. 'It's all right, Phil. It can't be helped. Er, how many people knew you'd be at the hospital this afternoon?'

'Quite a few,' Phil told him sheepishly. 'I reckon I told everyone at the pub, last night, I was that excited. They was placing bets on whether it'd be a boy or a girl.'

'Never mind. How did it go, anyway? Boy or girl?'

The farmer looked a little crestfallen. 'We still don't know. They couldn't see.'

It was another twenty minutes or so before Linc and his father left South Lodge Farm, and thankfully

Sylvester seemed to have given up the idea of visiting the mill that evening. They drove back to the house discussing the problem of Jim Pepper, and Linc went on to the Vicarage to find that Noddy and Magic had already been neatly plaited, and Ruth had all but finished loading the horsebox.

He apologised unreservedly, helped check everything on board, then put up very little resistance before accepting an invitation to the house for a meal. Ruth had already been over to walk the cross-country course that afternoon, and went over it fence by fence with him during supper.

The mood when they set off for the event the following morning was light-hearted. Quite apart from the usual excited anticipation of the challenges ahead, Abby was showing signs of increased brain activity, which her consultant viewed as very promising, and Ruth was buoyed up with optimism.

Linc and she were joined in the cab of the horsebox by Nikki, who'd offered to groom for them both. Nikki had apologised very prettily to Linc the day after the dinner party. She confessed to having no memory of having behaved badly, and told Linc she was horrified when Crispin had informed her of it.

'I hope I didn't mess things up between you and Josie,' she said, and Linc assured her with, it had to be said, less than perfect truth that it was all forgiven and forgotten. He had decided that, given time, Josie and he would sort things out, if indeed it were meant to be.

An advance telephone call to the secretary, two

days before, had furnished them with their start-times, two of which were fairly early in the running order. In addition to this, they had set out at the crack of dawn to allow Linc to walk the course before the competition got under way. Consequently there were only a handful of lorries and trailers on the field when they turned the Hathaways' horsebox off the road and bumped across the grass under the directions of several enthusiastic young stewards in fluorescent tabards. Linc preferred an early start; always supposing they opened proceedings promptly, it meant less time for the inevitable hitches and delays to build up. Once ready to go, being kept waiting for more than a few minutes can result in both horse and rider becoming stale and losing the keen edge needed for competition.

On arrival, Nikki took charge of the horses whilst Linc and Ruth fetched their numbers and familiar-ised themselves with the general layout of the showground. Then, Linc set off to walk the cross-country course in double-quick time and Ruth, who was first to ride her dressage test, went back to the lorry to saddle Magic.

Fifty minutes after arriving she presented herself at the arena, impeccably turned out in breeches, boots and black coat. Her long hair, neatly confined in a net, almost exactly matched Magic's gleaming chestnut hide and Linc thought they presented a lovely picture, which was only slightly marred by the mare's shying at the shiny white boards that marked the perimeter of the rectangular arena. Once they got started, however, they produced a very credit-able test, which Linc knew he had little hope of matching. Magic was a lot more animated and her paces more showy than Noddy's.

Twenty minutes later Linc rode his test, desperately trying to instil some sort of enthusiasm into his horse while giving an outward impression of tranquillity and effortlessness. He had limited success. Even though it was still early, it was set fair to be a warm day and Noddy wasn't inclined to exert himself unduly in a discipline which he considered a dead bore. As the test progressed, Linc was aware that the penalties were steadily piling up and by the time they left the arena he knew he could expect no less than a cricket score, having turned many of the intended circles into oddball potato shapes, and cantered stubbornly round one end on the wrong lead.

Nikki came forward to hold the recalcitrant horse and commiserate as Linc jumped down with a rueful smile.

'Let's hope Hilary Lang wasn't around to see that!' he remarked, patting Noddy's brown neck.

'That looked like hard work,' someone said, and he turned to see Dee Ellis approaching.

'It was,' he agreed.

'Well, my boy should be full of energy anyway. I've been giving him a few more oats this last week,' she told him.

'More oats?' Linc nearly choked on the word. 'He . . . er . . . seemed quite perky last time.'

'Yes, I know,' she said indulgently. 'But he's got more to do this time. I didn't want him to struggle.'

Linc had his own ideas about who was likely to struggle but he kept his thoughts to himself. After all, the deed was done. There would be time enough to criticise Steamer's preparation when he blew his top in the dressage arena, as he might well do on that diet.

Promising to rendezvous with Dotty Dee at her lorry in plenty of time to warm up for Steamer's test, Linc made his way back to his own box with Nikki and the horse, for refreshments. As they passed the end of the row of trade stands a brindle-coloured bullet hurtled out of nowhere and leaped up at Linc, causing the normally placid Noddy to side-step in alarm.

'What the hell!' Linc exclaimed, swinging round.

The dog sat on his foot, looking up at him with a wide grin.

'Tiger!' Sandy Wilkes came striding over. 'Oh, it's you, Linc. He seems to have taken quite a liking to you.'

'Yeah, looks like it. He should be on a lead round here, you know. You'll cop it, if you're spotted! What are you doing here anyway? Are you trading? I didn't see your stand earlier.'

'Er, not officially,' Sandy admitted with a sheepish grin. 'But I'm letting it be known I'm parked in the car park if anyone needs anything.'

'You'll be lynched if the other traders find out,' Linc told him. 'Look, would you like to get your dog off my foot, I've got horses to ride.'

'Sorry.' Sandy hauled Tiger towards him and clipped a lead on to his collar. As he straightened up he looked critically at Linc. 'Hey, what happened to you?' he asked, gesturing at his own face by way of illustrating his question. 'That looks nasty.'

'You should see the other guy!' Linc retorted. The outward signs of the attack had, for the most part, faded into insignificance but he still bore a scar on his cheekbone and a dark mark under one eye. The deep bruising to the muscles of his torso and upper arms was proving much slower to heal, and he viewed the looming challenge of coping with Dee Ellis's grey with something less than wholehearted joy. 'By the way, Ruth's here,' he said, changing the subject.

'I know. I was on my way to find her. See you later.' With a cheery wave, and dragging a reluctant Tiger in his wake, Sandy struck off across the showground.

When Linc finally did haul himself stiffly aboard Steamer, he was pleasantly surprised, as he remembered he had been last time, by the big grey's manners. In the dressage arena he was forward-going but tried hard to do as he was asked. His level of concentration was evident in the activity of his ears and the way he busily mouthed his bit, spewing gobs of foam down his broad, dappled chest. Unfortunately, concentration notwithstanding, excessive mouthing and tail swishing incur penalties, and Steamer finished his test with a very average score, but Linc warmed to him for his generosity of effort.

He made a rapid change back on to Noddy and warmed him up for the showjumping phase, watching Ruth jump a clear round on Magic as he did so. Noddy, in his turn, jumped a careful clear and half an hour later was in the start box for the cross-country.

Ruth had returned from her round some fifteen minutes earlier to report that in general the course was riding well but that fence five was a bit tricky and, further on, Magic had had trouble shortening for the low bounce into the lake. Linc had digested the information, trying not to dwell on Steamer's treatment of the bounce fence at Talham.

As the steward began his countdown Noddy fidgeted and tried to rub his face on his knee. Linc pulled his head up and made him walk forward round the starting box. The horse's legs were liberally smeared with grease and he'd already managed to get some in his eye while they were waiting. Nikki had had to rinse it out with warm water. Linc didn't want to risk his doing it again.

'Three, two, one – good luck!' the steward called cheerfully, and Noddy and Linc were off and running.

The first three or four fences were relatively easy and the fifth was a combination of obstacles amongst the trees, which held no problems for Noddy. He skipped through with ease, and Linc patted his neck, pleased with him. Out here in the open country, with room to gallop and natural fences to jump, the lop-eared brown horse came into his own. He had a long, ground-eating stride, and the ability to adjust it to meet the jumps right, without being told. The bounce over two logs into the lake troubled him not at all, and he crossed the finishing line inside the optimum time and still full of running. Even though Linc knew his dressage score would keep him out of the placings, he was very satisfied with the horse's performance.

He wasn't so satisfied with his own condition, however. Dismounting from Noddy he felt a little light-headed and rather as if the stuffing had been knocked out of him and could only surmise that Beanie's attentions, the week before, had affected him more than he'd realised.

Nikki took charge of the horse, running his stirrups up, loosening the girth and throwing a cotton sheet over his back to cool him down gradually.

'Thanks, Nik, you're a star,' he told her, gratefully. 'Can I leave him to you? I'm just going to get a bite to eat before I tackle Steamer.'

'No problem,' she said cheerfully, and departed for the lorry.

He had, in fact, only twenty minutes or so to spare before warming the big grey up for action, and spent it buying hot, sweet coffee and a bag of freshly made doughnuts.

'You'll get fat!' a voice commented behind him.

Linc swung round.

'Josie!' he declared delightedly. 'I didn't know you were here.'

'I've only just arrived,' she said, smiling at him with no trace of her recent reserve. 'I got back from London at eight o'clock this morning. So, are you going to offer me one of those? The smell is making my mouth water!'

Linc didn't bother analysing her behaviour. She looked gorgeous in designer-faded jeans and a stretchy slash-necked tee-shirt, and he was just over the moon that she was there. He held out the paper bag with its sugary contents.

'Is this the proper diet for a model?'

'Bugger that!' she announced. 'I'm starving! What's your excuse? You don't normally eat during a competition, do you? Ruth never does.'

'Energy food,' he said succinctly. 'I'm due to ride Dotty Dee's horse in a minute.'

He had told her about his previous encounter with Steamer, and now she frowned at him.

'Are you fit for that?'

'To be honest, I'm not sure,' he admitted frankly. 'I guess we'll find out.'

Taking a chance, he reached for her hand as they walked back towards the lorry park. She didn't appear to object, and by the time he came up with Dee and Steamer, he was on cloud nine.

The big grey's good behaviour lasted for the duration of the showjumping phase, which he completed with no additional penalties, but as soon as they began to prepare him for the cross-country his growing excitement was palpable. Dee checked his protective boots were fitting snugly and that the metal studs in his shoes were tight. Grease was applied to the front of his powerful, iron-grey legs, and his nose, mouth and eyes were sponged out with cold water. Finally, as Linc pulled on his gloves and mounted, she tied a bootlace from the head-piece of his bridle to his topmost plait.

'There's a confidence booster,' he observed.

'Better safe than sorry.'

'What's it for?' Josie had been watching with interest.

'It's to stop the bridle being pulled off over his ears if I fall off,' Linc told her.

'Let's hope you don't need it.'

'Amen to that.'

Linc's number was called and he rode into the start box where Steamer stood like a rock with his head up and muscles quivering with nervous energy. With ten seconds to go, Linc took a stronger grip on the reins and turned him in a circle.

'Three, two, one . . . good luck!'

Dee and Josie echoed the starter's call and with a lurch Steamer was off, accelerating like a drag racer. Having experienced it before, Linc was at least not caught unawares, but he soon found that anticipation of the problem went almost nowhere at all towards coping with it.

The first fence, low as always and made up of oil barrels and a rail, rushed at them and was negotiated somewhere mid-stride, with no discernible interruption to their forward progress. The second and third fences went much the same way, but they met the fourth obstacle on entirely the wrong stride and Steamer clouted it hard, his momentum causing him to stumble and nearly pitch on his nose.

Linc, realising some way out what was on the cards, sat back a little and managed to stay in the saddle, taking advantage of Steamer's momentary loss of impulsion to shorten his reins still further and sit down hard, driving him into the bridle. It took all his strength and wrenched his damaged muscles unmercifully, but it worked. The big grey came up short, snorting with indignation, and by anchoring his thumbs in the neckstrap of Steamer's breast-girth Linc was able to keep him steady most of the way to the combination of jumps which formed fence five.

Once Steamer realised that several rails were involved, he concentrated and accepted a certain amount of guidance, with the result of making the whole thing look easy. As they galloped away towards the sixth, Linc slapped the hot, dappled neck and heard the announcer say in unemotional tones, 'Lincoln Tremayne and Night Train are safely through the Valley Copse complex and heading for the Bullfinch.'

This matter-of-fact report on his progress was so far removed from his frantic battle for control of the exuberant grey that it seemed almost surreal. As they thundered down a couple of hundred yards or so of clear turf, Linc wondered with amusement if the disembodied voice behind the public address system would still sound so flat if it had to say, 'Lincoln Tremayne and Night Train have missed fence six, left the course and are heading for Swindon.'

As it turned out, they negotiated the next few fences without mishap, and it occurred to Linc that Steamer might actually have given himself a bit of a fright by hitting the fourth so hard. They were now just over halfway round the course; the lake fence with its problematical bounce-in loomed, and Linc's whole body ached with fatigue.

They burst from the trees, travelling down the long slope towards the lake, and with each stride his control of the horse slipped a fraction more. It was exactly the situation that Linc had hoped to avoid. The sensible course of action was undoubtedly to pull the horse into a circle until he slowed up, but circling once inside the penalty zone meant twenty points added to their score, and now Steamer had seen the jump, Linc wasn't sure he had the strength to turn him anyway.

By the time they reached the first of the two logs,

Steamer was flying. At the last moment he seemed to see the second log, bunched his quarters, stretched his forelegs out and launched himself skywards. After what seemed like an age suspended in mid-air, horse and rider landed in the brownish water of the lake with a colossal splash that must have drenched the photographer who crouched nearby.

How the horse kept his feet, Linc would never know, but somehow he did, and as the weight of the water dragged at his legs, Linc was able to recover from his position up by the grey ears and turn him in the direction of the exit fence and dry land. Seconds later they were out and powering up the bank on the far side to the accompaniment of a huge cheer from the ranks of spectators. The incline allowed Linc a little breathing space and by the time they had made it safely to the other side of a bank and rails near the top of the hill, Steamer had worked off his excessive energy and settled to a pace that was brisk but no longer potentially suicidal.

It occurred to Linc, as they flew the end-to-end park benches that made up the last fence, that here was a horse tailor-made for the gruelling world of three-day eventing. Quite possibly, two sessions of roads and tracks, totalling an hour or more, with a couple of miles over steeplechase fences in between, might temper the air of wild excitement with which he approached the cross-country course. And in spite of the nerve-shredding round he'd just experienced, Linc found himself hoping that he'd be the one to find out.

Once across the finishing line, Steamer relaxed

his jaw and slowed his pace, dropping back to a walk in a very few strides and turning with obvious affection to meet Dee as she hurried forward with Josie a pace or two behind.

'Bloody hell!' Josie exclaimed explosively. 'I can't believe you got round in one piece!'

'That makes two of us,' Linc agreed with a slight smile.

'Have you seen your time?'

He shook his head. If the truth were told he was having a little trouble focussing on anything just at that moment. There was a buzzing in his ears and his vision was a patchwork of dark and light.

Kicking his feet free of the stirrups, he swung his right leg back over Steamer's rump and slid to the ground, keeping hold of the saddle to steady himself as his knees threatened to give way under his weight. For three or four seconds the dark blotches were in danger of eclipsing the light ones completely, then they slowly cleared.

'You were nearly half a minute inside the optimum! Hey, are you all right?' Josie put a hand on his arm.

'Yeah. Just give me a sec.'

'Perhaps I should have given *you* the oats,' Dee suggested, smiling broadly. 'You look exhausted, but Steamer looks as though he could go round again.'

'It would probably do him good!' Linc said with feeling. 'He's a complete maniac!'

'But he got round. You're a clever boy,' she told the horse, apparently writing off Linc's part in the achievement.

Once the formalities had been observed, Dee

happily led her 'clever boy' off towards her lorry and the promise of a carrot, and Linc made his weary way back to find Ruth. Josie fell in beside him and slipped her arm through his.

'Lean on me, if you like,' she offered. 'You look all in.'

'I should have had more doughnuts,' he joked, trying, nevertheless, not to use her as a support. 'Wherever we go you seem to end up helping me home!'

Back at the lorry, Noddy and Magic were already loaded and contentedly munching hay. Ruth, Nikki and Sandy were all sitting on the lowered ramp enjoying the sun and eating ice creams.

'How'd it go?' Ruth called. 'We heard that you'd got round, but not much of the stuff before that. Was he good?'

'In a manner of speaking,' Linc said. 'He went clear anyway.'

'Oh, well done!'

'You look cream-crackered,' Sandy remarked. 'Absolutely fished!'

'*Fished?*' Ruth echoed, incredulously.

'Fish pasted. Wasted,' Sandy supplied, adding proudly, 'I made that one up myself.'

'Actually it's quite descriptive,' Linc said. 'Fished. I wouldn't mind but the horse looked as fresh as a daisy!'

Ruth drove the lorry on the homeward trip. It was only a small two-horse box and therefore not subject to HGV restrictions, and Linc was quite happy to leave the driving to her. Josie had to return, as she had come, in the E-type, but the kiss she had given him on parting, albeit on the cheek, left him in a haze of pleasurable contentment.

On the way home, the three of them chattered lazily about anything and everything. Nikki hadn't heard about the fire at South Lodge Farm and was interested to learn of Jim Pepper's possible involvement.

'I thought he'd moved away,' she said. 'Until I saw him coming out of The Wheatsheaf the other day with that forester chap.'

'Jack Reagan?' Linc asked sharply.

'Is that his name? Big chap; dark curly hair? Yes, it *is* Reagan, isn't it? I remember now.'

'And they were together?'

'They seemed to be. Unless they just happened to come out at the same time. But, no – because Reagan kind of slapped him on the back as they parted. I didn't think much of it at the time, but I suppose it *was* a bit odd . . .'

'When was this? Can you remember?'

'Um . . . I'm not sure. I think I was on my way to the gym but I can't remember which day. It could have been Tuesday or Thursday. With Mum here my usual routine's gone to pot.'

'So why the sudden interest in keeping fit?' Linc quizzed her. 'Cris says you've got a personal trainer.'

'Yes, Terry Fagan. He used to work as a bouncer for my father but he's a trained fitness instructor now.'

Ruth was impressed. 'Wow! That's the *in thing*, isn't it? All the celebrities have them. A few years ago it was personal shrinks, now it's fitness coaches.' She put on a plummy voice. 'No trainer? But, dahling, you must! Everybody has one.'

Nikki laughed. 'It's not like that. I've known Terry for years. He moved down here and wanted a reference for a job at the Silver Pine, and it just went from there.'

That explained her show of affection for him outside the leisure centre, Linc thought, but he couldn't help wondering how far it had gone 'from there'.

As Ruth parked the lorry in the Vicarage stable-yard, the work began again. A one-day event, with its three separate components, is quite a strain on a horse and the tough nature of the cross-country course lays it open to all kinds of cuts, grazes and bruising. Noddy and Magic needed hosing down to remove the last traces of grease before having their legs meticulously inspected for signs of injury. Having satisfied themselves that none had been sustained, Linc and Ruth applied cooling poultices to Magic's slightly filled legs while Nikki made up a small, easily digestible bran mash for the horses.

With three of them on the job, the lorry was soon emptied and cleaned, and the tack wiped over, and with Ruth promising to give both horses another, more nutritious feed later, Linc left Noddy rugged up and munching on a haynet, and drove Nikki back to Farthingscourt.

'Pity you didn't win anything,' she remarked after a few moments. 'They all went so well. Even that mad thing you rode last!'

'Steamer could be the best of the lot, if I could only get him settled. I'd like to try him in a different bit, but Dee says he's the same whatever you put in his mouth.'

'Well, *I* wouldn't fancy riding him,' Nikki said.

When Linc had first met her she'd competed a little on a horse that her father had bought her, but had soon given up, freely admitting that she hadn't the nerve for eventing.

'He's not a woman's ride,' Linc said. 'I can't think why Dotty Dee ever bought him for her daughter. He's just too strong. I'm not at all sure he's not too strong for me. I'll have to go and see your fitness trainer!'

'Well, you could. Why not?'

'Time,' Linc answered succinctly, turning past Sykes's cottage into the drive.

'So, how's it going between you and Josie?' Nikki enquired.

'Okay, I think.'

'Are you serious about her?'

'It's early days,' he said cautiously. 'But, yes. I think so.'

'She's very pretty. So is Ruth. What about the one in hospital, is she pretty too?'

Linc considered this. 'I think she will be. She's still growing up.'

'Will you go on trying to find out who attacked her? Now they've warned you off, I mean.'

'I don't know if there's much more I *can* do,' Linc told her frankly, as they swept over the bridge and round in front of the house to the courtyard beside.

'But it hasn't put you off, has it?' she persisted. 'You'll still go on trying?'

'Yes, I suppose so.'

He switched the engine off and looked across at Nikki who looked concerned.

'I think your father's right. You should leave it to

the police,' she said. 'These people are obviously dangerous. You will be careful, won't you?'

'I will,' Linc promised, quite touched. 'I'm nobody's hero, I can tell you.'

8

Sunday was a very busy day. The sun was out and visitor numbers were substantially up on the previous week as the holiday season began to get into full swing. School holidays made little difference to the takings at Farthingscourt, for the estate had so far managed to resist the commercial pressure to turn itself into the kind of all-purpose tourist attraction that appeals to the multitudes. Tearooms in part of the old kitchens and a picnic area beside the car park were its only concessions to the modern trend.

Linc had managed to pay Noddy an early visit, riding him out round the village at a walk to loosen his joints before turning him out into the Vicarage paddock for the morning. Ruth promised to fetch him in as soon as the heat and flies started to bother him, and Linc returned to his home and office.

By the time the last visitor had been seen off the premises, the show rooms checked for damage, loss and stowaways, and the part-time staff departed, Linc wanted nothing more than to stretch out on his bed and sleep. Aside from the normal hassles of an opening day, his father had been more than usually difficult. Curt and hard to please, he'd made Linc pay all day for Saturday's sport.

He was wearily ascending the back stairs when his mobile trilled.

'Damn!' he muttered, toying with the idea of turning it off unanswered but his conscience wouldn't let him. It might be important.

'Yeah?'

'Oh, dear, have you had a bad day?' It was Josie.

'It's getting better,' he assured her. 'Sorry. I didn't mean to be rude.'

'Well, I don't know if you're free, but we're having a barbecue and we wondered if you'd like to come . . .'

Linc hesitated, doing a mental inventory of his aches and pains and coming up with a depressing total.

'Look, Josie, normally I'd love to but I really don't feel up to making polite conversation this evening.'

'Well, you don't have to,' she said brightly. 'It's only family. Oh, and Sandy's coming, but that's all. It's just such a lovely warm evening and we haven't done anything like this for absolutely ages with Abby being in hospital. You can crash out on the seat-swing or in the hammock and be waited on hand and foot.'

The idea was growing more alluring by the moment. Linc considered the alternative; a meal alone in his flat or with his father in his private dining room, which – in his present mood – wasn't the most cheery of prospects.

'Okay, thanks. You've talked me into it,' he said. 'What time?'

'Whenever you're ready. Dad'll be ages getting the barbecue going if I know him.'

It was, in fact, a little over half an hour later when Linc arrived at the Vicarage having showered and changed. He was greeted with informal pleasure by Josie's mum, Rebecca, who accepted his gift of a bottle of white wine and ushered him through the house and out through the Victorian-style conservatory on to the patio at the back. Here, in spite of his daughter's pessimism, David Hathaway had the brick-built barbecue going strongly, and quantities of sausages, chops and kebabs already sizzling away with mouth-watering aromas.

Linc was met with a warm welcome, not only from the humans assembled there but also from the Hathaways' spaniels, Dorcas and Sukey, and the familiar wide-smiling, brindle form of Tiger.

'Hello, rascals,' he said fondly to the dogs, and Tiger planted himself, predictably, on his foot.

'I was going to leave him in the car,' Sandy told him, removing the dog. 'But I was shouted down.'

'Absolutely!' Ruth exclaimed. 'In this house, dogs are people. We'd no more leave them out of the fun than we would Hannah and Toby. In fact,' she added with a mischievous sideways glance at her brother and sister, 'we'd probably be more likely to shut *them* away!'

Linc grinned at the cries of indignation that greeted this, and moved forward to exchange kisses with Josie.

'Come,' she instructed him, taking his arm and

leading him firmly across to the seat-swing by the garden wall. 'Sit. I've told everyone you're fragile and on no account must you be asked to move.'

'I'm not that bad!' Linc protested, embarrassed. 'I was just feeling tired and a bit lazy, but I'm glad I'm here now.'

'Truly?'

'Truly,' he confirmed, sitting obediently on the cushions under the fringed canopy.

'Good.' She smiled and his heart did cartwheels.

'Grub up!' came the shout from the barbecue area, and Linc made to get up.

'Oh, no, you don't!' Josie stated. 'I'll get yours.'

'Has anyone ever told you you're a bossy woman?'

'Frequently, so you'd better get used to it! That is . . . if you want to,' she faltered, turning pink under her golden tan. 'I'll go and get the food.'

Linc watched her go, enjoying the sway of her slim hips and the tantalising glimpses of long brown legs under the red and gold sarong she wore. He must still have been smiling a couple of minutes later when Sandy appeared with a laden plate and sat down on the other end of the swing.

'I was going to say a penny for 'em,' he remarked. 'But by the look on your face I'd say they were worth a lot more! Aren't you eating?'

'Josie's getting it.'

'Quite right. Start the way you mean to go on,' Sandy approved. 'She says you're feeling a bit under the weather – nothing catching, I hope?'

'No. Just tired.' Linc quickly moved his feet as Tiger tried to sit on them again.

Ruth approached with a plateful of kebabs and

garlic bread. She wore a floaty, gypsy-style outfit and no shoes, and Linc thought she seemed happier than he'd seen her look since her sister was attacked.

'How's Abby today?' he asked as she sat down.

'The doctors are really pleased with her,' Ruth replied. 'They say her brain is very active – which is a good sign – and the wound on her head is healing well. I think it's just a matter of time.'

'That's great.'

'How's your investigation going?' Sandy asked Linc.

'Very slowly,' he admitted. 'I don't think I'm in old Sherlock's league.'

'But you're still looking?'

'For what it's worth. Actually, it will be interesting to see if Abby can remember anything herself, when she comes out of her coma.'

'Do they think that's likely? That she'll remember, I mean.'

'Probably not, I gather. Also, she was hit from behind, so it's quite possible she never saw the thieves at all.'

'If you ever want any help – I mean, if there's anything I can do – please let me know,' Sandy said. 'I've got a lot of contacts. You get to know a hell of a lot of people in my line of work. I'd like to help.'

'Thanks. I might take you up on that.' Linc was quite frankly surprised. Although good-natured, Sandy had always struck him as a fundamentally lazy person, who went through life taking the easy option wherever possible.

Sandy nodded, then put his arm round Ruth's shoulders and gave them a squeeze.

'Still, the main thing is, she's getting better,' he said. 'And I haven't heard of any raids lately, so perhaps the bastards have moved on. Let's talk about something else, shall we?'

Josie reappeared with plates full of goodies, and the evening progressed in the way of many impromptu outdoor get-togethers, into a lazy haze of food, wine, flickering patio lights and pleasant, rambling conversation, which no one would after-wards recall.

Sandy left just after midnight and Linc shortly after, walked to his car by Josie with her arm through his and her head on his shoulder. Whether it was the wine or not, Linc didn't know, but it seemed the most natural thing in the world to pull her close and kiss her goodnight in a fashion that had nothing in common with the polite, social kisses they had so far exchanged.

When he reluctantly drew away from her and got into the Land-Rover for the homeward journey, Linc felt as though a major piece of his world had just slotted into place.

'Are you all right to drive?' she asked, putting a hand through the open window and touching his cheek.

'Unless there was any hidden alcohol in that fruit punch,' he said. 'I didn't have much wine, though to be honest I feel away with the fairies! It's your fault. If I drive off the road, I'll blame you!'

First thing Monday morning Linc received a visit from Rockley. He was in his office sifting through the day's mail when Mary showed the inspector in, offered coffee, and discreetly withdrew. Linc rose from his chair, shook hands and waved the detective into the one opposite, which was the twin of his own and often occupied by Mary.

'Mmm. Comfy chair,' Rockley commented as he settled into it.

'Bad enough being stuck in here for hours. No sense being uncomfortable as well,' Linc observed, sitting back down. 'What can I do for you?'

'I just came to update you on our investigations, really,' he said, running his hands approvingly along the leather-upholstered armrests. 'Where did you get these? I wouldn't mind one myself.'

'You'd have to ask Mary. They were here when I took over. So, what have you found out?'

'Nothing much,' the DI admitted. 'The Greyhound Racing Board was very helpful, but none of the Barneys or Barnabys on their records fit the bill, as far as we can determine.'

'And you came all the way out here to tell me that?'

'Well, actually, the station's being honoured by a visit from some of the top brass this morning, and as it isn't absolutely essential that I be there, I thought I'd make myself scarce.'

'Ah,' Linc said, amused. 'So, what's your next step?'

'Well, it would be a great help if you'd tell me where you got your information . . .'

'Sorry.'

'We can be discreet too, you know.'

'I gave my word,' Linc stated firmly.

A light tap on the door, and Mary came in bearing a tray with two mugs of coffee and a plate of chocolate digestives.

Rockley sucked breath in through his teeth and shook his head.

'Got to think of my waistline,' he protested, but thinking of it didn't appear to inhibit him for long. By the time the door had clicked shut behind Mary, he had helped himself to a biscuit and was dunking it in his coffee.

After a necessary pause, Rockley picked up where he'd left off. 'Ah, but kids don't remember that kind of thing,' he said, watching Linc closely.

Linc checked his instinctive response. The man was clever.

'I didn't say it was a child,' he responded mildly. 'You'll have to try harder than that.'

'Can't blame me for trying. So what about you? Any more threats?'

'No. I said I'd tell you if there were.'

'So you did.' Rockley helped himself to a second digestive. 'But you have to admit you can be a little – how shall I put it? – *selective* with your reports.'

He offered the plate of biscuits but Linc shook his head.

'Don't tell me you're watching your weight,' Rockley said disgustedly.

'No. I just don't like them.'

'Oh.' He looked as if the idea was unthinkable. 'Then you've finally taken my advice and decided to leave things to us? No more snooping round the greyhound tracks?'

'Well, I did go racing the other night,' Linc confessed. 'In my capacity as a prospective owner. But I obviously didn't upset anyone, because there's been no comeback.'

'You know,' Rockley said, thoughtfully dunking

his third biscuit in what remained of his coffee, 'you're just as stubborn as your father.'

'Let's leave my father out of it, shall we?' Linc suggested. 'Do you need more coffee?'

'Giving you a hard time, is he?'

Linc drained his own mug and sat back, saying nothing.

'We've had no luck in tracing any of the youths who attacked you last week,' Rockley went on after a moment. 'We sent an officer there on Saturday night in the hope of finding some of the same people out and about. But although one or two people remembered seeing a group of youngsters at around that time, none of them witnessed the assault, and none was able to put names to any of the faces.'

'And who can blame them?' Linc remarked.

Rockley shrugged. 'Yeah, I guess, but it makes my job nigh on impossible at times.'

He polished off a fourth digestive, dry, and with a long regretful look at the remainder, said he supposed he'd better be going, and stood up.

Linc saw him out, resisting an impulse to offer him the rest of the biscuits in a 'doggy bag'.

After a morning spent in the office, dealing with general administration, Linc was glad to escape to the mill after lunch. His joy was tempered somewhat by his father's decision to accompany him; his mood hadn't noticeably improved over-night.

Long discussions with Saul, the millwright, a detailed inspection of the work in hand, and the news that the restoration was, so far, within schedule and budget, seemed to mollify him, however, and by the end of the session Linc seemed to be back in his good books.

The millpond, now completely drained and scraped clear of silt and vegetation, looked vast and somehow degraded, a line on the stonework showing where the water normally reached. Work on shoring up its banks was well under way and Linc looked forward to the day when it could be refilled, and the ducks and swans return.

The renovation of the roof of the mill building was now well underway, with half of it under bright blue plastic sheeting and the other half sporting neat rows of tiles. The weather, to date, had been kind to them. Over three storeys up, four men in shorts, hard hats and not much else, moved easily across the timbers, apparently oblivious to the danger.

The millwright was only there part-time in an advisory capacity to oversee the work on the mill furniture and machinery, and he departed on other business when the inspection was over.

Linc and his father left shortly after; Linc driving back to the house to drop Sylvester off, then going on to South Lodge Farm to meet the insurance assessor. On the way back, after stopping for a cup of tea in the farmhouse with Phil and Cindy Sutton, he happened to see Jack Reagan tying up beans in the garden of his cottage, and drew to a halt alongside.

It had only just gone half-past four, and as he got out of the Land-Rover he smiled to himself, imagining the forester swearing under his breath at having been caught out knocking off early. Personally, he didn't mind the odd liberty being taken with working hours, especially among the long-serving staff, although he knew his father was far less tolerant. 'Give them five minutes – they'll take an hour,' he'd said once, when the subject arose. But Linc knew for a fact that Reagan often worked unpaid overtime to get a job finished, and was prepared to trust him.

The forester met him at the gate, wiping grubby hands on his jeans and looking slightly wary.

'Sir?'

'Hello, Jack. Your garden looks nice.'

'Thank you.' He didn't try to justify his early finish, and Linc thought better of him for it.

'I just wondered if you'd seen anything of Pepper since Friday night. Is he still hanging around the villages?'

'I don't know, sir. I don't go out much of an evening these days, since the baby was born.'

Linc hesitated. How to mention what Nikki had seen without it sounding like an accusation? He put an undertone of disappointment in his voice. 'Oh, you wouldn't know which pub he usually frequents, then? I'd like to keep an eye on him.'

Reagan pursed his lips. 'I did see him in The Wheatsheaf at lunchtime a week or so ago, but when he saw me come in, he drank up and left.'

'You had lunch there?' Linc probed.

'Yes. I was working over that way, and Lynne had gone to visit her mother.'

He looked and sounded slightly resentful at being questioned, and Linc couldn't really blame him.

'Is the food good there? I was thinking of taking a friend out for a meal.'

'Their steak and ale pie is the best I've ever had,' the forester said, relaxing. 'Er, Lynne's just put the kettle on. Would you like a cup of tea?'

Having recently consumed two cups at South Lodge Farm, Linc declined and could almost see the shutters come down on Reagan's face once more. He explained, but it seemed the damage was done; the forester's overture of friendship had been, in his eyes at least, rebuffed, and Linc had the feeling that it would be a long time before it was offered again.

As he got back into the car he was conscious of a faint disappointment. He had hoped Reagan would come clean about his meeting with Pepper, but he obviously hadn't. Nikki had seen them leave The Wheatsheaf together and yet Reagan claimed that Pepper left the pub as soon as he arrived. It was understandable, Linc supposed, that the forester should be wary of admitting that they'd talked but it made Linc even more suspicious of what they had talked about.

He shrugged off the negative thoughts and looked forward to his evening. He and Josie had spoken on the phone earlier in the day and arranged to go out for a meal, dropping in to see Abby on the way. But first, Linc had another appointment. He'd called Barney Weston earlier in the day to say that he'd decided to take him up on the offer of one of the Green Baize saplings and the trainer had suggested he come over and choose which one he wanted.

Linc was surprised at the degree of excited anticipation he felt at the prospect, which had, after all, started out as a whim. Apart from Rockley, he had told no one about his venture into owner-ship, and decided to keep it that way for the time being.

One was black and one fawn, both male, and

according to Barney they were equally well put-together from the running point of view. In the end, Linc went on instinct for the fawn one, backing it up with the knowledge that Abby seemed drawn to feisty animals, and of the two, this seemed slightly more forward.

'I had a name in mind,' he told Barney. 'Are they already named or can I choose?'

'No. I usually register the names just before they start their trials.'

'So, are there any rules, or can I choose what I like?'

'There are rules, of course, but the most difficult thing is finding something not already in use. It's best to have several choices. What had you in mind?'

He noted Linc's suggestions, promising to submit them in the near future, and after refusing yet another cup of tea, Linc drove back towards the Vicarage to pick up Josie.

For all the doctors' enthusiasm, Abby didn't look any different to Linc than on his last visit. If anything, he thought, her face seemed a little thinner, the dark circles under her eyes more pronounced. There had been no movement from her for a couple of days now and there was no sign that she was aware of their presence, but even so he felt an irrational sense of guilt that he was there with Josie. After ten minutes or so, he told her he would wait downstairs, and after leaning forward to whisper a few rallying words in Abby's ear, dropped a kiss on her brow and left the room. As he shut the door he saw Josie lift her sister's hand to her lips, and the expression in her eyes made his throat ache in sympathy.

Business took Linc into Blandford the next morning and, having lost her car to her mother for the morning, Nikki begged a lift.

'Crispin won't lend me his,' she complained as she settled into the leather upholstery of the Morgan, recently returned from the restorers.

'I'm not surprised,' Linc commented with amusement. Crispin's second-hand Porsche was the apple of his eye and, devoted though he was to his wife, it didn't blind him to the fact that her driving was somewhat erratic at the best of times, and downright awful at others. It was not unknown for her passenger to have to grab the wheel if she happened to be distracted by something or someone at the side of the road. She tended to drive where she was looking, instead of the other way round.

Among other things, Linc's business in Blandford involved a meeting with his bank manager about further funding for the mill project, which was completed in half the time he'd expected. He had just emerged on to the high street and was regretting having told Nikki he'd meet her in an hour and a half when he was hailed by a friendly voice. He turned to see a corpulent, suited man in his late-fifties, and recognised Mike Farquharson, his father's wine merchant.

'Hello, Mike. How are you?'

'Fine. Fine. I haven't seen you for ages,' Farquharson said as they shook hands. 'Your father told me you were home, of course; said you were doing old Clive whatsisname's job, but I haven't seen you around.'

'Don't come into Blandford much,' Linc told him. 'But I had to see the bank manager today.'

Farquharson grimaced. 'Just on my way to the bank myself. Shan't be long though. How d'you fancy a quick drink?'

Linc raised his eyebrows and looked at his watch.

'Yes, I know. Better be coffee, I suppose,' the merchant acknowledged wistfully. 'Mind you, Hopgoods down the road there do a very good Irish coffee . . .'

Ten minutes later, settled in a comfortable chair in a corner of Hopgoods restaurant-cum-coffee bar with a cappuccino in front of him, Linc brought Farquharson up to date with his activities over the last few years. He finished by telling the older man all about Noddy and his dream of eventing glory.

'Ah, now I knew you were still riding. My niece saw you at an event a few weeks ago and I made the mistake of mentioning it to your father.'

'Ah.'

'Yes. *Ah*,' Farquharson said heavily. 'I didn't realise he still felt so strongly about the whole business. While you've been away the subject just hasn't come up, I suppose. I used to ask what you were doing and he'd say, "I've no idea, he doesn't tell me."'

'Mmm. That sounds about right,' Linc agreed. 'And he never asked.'

'Well, I'm afraid I might have put my foot in it,' the vintner confessed. 'Before I discovered how the land lay, I blundered in and suggested that the company might sponsor you. I honestly thought he'd be pleased . . .'

'Sponsorship?' Hope rose and then just as quickly waned. 'Oh, dear. I imagine you got a frosty reception.'

'You could say that. He didn't answer directly, but he reminded me of all the years of custom Farthingscourt has given Farquharson's, and said how much he hated change . . . It was sort of left in the air but I had no doubt as to what he meant.'

'He threatened you?' Linc demanded furiously. Farquharson's Wines & Spirits had been vintners to the Farthingscourt Estate for the best part of two hundred years, Mike Farquharson taking over the reins on his father's retirement some ten years before, and Linc knew his own father regarded both of them as friends as well as suppliers. The knowledge that he would go so far as to use intimidating tactics to bend them to his will shocked Linc.

'I probably shouldn't have mentioned it to you,' Mike put in hastily. 'We more or less let the subject drop and he seemed okay when I left. Best not stir it up, d'you think?'

Linc's own inclination at that moment was to face the Viscount with it as soon as he got home, but the anxiety in the wine merchant's face made him think again. He could be pretty sure his father wouldn't be swayed on the matter, and Linc's letting on that he knew might well spell trouble for Mike.

'I can only apologise. I'm afraid my riding is a taboo subject at home, but I'm very grateful for the offer anyway.'

'Yes, well, maybe one day . . .'

Linc smiled and shook his head. 'I can't see it, Mike, really. But, thanks. So how are things with you?'

The conversation turned and Linc took care not to let his lingering annoyance show. It was bad enough that his father should turn Mike's offer down without consulting Linc, but to do it in such a way was unforgivable.

As a consequence of stopping for a chat with Mike Farquharson, Linc actually got back to the car ten minutes later than he had told Nikki but even so, he was fractionally before her. She appeared, laden with carrier bags, as he set off along the second row of vehicles, looking for the Morgan. One of the disadvantages of driving such a low-slung car was the difficulty involved in finding it in a car park, if you hadn't made a precise note of which row you'd left it in. Sometimes, from a distance, the Morgan's position looked like a vacant space.

Nearly all the cars in the park bore leaflets fluttering under their windscreen wipers, as did Linc's when he eventually tracked it down.

'What's that? Buy one – get one free at the local tandoori?' Nikki asked as she came up. 'Or cut-price double glazing if you allow three lots of people to come and view the results? Hey, that would shake 'em, if you asked for a quote for Farthingscourt!'

Linc laughed, but the smile died on his lips as he removed the leaflet and found a fold of newsprint tucked behind it.

'What's the matter?' Nikki was watching him.

'Er, nothing really.' Linc palmed the paper and read the leaflet. ' "Flower and Vegetable Show.

Special prizes for first-time exhibitors". There you are, you could enter one of your flower arrangements.'

Nikki made a face. 'You'll have me joining the WI next,' she said.

'Nothing wrong with the WI,' Linc told her, easing himself into the car.

He waited until he'd dropped Nikki off before looking at the scrap of newspaper. The First Viscount Tremayne, with his taste for grandeur, had built Farthingscourt with four lodges; one roughly at each compass point, although they were all, for geographical reasons, slightly offset from the centre. Nikki and Crispin shared the cottage known as North Lodge, which in common with West Lodge guarded a gate currently kept shut and locked to minimise access to the estate.

As Nikki let herself in through the pedestrian gate beside the thatched cottage, Linc took the newspaper from his pocket and unfolded it. As before, it was part of a single sheet with several words picked out in Day-Glo yellow. As before, it was short and to the point.

You don't listen. Now you must watch your back.

Linc regarded it gloomily. It was bad enough being warned off when he'd been actively snooping, but this time he had no idea what he was supposed to have done. As he stowed the newsprint in his wallet he couldn't resist a quick glance round, as if to check that the author of the note wasn't watching him at that moment. What he found additionally disturbing was that today he'd been driving the sports car for the first time since the night of the raid at the Vicarage. It had been too dark then to identify the Morgan, so either someone had been making enquiries about him or he had been followed when he left Farthingscourt earlier that morning. Neither option left him feeling especially comfortable.

Estate commitments kept Linc busy over the next couple of days. A group of workers from the local branch of the conservation volunteers was due to arrive on the Friday night for a weekend doing path restoration and undergrowth clearance around the mill. Accommodation had been arranged for them on camp beds in the village hall complex at Farthing St Thomas, the next village north of Farthing St Anne, but there were a number of other matters to be taken care of. One of these was the organisation of a dance for them on the Saturday night in the main body of the hall. Thankfully, Nikki had offered to take that on.

It was Thursday evening before Linc had a chance to see Josie again. They had decided to go out for another meal but she had also expressed a wish to see the mill, so he picked her up from the Vicarage in the early evening and headed back towards Farthingscourt.

Passing Sykes's cottage at East Lodge, he continued along the lane towards Farthing St Thomas, pausing on top of the bridge over the millstream so she could see where it rushed down into Valley Wood. It ran in its own mini-gorge here, the banks dropping away steeply, each side of the bridge, to the streambed some fifteen feet below the level of the road.

With the young leaves on the surrounding trees casting dappled shade on the water it was an idyllic spot, but some twenty years before it had been the talk of the villages when a local man, subsequently known as River Joe, had driven off the road here on his way home from the pub. His pick-up truck had tipped over and come to rest on its roof in the stream, where it stayed undiscovered until some children found it the next morning. The driver, held just clear of the water by his seatbelt, had lived to tell the tale, and the story earned him a number of beers in the following weeks.

'It's lovely, isn't it?' Josie said. 'We used to cycle along this road as kids and mess around on the bridge, but since I've been driving I've never even stopped to look. How far downstream is the mill?'

'About a quarter of a mile and about forty feet lower down.'

He put the Morgan in gear and drove on, turning into Mill Lane a hundred yards or so further down the road. Here, a decade's overgrowth of rhodo-dendrons had been hacked ruthlessly back to allow access to the lane which had been gated and largely unused in all that time. The gravel lane, with Valley Wood on its left and a coppice known as Millersholt on its right, progressed roughly parallel with the stream before swinging downhill to pass close to the mill itself.

Linc pulled into the car park and he and Josie got out and walked round the outside of the mill building and the pond, where he showed her the dam and the bypass pipe. Coming back, they inspected the headrace through which water from the pond would one day pour to activate the huge breastshot wheel. For now the magnificent wheel hung idle on its axle, the wheel pit below it dry and scraped clear of the accumulated muck of ages.

'It hits the wheel just above halfway up and the weight of the water turns it backwards, sloshing out at the bottom into what's called the tailrace, which takes it back to join the stream.' Linc paused. 'Am I telling you what you already know?'

'No. Please, go on,' Josie said. 'How long will it be before you can get it going again?'

'Actually the mechanism seems fine. We gave it a good greasing and tried it out, and basically it works. One or two of the gear wheels need some attention – new cogs and the like – and the stones need dressing, but it's more structural restoration that needs doing. The roof and the garner – that's the top floor where the grain is stored – are the worst. Saul, the millwright, reckons another month and we should be more or less there.'

'I bet you can't wait,' Josie said, eyes shining. 'Do you think I could come and watch?'

'Of course.' Her easy assumption that their relationship was to be long-term filled him with a warm glow of contentment. 'I'll reserve you the best seat in the house.'

They continued the tour, going over as much of the inside of the mill as was safe and Josie seemed fascinated by all of it.

'Once the water is flowing again, how do you stop all this working if you haven't any grain to mill?' she wanted to know. 'Is it just a case of shutting the sluice-gate?'

'That's right. But if you just want to stop one pair of stones there's a thing called a jack ring that lifts the stone nut out of gear.' He showed her how a lever operated a metal collar under one of the smaller cogs. 'It's all so simple but it works.'

He explained how the grain was fed into the eye of the runner stone by a wooden chute called a shoe, regulated by the rhythmic tapping of a metal bar known as the damsel.

'As the stone rotates, the damsel gently taps the shoe to keep the grain running evenly. Millers say it got its name from the constant chattering it makes,' he said with a sidelong look at Josie. 'It's where the term "chatterbox" comes from.'

'I shall ignore that remark as a piece of typical male chauvinism,' she informed him. 'But you've obviously done your homework – I'm impressed!'

'Well, I've had this in mind for a long time. I visited several mills while I was working away and now I follow Saul round whenever I get the chance. There's nothing he doesn't know about the workings of a mill. I think it's fascinating. I've half a mind to give up estate management and become a miller myself.'

'What would your dad say to that?' Josie quizzed him with amusement.

'Well, I can't do anything right as it is,' Linc said, a touch of bitterness slipping past his guard. He regretted it instantly as the smile left Josie's eyes. 'Sorry. Family stuff. Anything else you want to know?'

She studied his face for a moment as if she would say something, then turned and ran her hands over the wooden casing, or tun, that enclosed the stones.

'How often do the stones need dressing – that's re-cutting the grooves, isn't it?'

'Yes, that's right. It depends on the type of stone. These are French burr, Saul's going to do them next week and they'll grind for maybe three hundred hours before they need doing again.'

They left the stone floor and came down the stairs and out of the building to stand in the evening sunshine on the narrow bridge downstream of the wheel.

Josie sighed. 'I love these old places. I wish I had a machine that could let me turn time backwards fifty years at a time, just to see how things used to be.'

'Pretty harsh, I'd say,' Linc commented. 'Hard work, poor conditions, cold, damp . . .'

'I know. I didn't say I wanted to *live* in the past, just look at it. Anyway, people must have been happy then, too. After all, we think we've got it all these days but who's to say future generations won't feel sorry for *us*?'

'True.' Linc hadn't thought of it like that.

'So I shall continue to think of old Dusty Miller, carrying his candle across to start up the mill in the chill dark hours of the early-morning . . .'

'Now I *would* feel sorry for him if he did that,' Linc exclaimed. 'Candles are the one thing you won't find inside a mill.'

Josie looked puzzled.

'The flour?' he prompted. 'Haven't you ever heard of the combustible properties of fine dust? The mill would have gone up like the Fourth of July! In fact, several did, according to Saul.'

'Of course. You know, I never thought of that. Poor old Dusty Miller!'

'Well, at least it would have warmed him up,' Linc remarked, as they made their way back to the car.

Josie stopped and looked back at the beautiful old stone building. 'You know, I was just thinking this would make a terrific location for a fashion shoot. You could make a bit of extra money out of it. I know one company in particular who are always looking for places like this.'

Linc was doubtful. 'Wouldn't it be a bit disruptive?'

Josie shook her head. 'Take a day, maybe two. Easy money. D'you want me to suggest it? No obligation.'

'Maybe. I'll think about it.'

Although he hadn't mentioned it to his father, the business of the lost sponsorship still rankled with Linc and so when Nina Barclay phoned with the eleventh-hour offer of his partnering Hobo over a local hunter trial course on the Saturday, he accepted with little hesitation. It was in the back of his mind that, with the conservation working party visiting the mill and the house open to the public, he ought to stick around, but what the heck! Sykes was very capable of dealing with any issues that might arise and, after all, he wouldn't be gone more than a couple of hours.

His father wasn't pleased when he found out, and to add to his displeasure, Nikki and her mother decided to go along and watch. Beverley had done a little eventing when she was a girl and had often groomed for her daughter in the days when *she*'d competed, but in view of her hostility towards him,

Linc felt it was more likely boredom that had prompted this outing, rather than any wish to cheer him on. Perhaps, he thought uncharitably, she hoped to see him bite the dust.

If that had indeed been her motivation then it was her lucky day. There had been a heavy shower in the night, and in spite of wearing large studs, Hobo marred a lovely round by sliding into a ditch and then falling sideways as he struggled out.

Linc was tipped off unceremoniously but although the ground was pretty hard under the greasy surface he was unhurt and able to remount straight away. Had the event been affiliated, the rules would have forced him to retire but as it was he was able to continue his round, pulling up with an apology to Nina for the mistake, even though there was nothing he could have done. Beverley said little about it but wore an air of great contentment for the duration of the journey home.

The three of them arrived back at Farthingscourt just before one o'clock and walked straight into the aftermath of an incident.

As Linc drove the Discovery up the drive towards the house he could see Geoff Sykes standing at the top of the steps by the front door. He hurried down as the vehicle drew closer and something in his expression made Linc pull in and stop, rather than continuing round to the stable yard.

'Geoff? What is it?' he asked, opening the Land-Rover door.

'Thank God you've come! It's your father, sir. He's had an accident.'

Linc went cold. 'What's happened? Is he all right?'

'Tyre burst on the Range-Rover and he drove into the ditch over back of Piecroft Copse,' Sykes told him. 'Cracked his head on the doorframe. Wasn't wearing his seat-belt, of course.'

'Where is he now? Hospital? When did it happen?' Linc had got half out of the Discovery but now he sat back in.

'No,' Sykes said, looking even more agitated. 'That's just it. He won't go to the hospital. Says he's all right. You know how stubborn he can be – beggin' your pardon, sir, but you know how it is. Mary's with him upstairs, she sent me to wait for the doctor.'

'Yes, I know how it is,' Linc agreed. 'I'll go on up.'

He became aware that a small group of paying visitors had assembled, just within earshot, and were drinking in the drama.

'Good morning,' he called brightly. 'Do feel free to go on in.'

The tourists returned the greeting and hurried off towards the steps as Linc pulled the Land-Rover door shut and drove round to the yard.

He took the backstairs two at a time and marched briskly along the worn carpet of the east wing corridor to his father's bedroom, where he met Mary coming out.

'Ah, Linc,' she said in tones of relief, shutting the door behind her. 'Your father's in there. Did you see Geoff? The doctor hasn't arrived yet, I suppose?'

'No. Geoff told me what had happened. Shouldn't he be in hospital?'

Mary pulled an exasperated face. 'If you can

convince him to go, you're a better man than me.'

'Being awkward, is he?' Linc asked.

'Awkward,' she stated, 'is the polite word for it! But seriously, I think he's probably okay. We'll just have to see what the doctor says. He's cut his forehead, which might need a stitch or two, but he swears he didn't black out. I think he's just badly shaken, but it hasn't improved his temper, I know that!'

'Poor Mary,' Linc said, putting his hand out impulsively. 'He doesn't deserve you, you know?'

For a moment, she looked deeply touched, then she gathered her usual business-like cloak around her once more. 'You'd better go in. Maybe you can coax him out of it.'

Linc had grave doubts about that but he promised to try, and went on in.

He found his father shoeless but still fully dressed, lying on top of the counterpane on his four-poster bed, with the two wolfhounds on the floor beside him. They thumped their tails softly as Linc approached.

'Hello, boys,' he murmured.

Someone, presumably Mary, had taped a lint dressing on to the patient's brow, and he was reclining against his pillows with his eyes shut, apparently unaware that Linc was there. He looked pale and the shock of the morning's events had left his features looking gaunt. For the first time it was brought home to Linc that his father was getting old, and the realisation softened the tone with which he greeted him.

'Hi there. What have you been up to?'

Sylvester's eyes opened and focussed on his son.

'Oh. It's you,' he muttered unencouragingly.

'How are you feeling?'

'I've got a splitting headache and I think I've broken my thumb,' he said, closing his eyes once more.

'I expect the doctor will be here soon,' Linc said. 'He'll give you something for the pain.'

'If you'd been here where you were supposed to be, this would never have happened,' his father declared, opening his eyes again and glaring at Linc. 'Sykes would have been free to go instead of me having to.'

With an effort, Linc ignored this unfairness.

'What happened? Geoff said a tyre burst.'

'Or somebody burst it.'

That gave Linc a jolt.

'What? What d'you mean?'

'I mean somebody shot it out,' Sylvester averred. 'Reagan phoned. Told Sykes he thought he'd seen Jim Pepper out near Home Farm. Wanted you to go in case there was trouble, but of course you weren't here. You were too busy out playing with your horses! I said I'd go, but when I was halfway there this happened.'

'But what makes you think someone shot at it?' Linc asked, frowning. 'If you have a blow-out it can sound like a pistol shot, you know.'

'I know that,' he snapped. 'I'm not a fool, you know! But I wasn't going that fast. I'd slowed down a bit because I thought I caught sight of someone in the bushes at the side of the road. If I hadn't, I'd probably have been killed!'

Linc didn't know what to say. He turned away to look out of the big rectangular-paned window on to the neatly planted beds of the formal garden below.

Now you must watch your back, the note had warned. Was this what it had meant? If the tyre had indeed been shot out, then had his father been the intended target at all or, driving one of the estate vehicles, had he been mistaken for Linc? After all, when Reagan made the call he would have expected it to have been Linc who responded.

Reagan? Did that mean *he* was involved? Or Pepper? But that didn't make sense; Jim Pepper's feud against the Tremaynes could have nothing to do with the warning notes.

'How did you get back?' he asked his father.

'Reagan came and found me. He's gone back to get the tractor and pull the Range-Rover out.'

Linc turned. 'I'm not sure he should do that. Better let the police see it *in situ* first. Has anyone called them?'

'I don't suppose so. I didn't tell Mary about the shot, she'd only have worried. Can't see the sense in calling them anyway. We know who's behind this: Pepper and that no-good son of his.'

'Nevertheless, as you said the other day, the police ought to be told. We haven't any proof and just maybe they can find some. I'll go and ring Rockley and I'll tell Reagan to hold on, if it isn't too late.'

'Oh, all right. Do what you want – you always do! Where's that blasted doctor got to? This hand hurts like the blazes!'

'That blasted doctor has just arrived,' Dr Small said, advancing quietly into the room and closing the door behind him. 'He got held up treating a child with a nasty reaction to an insect bite. My apologies.'

'Yes, well, I expect you *are* busy,' the Viscount admitted with a touch of embarrassment, and the young doctor winked at Linc in passing.

Smiling, he left the room and almost bumped into Mary, who was waiting just outside.

'Did you manage to settle him down at all?' she asked anxiously.

'Not noticeably,' Linc confessed. 'It appears that I'm almost completely to blame for the whole incident. If I hadn't been out "playing with my horses". it would never have happened.'

'Oh, dear! I did hope he wouldn't say that to you,' Mary said. 'He said it several times when we were waiting.'

'Don't worry. I'm used to it,' he assured her. 'And now, just to make him more annoyed, I'm going to phone Rockley. This has got to be looked into.'

Rockley was off duty, so the Viscount was attended by an officer he didn't know, which darkened his mood still further. Linc had been too late to stop Reagan moving the Range-Rover but DS Manston organised a search of the crash area and arranged for the vehicle to be taken in for forensics to examine.

Manston, a solidly built forty-something who had a deceptively open and childlike countenance, struck Linc as a very shrewd man. He arrived within fifteen minutes of Linc's call, for which he had no doubt his father's title and irascible reputation were responsible, and took the measure of his man almost immediately. The Viscount had transferred to the library to receive Manston, against Dr Small's advice, and Linc left them to it, intending to catch the policeman as he was leaving.

As it turned out, Manston was keen to talk to him, which was just as well because he'd been called to his office to take an important phone call by the time the policeman had finished interviewing his father.

Manston rapped on the pine door, opened it and leaned round.

'Mr Tremayne, may I have a word?'

'Sure. Come on in,' he invited. 'And call me Linc, please.'

In stark contrast to his senior, Manston declined all offers of refreshment but, to Linc's amusement, he too commented on the chair.

'I'm beginning to think the seating at your station must be abysmal,' Linc remarked. 'Perhaps they don't want to encourage you to spend very long in it.'

'Probably.' Manston smiled. 'Now, this business with your father. Have you got any thoughts on it?'

'He seems fairly sure it wasn't an accident.'

'Yes, he does. And he's prepared to name names.'

Linc pursed his lips. 'Jim Pepper. Yes, it could have been . . .'

Manston's interest sharpened. 'But?' he prompted.

Linc unlocked the top drawer of his desk and took out the latest sheet of newsprint.

'I found this under my windscreen wiper the other day. I presume Rockley has told you what's been going on?'

'He has.' Manston took a polythene bag from his

pocket and put his hand in it before reaching for the paper. 'When exactly did you get this?'

'Er, Tuesday, I think it was. I'd parked in Blandford and it was there when I got back.'

Manston scanned it. 'And you didn't think we'd be interested, I suppose.'

'Yeah, I'm sorry. I've had one of those weeks. But, to be honest, the other notes haven't thrown up much information so I didn't think it was urgent.'

'And you think today's incident may have something to do with this?'

'I'm not sure.' Linc frowned. 'Today sounds more like Pepper's work, especially in light of what Reagan saw. But I don't think Pepper has anything to do with the notes.'

Manston enclosed the newsprint in the polythene bag and sealed the top.

'You would seem to lead a very complicated life, Mr Tremayne.'

'It's certainly getting that way,' Linc sighed.

'And what did you do to provoke this?' Manston asked, gesturing at the warning note.

'Nothing that I'm aware of. I've pretty much run out of ideas. That's what makes it even more puzzling.'

'But it doesn't bother you unduly?' Manston queried, looking at him oddly.

'Not much I can do about it,' he observed matter-of-factly.

The detective gathered together his pen, pocket book and the polythene bag, and stood up, smiling slightly. 'I see what the DI meant about you now. Well, I'll be off. We'll be in touch about the Range-

Rover or if this turns up anything new. And,' he added, pausing by the door, 'if anything else happens or you remember something else you should have told us, perhaps you'll give us a call? Our clairvoyancy department is a bit short-staffed at the moment.'

Linc grinned. 'Yeah, yeah. Give my best to Rockley when you see him. No news your end on the Abby Hathaway case, I suppose.'

Manston shook his head. 'Nothing much to report, I'm afraid, but that doesn't mean we're not doing anything. The investigation is ongoing, so leave it to us, okay? And try to stay out of trouble for five minutes.'

9

Trouble was the last thing on Linc's mind that evening as he dressed to go out. He had a table booked for eight-thirty at his favourite restaurant, and after dropping in on the conservation workers' shindig in Farthing St Thomas's church hall, he would be off to pick up Josie. There wasn't strictly any need for him to turn up at the party but he wanted to thank the volunteers personally for the hard work they were cheerfully putting in at the mill. He felt, too, that he owed it to Nikki at least to put in an appearance, after she had gone to the effort of organising the evening.

When he left the house just after half-past seven it seemed set fair to be a fine evening but by the time he got to Farthing St Thomas, just a couple of miles away, a strong breeze had sprung up, carrying with it a few spits of rain. Linc parked the Morgan and pulled the soft-top into place before going into the hall. Inside, the party was already underway. Balloons and streamers decorated the walls and ceiling, and in the kitchen area a trestle table groaned under the weight of a huge buffet. As usual, Nikki had excelled herself.

Because most of the group was actually bunking down in the anteroom of the hall for the weekend, they had helped set everything up and consequently the drink was already flowing and spirits high. A local DJ had been hired and was operating from the tiny stage but, in common with most of the parties Linc had ever been to, people were much more inclined to chat than dance at this stage of the evening.

The conservation group consisted of between thirty and forty individuals of diverse ages and backgrounds who, it was impossible to think, would ever have found themselves socialising under any other circumstances. But as Linc moved among them it seemed that, having been thrown together, the eclectic group was interacting really well. As the alcohol consumption rose, releasing inhibitions, some of the younger volunteers began to take to the dance floor and amongst them there were a few faces that Linc felt he'd seen before, though he couldn't imagine where.

He moved across to the makeshift bar area where Crispin was helping Nikki dispense polystyrene cups full of fruit punch or beer. Bowls of nuts and crisps stood on every available surface, and in the kitchen behind the bar Linc could see Beverley arranging sprigs of parsley and twists of cucumber on the plates of sandwiches and sausage rolls. Typical of her to try and add a bit of spurious sophistication to what was a fairly rough and ready affair.

'Is it my imagination or are there a few more here

than we started with?' Linc queried, in something only a couple of decibels lower than a yell. It seemed inconceivable that so few people could make so much noise.

Crispin nodded, leaning close to his brother's ear. 'One or two of the youngsters from the village have found their way in but I've had a word and they've promised to behave. I feel a bit sorry for them, there's not a lot for them around here.'

'Okay.' Linc made the thumbs up sign. It was easier than trying to make himself heard.

'Hope you've got the hood up on that car of yours,' Crispin added, matching his actions to the words. 'It's been raining quite hard.'

'Yeah, she's all covered up.'

'Have you tried Nikki's punch?' He proffered a cup.

'Thanks.' Linc took it and sniffed appreciatively. 'What's in it? Don't forget I'm driving.'

Crispin smiled, shook his head and gave him the thumbs up, which Linc took to mean it was fairly safe, but before he had the chance to take more than an experimental sip, his attention was claimed by the group co-ordinator who wanted a word with him and his signature on a form.

'We need to go somewhere a bit quieter,' Linc said, leaning towards the man and indicating the doorway into the anteroom. He placed his drink on Crispin's table, close to the huge stainless steel punchbowl, pointed at it and yelled, 'Back in a minute.'

Crispin grinned. 'Yeah, maybe.'

It was, in fact, nearer fifteen minutes before he was able to get away from the man, by which time the meaning of Crispin's obscure remark had been made very clear. The group leader, though pleasant enough, suffered from acute verbal diarrhoea and Linc had to resort to looking at his watch and exclaiming theatrically that he had to be somewhere else. Returning to the main hall, he edged round the dancers and paused beside his brother.

'You could have warned me!' he bellowed, and Crispin laughed, then raised an eyebrow and nodded significantly. Linc looked over his shoulder and spotted the talkative man on the far side of the room, scanning the crowd as if searching for someone.

'Oh, Lord!' he groaned. He turned his back, hoping he hadn't been seen, and picked up his cup of punch. He would have had difficulty in saying what had gone into the reddish liquid; fruit juice, certainly, and at least one source of alcohol, but there were undertones of something else that he couldn't identify, too. He became aware of Nikki watching him anxiously and smiled at her. 'That's great!' he mouthed. 'What's in it?'

'Secret recipe,' she told him, beaming happily. 'My dad used to make it. How long can you stay?'

Linc looked at his watch and then held one hand up, fingers spread to signify five minutes.

Nikki's mother had come out of the kitchen now and was standing beside her, regarding Linc with a look that could have curdled milk. He wondered if she was ever going to forgive and forget and then, in progression, decided that he really didn't care, just as long as she soon went back to Surrey and remained there.

After a couple more minutes, he wearied of

229

battling against the noise to try and make conversation with Crispin, and seeing the volunteer leader heading his way, took a last swig of the boozy, fruity concoction, put the cup down, waved and made for the door.

The air outside was wonderfully cool after the crowded hall, and even the light drizzle felt refreshing. He headed for the Morgan, gratefully leaving the noise behind him and reflecting that he was getting too old for discos. Across the car park, a man sat at the wheel of a car. Thinking he looked vaguely familiar, Linc raised a hand in greeting. The other man responded by rudely turning his head away.

'Suit yourself,' Linc muttered under his breath.

Lowering himself into his car, he slammed the door, shaking the raindrops off the fabric roof. For a moment he just sat, feeling all of a sudden weary and a little light-headed. He wondered if he'd hit his head when he fell off Hobo that morning, but didn't think he had.

'Food. That's what I need,' he told himself firmly, and turned the key in the ignition. What with riding at the hunter trial that morning and the drama of his father's accident – if accident it had been – he hadn't had much time for eating, and by late-afternoon, when he had begun to feel really hungry, his dinner date with Josie was only an hour or two away.

He reversed out of the parking space, giving himself a shock as he nearly scraped a neighbouring vehicle.

That wasn't like him; he prided himself on being a good driver. He hoped the rude man hadn't noticed. With extra care he swung the Morgan round and headed for the exit, where he stopped for a moment, trying to remember which way he needed to go.

Josie. That was it. He was on his way to pick Josie up. All in all, he thought it might be an idea to beg a cup of sweet coffee at the Vicarage before they set out. It seemed his blood sugar was pretty low. He felt decidedly muzzy.

The car stalled, and he blinked and shook his head to clear it. He was getting nowhere fast. Taking a deep breath, he started the engine once more and drove out into the lane. In spite of the light rain, a gleam of evening sunlight was slanting through the trees, flashing intermittently into his eyes with a hypnotic effect. He reached into the glove shelf for his sunglasses and put them on.

That was better.

Soothing.

He closed his eyes for a moment against the growing turmoil in his head; too befuddled even to wonder what was causing it.

The strident blare of a car horn made him jump and his eyes snapped open as the vehicle swished by. Over-reacting, he steered left and the Morgan bumped up on to the verge for a few yards, scraping its undercarriage, before regaining the road.

His vision was a swirling pattern of light and dark, breathing was an effort and his stomach felt ghastly.

Home.

Farthingscourt.

He knew that was where he should go, but try as he might he couldn't keep his eyes open. He put his foot on the brake as a sensation of overwhelming drowsiness came over him and he began to slide into a bottomless, dark pit.

A bell was chiming.

Each strike of the clapper sent a red-hot pain through Linc's skull.

He groaned and someone spoke, but it sounded distant and distorted, like a voice underwater. He couldn't make out any words and couldn't be bothered to try.

He felt suddenly urgently sick and retched, the effort pulling his head towards his knees. Instantly, hands grasped him and his world turned upside down. Blackness closed in once more.

Running water; a stream or a fountain.

Linc forced his eyes to open a millimetre or so. The water was white and swirling. It filled his vision, sparkling with reflected light. It was blinding; it hurt. He shut his eyes.

Nausea rose and he retched dryly. His stomach was empty, except for the burning, and that wouldn't budge.

He seemed to be bent over. Something hard was pressing against his chest but when he tried to move, to ease the discomfort, his muscles refused to obey.

He groaned once more, the sound barely audible, and was rewarded by the return of the nightmarish, echoey voices. The unseen hands pulled him upright but his head lolled forward out of his control, until another gentle hand lifted his chin.

Upright wasn't good. What little he could see

under his half-closed eyelids tilted and swam, and the voices faded once more.

Crispin was sitting beside Linc's bed.

Actually it was somebody else's bed, not his. The ceiling was lower in his own bedroom and slanted down to meet the wall. This one was much higher; was it Crispin's room, perhaps? Linc couldn't recall what the upstairs rooms were like in the North Lodge cottage.

He rolled his eyes to bring his brother into view once more. He was looking away, towards the window, apparently lost in thought. It appeared to be daylight outside.

'Hey, Bro,' Linc said. At least, that was his intention. In reality, all he made was a whisper and the discovery that his throat was very sore.

It was enough to get Crispin's attention.

'Linc! Wow, finally! I thought you were going to sleep for a week. How d'you feel? No. Scrap that. Silly question.'

'Very silly,' Linc croaked. He glanced up at the ceiling again. 'Where am I?'

'Er, I think it's Abby's room,' Crispin told him. 'I think that's what they said.'

Linc frowned. 'The Vicarage?'

'Yeah, of course. My God! You *were* out of it, weren't you? Sandy brought you here.'

Sandy? Why *Sandy* of all people? Linc tried to make sense of it but couldn't. The effort made his head pound.

'What time is it?'

Crispin put his hands behind his neck and arched his back, stretching the muscles. 'Nearly nine o'clock. I've been here for ages. Ever since you stopped throwing up in the kitchen sink – about one o'clock, I think that was.'

Linc frowned again. 'I don't remember that.'

'Then you're the lucky one!' his brother said with feeling. '*I* shan't forget it in a hurry, I can tell you. It was grim!'

'The kitchen sink?' Linc's lip curled in distaste.

''Fraid so. We didn't have time to get you any further.'

'We?'

'Me, Sandy, and the doctor . . .'

'Doctor Small?'

'No. The doctor on call. Can't remember his name. Came from miles away. Apparently Josie called him when she called me, soon after Sandy brought you in, but he didn't get here until nearly midnight.'

'Oh, God! Josie?'

'Yeah. You're certainly putting that relationship to the test! She's quite a girl, though! And her sister, Ruth. You'll be relieved to know that the parents were out, at the hospital, I gather.'

Linc was silent for a moment, horrified at the picture Crispin was painting. He became aware that his brother was regarding him oddly.

'The doctor asked us if you could have taken anything – you know, drugs and stuff. He thought it might be an overdose at first. We said absolutely not.' He paused awkwardly. 'You didn't, did you?'

'You have to ask?' Linc was momentarily hurt but then reason reasserted itself. What with university and then his moving away, he and Crispin hadn't seen a lot of each other as adults until five months ago. Could Linc really blame him for a moment's doubt? How well did they actually know one another?

'No. That's what we said,' Crispin said, looking relieved. 'I'm not sure he believed us, though. He took a blood sample and was making noises about carting you off to hospital at one point. I think he was in a bit of a panic because he hadn't got here sooner. Not that it was his fault, poor bloke. He was on the other side of the county, and as far as he knew you were just drunk.'

Linc was feeling a little better now. He manoeuvred himself up into a sitting position, which made the muscles in his arms, shoulders and stomach feel as though he'd just put them through a stiff workout. After spinning a time or two, his head settled to a heavy ache, and he felt as weak as a cat. Somewhere along the line, someone had changed him into a pair of pyjama bottoms.

Crispin watched the discovery, and grinned. 'Don't worry, I did that. So what *did* happen to you? You seemed okay when you left the party.'

Linc tried to think back, but all that came to him was an assortment of muddled images. He vaguely recalled riding Hobo at a hunter trial, and his father in bed with his head bandaged. When had that been?

'I don't remember a party,' he admitted finally. 'I don't remember anything. It's scary.'

'Well, you only stayed for twenty minutes or so, and you certainly weren't drunk when you left. You'd only had a cupful of punch and left half of that. That would have been about eightish.

According to Sandy, it couldn't have been later than quarter-past when he found you.'

Linc shook his head helplessly. 'I don't remember any of it,' he repeated. 'Could someone have put something in my drink? Who was there?'

'Just the conservation group and a few youngsters from the village,' Crispin said. 'I can't imagine any of them doing something like that. I mean, it wasn't just a case of getting a bit tipsy. You were really bad there for a while.'

Linc looked broodingly at the bright squares of the window and something Crispin had said earlier came back to him with a jolt.

'Nine o'clock! What day is it?'

'Sunday.'

'Oh, God! I should get home. It'll be time to open . . .' His voice faded. 'Does he know?'

'Dad?' Crispin shook his head. 'No. I almost called him, but once you were through the worst I thought it best not. If he asks, just say you had one too many and stopped over here. I'll back that up and so will Nikki.'

'Thanks.' Linc was sincerely grateful.

'Anything for a quiet life.'

'Amen to that.'

The door opened softly and Josie peered round it.

'Oh. You're awake. How're you feeling?'

'Much better now, thanks.' He hesitated, half-embarrassed. 'Josie – I'm *so* sorry about all this. I don't know what happened, I can't remember a thing. From what Crispin says, I've been the house-guest from hell!'

'It *was* pretty terrifying,' she admitted. 'The doctor was ages coming. I rang him twice. He just said to keep an eye on you, and that you'd probably sleep it off. But I wasn't sure about that. It wasn't normal sleep. Your breathing was so shallow and we couldn't begin to wake you. I was on the verge of calling an ambulance when he finally turned up. I was never more thankful to see anyone in my life!'

'I'm sorry,' Linc repeated. 'Crispin says Sandy brought me here. How on earth did that happen?'

Josie sat on the end of the bed. 'He knew Mum and Dad were going to be out and was on his way here with a video and a bottle of wine to keep Ruth company while she was babysitting. He says he found you in your car on the side of the road near the bridge. You know, where we stopped the other day.'

She looked enquiringly at Linc, who shook his head.

'I still don't remember.'

'Well, apparently you were pretty lucky. He said if the car had rolled forward another couple of feet you'd have ended up in the stream like old River Joe. Anyway, Sandy said it would have been a struggle to get you into his car, so he drove you here in the Morgan.'

'I wouldn't have given much for your chances if you *had* gone that extra yard,' Crispin observed mordantly. 'If your car had tipped over like River Joe's pick-up, that soft top wouldn't have been much protection.'

There was a moment of thoughtful silence and then Josie said, 'The doctor thought you might have OD'd. When you started to be sick, he said it was probably a good thing. Crispin says you weren't drinking. Was it something you ate?'

'Linc wonders if someone slipped him a Mickey,' Crispin put in.

'It was bloody stupid, if they did!' Josie said explosively. 'Who? And for that matter, why?'

Linc sighed. 'That's where the theory falls short,' he admitted.

'Well, if they did, they ought to be brought to book for it. You could have been killed. I hope you're going to report it.'

A vision of DI Rockley armed with his pocket-book flashed into Linc's weary brain and he shrank from the prospect. 'Oh, not again!' he protested, rubbing his aching forehead.

'But you must!'

'I really think she's right,' Crispin added.

Linc gave in. 'All right. I'll do it on the way home.' He flipped back the duvet, prior to getting out. 'Er . . . what happened to my clothes?'

Sunday at Farthingscourt had to be got through. In spite of Josie's protestations that he should stay in bed for the day and see the doctor again, Crispin drove Linc home via the police station, to arrive only a short while after the doors opened to the public at ten-thirty.

He had a cool shower, which did little to improve the fog that hung over his brain, and trudged through the first part of the day feeling as though he had a massive hangover. His father, who he saw briefly early on, appeared to notice nothing amiss but, coming into the office a little later, Mary looked hard at him and asked if he'd had a bad night.

'Yeah, a bit rough,' he told her.

'Too much to drink?' she asked, with what

seemed to be genuine sympathy, even though Linc couldn't imagine her ever having been the worse for wear.

'Something like that,' he said, wishing it were as simple as that. With his brain only capable of operating at maintenance level, he had not attempted to sort out the implications of the previous night's events.

'Mmm. I saw you sneak back in this morning, but I don't think your father noticed. He's still pre-occupied with what happened yesterday.'

'Yesterday?'

'The Range-Rover . . . Don't tell me you've forgotten! Gosh, it must have been a heavy night!'

'Of course. Sorry.'

He was sitting at his desk staring at paperwork that kept blurring on the page, and when Mary had finished what she was doing, she moved the papers and put a cup of coffee in front of him, suggesting that he recline his chair, shut his eyes and take it easy until he felt better.

'The paperwork can wait and Geoff can manage perfectly well. He always does when you're riding at the weekend. I'll call you if there's a problem.'

'Thanks. I might just do that.'

As the door closed behind her he took a sip of his coffee, adjusted his chair slightly and leaned back against the headrest. He had no intention of sleeping; he just wanted to close his eyes for a moment to try and ease the heavy pounding in his skull. The showers had cleared away overnight and day had dawned bright and sunny, the light intensifying his discomfort. Scarcely aware that he was doing it, his hand located the edge of the curtain and twitched it half-across. The resulting shade was blessed . . .

'. . . and when you *are* here you're half-asleep!'

Somebody had come into the office. Linc fought his way up through the layers of sleep.

'Lincoln!' Sharply.

It was his father. *Damn.* Of all people it had to be him. Apart from the cut on his forehead, which had been closed with adhesive strips, he looked none the worse for the previous day's experience.

'Are you listening to a word I'm saying?'

Linc was never at his best when suddenly woken up. It was as if the part of his brain that controlled tolerance and tact was the last to start functioning.

'Oh, for God's sake!' he groaned. 'What do you want?'

It could have been worse; he could have said the first thing that came into his head, which was, *Oh, sod off and leave me alone!*

'A little respect would be a start!' Viscount Tremayne obviously didn't appreciate his narrow escape. He drew back the curtain, flooding the office with sunlight, and Linc winced and turned his head away.

His father frowned. 'Are you hung over?'

'In a manner of speaking . . .'

'Don't be flippant! Either you are or you aren't.'

'I think someone spiked my drink last night,' he said, rubbing one hand wearily across his eyes. He had hoped to avoid the subject but it was plain he couldn't. He knew from experience that if his father were in interrogative mode, he would keep probing until he had the whole story, and any attempt to

240

foil him would be regarded as proof of a guilty conscience.

Linc found he was drifting again and concentrated with an effort. His father was regarding him searchingly.

'When? Last night? Where?'

'At the conservation do.'

'At the party? Well, have you any idea by whom? Or why?'

Linc shook his head. It had been occupying his mind all morning – or at least, that part of it in which he'd been able to marshal any sensible thought processes at all.

At the police station, Manston had been on duty once again. He'd taken the incident very seriously and asked Crispin to furnish him with a full list of the partygoers by the end of the day. He also wanted to know the name of the doctor who had attended Linc at the Vicarage, and was interested to hear of Sandy's part in the drama.

Crispin told Manston that Linc had left his cup of punch on the drinks table while he went off to talk to the volunteer group leader, and Manston immediately wanted details of everyone who had approached the table at that time. Crispin did his best, but as he couldn't fit names to the faces of those who'd been at the party, he wasn't much help.

'Would your wife be able to help us?' Manston wanted to know.

'Well, she might,' Crispin said doubtfully. 'She organised the whole thing, so she had more to do with them than I did, but she was here, there and everywhere, all evening.'

'But you didn't leave the table at all?'

'No. Yes – wait a minute – I did! Someone came to tell me my car alarm was going off, so I nipped out to the car park to switch it off,' he said. 'But I was gone less than two minutes.'

'Plenty of time for someone to slip something in your brother's drink, though, if they'd been watching for an opportunity,' Manston pointed out.

'Well, yes – I suppose so, but Nikki was around somewhere and Beverley had come over by then, too. My mother-in-law, Beverley Pike,' he added, seeing Manston's questioning look.

As Linc could still not recall anything about the party or what followed, Manston had sent them on their way.

But even if opportunity had been found, the question of motive remained. Who, at the party, could possibly have wanted to render Linc helpless? And to what end?

'Linc! Good God, it's like trying to talk to a zombie! I asked you if you'd reported it.' The Viscount's patience, never his strongest point, was wearing dangerously thin.

'I'm sorry. Yes, I did, *and* I've seen a doctor,' Linc told him. 'So now you know as much as I do. All in all, it was probably just a misguided prank.'

'Is that what Rockley thinks?'

'It was Manston, and he didn't precisely say,' Linc hedged. 'He said they'd look into it, but there were several gatecrashers there last night – mostly kids from the village – but it makes it very difficult to account for everyone.'

'So you've had no more warning notes?'

'Not since the last one.' Linc was troubled by a

twinge of guilt but ruthlessly smothered it. After all, it was technically true.

His father was regarding him steadily, as if unsure whether to believe him, and Linc returned the look, trying not to imagine, as he had done in his childhood, that his father could see inside his head and would know he was lying.

After what seemed an age, the Viscount shrugged and turned towards the door, saying, 'Well, you'd better take the afternoon off and sort yourself out. Get some sleep, you look as though you need it.'

'I'll be okay . . .' Linc began, but his father turned and fixed him with a quelling eye.

'I'm your employer and you'll do as you're told,' he said with finality.

More or less banished to his room for the afternoon, like a school-aged kid, Linc nevertheless found the lure of a couple of hours of rest in a darkened room too much to resist and stretched out on his bed. His body had other ideas, however, and he slept for a full eight hours, only waking when his mobile phone trilled on the bedside table. It was Josie, concerned that she hadn't heard from him but relieved that he'd been resting.

Monday found Linc still a little fragile but generally much improved, so he got up at his usual early hour and drove over to the Vicarage to ride Noddy. He arrived to find Ruth tidying away the mucking out tools, accompanied unusually by Hannah. He looked at his watch in surprise.

'Am I late or are you early?' he asked, getting out of the car. He hadn't seen Ruth the previous morning and had dreaded the awkwardness of their meeting after the gruesome business of Saturday night, but it seemed she had other things on her mind.

'No, I'm early. I fed them all at six, so you can ride if you want. We're all going to the hospital. Mum called – something's going on with Abby. They think she might be waking up!'

'Really? That's brilliant! Go on then, you go. I'll finish up here.'

'You don't mind?'

'Don't be daft!'

'Oh, thanks.' Already halfway across the yard, Ruth paused. 'Are you all right now? After the other night, I mean. That was horrible!'

'We thought you were dead at first!' Hannah put in, with ghoulish relish. 'You looked like a corpse.'

'Hannah!' Ruth exclaimed, crossly.

'I felt like one,' Linc responded. 'But I'm much better today, thanks. Now go!'

'We'll ring you if there's any news,' Ruth said, backing away and dragging her sister by the hand. 'Are you sure you don't mind?'

Linc waved her on and went to get Noddy ready, trying to keep the leaping hope under control. Dreadful if it was yet another false alarm.

By the time he'd ridden and rubbed Noddy down, there had still been no word and the first thrill of excitement had settled into a wary anticipation. What if the change in her condition signalled not a return to consciousness but a deterioration? The effect it would have on the rest of the family didn't bear thinking about.

It was nearly nine o'clock when Linc left the Vicarage, having done all he could, and he decided to head on to Shaftesbury to see Sandy. Making a slight detour, he called in at the excellent Post Office and general stores in Farthing St Thomas, where he bought a bottle of Scotch and a bacon roll. The first he stowed in the roomy glove compartment of the Discovery, the second he ate whilst he drove. In theory, it wouldn't have taken much longer to call back to his flat at Farthingscourt but in practice he'd have been lucky to get in and out without someone finding something that needed his urgent attention, and wanting to know where he was going and why.

When he reached the industrial park, he found the forecourt to Sandy's unit already taken up with the saddler's own lorry and a white BMW that he vaguely remembered having seen there before. He searched his memory and came up with a mental picture of a tall, well-built man in a leather coat. Nobody he knew.

He parked the Farthingscourt vehicle on the other side of the lorry from the BMW and started to get out, then hesitated. He'd walked in on Sandy's visitor last time; perhaps he'd give them a moment or two. So he sat in the warm sunshine watching a busy colony of house martins coming in relays to a series of mud nests, high under the metal overhang of the building, his mind returning to the puzzle of Saturday night. He couldn't see how it could have anything to do with the warnings he'd received, but if not it seemed completely pointless.

Either way it had left a lot to chance. Given the state he'd been in, he might very possibly have driven off the road and into a handy tree, but it was just as likely he would do what in fact he did do –

gradually lose consciousness and bump on to the verge, stalling the car in the process. The thought of what might have happened if he'd travelled that extra yard or two still made him go hot and cold. But that could never have been planned for

And if he hadn't left the party early, what then? After all, whoever slipped him the Mickey Finn could have had no way of knowing how long he'd stay. Crispin had told Manston that Linc had left just a couple of minutes after drinking the punch, but he might have stayed there all evening for all anyone knew.

Was the object to make him a laughing stock? Was one of the conservation group an ardent republican, who might gain satisfaction from putting one over on a member of the hated aristocracy? But surely such a person wouldn't have volunteered to work on the estate in the first place.

Or was the intention more sinister still? Apparently, hounded by the garrulous group leader, he'd drunk less than half a cup of Nikki's punch before he left. If he'd drained the cup would he still be here to tell the tale? Manston was very keen to know what his blood tests revealed. Was the violence of Linc's reaction in keeping with the substance he'd consumed or was it an individual response, compounded by his not having eaten for several hours?

The door of the unit opened, interrupting his thoughts, and an unfamiliar voice said testily, 'Well, if you'd just used your head, there wouldn't still *be* a problem!'

From where Linc sat, he couldn't see the owner of the voice because Sandy's lorry was in the way.

He could just see part of the open doorway if he craned his neck but didn't particularly want to be caught doing anything so bad-mannered.

Still inside the unit, Sandy's reply was indistinct, but Linc had no problem hearing his visitor's response to it.

'Oh, no! Don't try and shift the blame. You *both* fucked up! But *you* had a chance to put things right and you didn't – that's what pisses me off!'

Sandy's voice came again, protesting, but the other man cut across him.

'No. That's not good enough. I'm going now, and I don't want to hear from you unless it's good news.'

After a moment a car door slammed and its engine roared into life. The white BMW backed out of its space and on a long fluent curve, accelerated out of the park.

There was a crash from the unit and Linc looked back to find that Sandy had slammed the metal door shut. In fact, he did it with such force that it failed to catch and bounced open again. It was obviously not a good moment, and if he hadn't made a special journey to see the saddler, Linc would have thought twice about going in. As it was, he retrieved the Scotch from the glove compartment, shut and locked the Land-Rover and headed for the swinging door.

Sandy had gone into his office, leaving the door ajar, so Linc knocked lightly on it and peered round.

The saddler was sitting at his desk with a whisky bottle and empty tumbler in front of him and a stormy expression on his good-natured face. The bottle held only an inch or so more liquid.

'Refill?' Linc suggested, holding his bottle out with a smile.

'What?' Sandy looked up, scowling.

Linc put the Scotch on the desk in front of him. 'By way of a thank you for the other night. Looks like I was just in time, too.'

Sandy's scowl dissolved into a beatific smile. 'There is a God!' he declared. 'Will you join me?'

'Er, I'd prefer a coffee, if you've got some. I'm still feeling a little fragile.'

'Sure.' Sandy emptied the first bottle into his glass, took a swig and stood up. 'You certainly learn your lessons the hard way. Sit.'

'Actually, I hadn't been drinking,' Linc informed him, making use of the chair on his side of the desk. 'I think someone must have slipped me a Mickey at the party.'

'Nice of them!' Sandy observed. 'You were well out of it when *I* found you, that's for sure! I tried to wake you but you were dead to the world, so I thought it was best to take you on to the Vicarage with me.'

'In my car.'

'Yeah, well, I didn't think you'd want it left there, and since you were already in the passenger seat, it seemed the simplest thing to do.'

'I *was*?' Linc couldn't imagine why he might have changed seats; not easy in a Morgan, without getting out and walking round.

'Yeah, *I* thought it was odd,' Sandy remarked. 'Thought perhaps someone else had been driving but there was no one around.'

He looked at Linc as though he was expecting

248

him to provide an answer to the puzzle but he had none to offer.

'I'm sorry. Your guess is as good as mine.'

'Oh, well, people do strange things when they're stoned,' Sandy observed placidly as he switched the kettle on and located a mug. He peered inside this and then tapped it upside down before spooning coffee granules into it.

Linc decided it was probably better not to ask.

'Got any idea who planned that little surprise then?' the saddler went on.

'None at all. But I'd certainly like to come up with them in some lonely spot . . .'

'I bet.' He found milk in a mini-refrigerator next to the microwave, and sniffed it cautiously. Linc began to think the whisky might have been the better option after all.

There was a scratching at the door and when Sandy opened it, Tiger trotted in, tail waving happily. He made a beeline for Linc's feet and parked his brindle rump firmly on them.

Sandy smiled. 'He's happy now. Al doesn't like dogs and Tiger tends to growl at people who give off the wrong vibes, so I had to shut him out.'

There are dogs and dogs, Linc thought, sympathising with Sandy's late visitor on that point, at least. Nevertheless, old habits die hard, and he found himself fondling Tiger's ears as he talked.

'He didn't sound a particularly happy bunny, as it was,' he commented. 'I'm sorry, I couldn't help overhearing. He wasn't exactly discreet when he left. Is it anything I can help you with? I feel I owe you.'

'Rubbish! What was I supposed to do? Leave you there?'

'I don't know. But thanks anyway. And your friend Al?'

'No. It's okay. I can handle him. He just gets a bit hot under the collar. He'll calm down. Nothing you can do.' Something struck him as funny and he chuckled.

'What's the joke?'

Sandy shook his head, handing Linc his coffee. 'Nothing really. Actually, one thing you *can* do . . . Stop sending the bottles round here. It's bad for my reputation!'

'Bottles?' Linc was bewildered.

'Bottles and stoppers – coppers,' Sandy translated. 'They were round again today, asking about Saturday. Honestly, you do a bloke a good turn and all you get is grief!'

'Yeah, I'm sorry. I should have warned you. They said they'd want to talk to you. But surely they didn't give you a hard time?'

'No, not really.'

Linc sipped his coffee. 'So what's with the rhyming slang? You're not a cockney, are you? You don't sound it.'

'My old man was. I used to sound just like him but I found some of the hoity-toity horsy crowd didn't approve, so I try and remember to talk proper when I'm "ite and abite"!'

Linc laughed. 'Well, I'm just glad you were "ite and abite" on Saturday night,' he said. 'Or God knows where I'd be now!'

Sandy started to say something but was interrupted by the shrill tone of Linc's mobile phone. He paused while Linc retrieved it from his pocket and looked at the display.

His heart skipped a beat as the caller was identified as Josie and, apologising to Sandy, he answered it.

'Linc! It's happened! She's awake!' Josie was half-laughing and half-crying. 'She opened her eyes and smiled at us! She said "hello"!'

'Oh, Josie, that's wonderful! She made it! I knew she would. Didn't I say she was a tough cookie?'

'You did. But it's been so long. Oh, I can't believe it! This is the best moment of my entire life! We've all been laughing and crying – we can't stop!'

'I suppose it's family only, at the moment?'

'Yes. I'm sorry. And *we* were only allowed to stay for a short time. She's got to rest and then there'll be tests to do and stuff. But I just had to tell you . . .'

'Thanks. Give her my love. Will I see you later?'

'Probably. I'll give you a ring. 'Bye then.'

''Bye.' Linc cut the connection and looked across at Sandy. 'Abby's made it. She's come round!' he said, and his voice cracked a little with the emotion.

'That's brilliant! What a relief!' the saddler said, smiling. 'Will she be okay? I mean, has she said anything yet? I know they were worried – you know – about brain damage.'

'Well, she said hello,' Linc told him. 'So that's a start. It's looking good but I guess only time will tell.'

'Yeah.' Sandy looked thoughtful. Then he raised his glass. 'Well, here's hoping!'

'I'll drink to that. Even if it *is* just coffee.'

10

Realising that the Hathaway family probably needed space and time to take in their marvellous change in fortunes, Linc resisted the temptation to contact Josie later that day. The next morning he sent her a text message, simply asking if everything was still all right.

The answer came back promptly: *Yes. Everything fine. Am at Hosp. Call u L8R. J xxx*

She actually called less than an hour later, full of bubbling happiness. Abby, it appeared, was far better than anyone had dared hope and improving all the time.

'She can't remember anything much about the night she was attacked,' Josie told him. 'Rockley came to speak to her but she couldn't tell him anything new. The doctor didn't let him stay long because of upsetting her. She's very easily tired and rather emotional.'

'That's not surprising, I suppose,' Linc said. 'It's incredible, really, that she's as well as she is after – how many weeks is it?'

'Four weeks, four days,' Josie supplied. 'It's hard to believe. I think it's going to take a while for Abby to get her head round it, too.'

'Will you be at the hospital all day?'

'No. I'm on my way home now, actually. We have to be careful not to overtire her. She's still very weak.'

'Well, I don't know whether you feel like it but Farthingscourt is hosting a musical soirée this evening, and I wondered if you'd like to come. It's part of a season of concerts in stately homes and we've been lucky enough to land Mischa Barinkov playing Rachmaninov's Piano Concerto. You know, Number Two, the famous one. It should be lovely – if you like piano music, of course.'

'I love it. And Rach Two is my absolute favourite. What time do you want me?'

All the time, was the answer that sprang immediately to mind, but Linc bit his tongue. 'Half-past seven for eight,' he told her. 'There's a buffet supper afterwards, so it should be a good evening.'

The evening was indeed a great success. It was the first time Farthingscourt had participated in the concert series and tickets had sold out weeks before. It was stipulated that people should turn up in eveningwear and, with very few exceptions, they did. Softly lit, and with its richly dressed occupants, the state drawing room at Farthingscourt looked almost as it must have done in its heyday, in the time of St John, the ill-fated Third Viscount.

Even in a room filled with glamorous people, Josie turned heads in a long slim dress of burgundy silk. Her modelling experience gave her an air of calm elegance and Linc guessed that he was the envy of many of the other men. He'd have been less than human if he hadn't enjoyed the sensation.

The young Russian pianist gave a beautiful performance on a Steinway that had been loaned to Farthingscourt for the occasion, and the applause was long, rapturous and entirely genuine.

When Linc turned to look at Josie at one point during the recital he was touched to see her eyes shining with unshed tears.

'No need to ask if you enjoyed that,' he murmured, as they stood up to file into an adjacent room where the kitchen staff had set out a buffet on two long refectory tables.

'Oh, it was beautiful! What a gift to be able to play like that! And he's only – what? – nineteen.'

'Yes. It makes one wish one'd practised more as a child, doesn't it? My mother was a very passable pianist. She would sing, too.'

'I wish I'd met her. She looks such a lovely person in that portrait. I'm really glad you showed it to me.'

'Would you like to see it again?' Linc asked. 'We can slip away after supper. I'll show you the rest of the house, too. The bits we didn't get round to before.'

'Yes, please. I'd like that.'

They joined the queue for the buffet and, in due course, took their food and wine to a window seat where they were joined by Crispin and Nikki. But when the second part of the evening's entertainment was announced and the guests drifted back to the drawing room, Linc and Josie waited behind and then made their way out into the hall.

'There's only about forty minutes more and it's

mostly chamber music. You don't mind missing that, do you?'

'Not at all. Chamber music isn't really my thing. I'd rather remember that wonderful piano playing,' Josie assured him.

'I'd like to have been able to introduce you to him but his manager told us he'd be whisking the poor lad off to appear on some late-night chat show as soon as he'd taken his bows. I should imagine they'll be cutting it fine, even then. He's doing the publicity thing for his upcoming tour. It must be a bit daunting when you don't speak very much English.'

They climbed the main stairs to the first floor and entered the long gallery. Linc flicked a switch to illuminate the portraits and they made their way along, pausing at each picture. Josie seemed genuinely fascinated, wanting to know as much of the Tremayne family history as Linc could dredge up from his memory.

Stopping every few feet, they made slow progress, but as Linc's hand lay on the body-warmed silk of Josie's hip, and she had hooked her thumb in the back of his waistband, he was not about to complain.

'And here's the infamous St John, your alter ego,' she teased. 'What a romantic figure he is, to be sure. I think you should try your hair like that. You'd look rather dashing with long hair tied back with a ribbon.'

'There are some things I won't do, even to please you,' Linc responded firmly. 'And growing my hair is one of them. Besides, I don't think I would look so dashing on dressage day at a three-day event, if I had to put it in a hairnet!'

Josie giggled. 'You may have a point there.'

They wandered on, talking in muted tones, heads close together, eventually reaching the far end of the gallery.

'Whereabouts are your rooms? In the dungeons with the rats and spiders?'

'No. The opposite. Up in the roof. The old housemaids' dormitory.'

'Bare boards and a straw mattress?'

'Yes, but the housekeeper lets me have a blanket in the winter. And I'm lucky to have found employment at all in these hard times,' Linc said, putting on a Dorset accent. 'Actually, it's not at all bad up there. Do you want to come and see?'

'Er . . .' Josie hesitated, avoiding eye contact. 'Is this an invitation to come and see your etchings?'

Linc's heart rate doubled. 'That depends.'

'On what?' She was studiously inspecting a marble statuette.

'On you,' he said carefully. 'You're welcome just to sign up for the standard package, comprising guided tour of the apartment, view from the window – not great in the dark, I admit – a cup of coffee and a biscuit. Or you can go for the deluxe version which is a made-to-order package and may take considerably longer.'

'Um, I think I'll start with the standard deal, if that's okay?'

'Of course it is,' Linc assured her, gallantly hiding his disappointment. He crossed the corridor and opened a small door in the panelling. 'This way, madam. Mind the stairs, they're rather steep.'

At the top of the narrow flight of steps they emerged through another small door into Linc's living room and he watched with pleasure as Josie's eyes lit with surprised appreciation.

He'd adorned the basic canvas of natural oak beams, cream-painted walls, stripped floorboards and dark leather suite with colourful rugs, tapestries and cushions of South American origin. He was rather pleased with the overall effect himself, and Josie's reaction was gratifying.

'Wow! It's lovely! Did *you* do all this?'

'Yes. Don't sound so surprised,' Linc replied indignantly. 'Come and see the kitchen while I rustle up a cup of coffee.'

The kitchen followed the theme, with aged oak cupboards, granite worktops, cream walls, and tiles in hot, peppery colours behind the sink and cooker.

'Go and have a look at the rest,' he suggested, taking mugs out of the cupboard and putting the kettle on to boil.

Josie wandered off down the passageway that led to a small study, a big airy bedroom with a sloping ceiling, and a neat en-suite bathroom with a roof light over the roll top bath. Linc had spent many a blissful half-hour soaking in there and gazing up at the stars.

She came back just as he was putting the milk back in the fridge.

'It's absolutely gorgeous!' she exclaimed. 'I'm green with envy!'

Linc was pleased. He handed her a mug and led the way back to the sitting room.

'I thought you said there was a biscuit included in the standard package,' Josie reminded him playfully.

'I lied. Though I might have a bit of cake somewhere.'

She shook her head. 'No, I'm fine, really.'

Linc sat on one end of the sofa and, after a moment, Josie joined him, kicking off her shoes and curling her legs up beside her. They sipped coffee in companionable silence for a minute or two and then Josie looked sideways at him with what could almost have been described as a shy smile.

'So what does the deluxe package consist of?' she asked softly.

'Ah, but I didn't think madam was in the market for that,' Linc countered.

'I'm an impulse buyer. Sell it to me.'

'I can do better than that,' he offered, leaning across and taking her mug out of her hand. He placed both mugs on the low table. 'I can give you a free demonstration. No obligation to buy.'

Josie slid over the smooth leather seat to nestle within the circle of his arm.

'That sounds fair enough.' She undid one of the buttons on his cotton shirt and slid her hand inside. 'Is it okay to handle the goods?' she murmured, her head somewhere beneath his chin.

Linc took a deep steadying breath.

'Oh, yes. That's part of the deal,' he assured her.

Linc woke first in the morning and lay looking up at the squares of sunlight on his bedroom ceiling with a feeling of rare contentment. Snuggled by his side, Josie slept on. Turning his head, he could just see the dark sweep of her lashes on her golden skin. As if aware of being watched, she suddenly stretched luxuriously and opened her eyes.

'Morning,' he said softly. 'So, what did you think of the deluxe package? Can I interest madam in signing up for further tours?'

'Um . . . I might need to think about it,' she hedged. 'You know, shop around and compare prices.'

There was a moment's silence, then Linc asked, 'Is madam by any chance familiar with the phrase "hard sell?"' and rolled over to pin her arms on to the pillow, either side of her head.

Some minutes later, when things had quietened down, Linc lay looking at her from under his lashes.

'What?'

'I was just wondering what you'd say if I asked you to marry me,' he replied frankly.

She blinked, then said matter-of-factly, 'I'd say yes.'

'Just like that?' Linc queried. 'Don't you even want time to think?'

'I've already done that,' she told him. 'That first time you showed me round and I saw the portrait of your mother, I tried to imagine what it would be like to come here as a bride and I just couldn't get my head round it. That sounds arrogant, I know, because I don't suppose the thought had even crossed your mind then, but I knew *I* was getting involved and I needed to sort myself out. If I couldn't handle the idea of Farthingscourt and the title and everything then I was on a hiding to nothing. Whichever way it went with you, I was going to lose.'

'That was when you went away to London?'

'Yes. I needed space to think. Though I did need to go anyway, to sort out something about the flat.'

'And?'

'And I decided that it was too late anyway. I decided that I'd take my chances, because if it came to it and the feeling was right, then nothing else mattered.'

'And it feels right?'

'It's always felt right,' she stated simply. 'Hey, this is very one-sided! What about you? When did you know?'

'I think, in the restaurant in Shaftesbury. Though I thought what happened later might have blown it for me. And as for the other night . . .'

'You certainly know how to show a girl a good time!'

'Don't I just,' he said ruefully.

'And what about your father? Will he approve?'

'He likes you. Not that it would make any difference if he didn't.'

Josie shook her head. 'You say that, but I don't think it's true. I think you both care a lot more about each other than you let on.'

Linc adopted a stern tone. 'For God's sake, woman! I want a wife, not a psychoanalyst!' he declared, then grunted as a slim fist hit him in the solar plexus.

They decided to announce the engagement at the weekend, when the excitement over Abby had died down a little, and when it might be possible to arrange an informal gathering of the two families.

'How do you think your parents will take it?' Linc asked.

'Well, it seems as though you're almost part of the family as it is, so I shouldn't imagine they'd kick up *too* much of a fuss,' she said, affecting an offhand manner. 'Although I think Daddy always rather hoped I'd marry a doctor or a lawyer.'

'Oh, dear. Perhaps you'd better try and sneak back in quietly and we'll forget all about it,' Linc suggested.

Josie snorted. 'Not much chance of that with Hannah around! She'll no doubt bring up the subject at the next family meal.'

Linc laughed. 'Not destined for the diplomatic service, young Hannah.'

'You can say that again! Gossip columnist for a national daily, I'd say!'

Josie had been all for leaving early, by the back stairs and side door, but as Linc pointed out, her car was clearly visible to any interested observer, parked in the stableyard where she had left it the night before.

So she had toast and coffee with him, enjoying the view from the kitchen window, and followed him downstairs with a casual air, as if she regularly stayed over. In fact, her masterly performance was all but wasted because the only person they met on their way out was Mary, and she greeted the pair without so much as a lifted eyebrow.

'Does Mary live in the house?' Josie asked, as she and Linc emerged into the bright stillness of a perfect May morning.

'No, she has a cottage in the yard but she often eats with my father. They seem to have got quite close in the last few years. I've noticed the difference since I've been back.' They had reached her car. 'So, I'll see you in a minute, okay?'

'Okay. I'll tell Noddy you're on your way.' Josie

smiled and made to turn away but Linc caught hold of her arm and pulled her back.

'Where do you think you're going?' he demanded.

She laughed, put her arms round his neck and kissed him soundly. 'That better?'

Linc nodded. 'It'll do for now.'

'I think last night went rather well, don't you, Mary?'

Linc had ridden Noddy and was back in his office attending to his mail.

'Mmm. It certainly seems to have gone well for you anyway,' she observed, eyes twinkling.

'Miss Poe! Most secretaries would be severely reprimanded for a comment like that!'

They both knew she was a lot more than a secretary to the Tremaynes, both Senior and Junior.

'She's a lovely girl. You're serious about her, I take it?'

'Well, I've asked her to marry me,' Linc said. 'It doesn't get much more serious than that! But don't say anything to anyone just yet. We'll probably announce it at the weekend.'

'Oh, Linc, that's wonderful news! Your father *will* be pleased. No, don't worry, I won't say anything.'

He put down the last of the morning's correspondence and stood up. 'Do you really think he will?'

Mary nodded. 'I'm sure of it. He's very taken with Josie. He said as much to me the other day.'

'Well, it's a good job he talks to you or I'd never know what he's thinking,' Linc said with a touch of bitterness. 'I think this family would fall apart at the seams if it wasn't for you. Would have done long ago, come to that!'

'Linc . . .'

Mary stopped, maybe searching for the right words, and he cut in, saying briskly, 'Well, anyway, I must get on. I'm supposed to be meeting the heritage guy at the mill in five minutes, so that's where I'll be if anyone wants me.'

The 'anyone' turned out to be DI Rockley. He arrived just as Linc was winding up his meeting at the mill, having first called at the house and been forwarded by Mary. When the man from English Heritage got into his car and went on his way, Rockley emerged from his and came over to where Linc stood, glancing appreciatively at the mill buildings as he did so.

'Always wanted to live in a mill,' he remarked.

'You can have this one if you want,' Linc offered, as they began to walk along the front of the building.

'Having trouble?'

He shook his head, sighing. 'No, not really. Just endless red tape. This would have been finished by now if it wasn't for form-filling and waiting on visits from this or that official. It's such a waste of everybody's time. If they didn't have to pay all these people the grants would be twice the size!'

Rockley nodded in sympathy. 'The world is slowly being dragged to a halt by red tape. And the police force is a prime example. How long before you get this beauty going again?' They had reached the first footbridge and he was looking at the wheel.

'Next month, all being well, but there are no guarantees.'

'Are you having a grand opening? I'd like to come, if you do.'

'I'll let you know,' Linc promised. 'So, what can I do for you? Or are top brass visiting the station again?'

They wandered on to the second bridge and paused to watch the water gushing from the pipe into the by-pass stream.

'Manston tells me you've been in trouble again,' Rockley commented.

'Yes, but not of my making.'

'Have you heard from the doctor?'

'Not yet. Have you?'

'As a matter of fact, yes. And he had nothing to tell. The results of your blood test showed no suspicious substances in your system.'

'There must have been! I wasn't drunk, if that's what you think.'

'No. That would have showed in your test, too.'

Linc was bewildered. 'So what are you saying? That I had some sort of attack or seizure?' The thought was deeply disturbing.

'Not necessarily. There are a couple of substances that are very difficult to detect. Rohypnol and GHB; the date-rape drugs. Because their effects can mimic those of alcohol abuse, they often go unsuspected, and unless specific tests are carried out within a few hours, their use is almost impossible to prove.'

'But the blood test . . .?'

'It has to be a urine test,' Rockley stated. 'And it isn't something that hospitals are set up to test for. Usually it's done by a police lab. So you see, unless someone has, or is given, an amount which constitutes an overdose, such as in your case, these drugs probably wouldn't even be considered.'

'Would it have been in my drink?'

'Probably. GHB in particular is very easy to disguise. It's a clear liquid, and although it has a salty taste, you need so little of it, you could put it in almost any fruity or alcoholic drink and the recipient would be none the wiser.'

'Like fruit punch.'

'Yes, like fruit punch.'

'But why do it? What did they hope to achieve? Not . . . not rape, surely.' Linc could hardly bring himself to say the word and his face reflected the abhorrence he felt.

'It's unlikely.'

Rockley bent and picked up half a dozen stones from the path and began to toss them, one by one, into the running water.

'Although it is known as a date-rape drug, GHB – Gamma hydroxy butyrate – is quite widely taken in our larger cities as a recreational drug, because in low to medium doses, as I said, it produces an effect not unlike that of alcoholic intoxication. The problem is that as a liquid GHB comes in very varied degrees of concentration. Unless you know and trust your source it is frighteningly easy to overdose.'

'But where does it come from? It's a banned substance, obviously, so . . .'

'Ah, but it's not.' Rockley dropped the last of the pebbles and turned to face Linc. 'It's a prescribed sedative. But it's unfortunately also fairly easy to make and there are internet sites that tell you exactly how to go about it. The boys at the lab tell me it's basically a degreasing solvent mixed with drain cleaner!'

'Oh, God! No wonder I was ill!'

'They also tell me that it's a substance produced in minute quantities by the body itself, but that doesn't, as some of its proponents argue, make it safe to consume. The main danger is that it's extremely dose-sensitive, and by that I mean that the dose needed to induce dangerous effects is only slightly greater than the dose some people regularly enjoy taking. Any other contributing factors, such as combining it with other drugs, or alcohol consumption, or even something as simple as taking it on an empty stomach, can drastically increase the effect it has on an individual.'

'I don't know whether I'd eaten,' Linc told him. 'But I suppose there was probably alcohol in the punch. I don't remember.'

'Your sister-in-law said there was a little.'

'I still don't see the point of it all.'

'Well, as a date-rape drug it renders the victim extremely susceptible to suggestion. They experience a lack of inhibition and find it almost impossible to exert their own will. To add to our difficulties, victims also suffer amnesia. It's a bugger! The effects of overdose are – among other things – prolonged unrouseable sleep, possible respiratory disorders, vomiting, and death. Many hospitals don't recognise the symptoms and there have been a number of fatalities in the States – where it's no longer available on prescription, by the way.'

Linc was frowning, struggling to take it all in.

'So, given that I fit all the criteria, what do you

think the intention was? Was the overdose deliberate?'

Rockley sighed. 'I wish I could tell you. Whatever the answer, I'd say you were lucky your friend Sandy Wilkes came along.'

'He said he found me in the passenger seat,' Linc mentioned, remembering.

'Yes. It was in his statement. Any idea why?'

Linc leaned over the railing, staring at the water. The idea forming in his brain was unpalatable, to say the least, and he was reluctant to give voice to it, as if doing so would somehow give it substance.

'What if I changed sides because I was told to; so someone else could drive the car with me in it.' He paused, thinking hard.

'Go on,' Rockley prompted.

'Well, what if the car was stopped by the bridge on purpose and I was supposed to get back into my side but by then I was unconscious?'

He looked up and found Rockley watching him intently.

'Do you remember old River Joe? I can't recall his real name, but you remember what happened to him?'

Rockley nodded. 'Indeed I do. And I'm right with you. If you'd gone over into the river in your car, with its soft-top, you'd have been very lucky to have got out alive.'

Linc was appalled at where this was leading, but he'd gone too far to stop now. 'It's a very quiet lane,' he went on. 'If there *was* someone else, they could quite reasonably have expected to have plenty of time to set it all up. Especially if I was unconscious. It was just a matter of luck that

Sandy came along at that moment. He said he didn't see anyone else, but maybe whoever it was panicked. It would be easy enough to drop down into the river and under the bridge until the coast was clear.'

'And if it had gone to plan, it would appear that you'd driven off the road accidentally. Sad, but it had happened before. By the time you were found there would quite possibly be no trace of the drug in your body to give the game away, even if anyone thought to test for it.' Rockley paused. 'It's certainly possible. In fact, I'm very much afraid you could be right. But why, Linc? Tell me. What have you done or found out? Why should someone risk so much to get rid of you? Because that's what it boils down to, you know. Someone is terrified of what you might do or say. So, if you know anything – anything at all – you must tell me.'

'I wish to God I could!' Linc exclaimed. 'But I honestly don't. I'm not exactly ecstatic about the idea that someone may be trying to bump me off! You heard about the latest note, I suppose?'

'Yes. Forensics have had a look at it and come up with absolutely zilch, except that it apparently comes from the *Mail* instead of the *Sun* this time. I'm not sure if there's any significance in that or not.' He groaned, running his fingers through his hair. 'I'm finding it hard to think straight at all at the moment, to be honest. We've got a new Chief Super and he's determined to make his mark. Talk about a new broom . . . It's enough to drive you mad. Or, in the words of one of my younger colleagues, "It's doing my head in." I suppose he'll get over it eventually.' He sighed heavily and looked at his watch. 'Well, I must get going. And you, to quote the last note, "Watch your back", okay? We're doing what we can but we haven't had a lot to go on and quite frankly it's baffling. You say you've not been nosing around . . .'

'And I haven't.'

'Then why do they still feel threatened? Why risk breaking cover to attack you, when there's no real need? Especially now young Abby's on the mend. Are you sure you've told us everything?'

'Absolutely,' Linc assured him.

'Oh, well . . .' Rockley sighed, turning away from the stream and back towards his car. 'As I said, look after yourself. Try to stay away from lonely places, dark alleys and the like. We'll be in touch.'

He held out his hand and Linc shook it. The night they had first met, he would have taken long odds against ever liking the detective, but surprisingly he found he now did.

'Have there been any more tack thefts recently?' he asked.

'No. Not on my patch. They've either moved on or decided to lay low for the time being. Why?' the detective added suspiciously.

'Just curious.'

'Hmm.' Rockley didn't sound convinced, but nevertheless, after a long hard look at Linc, waved a hand and moved away.

Linc reviewed their conversation in his mind as he watched the big silver car nose its way out of sight into Mill Lane. Then suddenly there was a slithering noise from above, followed by a warning shout, and he flashed a glance upwards even as he ducked sideways into the shelter of the wall. Two tumbling, spinning black shapes missed him by a whisker, shattering dramatically on the stones at his feet.

A roof tile, or two – it was difficult to tell, the pieces had scattered over quite an area. Linc prudently waited a moment and moved a foot or two along the wall before venturing away from the protection of the overhang. Looking up, he could see two of the roofing team gazing anxiously back at him and waved a hand.

'Bloody hell! You all right, mate?' one of them called. 'It didn't hit you, did it?'

Linc shook his head. 'No. You'll have to try harder than that!' he called in reply. But, joking aside, he should have been wearing a hard hat on site. It was a stipulation of the contractors, the grantors, and the funding partners.

'Bloody thing snapped in two when I picked it up,' the workman shouted. 'Must have been a dud, sorry.'

'S'okay. How's it going?'

'Pretty good. End of the week, I reckon.'

'That's brilliant! Well done!' Linc waved a hand and moved on, pleased. They were ahead of target. Weather permitting, they would finish a full two days early.

As he reached the Discovery, he paused.

'Watch your back' Rockley had advised; the note had said the same. Not much point watching his back if the danger came from above.

It may only have been an accident but if he'd been a fraction of a second slower, the tile could have split his skull.

His reactions had saved him again, but Linc wondered, with a shiver, just how long his luck could hold.

11

The Hathaways were still basking in the euphoria engendered by Abby's return to consciousness when they were cruelly knocked back by the news that, in her weakened state, she had succumbed to an infection and was once more seriously ill.

It was Ruth who gave Linc the news when he arrived to ride Noddy on the Friday morning.

'The doctors are worried that she could go down with pneumonia,' she reported, looking even more tired and dispirited than she had in the days following the attack. 'It's awful. We were all so happy. So sure that everything was finally going to be all right. Why did this have to happen? Haven't we been through enough? Hasn't *she*?'

Linc didn't know what to say. There didn't seem to be anything that wouldn't sound trite and unconvincing, so instead he went to her and put his arms round her.

'Is there anything I can do?' he asked.

Leaning against him, Ruth shook her red-gold curls. 'You're doing it,' she said into his fleece.

'Where's Josie?'

'She drove Mum to the hospital this morning.' Ruth stepped back, looking up at him. 'Mum's in a state. It's like she'd been strong for so long and then she just relaxed. I heard her telling Dad she didn't think she could cope with any more. It's awful. When you're a kid, no matter what happens, you can always turn to your parents for comfort, then suddenly one day you find that they don't have all the answers – that they need comforting themselves, and it's kind of scary. I suppose it's called growing up,' she added, with a flash of a self-conscious smile. 'But just at the moment I don't want to.'

'It's been hard on all of you,' Linc said softly. 'But you're a wonderfully strong family. You'll pull through.' They would, too. Whereas his own family had all but fallen apart after the death of one of its members, he felt that even should the worst happen, the Hathaways would survive.

'Oh, Josie said to tell you she's very sorry but she won't be able to groom for you at Coopers Down tomorrow. She'll ring you later anyway.'

'That's no problem. I'll manage. Or I might even ask Nikki again. I think she quite enjoyed it.'

'I shan't take Magic. I just feel I want to be around, in case . . . well, you know.'

'Yeah, I know.'

When Josie did ring Linc it was to report no change in her sister's condition, but then Ruth came on the line to ask if he'd like to ride Magic in the following day's competition. Linc had initially protested but Ruth seemed very keen that he should, so he agreed with, to be honest, no real reluctance. The mare was

273

fun to ride and, at sixteen hands, was well up to his weight.

So Linc set off for Somerset early on Saturday morning with Noddy and Magic in the back of the lorry, and Nikki, who had happily agreed to groom for him, with him in the cab. The downside of the arrangement was that Beverley had decided to offer her services too, in spite of Linc's assuring her that there was no real need. Nevertheless, with Dee Ellis and Steamer also attending, he looked forward with pleasure to a busy day.

It was unfortunate that the long spell of fine weather had chosen the Friday afternoon to break, and after a night of intermittent rain, the going remained hard underneath but had become slippery on top. Even so, the morning proceeded with no more than the average number of minor panics and crises.

Surprisingly, Crispin turned up before the day was very far advanced, camera in hand, as always, but rather than take shots of the horses in action, proceeded to photograph all the hustle and bustle of the preparation for competition. It was, he said, for his 'Sporting Life' exhibition.

Steamer was Linc's first ride of the day and, as before, the big grey did his very best to comply with his wishes in the dressage. The result was a test that was accurate but a little lacking in finesse, but the judges for once seemed to recognise his effort and their marks were better than Linc could have hoped for.

'Bless him! He had his tongue out like a little boy concentrating on his maths,' Dee exclaimed, patting her horse fondly as she met them outside the arena.

Magic was scheduled only two horses later and in spite of the interruption in her warming up, the showy chestnut produced a super test and went into an early lead.

Both horses managed uneventful and penalty-free rounds in the showjumping, and Linc just had time to coax an unwilling dressage performance out of his own horse before mounting Steamer for the cross-country phase of the event.

It had to be said that he entered the start box with some trepidation, because first reports from the course suggested that a combination of the slippery conditions and some challenging fences were resulting in a higher than usual number of retirements and disqualifications.

Steamer stood waiting for the off, stock-still and quivering, and with his rump turned towards the first fence. This was Linc's latest ploy to stop himself from losing control the instant the starter sent them on their way.

It wasn't a huge success. He wouldn't have believed that any horse could turn himself through one hundred and eighty degrees so quickly. Almost before the words 'Good luck' had left the official's mouth, Steamer had whipped round and was running. Linc recovered his balance and managed to haul in an inch or two of rein as they approached the straw-bale first fence but he made no noticeable impression on the big grey's speed. Steamer took the first three obstacles as if he were steeplechasing and Linc resigned himself to another white-knuckle ride.

The course at Coopers Down was indeed tricky in parts. When Linc had walked it earlier in the day in the company of two fellow competitors, they had earmarked five potential hazards, one of which was the fourth fence, an innocuous-looking tree trunk at the top of a slope followed by another at the bottom. The problem lay in the slope. Even trying to walk down it, one of Linc's companions had slipped up and completed the journey on his backside. After the merriment had subsided, they all agreed that after a dozen or so horses had slid down it the incline would be treacherous.

It had been Linc's plan to approach the combination on a short, bouncy stride, to start with as much balance as possible.

Ah, well . . .

With no deference whatsoever to Linc's wishes, Steamer flew the first tree trunk, landing halfway down the slope and sliding the rest of the way with splayed forelegs to meet the second trunk with a resounding smack moments later. His momentum carried him forward and he half-fell over it to land on his knees the other side. Linc found himself with his face buried in the horse's unplaited mane, just behind the long grey ears. With a lurch forwards and sideways, Steamer made it to his feet, throwing his head up and tipping Linc back into the saddle as he did so. Showing commendable presence of mind, he used the grey's temporary state of unbalance to his advantage, shortening the reins and sitting deep, trying to force the horse to adopt a rhythm of *his* choosing for a change.

He was partially successful. His approach to the fifth, a massive pole over a ditch lined with railway sleepers, was almost sensible, and they made it through the other problem fences without incident, but with each jump Steamer seemed to gain a little speed. By the time they reached the last he was travelling so fast that he skidded on the turn to it and missed it altogether. They swung round to come to the fence again but the damage was done. Twenty penalties for circling. Effectively out of contention.

Dee Ellis wasn't dismayed. In her eyes Steamer could do no wrong. Blaming the weather exclusively for his mistakes, she hugged him and fed him Polo mints before leading him off to her lorry. Wondering what, if anything, could be tried to steady the horse, Linc trudged back to link up with Nikki and Magic.

At the end of the dressage, Magic had only slipped two places, and to Linc's surprise and delight the chestnut produced a faultless cross-country round to finish on her dressage score. Whatever anyone else did, she couldn't finish lower than third.

Ruth would be over the moon.

Noddy had jumped an adequate but cautious round in the showjumping arena and Linc suspected that he wasn't happy with the state of the ground. Some horses adapt much more easily to slippery conditions than others. Noddy was behaving like an OAP on an icy morning. Linc put the biggest studs that he had into the brown horse's shoes and prepared to nurse him round the cross-country course for the sake of experience.

Nikki offered to warm Noddy up while Linc sat in the lorry cab drinking coffee from a flask and eating a ham and cheese roll. Magic was standing quietly in the back, munching on a full haynet. Presently, with an apple in his hand, he went in search of his horse and found him being held by Nikki while her mother greased him up and checked his bandages. He glimpsed Crispin off to one side, still happily snapping.

'Getting down and dirty, eh, Beverley?' Linc joked, feeding his apple core to Noddy.

'I was brought up with horses,' she reminded him, straightening up and wiping leg grease off her fingers on to an old tea towel. 'I've tightened his girth up one hole but I think it'll go up again.'

'Thanks, I'll do it when I'm on.' Linc went round to Noddy's near – or left – side and checked the stirrup length. Somebody had already adjusted the leathers from Nikki's length to his. 'Wow! What an efficient team,' he said, impressed.

'We do our best,' Nikki declared jauntily. 'Is Magic okay?'

'Yes. The girl in the next lorry has promised to keep an eye on her. I gave her your mobile number in case of emergencies.' Linc swung on board Noddy, found his offside stirrup, then moved his leg forward to lift the saddle flap and tighten the girth, which under his weight, went up another hole. Noddy cow-kicked and sidled, a sure sign that he was beginning to wake up for his favourite part of the proceedings.

'Just stand still!' Nikki told him firmly. 'Ugh, you old slobberchops! You've gobbed all over me! Come here, let me tidy you up, you mucky horse.'

A quick wipe over the face and nostrils with a wet sponge and Noddy was ready to go. As Nikki let go of his head he immediately tried to rub his nose on his greasy legs but Linc hauled him up and sent him forwards. After ten minutes or so of walking and trotting in circles he was called into the starting box to await the countdown.

Making his way across, Linc called out to Nikki, 'He keeps shaking his head. Can you just wipe his face again?'

'Number one hundred and seventy, into the starting box, please!' The steward sounded impatient at being obliged to repeat himself. It had begun to rain steadily once more and tempers were shortening.

Nikki came forward with a tea towel, mopped Noddy's face and checked that his forelock wasn't trapped by the bridle and pulling uncomfortably. She slapped him on the neck.

'He seems fine,' she said. 'Good luck.'

Linc rode into the start box but Noddy still seemed bothered by something. Linc wondered if it was a fly, and decided that once they were on the move, the horse would probably forget all about it.

'Thirty seconds.'

Noddy stopped abruptly and tried to pull enough rein through Linc's fingers to get his head down to his knee and rub. Linc pushed him forwards again. The last thing he wanted was for Noddy to get the leg grease in his eyes.

'Twenty!'

Noddy shook his head once more, then tossed it upwards. Linc patted him soothingly.

'Five . . . four . . . three . . . two . . . one . . . good luck!'

Diving his head down sharply, Noddy jumped into a canter and they were away.

As they approached the first fence, it appeared

that whatever had been annoying the horse had gone, but as they landed and continued towards the second, he shook his head again briefly, the movement throwing him off balance for a moment. Linc steadied him, letting him pick up his rhythm once more, and they cleared the next safely.

All was not well, though. Noddy had begun sweating heavily and after a stride or two he again became preoccupied with whatever was bothering him and rapped the top rail of the third pretty hard. Linc hoped he'd be a bit more careful with the tree trunks of fence four but it wasn't looking good. Leaning hard on the bit he was gaining speed and as the solid mass of the first log came into view, Linc had to sit down hard and take a pull, forcing the brown horse's head up so that he could at least see the jump. Even so, Noddy hit it a resounding whack as he went over. He careered down the slope, slipping and sliding on the slippery ground, and cracked his knees on the second trunk as well, pecking on landing.

Linc felt enough was enough. Something, maybe a bee-sting, had badly upset the horse and he had no intention of risking either of their necks by trying to continue. As Noddy regained his balance, he shortened his reins right up and tried to pull him to a halt, but the horse was having none of it. He shook his head so violently that he almost fell over and then plunged forward, ripping the reins through Linc's fingers and heading at a ragged gallop towards the rail and ditch of fence five.

Although he was pulling uncharacteristically hard, Noddy seemed now to have stopped his frantic head-shaking, and Linc allowed himself to hope that the crisis was over. Battling reins that were slippery with sweat, Linc managed to get Noddy's head up but they were less than five strides from the fence and he had to make a split-second decision. Clenching his jaw, he sat down and rode the horse forward.

Noddy approached the ditch and rail on a long stride and met it perfectly.

But he didn't take off.

It was as if he hadn't seen it. In the last couple of strides when he should have pricked his ears, lowered his head and got his quarters under him, he just kept galloping.

His front legs went into the five-foot-wide ditch, he hit the massive rail at chest height with a grunt of shock, and his back legs kicked skywards as his momentum carried him over and down.

Linc let the reins slip as he felt the horse falling but there was nothing he could do to save either of them. Noddy's neck and long brown ears disappeared leaving him perched high, and battered turf and railway sleepers hurtled to meet him.

The ground hit him sickeningly hard between the shoulder blades, rattling his teeth and driving the air from his lungs. He was briefly aware of seeing the edge of the ditch against the pale grey sky before it was blocked out by the dark mass of Noddy's falling body.

Someone somewhere clearly said, 'Oh, shit!' then awareness left him.

Somebody was stroking his hand.

It felt rather nice, and as thinking was, for the moment, too much trouble, Linc just lay with his eyes shut, enjoying the sensation. When the movement ceased he felt an inordinate sense of loss.

'No. Don't stop,' he mumbled, lifting his eyelids a fraction.

White sheets, green coverlet and a metal bedstead.

Hospital. Damn!

'Linc!' Josie leaned towards him, smiling with relief. 'Thank God! Stay there, I'll call the nurse.'

Linc had no intention of going anywhere just at that moment but he didn't think he wanted a nurse, either. He opened his mouth to say so but Josie had already gone and was calling down the corridor.

'You didn't manage to kill yourself this time. Will you finally stop now?'

With a shock of surprise, Linc turned his head to the other side and located his father, sitting in a chair by the window and looking at him with an expression of bitter reproach.

Linc searched his memory and came up with a one-day event. Noddy had fallen with him – a nasty fall. 'How's Noddy? How's my horse?'

'Forget the bloody horse and answer my question! Will you give up?'

Linc looked at him bleakly. So much for paternal concern. He hadn't even asked Linc how he felt.

Sylvester stood up.

'Well?' he asked abruptly.

'No,' Linc said quietly, and looked beyond him to the window where, beneath the half-lowered blind, the outside world was gloomy and wet. He fought the temptation to look back, and after a moment his father got up and left the room without another word.

'Linc? Are you okay?' Josie had come back. 'Where's your father going?'

Linc looked at her and shook his head wordlessly, ashamed to find his eyes blurring with a sudden rush of tears. God! He couldn't remember the last time he'd cried. Even as a child he rarely had. There was no point when there was no one to cry to.

'The nurse is just coming.' Either Josie hadn't noticed, or she was pretending she hadn't.

Linc closed his eyes and steadied himself. He knew it was shock that had weakened his defences. Josie took his hand again and he squeezed hers, looked at her and smiled.

'I'm sorry. I keep doing this to you, don't I?'

'You do rather. Actually, I'm beginning to think you might do better to marry a nurse,' she said.

Linc summoned a smile in response. 'You might be right. How's Noddy? Do you know if he's okay?'

'Well, he's a little sore but he doesn't seem to have broken anything, according to Nikki. Which reminds me – I should ring her. She was desperately worried, poor girl, but she had to get the horses home.'

'Oh, my God!' Linc exclaimed in real alarm. 'The lorry! Nikki mustn't drive the lorry! She's bad enough in a car!'

'Calm down. She didn't have to. Apparently Crispin was there.' Josie fished in her handbag, frowning. 'Damn! I've left my mobile at home. I'm always doing that. I'll just nip down the hall . . .'

Linc closed his eyes. His head ached and he felt unutterably weary. It was hard to believe that, after everything else that had happened, he should end up in hospital as the result of a riding accident.

Miserably he considered the ever-widening gulf between him and his father. Frankly he was surprised the old man had even come to the hospital, given his harsh comments on the subject in the past.

There was nothing to be gained by dwelling on the matter. If he intended to continue eventing – as he assuredly did – then the breach with his father was a consequence he would just have to go on living with. He switched his thoughts instead to Noddy's strange behaviour. Something had badly upset him, but what? He was normally such a placid horse.

A nurse appeared, cheery and efficient, checked him over, told him he'd live to fight another day, made a couple of notes on the clipboard at the end of his bed and left again, her soft-soled shoes squeaking away down the corridor outside.

Linc went back to his thoughts.

Footsteps on the lino. Josie was back. He opened his eyes and she smiled at him. 'Nikki sends her love. She was so relieved she burst into tears,' she reported.

'Do they know what upset Noddy yet?'

'No. Not exactly. Nikki wondered if he might have got an insect down inside his ear. A wasp or a horsefly, perhaps. I'll tell you what, though, she gave me one bit of good news. You and Magic won your class! Just wait till I tell Ruth, she'll be over the moon!'

'That's great! Trust me to miss my big moment, though.' Linc put his hands on the mattress, either side of his waist, and tried to shift his weight up the bed a little. His back and neck felt very sore and he winced.

'Ouch!' Josie said, wincing in sympathy. 'Does it hurt very much? The doctor didn't think you'd done anything serious but he said they'd X-ray you when you came round. It'll be tomorrow now, I suppose.'

'How long have I been here? Where are we, come to that?'

'Yeovil General. And it's just gone half-past five. Nikki rang your father just after three, and Mary rang the Vicarage to let me know. I'd only just got in from seeing Abby, so I jumped back in the car and came over here. Your father was in a bit of a state when I got here.'

'Abby!' Linc exclaimed, remembering. 'How is she?'

'Holding her own. They think she'll be okay. Now, I'm under strict instructions from your nurse not to keep you talking for too long, so I'm going to get myself a cup of coffee and I'll be back later.'

Linc was given the all clear and allowed home at midday the following day, with the proviso that he should spend the rest of the day in bed and take it easy for at least another two or three.

He was making himself a cup of coffee in the kitchen of his apartment that afternoon when his father knocked and announced himself. Linc cursed under his breath.

'Come in,' he called from the kitchen doorway. Then, as he did so, 'Can I get you a coffee?'

'Er, tea, please. Earl Grey.'

'Have a seat,' Linc suggested, but Sylvester followed him back into the kitchen.

'I thought you were supposed to be in bed.'

'I was bored.' Linc rummaged in the cupboard for the packet of Earl Grey he'd bought soon after he'd moved in. This was the first time he'd had occasion to use it. He wasn't keen on fancy teas himself but he knew it was his father's favourite.

'You look very pale.' He even managed to make *that* sound like an accusation.

'Being knocked out obviously doesn't agree with me,' Linc observed flippantly.

His father seemed strangely ill at ease. He wandered out into the sitting room again and Linc could hear the boards creaking as he moved around.

When he carried the mugs through, Linc found him staring at a framed photograph that stood on top of the bookcase and groaned inwardly. The print was of him riding Hobo at the Talham Horse Trials. Putting the mugs down on the coffee table, he sank back in the nearest sofa and awaited the inevitable recriminations.

There was a long silence and Linc was about to draw his father's attention to his cooling Earl Grey when he spoke.

'Why do you do it, Linc? What are you trying to prove?'

'I'm not trying to prove anything,' he said, exasperated. 'I do it for the same reason Mum did – I love it.'

His father turned to face him. 'But you know what happened to your mother – why must you tempt fate? Are you trying to break me completely?'

Linc was shaken by the anguish in his face. Up to now his opposition had always been expressed in such antagonistic terms it was easy to miss the underlying fear. Even so, Linc couldn't go through life being hemmed in by someone else's anxieties.

'No! That's not what this is about!' he protested. 'This is about *me* and what *I* want to do. Eventing is my passion. I want to get to the top; to ride at Burghley and Badminton, and maybe – just maybe – ride on the British team one day. I might not make it, but nothing you can say will stop me trying!'

'And what about yesterday? That nearly put a stop to you for good! From what Beverley says, if you hadn't landed in the ditch, the horse would have come down right on top of you! What would have happened to your precious dream then?'

'Bugger Beverley!' Linc exclaimed furiously. 'Why can't she keep her bloody mouth shut?'

'For once we agree. But the fact remains, people are killed eventing. Oh, I don't just mean your mother – it happens every year.'

'People are killed doing all sorts of things. If you let statistics rule your life you'd never get in a car, for God's sake!'

'Cars are a necessary evil. You don't *have* to ride,' his father pointed out.

'Well, I choose to!' Linc retorted. 'And while we're on the subject . . . I saw Mike Farquharson the other day.'

'Ah, he ran to you with that little story, did he?'

'No, he didn't. We met by chance and had a cup of coffee together. How dare you turn down an offer of sponsorship on my behalf?'

'I didn't. He decided against it.'

'After you threatened to withdraw your custom! How low is that?'

'I may not be able to stop you killing yourself on your bloody horses, but I'll be damned if I'll help fund it!' The Viscount had stepped forward to stand looking down at his son, with his hands on the back of the other sofa. Now he turned away and went to the door.

'You haven't drunk your tea.' Suddenly Linc didn't want him to go. For once, everything was out in the open but it was all too ragged and raw to be left like that.

'I find I'm not thirsty after all.' Sylvester opened the door and then paused. 'You're too much like her, you know. All fired up and passionate about things you care about. So alive! But then one day – she wasn't . . .'

As the door shut behind him, Linc sighed unhappily. It had been the best opportunity he'd ever had to put his own point of view across, and what had he done? He'd lost his temper and said a lot of things that would have been better left unsaid. With a muttered curse, he slammed his fist down on the coffee table and then glared at the slopped tea.

There was a tentative knock at the door and Mary peered round it.

'May I come in?'

'You can but I'm not very good company,' he warned her.

'Oh, dear. You didn't quarrel, did you?'

'No. Well, yes, I suppose we did. I don't know. I just can't seem to say the right thing.' His head was aching now and he massaged his forehead.

'Is that tea going begging?'

'Yeah, Dad didn't touch it, but I'll make you some fresh.' He started to get to his feet but Mary waved him back.

'This'll be fine, but – call me a Philistine – I

absolutely can't drink it without sugar.' She picked up the mug and disappeared into the kitchen, emerging shortly after with a spoon in her tea and a couple of the painkilling tablets the hospital had prescribed for Linc. These last she put on the table in front of him.

He looked at them bemusedly.

'Are you a mind-reader or something?'

'No. Simple deduction. A row with Sylvester is enough to make anyone's head ache, even if they hadn't landed on it from a great height just the day before!'

Linc took the tablets gratefully, affecting not to notice Mary's unconscious use of his father's first name.

'Oh, I wish I'd handled it differently. It's the first time in – what? – seventeen years that he's even *tried* to talk about it and I made a real pig's ear of it. It was just so unexpected. I guess yesterday shook him up a bit . . .'

'Mmm. That and something your young lady said to him.' Mary sat down opposite him.

'Josie?'

'Yes. At the hospital.'

'What did she say?' Linc was intrigued.

'I'm afraid you'll have to ask her,' Mary told him. 'She'd come out to use the phone but when she saw him she came straight over and demanded to know what he'd been saying to upset you. It was obviously private so I made myself scarce, but whatever she said, she certainly got under his skin. He was very thoughtful on the way home.'

'Oh, dear. I didn't want to involve her in all this.'

'I think she wants to be involved. And anyway, no

one could ever accuse her of being a fair-weather friend, could they?'

Linc chuckled. 'That's for sure.' He leaned back into the sofa, closing his eyes and wishing that the hospital had given him something a bit stronger and faster-acting.

Mary read his body language. 'Right. Back to bed with you. Pull the curtains and go to sleep. Now!' she added, when Linc merely nodded without moving.

'Yes'm!' he said with a mock salute, but nevertheless obediently got to his feet and headed for his bed.

By the next morning Linc's headache had settled to more bearable proportions. He got up at the usual time and made his way to the Vicarage before anyone was around to try and talk him out of it.

Ruth and Josie were mucking out the horses and both of them told him severely that he should have stayed at home, resting.

'But I wanted to see how Noddy was doing.'

'He's feeling a bit sorry for himself,' Josie reported, coming forward to kiss Linc. 'Just like his master, I expect.'

'Oh, his master's suddenly feeling much better,' he told her, drawing her back for a second kiss. She looked fresh and beautiful with no make-up and her hair in a loose plait, and his spirits had indeed risen a notch or two at the sight of her.

They walked across to Noddy's stable together and Linc went inside. Noddy turned to look at him, trailing a length of hay from his chomping jaws. Linc held out a Polo mint and, after a moment's hesitation, the horse came over to take it from him.

'Oh, poor boy! He *is* stiff, isn't he?' Linc observed. 'And he's a bit sore round his mouth, too. Nikki must have forgotten to put the Vaseline on.'

'Yes, he is a bit, but his eyes are much better. They were really sore yesterday. They just wouldn't stop running.'

'Maybe that's what made him behave so oddly. But I'm not happy with the way he's walking. I think we ought to have the vet out, don't you?'

'He came out yesterday,' Josie told him. 'I didn't tell you because you were supposed to be resting and I thought, knowing you, you'd probably come haring over here if I did. I was going to ring you today to let you know. Anyway, he thinks it's probably just severe bruising and should start to improve over the next few days. If it doesn't, he'll want to X-ray him. He's given us some anti-inflammatories for him, and he's allowed to go out in the paddock and mooch around for a few hours each day. So you see, it's all in hand. We're looking after Noddy; all you've got to do is look after yourself. Which, I must say, you don't seem to be too good at!' she added with a sideways look. 'You know, I wouldn't mind if our life together became just a little less exciting as time went on. That is if you survive long enough to make an honest woman of me!'

Linc laughed. 'It's just an extraordinary set of coincidences. Believe it or not, I've led a fairly humdrum existence up 'til now. By the way, have you said anything to your folks yet?'

Josie shook her head. 'No. We agreed to wait, didn't we? Then of course Abby's illness postponed it, to say nothing of you throwing yourself off your horse . . .'

'If I wasn't so fragile, I'd make you pay for that remark, Miss Hathaway! By the way, how is Abby?'

'Not too bad. She's very weak but improving all the time. The doctor's pleased with her anyway.'

Deciding that no further treats were forthcoming, Noddy turned stiffly round and returned to his haynet. Linc looked at Josie.

'Dad came up to my flat yesterday. He was in a strange mood. Mary tells me you had words with him at the hospital. What exactly did you say?'

Josie coloured a little and looked at her feet. 'It was private, really.'

'Secrets already?' he queried, raising an eyebrow.

'Now that's not fair!' she protested. 'Actually, I think I was probably rather rude but it just made me so cross the way he was treating you. I said . . . well, I said if he keeps on pushing you away and something *does* happen, then he'll be left with nothing; not even memories. I asked him if he thought that was what your mother would've wanted. It was a bit melodramatic, I know, but I was just so mad at him for upsetting you like that. Have I blown it with him, do you think?'

Linc put his arms round her. 'No, I don't think so. He didn't mention it to me. Mary thinks you gave him something to think about.' He dropped a kiss on her soft dark hair. 'Thank you for going into battle for me, but you didn't have to, you know. I'm used to him. He just caught me at a bad moment.'

Linc was in the office after breakfast when Rockley rang.

'Ah, Linc. How are you? Been keeping out of trouble, I hope?'

'Er . . . yes. More or less,' he lied.

'Well, I thought you might like to know that forensics confirmed the tyre on your father's Range-Rover *was* shot out and, what's more, we've found and arrested the culprit.'

The DI sounded pleased with himself. Justifiably, in Linc's opinion.

'And who was it? Jim Pepper?'

'Mr Pepper, yes. But Junior, not Senior. Davy Pepper, his son. We searched the house and came up with two unlicensed firearms, and ballistics found a match with Jim Pepper's .243 rifle and a cartridge case found at the scene. However, the fingerprints on the cartridge were Davy's and he's made a confession of sorts. He claims he was out ferreting and the gun went off by mistake when he tripped.'

Linc snorted. 'Since when did anyone need a rifle to go ferreting? Poaching would be nearer to the mark, if you ask me! He had no right to be on Farthingscourt land anyway, he's been warned off countless times.'

'Well, my guess is that the opportunity presented itself and he took it. He was probably trying to win some brownie points with his father. He seems to be somewhat in awe of him. He was in a dreadful state when we turned up with our warrant. Fingerprinting him wasn't much more than a formality.'

'Poor kid. I don't think he's the brightest,' Linc said. 'What did Pepper Senior have to say?'

'He was spitting! I'd keep out of his way for a day

or two, if I were you. Anyway, I thought you'd like to know.'

'Thanks. I'll tell my father.'

'Right. And you? No more threatening notes or murderous incidents? Do you remember any more about last Saturday?'

'No, no, and no,' Linc replied succinctly.

'Well, you've got my number . . .'

'Yep. Nine, nine, nine.'

'Quite,' Rockley said.

Rather than try to organise a formal get together of the two families, which would have given the game away anyway, Linc and Josie decided to announce their engagement over coffee one morning at Farthingscourt. The younger children were back at school, and as Abby continued to improve, Linc had the idea of inviting Josie's parents and Ruth on a private tour of the house, making sure it would be a day when his father was in.

He suggested it when they rode out the next morning, on Magic and Cromwell.

'They'd love that,' Josie told him. 'But are you going to warn your father in advance – about our engagement, I mean? Just in case he reacts badly.'

'Don't worry, he won't. And besides, it's a done deal. You're not getting out of it now!'

'Well, I know *my* family will be over the moon.'

Linc looked pensive. 'All of them?'

She turned to look at him.

'You're thinking of Abby.'

'Mmm. I'd hate to upset her, just when she's finally getting better.'

'She's growing stronger every day. But I suppose we could wait and tell her later . . .'

Linc shook his head. 'No. If anything, I think we should tell her first. Will I be allowed to come and see her soon, d'you think?'

'I don't see why not. I'll ask when I go in this afternoon.'

'Thanks, I'd like that.'

On Wednesday afternoon, in complete contrast to Linc's last visit, the hospital room was filled with colour and light. Gone was the hushed atmosphere of unspoken dread, the monotonous beeping of the life-support equipment and the 'there but not' presence of the girl in the bed. Now the room was awash with sunlight, flowers and get-well cards. It was also, Linc saw with mild irritation, awash with members of her family. Not only Josie, who he'd arranged to meet, but also her parents and Hannah – who should by rights have been at school. He and Josie really wanted to speak to Abby alone.

Abby herself, though still white and frail, was talking to her mother when Linc let himself in. Her hair had been washed, someone had painted her nails, and around her neck hung a pretty crystal on a chain, which Linc knew had been a present from Ruth who believed in the healing power of such things. Josie looked up with a smile which was half-welcoming, half-apologetic, and Linc moved forward with his own gifts of flowers, a huge card and a book on advanced pony driving.

'Hi, Abby. You don't look as though you need these,' he joked, holding the flowers out. 'I think you've got a better stock here than the florist had!'

Her thin face turned towards him, brows drawn down over her dark-circled eyes as if she couldn't place him for a moment. Then, inexplicably, she drew back against her pillows with a look of panic, reaching out blindly for her mother at her side.

'No!' she whispered. 'Mummy, what's he doing here? Why's he here?'

Rebecca Hathaway's face reflected the shocked bewilderment Linc was feeling.

'It's Linc, darling. He's come to see how you are. He's been worried . . .'

'No!' Abby cut in sharply, grasping Rebecca's hand with her own emaciated one. 'He was there! I saw him. Please don't let him near me! Make him stay away!'

'Abby?' Linc took a step closer, completely mystified by her reaction. 'What's the matter? You remember me, surely?'

His approach seemed to unnerve her still further. Her voice rose higher. 'Stay away! Mummy . . .'

This last was an entreaty, quickly followed by a collapse into tears as she twisted round to bury her face in Rebecca's jumper. Her mother put a comforting arm around Abby's shoulders, looking up at Linc with troubled eyes and a tiny, confused shake of her head. On the other side of the bed Josie reached out to stroke her sister's hand, and Hannah sat with her mouth open, drinking in the scene with round-eyed fascination.

It was Abby's father who got to his feet and faced Linc at the end of the bed.

'I think you'd better go.'

He opened his mouth to protest, but David Hathaway's gaze was uncompromising. Linc gave way. After all, it was Abby's well-being that was important.

'All right,' he said quietly. 'I'll go. I'm sorry I've upset her. I've no idea why.'

He placed the gifts on a vacant chair and turned away, baffled and not a little hurt.

'Linc, wait!' Josie called. 'Let's go and have a cup of coffee.'

As the door shut behind them she caught hold of his hand and pulled him round to face her.

'She's confused, Linc. She doesn't know what she's saying. Don't let it get to you.'

'Did you see your father's face?' he demanded. '*He* believed her.'

'No, he didn't. At least, he won't when he's had time to think about it. They know you. They know you'd never get mixed up in something like that. Why would you? It's crazy! Daddy's reaction was just instinctive.'

Linc stood for a moment trying to marshal his thoughts.

'You'd better go back in. I'll go home and ring you later.'

'You will not!' Josie told him. 'You're coming downstairs for a cup of coffee. I'm not going to let you shut me out, so don't try it.'

They had, in fact, two cups of coffee each in the hospital lounge before Josie would let him go. None of the other Hathaways came down to find them, for which Linc wasn't sure whether to be grateful or sorry. Josie sat close to him with her hand on his thigh, not attempting to cheer him with any further reassurances, just comforting him by her presence. When he left her at the hospital door he put his arms round her and hugged her as if he would never let go.

'Thank you,' he murmured.

'For what?'

'For not asking me – you know . . .'

'I don't have to,' she said simply.

Linc was in his office the following morning when Mary tapped on the door and announced DI Rockley.

'Okay, show him in,' he said, standing up to greet the policeman, who came in, followed closely by DS Manston.

'Linc,' Rockley acknowledged him gravely as they shook hands.

'Have a seat,' Linc offered. Then, with a ghost of a smile, 'I'm afraid there's only one of those leather ones. You'll have to fight over it. There's an ordinary one over there.'

'Oh, no, I'll just pull rank,' Rockley responded. 'But actually I won't sit, thank you. I'm afraid I've got some rather disturbing business to discuss with you. Abby Hathaway has remembered, in part, the events of Friday the twentieth of April. And she has, I'm afraid, made an unexpected allegation.'

Linc's heart sank. 'She thinks I was there,' he stated. 'I know. But I have absolutely no idea why.'

'I'm afraid it's a bit more serious than that,' Rockley informed him. 'She was extremely distressed when I spoke to her but one thing was very clear. According to Abby, it was you who lashed out and hit her, knocking her to the ground. In short, she's accusing you of assault.'

12

Linc looked at the two detectives bleakly.

'So, have you come to arrest me?' he asked Rockley. 'Is that why you brought back up?'

'No, I'm not here to arrest you – though, strictly speaking, I should, given an accusation of this sort. I just want to go over the details of your statement again, to see if you've anything to add. DS Manston is working on another case with me and came along for the ride. Now, we can either do it here or you can come back to the station.'

Linc looked at his watch. 'I can give you twenty-five minutes. Then I'm afraid I've got an appointment. But – I warn you – I shall sit down, even if you don't.'

'Twenty-five minutes should be adequate,' Rockley agreed, sinking into the favoured chair opposite Linc. With a resigned sigh, Manston drew up the remaining seat.

Asking Linc to recount everything he could remember about the night of the attack, the two detectives proceeded to check this against his original statement with meticulous care.

'And you've absolutely no idea what kind of van or lorry it was?'

'No, how could I? It was dark, his lights were blinding me and it was as much as I could do to avoid a head-on collision,' Linc protested. 'You saw what he did to my car.'

'What the wall did to your car,' Manston said softly.

Linc had had enough.

'Look, why the hell would I want to take the tack from the Vicarage? My own saddle and bridle went too, remember? And the business with the bit – it doesn't add up.'

'Insurance? New for old. Or just plain greed. You'd be surprised the lengths some people will go to, to cover their tracks. Speaking generally, of course,' Rockley said. 'I'm not suggesting you did.' He observed Linc long and hard, frowning heavily.

'You've obviously been thinking about this since last night. What have you come up with? Why should Abby be so sure that you were her attacker?'

Linc had been thinking of little else.

'I told you, I've no idea. Unless she wasn't completely unconscious when I found her. I certainly thought she was – I mean, she didn't respond in any way but I suppose if she heard my voice . . .'

'That wouldn't explain why she's convinced that it was you who hit her,' Manston pointed out. 'She says she saw you.'

Linc shook his head. 'I can't explain that. I can only ask you to believe me when I say I didn't do it.'

Rockley favoured him with another long look. 'I

do believe you,' he said eventually. 'But professionally I have to keep an open mind. A judge isn't going to be interested in my hunches, so we have to get to the bottom of this as quickly as possible.'

'Well, it can't be quickly enough for me!' Linc assured him. 'Quite apart from the fact that my girlfriend's family are now looking at me as though I'm a leper! And who can blame them?'

Rockley got to his feet. 'Oh, I don't think it's as bad as all that. I spoke to David and Rebecca this morning and they're confused by this – as we all are – but they'll come round, I'm sure.'

There was a tap on the door and Mary leaned round it.

'Linc, Saul's here. Do you know how long you'll be?'

'Only a minute or two, Mary. I think Inspector Rockley is just leaving?' he replied with a questioning glance towards the officers.

'Yes, we are,' he confirmed. 'We'll be in touch if there are any further developments.'

'In the meantime, don't leave the country?' Linc suggested, without smiling.

DI Rockley held his hand out. 'Goodbye, Mr Tremayne.'

When Linc had finished his business with the millwright, he was about to leave his office when Nikki came in with the news that Jack Reagan was looking for him.

'Can't Geoff deal with it?' Linc asked with a touch of irritation. Amongst other things, Saul had brought unwelcome news of possible subsidence in the bank alongside the weir, and he was anxious to get to the mill and see the damage for himself.

'He particularly asked for you,' Nikki said. 'Something about Jim Pepper, he said, but I'll see if I can find Geoff, if you like.'

'No, that's all right. Where is he now?'

'He's outside in the yard, talking to Crispin. I'll get him, shall I?'

'Okay.' With a sigh, Linc sank back into his chair and closed his eyes. In spite of Saul's worrying report, he couldn't get his mind off the shock of Abby's accusation. How could she even *think* he'd hurt her?

There was a step in the doorway.

'Sir?'

Linc opened his eyes.

Hesitating on the threshold, one weathered hand trying in vain to smooth his rebellious dark curls, the forester looked ill-at-ease.

'Ah, Jack. What can I do for you?'

Before he could answer, Nikki came in. 'Anyone like a coffee? I'm just making one.'

Two affirmatives and she'd gone again, calling the same query to Crispin as she crossed the yard.

'Nikki says it's something about Jim Pepper,' Linc prompted. 'Sit down, man, why don't you? You know his son's been arrested, of course?'

Reagan sat, still looking awkward.

'Yes, sir. That's what started it.'

'Started what?' Linc strove to remain patient.

'Well, he's been making threats again. Phil Sutton told me that Pepper went absolutely ballistic the night Davy was arrested. Apparently he blames you.'

'Well, there's a surprise,' Linc murmured.

'Phil says Pepper was completely out of his skin by nine o'clock and when Pete at The Wheatsheaf suggested he went home to sleep it off, Pepper started throwing his dustbins around. Anyway, last night he was there again and drinking like there was no tomorrow. One or two of the lads escorted him home and apparently he was shouting the whole way about how it was your fault and that he was going to get even with you in a big way. They told me. They thought I should warn you.'

Linc sighed once more. The morning had started badly and was getting steadily worse. This he could definitely do without.

'Has anyone told the police?'

'Er, no. I don't think so,' Reagan said uncomfortably. 'The thing is, Jim Pepper has a nasty way of finding out who says what around here, and he particularly doesn't like snitches. Things happen to people who cross him, if you know what I mean?'

'Yes, I think I probably do,' Linc said heavily. 'Well, thanks for telling me. I'll have a word with Rockley sometime, but not just now – I've had enough of him for one day.'

'Two coffees,' Nikki announced brightly, coming back into the office. As it was a non-public day she was wearing hipster jeans and a figure-hugging lambswool jumper, and Linc noticed with amusement an appreciative gleam in Reagan's eyes as they followed her hip-swaying progress round the desk. Nikki's body language always became a couple of degrees more eloquent whenever there were admiring male eyes around.

Linc accepted his coffee and thanked her, then

turned his attention to the forester once more as she gathered up some empty mugs on her way out.

'I've been meaning to have a word with you about the old oak out on Piecroft Common. You know, the one the children play on. One or two of the branches look pretty rotten. I'd like your opinion. Can we go out and have a look at it – tomorrow afternoon, perhaps? It's no good trying to stop the kids using it, they've been doing it for years and their parents before them. But we might need to take a couple of those branches off. I just hope we don't have to have the whole thing down – they're bound to think we did it to spoil their fun.'

Reagan nodded. 'It does need looking at. What sort of time were you thinking of? I shall be at the timber yard most of the day, so it doesn't matter to me.'

'Okay. How about after lunch, then. Two o'clock? Good. Otherwise we'll just keep putting it off and there'll be an accident and hell to pay!' Linc wrote it in his diary and underlined it, before turning to other matters.

When he'd parted from Reagan, Linc headed for the mill to inspect the subsidence the millwright had mentioned. There was in truth little to see from the bank, and as Saul had said it was difficult to tell how bad the damage was. It had probably been caused by shrinkage now the pond was empty and had begun to dry out. Linc could only hope that there wasn't a cloudburst before they got round to reinforcing it. He had a word with the workmen on the roof and returned to his office for yet another meeting, this time with a picture restorer who was due to start work on cleaning all the pictures in the house. It was a job that would take months and cost tens of thousands of pounds.

By the end of the day he was dog-tired and happy to accept a spur-of-the-moment invitation from Crispin to spend the evening 'vegging out on the sofa' as he put it, with a few beers, a pizza and a DVD. With their atypical upbringing, it was the kind of normal, brotherly behaviour they'd missed out on.

'So where are Nikki and Beverley tonight?' Linc asked as they settled down in front of Crispin's top-of-the-range home cinema complex.

'They've gone to see a play. Beverley thought it would probably be terribly provincial, but she's gone anyway. I hope it isn't for Nikki's sake or she'll never hear the last of it.' Crispin made a face. 'If Bev's pining for the cultural delights of London, why the hell doesn't she go back there and leave us in peace?'

'Poor Cris!' Linc sympathised. 'Is she driving you mad?'

'Well, I wouldn't have minded if she'd only stayed the week, as she originally said, but she's made no mention of leaving, and yesterday, when Nik was telling her about the Georgian Fair, she started talking about what costume she would wear if she went to it! Honestly, I could have strangled Nik! I mean, that's not for another ten days or so.'

'You'll have to set a deadline. Can't you tell her you've got someone else coming to stay and will need her room?'

'She's not an easy person to lie to,' Crispin said. 'I've tried it and she always seems to know. She just keeps asking questions until she trips you up.

Besides, I don't want to upset Nikki at the moment. She's . . . well, she's in what you might call a delicate condition.'

'Pregnant?' Linc exclaimed, and his brother nodded, beaming. 'Well, congratulations! That's brilliant! I bet you're over the moon!'

Crispin nodded again. 'But a little bit apprehensive, too.' He paused, then corrected himself. 'Actually, to tell the truth, I'm absolutely bloody terrified!'

Linc laughed. 'You've got time to get used to the idea. When's the baby due?'

'Oh, not for ages yet. She's only nine weeks.'

'Is she pleased? I mean, was it planned?'

'Well, not as such,' Crispin admitted. 'But – yes, she's very happy.'

'What about the dragon?'

'Hmm. We haven't told her yet. We wanted to wait a week or two. Make sure everything's all right, you know . . .' He snapped open a can of beer. 'So how are things between you and the gorgeous Josie?'

Linc sobered up instantly. 'Aside from the fact that her sister's accused me of assault and her parents don't know whether to talk to me or not, everything's looking rosy.'

Crispin sat up. 'Who's accused you?'

'Abby. I went to see her in hospital and she threw a wobbly. Somehow she's got it into her head that I was there when she was attacked. In fact, she told Rockley that it was me that actually attacked her! She seemed genuinely terrified when she saw me – it was awful! And the look on her father's face . . .'

'But surely *they* don't believe you did it? I mean, they know you. Anyone who knew you would realise you'd never do anything like that.'

'She's their little girl,' Linc reminded him.

'Yes, I know . . . But what about Josie? What does she say?'

'Josie's been wonderful. Rock solid.'

'She's an amazing girl. I'll never forget that night at her place. I mean, you were so out of it, Bro, and then when you started throwing up we were all panicking but she stayed really cool. Even the doctor was impressed. If I were you, I'd marry the woman!'

'You never know, I might even do that,' Linc told him calmly. 'But I don't think her family would be very receptive to the idea just now.' In fact, he and Josie had decided, whilst drinking coffee in the hospital lounge, to put the announcement of their engagement on hold until happier times.

'No, probably not.' Crispin looked thoughtful for a moment, then brightened. 'Right. Enough of the emotional stuff! What we need is a dose of sheer escapism – bring on Rogan the Dark Destroyer!'

Linc cringed. 'You haven't . . .'

'Your face!' Crispin exclaimed, laughing. 'No, I haven't. Actually it's the latest James Bond. Didn't think you'd have seen it.'

Linc relaxed. It could have been a lot worse. 'No, I haven't. Put it on, little brother. Let's escape . . .'

When Linc parked the Land-Rover on the edge of Piecroft Common just after two o'clock the following afternoon, Reagan was nowhere to be seen. His own lateness was due to the fact that he'd mislaid his mobile phone and spent ten fruitless minutes looking for it. Nikki had been in and out of the house and office all morning and it occurred to Linc that she might have picked it up by mistake, but he couldn't find her either.

'Oh, she's having her hair done, I think,' Crispin told him, when asked. 'Don't ask me why, it looked fine to me as it was, but that's women for you.'

Piecroft Common, on the north-eastern edge of the Farthingscourt land, was and always had been a favourite playground for the estate workers' children and those of Farthing St James, the nearest village. Although at the moment the common was deserted, Linc had no doubt that soon after four o'clock this area of sheep-grazed turf and the old oak tree with its two rope swings would once again be host to numerous energetic youngsters.

He wandered along the edge of Piecroft Copse to where the old oak stood. The ground beneath the huge, dipping lower branches was smooth and bare, hollowed by the tread and scuff of countless scores of children's feet. Two short pieces of stick hung suspended from it on separate lengths of knotted rope, trailing their frayed ends on to the earth below. It all looked extremely hazardous but Linc remembered himself and Crispin playing on just such a swing when young and couldn't recall any serious injury having befallen either them or their friends.

At first glance the tree was strong and healthy but looking up into the branches, he could see two dead limbs, devoid of bark and foliage, and one that still supported leaves but was to all intents and purposes just a shell, its core rotted and fallen away. The trunk of the tree was enormous, fully six feet in girth, and bore the penknife scars of centuries of adolescent sweethearts in its rough bark.

Glancing at his watch, Linc turned away from the oak to look back to where he'd parked the Discovery. From this position, the vehicle was just out of sight round the edge of the copse and the common was devoid of life, the sheep at present turned out elsewhere.

'Come on, Jack,' he muttered. Although he could see the potential problems with the oak himself, Reagan was a trained tree surgeon and much better placed to estimate the severity and extent of the damage. It wasn't like him to be late, though. Even if his attitude was sometimes questionable, he was normally reasonably punctual. Surely he hadn't forgotten their arrangement altogether?

'Looks like he's not comin',' a rough voice observed from behind Linc.

He spun round and came face to face with the unshaven, yellow-teethed leer of Jim Pepper. His heart sank. How had this happened?

'Looks like it's just the three of us,' Pepper said. 'Nice and cosy, eh?'

Linc glanced from side to side but saw no one else. As far as he knew, Davy was still in custody.

'Oh, I'm sorry, I haven't introduced my little friend.' Pepper moved his right hand away from the leg of his navy boiler-suit to reveal a hefty, four-foot-long steel bar. 'Actually, it's not so little, is it?' he commented with an unpleasant smile. 'My mistake.'

Linc's spirits dropped even further. He returned Pepper's arrogant stare with an impassive one of his own, trying to concentrate on figuring a way out of the situation, but in reality not getting beyond wondering how fast Jim Pepper could run. He was fairly sure that reasoning with the man was a waste of breath, given his reported state of mind, and although he wasn't much more heavily built than Linc himself, the crowbar put all thoughts of physical contest firmly into the realms of crass stupidity.

'This is crazy,' he said, taking a step back. 'What d'you hope to achieve?'

Pepper stepped forward, lifting the bar menacingly.

'Satisfaction,' he said. Silly question, really.

Linc took another step back

'You're in enough trouble already. Don't make it worse.' He strove to keep his voice steady. 'Put the crowbar down and walk away.'

'Fuck you!' Pepper spat, stepping forward again.

That wasn't promising. Linc stopped moving. He could hardly walk backwards all the way across the common, even supposing Pepper let him. He wondered briefly what would happen if he took a step forward, but wasn't curious enough to find out. *Where the hell was Reagan?*

'What'cha going to do now, Mr *Honourable* Tremayne?' Pepper sneered. 'I don't think your friend Jack is coming. Or *is* he your friend, I wonder?'

Was he indeed? Linc's mind raced, remembering Nikki's report of seeing Pepper and Reagan together outside the pub.

'Maybe I know a thing or two you don't, Mr Public School Education.' Pepper pulled a crumpled sheet of paper from his boiler-suit pocket and waved it in the air. 'I bet you'd like to know what this says, eh? Maybe I'm not the only one who's fuckin' sick of being told what to do by a toff!'

Pepper jabbed the sharp end of the crowbar into the compacted dirt at his feet and Linc couldn't help looking at the three- or four-inch dent it made.

'Saw a man put one of these through his foot, once. Made a hell of a mess.' Pepper lifted the bar and lunged forward without warning, aiming the point at Linc's stomach.

Taken unawares, he stumbled back out of range, cursing himself in the next instant for not having tried to make a grab for the weapon. He steadied himself and waited with his hands spread in front of him, his curiosity over the possible contents of the note sidelined by more urgent concerns.

Pepper laughed derisively but hesitated, and it occurred to Linc that having got this far, the former estate worker quite possibly had little idea what to do next. It was one thing to make threats, but a heavy crowbar wouldn't be the easiest thing to wield successfully, especially when your opponent had the run of an extensive open space. It seemed that Linc's first instinctive reaction might well be the answer, after all. He was no great sprinter but he was confident he could outstrip the older man, especially if he insisted on holding on to the crowbar. If he discarded it, the competition would be closer, but Pepper without a weapon was an entirely more manageable proposition.

Linc took one more careful step backwards, poised in preparation to turn and run, and felt something bump gently against his back. Such was his state of tension that he didn't immediately think of the rope swing, hanging from the branches, but instead jumped in alarm and instinctively turned to meet the new threat. In that instant, Pepper attacked.

Honed by years of riding at speed, Linc's reactions saved him as they had done on the night Abby was assaulted. As Pepper moved forward, swinging his arm back preparatory to launching the crowbar like some overweight javelin, Linc caught sight of the movement on the edge of his vision. Even before his mind consciously had time to readjust he'd grasped the wooden crossbar of the swing and hurled it towards Pepper.

Because of the dragging effect of the rope, the stick didn't fly true but it achieved the desired result. Pepper ducked, and in doing so his aim with the crowbar was spoiled. The point lanced harmlessly past Linc, the whole shaft landing with a muted metallic ringing on the turf behind him.

Linc leaped at Pepper with his head bowed, catching him in the midriff with his shoulder, arms spread like a rugby prop-forward, and carrying him back and down to hit the ground with a satisfying thud. Pepper writhed beneath him, gasping obscenities and doing his utmost to throw him off. He was stronger than Linc had bargained for. In spite of the fact that he'd fallen with one arm twisted behind him, he was still making it very difficult for his captor to hold him down. Linc managed to shift until he was kneeling across Pepper's stomach and using both his hands to keep the man's one free arm pinned to the ground.

'You're breaking my fuckin' arm!' Pepper grated, through clenched teeth, trying to get his feet into play.

'Forgive me if I don't get too upset,' Linc told him. 'If you'd lie still it wouldn't hurt so much.'

Pepper didn't seem inclined to heed this advice, and gave Linc a rough couple of minutes before he finally conceded defeat.

'So what are you gonna do now?' he panted.

Linc honestly didn't know. This was where he needed his mobile phone more than ever. Breathing heavily, he sat on his boiler-suited captive and considered the possibilities.

It didn't take long. There were really only two: remain sitting on Jim Pepper until Reagan or someone else arrived, or let him get up and run the very real risk of having him break loose again. For the time being, he chose the former. For one thing, Reagan was – presumably – on his way; and for another, the longer he kept Pepper with his right arm trapped underneath him, the more useless it would hopefully become. Optimistically, Linc pushed the uncertain elements of his plan to the back of his mind.

'You're breaking my fuckin' arm, you bastard!' Pepper shouted at the top of his voice, his face livid. 'I'll sue you for assault!'

And probably win, Linc thought bitterly, but was saved the necessity of answering by the eminently welcome sound of a shout from the direction of the road.

'Over here!' he shouted in reply, twisting to bring deliverance into view. The voice had been unmistakably female but although he would have preferred Reagan or one of the other estate workers, he wasn't in a position to be too choosy. Now he could see that the person running across the turf towards him was in fact Nikki.

'Linc! Are you okay? What's happened?' she asked, slowing up a little breathlessly. Then, tilting her head to get a good look, 'Is that Jim Pepper?'

'It is,' he confirmed.

'So what happened? He didn't attack you, did he?'

'He tried, but he's not very good at it,' Linc said, deliberately adding a touch of scorn. He'd had a bellyful of the Pepper family.

Pepper's response to this was predictably obscene and Linc bounced on him a time or two.

'Shut up, okay?' he advised. 'I don't suppose you've got your phone on you, have you, Nik?'

'Yep. Well, actually, I've got yours,' she told him apologetically. 'The battery was flat on mine and I must have picked yours up thinking it was Cris's. That's why I came looking for you.' She held it out.

'Er, I think you'll have to do it for me. I'm a little busy.'

'Oh, right. Of course. So, who do you want me to ring?'

'I should think the police would be a good start,' Linc suggested dryly.

'Yeah, I guess so. What, nine, nine, nine? Or do you want your tame copper?'

'Nine, nine, nine will do. You didn't see Reagan anywhere around, did you?'

'Yeah, he's just coming. He called you on the mobile to say he'd got held up but I saw his pick-up coming just before I saw you.' The phone in her hand emitted a tinny voice and she put it to her ear.

314

'Er, police, please. And ambulance?' she queried, looking at Linc, who shook his head. 'No. Just police.' At the operator's prompting she gave details of their whereabouts and described the incident as attempted assault before ringing off, at which point Reagan came jogging up.

Pepper, hearing the forester's footfalls and possibly recognising his imminent arrival as the point of no return, suddenly renewed his attempts to shift Linc's weight and, catching him by surprise, almost succeeded.

'Jack! Get hold of his legs, will you? The bastard's so bloody strong!'

Reagan obliged, and with a further string of abuse, Pepper became still once more.

'What happened?' the forester demanded. 'What's *he* doing here?'

'Waiting for me, apparently. But how he knew . . .' Linc didn't feel it was the moment to voice the most obvious solution to that question. 'What we could do with now is some rope.'

'I've got some in the truck,' Reagan said.

'What about the swing?' Nikki put in. 'If anyone's got a knife.'

'I have.' The forester put his hand in his pocket.

'Why cut it down?' Linc enquired. 'It's long enough. Why don't we just tie his hands and leave him attached? Save us holding on to him.'

Pepper wasn't inclined to fall in with this plan but with the help of the burly Reagan, Linc managed to subdue his struggles long enough to bind him securely with the much-knotted but very tough blue nylon rope that formed the swing.

When they finally stood back to survey their

handiwork, Jim Pepper spat on the dirt at their feet and glared at Reagan.

'I'll get you, you double-crossing bastard!' he swore. 'Nobody sets me up and gets away with it!'

Linc glanced across at Reagan who shook his head and lifted his hands in apparent bewilderment.

'I don't know what he's talking about. I didn't set him up!'

Linc stifled his doubts. 'It's okay, ignore him. He's just trying to make trouble. Come away.'

Nikki touched his arm.

'Linc, you might want to see this,' she said quietly. 'I found it on the ground, just over there.' She had in her hand the piece of paper with which Pepper had taunted Linc earlier.

He took it and walked out from the shade of the tree into the sunlight, reading as he went. Behind him, the bound man laughed unpleasantly and called out something. Linc took no notice.

The note had been generated on a computer and printed on a sheet of A4 paper, of which the bottom half had then been torn off. It was not addressed to anyone, and said simply:

Friday 2 p.m. The old oak tree, Piecroft Common.
Do us both a favour, teach the bastard a lesson.
JR.

Linc frowned and read it through again. He looked up at Nikki and then at the forester, who was watching him intently.

'What? What does it say?' he asked.

Wordlessly, Linc handed it over and observed the

play of emotions on the other man's face as he took in the meaning of the words.

Reagan's dark brows dropped and his hand began to shake as he looked up at Linc.

'*Oh, no!*' he said with great emphasis. 'No. You're not putting this on me! I had nothing to do with it! There could be any number of people with those initials.'

'But not many who knew of our arrangement,' Linc pointed out. 'Unless you told anyone . . .'

'No!' Reagan declared, then perhaps realising that he was digging himself deeper, 'I mean, I don't know. I might have done – I don't remember. But I've never seen *this* before.'

Linc held out his hand for the note, and to his credit Reagan passed it over with only a moment's hesitation.

'What are you going to do with it?'

'I'm not sure,' he said, folding it and slipping it into the pocket of his jeans. 'I need time to think.'

'There's nothing to think about. I didn't write that!' the forester protested, black eyes flashing. 'Why would I?'

Only an inch or so taller but very much heavier, he gave the impression of towering over Linc, who could only be glad – if it *had* been a collaboration – that Reagan hadn't been there to back Pepper up.

'Jack, calm down. I haven't accused you of anything yet. Though it would help if I knew why you weren't here at two.'

'Some bastard let my tyres down; all four of them. It took me ages to pump them up. I've only got a foot pump at home.'

'So you were at home with Lynne?'

'Yes. No, Lynne was out or I'd have borrowed her car . . .' He tailed off, sounding defeated. 'You don't believe me, do you?'

'Linc, the police are here.' Nikki saved him the necessity of answering, which was just as well because he wasn't sure what to say. Reagan's excuse sounded slightly implausible but maybe that was in his favour. Surely if he'd planned the whole thing, he'd have sorted out a more solid alibi.

'Are you going to tell them?' Reagan asked urgently as they watched the approach of the police Range-Rover over the bumpy turf.

Linc looked at his anxious face and shrugged. 'Pepper will if I don't,' he said. 'Sorry, Jack.'

The Range-Rover pulled up beside them and two uniformed officers got out: one wiry and dark; one young, sturdy and blond. They looked vaguely familiar to Linc but he didn't know whether to be glad or sorry that it wasn't Manston or Rockley.

'Well, well. Someone's been busy,' one of them commented, gesturing towards the tree and its attached prisoner. 'Doing our job for us!'

'Well, I didn't think he'd wait around for you to arrive,' Linc explained. 'Not that you've been long, as it happens.'

'We were just down the road in St Thomas,' the policeman said, leaving the village prefix off, as many of the locals did. 'Mr Tremayne, isn't it? Constable Diller – we have met.'

'Ah, yes. The fire at South Lodge Farm,' Linc said, recognition dawning. 'In that case, you'll remember Jim Pepper, too.'

'Indeed I do,' Diller said. 'We've heard quite a bit about Mr Pepper lately, from one source or

318

another. What's he been up to this time? The girls on the desk mentioned attempted assault . . .'

Linc outlined what had happened, including the discovery of the note, which he produced for their perusal.

Diller read it, pursing his lips. 'JR. Any idea who JR might be?'

'Those are my initials, but I didn't send it!' Reagan, who had been standing listening, obviously couldn't stand the tension a moment longer.

Diller raised an eyebrow in his direction then turned his attention back to Linc. 'Who else knew of your meeting with Mr Reagan this afternoon?' he enquired.

'I don't think I actually mentioned it to anyone but I did put it in the diary, so anyone with access to the office could have known. Mary – my secretary, my father, my brother Crispin, Nikki here, her mother, Geoff Sykes was in to see me earlier . . . A number of people. The door isn't locked on non-public days and the diary's usually open on the desk. But I can't see why any of them would have told anyone else about it.'

'And Mr Reagan was late arriving for his meeting with you?'

'Someone let down my tyres!' Reagan half-shouted. 'For God's sake, can't you see, I'm being set up?'

'And who do you think would want to set you up, sir?' Diller responded calmly.

'Well . . . *I* don't know!'

The forester looked desperate, and Linc began to feel sorry for him.

'Constable, I don't know what's going on here

but I'm prepared to give Jack the benefit of the doubt for the time being. As I told you, he helped me deal with Pepper when he did get here.'

Diller looked sceptical. 'Well, he couldn't do much else, with the young lady here as a witness, could he?'

Reagan stepped forward angrily at this and Linc put out a hand to stop him.

'For goodness' sake, man! Don't make things worse.'

Constable Diller gave Reagan a thoughtful look and turned to Nikki. 'And you, young lady . . .' He consulted his notes. 'Mrs Tremayne. You were first on the scene. Did you see anyone else at all when you arrived? Anyone on the road? You came from . . .?'

'From St James,' Nikki told him. 'I was having my hair done and I came back this way to give Linc his mobile, which I'd picked up by mistake.'

'And how did *you* know where to find him?'

'From the diary in the office, like Linc said. It's not a private one.'

'I see. Well, it's just possible that whoever wrote this note – feeling as he obviously does about Mr Tremayne – might have come to see the results of his mischief-making. You know, the way arsonists like to stay and watch the fire.'

'Well, I don't *remember* having seen anybody,' she said, frowning. 'I don't think I even passed a car on the road – it's so narrow you have to pull in and I think I'd remember that.'

'Hey! What about me?' Pepper had evidently begun to think that even police custody was preferable to remaining tied to a tree.

'Read him his rights and cuff him,' Diller said to his silent, blond sidekick.

'You gonna believe everything that ponced-up bastard tells you?' Pepper demanded. 'Just because his father owns half the fuckin' county?'

'Are you suggesting that forensics won't find your prints all over that crowbar?' Diller asked. Then, when Pepper's only answer was another bout of swearing, 'No, I thought not.'

'I saw someone,' Reagan interjected suddenly. 'Yeah, I remember now. When I got out of the truck I could have sworn there was someone in the trees at the edge of the copse. It was just like a quick movement, but when I looked again I couldn't see anything. I'd forgotten about it with all this going on.'

The constable pushed his peaked cap back and scratched his head. His expression was openly disbelieving but he said patiently, 'Well, I suppose we'd better take a statement from you too, Mr Reagan. Exactly where did you think you saw this . . . person?'

By the time Diller and his quiet colleague had finished, Linc had had more than enough of the affair. Pepper was cut free of the rope swing and pushed, protesting, into the police Range-Rover, provisional statements had been taken and signed and eventually the two officers and their prisoner had departed across the common to the road.

Linc looked at Reagan, who was gazing bitterly after the disappearing vehicle.

'Well, Jack?' he said after a moment. 'What about this bloody tree?'

★

Having got his phone back from Nikki, Linc found a number of messages on it, including one from Nina Barclay, asking if he was still okay to ride Hobo on Sunday, and one from Barney Weston, inviting Linc to accompany him to the track again and updating him on the progress of his young greyhound. There was also one from Josie, saying that Sandy had taken delivery of the replacement tack they had all been waiting for and would be at the Vicarage that evening to fit it, if that was convenient.

Returning the calls, Linc confirmed his availability to ride Hobo, ignoring the little voice inside that was telling him that he must be running close to the edge of his father's tolerance where days off were concerned. Josie's phone was switched off but rather than ring the house and risk one of the others answering, he left a message to say he'd certainly be at the stables for Noddy's saddle-fitting.

In the event, he arrived at the Vicarage before Sandy did, and found Hannah sitting in the tackroom eating a packet of crisps. Linc was surprised. She wasn't in the habit of frequenting the stables for fear of being roped into helping out.

'Hello. Where is everybody?'

'They're washing up and stuff,' she told him between munches. 'Sandy's coming about half-past.'

Linc looked at his watch – twenty-past seven – and decided to give Noddy a brush over whilst he waited. He collected his grooming kit and a head-collar and went along to the brown horse's box, followed closely by Hannah who seemed disposed to be chatty.

Noddy was engrossed in a full haynet but turned his head enquiringly as Linc went in. He was still moving stiffly after his fall the previous weekend and Linc was beginning to think that his injuries would have to be investigated further.

As he set to work on Noddy's gleaming coat, Hannah kept up a rather one-sided conversation about anything and everything that came into her busy head. She didn't seem to require any more than sporadic input from Linc and he was listening with no more than half an ear to her disconcertingly sharp observations about the world and people around her when mention of Josie's name made him snap to attention.

'*What* did you say?' he asked sharply.

'They say Abby can come home soon. They just want to do a few more tests.'

'No, after that . . .'

'Oh. Well, Daddy says it's a shame Josie's got so fond of you because it'll upset Abby if she keeps bumping into you, but they can't really ask you to take Noddy away because of upsetting Josie.' She regarded Linc with her astute brown eyes, probing for a reaction. Apparently it didn't come up to her expectations and she tried again. 'Personally, I think Abby's a drama queen and should just get over it.'

Linc frowned at her. 'That's a bit hard, don't you think?'

'Well, it's obvious it wasn't you who hit her,' she said. 'Anyone can see that.'

'Thanks.'

'Well, you wouldn't need to break in, would you? You've got a key,' Hannah reasoned, brutally frank as always.

Linc hid a smile. 'Your sister isn't thinking straight at the moment. It's not really surprising after all she's been through, is it?'

'Hannah!' The shout came from the direction of the house, and as Hannah turned, Linc looked over her shoulder and could see Ruth coming across the yard. 'Where did you get to, you lazy little cow? One sight of the washing-up cloth and we don't see you for dust!'

'I was talking to Linc,' Hannah said defensively.

'Consorting with the enemy,' Linc put in with a touch of bitterness.

'Oh, Linc, that's not true!' Ruth said reproachfully. 'No one believes that.'

'Daddy does,' Hannah announced.

'No, he doesn't!' her sister exclaimed. 'And neither does Mum. Don't listen to her, Linc. She's just a troublemaker! And it's high time she grew up and learned to keep her mouth shut!'

He was inclined to agree but the fact remained that Hannah, for all her faults, was invariably truthful, and so he had to believe what she said she'd heard.

The arrival of Sandy's lorry precluded further conversation. As the engine noise died away, he opened the driver's door and jumped out, preceded by Tiger, who homed in on Linc with squeaks of joy, his stumpy tail wagging furiously.

'Ah, you've got a friend for life there!' Sandy called out, and Linc pulled his foot out from beneath the muscly rump and wished the thought gave him more pleasure.

'Ruthie m'darlin',' Sandy greeted her, putting

his arm round her shoulders and planting a kiss on her cheek. 'How are you?'

'A bit heavy-eyed after last night, to tell the truth. We went clubbing and danced the night away,' she added for Linc's benefit. 'I haven't done that for absolutely ages!'

'It was more exercise than *I've* had in years!' Sandy agreed, laughing. 'But it was good to see you let your hair down.'

They fitted Magic for a saddle first, trying three before Ruth was happy with one, and chatting all the while about Linc's burgeoning eventing career. They had just put a headcollar on Cromwell when Josie finally appeared.

She greeted Linc with a smile and a kiss on the cheek as he stood holding the grey horse, but he thought he detected a slight reserve and signs of strain around her eyes. His heart sank.

Sandy said 'Hi' to her and took up the conversation where he'd left off. 'Yeah, I don't think you can really reach the top unless you're a kid with stinking rich parents or you find yourself a sponsor,' he said, agreeing with a remark Linc had made. 'I'd offer myself but I don't think my level of sponsorship would benefit you much! I might run to the odd sack of horse feed and a set of shoes, but that's about it! Are you going to hop up and try it, missus?' He looked at Josie.

'I thought Noddy looked a bit sorry for himself this morning,' she said, accepting Linc's offer of a leg up on to Cromwell's back. 'What are you going to do about his saddle?'

Linc shook his head. 'We'll have to leave it, I think. I don't really want to sit on him if he's uncomfortable and we can't fit the saddle properly without.'

'No problem, I'll hang on to the two I brought for him. I won't have any trouble selling the one you don't want.' Sandy moved the grey horse's mane to get a clear view down the front of the saddle, checking for a good clearance of the spine. 'How does it feel to you?' he asked, looking up at Josie.

She shifted her weight, settling deeper into the soft leather seat. 'Can you lead him forward, Linc?'

After a circuit of the yard, she nodded to Sandy. 'That's fine. Very comfortable. What do *you* think?'

'It's a very good fit, considering his build. Isn't your mum coming down?'

'No. She's busy. Said she's happy to leave it to me.'

It seemed to Linc that her answer was just a little too casual and she was careful not to meet his eyes, but it might have been his imagination.

When Sandy had gone, Linc offered to help Josie fill the haynets for the night and Ruth tactfully went up to the house, leaving the two of them alone. Hannah was nowhere to be seen – for which he couldn't help but be thankful.

Josie said little while they stuffed the nets with sweet-smelling hay but afterwards, straightening up and picking bits off her jumper, she asked Linc if he wanted to come up to the house for a cup of coffee.

'Er . . . no, I think I'd better be getting back.'

She paused, looking searchingly at him. 'Not because of Mum and Dad?'

Linc couldn't deny it. 'I don't blame them, but I don't want to make things awkward.'

'Linc, they don't really think you did it, you

know. What Dad said at the hospital – he was just protecting Abby.'

'I know he was, but I can't forget the look on his face . . .'

Josie put her arms round his neck and leaned forward until their foreheads were touching. 'Oh, Linc, I'm so sorry. And we were so happy . . .'

Her use of the past tense didn't escape him but he didn't comment on it.

'I just wish I could figure out why she said it,' he murmured after a moment. 'What are we missing? Why was she so sure?'

Josie shook her head slightly, then lifted her chin to kiss him.

Linc responded with sudden, leaping passion and when they finally drew apart, gazed deep into her eyes and said, 'Come home with me?'

There was an infinitesimal withdrawal and Josie's eyes fell. 'Linc . . .'

Immediately he released her and stood back.

'No, it's all right. I understand. I've got things to do anyway.'

'It's just . . . the way things are . . .'

'It's all right,' he repeated. 'I'll give you a ring in a day or two.'

He turned away and she didn't call him back.

13

That Saturday was Linc's thirtieth birthday.

Having spent the last few years away from home, he'd grown used to birthdays coming and going with the minimum of fuss and, somewhat naïvely, had hoped the same would be true of this one.

Being a public day at Farthingscourt, it was business as usual, although Linc knew his father had a long-standing engagement that meant being in London for the best part of the weekend. So it was that when he called in to the library for what had become their habitual morning meeting, it was more in anticipation of wishing his father a safe journey than in any expectation of a birthday surprise.

'Hear you had a turn up with Pepper yesterday,' the Viscount began as Linc settled himself into the wingchair opposite his desk. 'Have we seen the last of him now, d'you think?'

'For a while, I should imagine. Caught in the act like that.'

His father grunted. 'Didn't hurt you, did he?'

'No, but not from lack of trying. I'm just glad he chose a crowbar for a weapon and not a hatchet! I don't think he thought it out very carefully.'

'And Reagan? What do you make of that?'

Linc hesitated. 'I'm not sure. If he *was* behind it, it was very clumsily done. But it seemed to me he was completely bewildered by the whole thing. After the police had gone and we could actually get on with looking at the tree, he went from being angry to almost kind of dazed, as if he couldn't quite get his head round it. He didn't try and talk his way out of it or anything.'

'But they were his initials on the note.'

'Yeah, but that's what I mean by clumsy. After all, with Pepper in the frame of mind he was, a simple time and place would have sufficed, I would have thought. He didn't really need to take the chance of putting what was to all intents and purposes his name to it.'

'But why would anyone try and set him up like that?'

'I wish I knew,' Linc said, sighing. 'But I can't think Jim Pepper would've bothered to make it up himself.'

'No.' The Viscount was thoughtful for a moment, then shook his head as if to clear it. 'Anyway, other business. If I remember rightly, it's your birthday today.'

Linc grimaced. 'The big three-oh. I'd hoped nobody would remember.'

'Well, as a matter of fact, it was Mary who reminded me,' his father admitted. 'But, whatever . . . I decided that rather than buy you some expensive toy that you probably didn't want, I would give

329

you something a bit more meaningful, so I thought you should have this.' He opened his desk drawer and removed a black drawstring pouch which he passed to Linc. 'It's been in the bank with the other things. It's up to you what you do with it – wear it or put it back – but by tradition it should belong to the heir.'

Linc took the soft leather bag and pulled the top apart. Tipping it, a heavy gold ring fell out on to his palm, and as he dropped the pouch and turned the ring over he could see the elaborately chased design with the huge emerald at its centre. It was the ring that featured in so many of the portraits in the Long Gallery; most notably that of St John Tremayne, the family black sheep.

'Wow!' Linc breathed, almost reverently. 'That's amazing! Thank you. Thank you so much. I didn't expect anything like this.'

His father looked half-embarrassed. 'Well, it's yours, for God's sake! Should have had it before now, by rights, but you weren't here, were you?'

Linc suppressed a wry smile. Since his uncharacteristic show of emotion after Linc's accident, his father had been more distant than ever. This brusque retort was more like the man he knew.

'Well, thank you anyway. It's nice to have. I wasn't even sure it was still in the family.'

Lord Tremayne grunted. 'Even that wastrel St John knew better than to gamble away the Farthingscourt Emerald.'

'I'll look even more like him if I start wearing this. Perhaps I should get my ear pierced so I can wear the earring, too . . .' he mused.

His father treated him to a withering look but

330

didn't rise to the bait. 'So, what are you doing with yourself today – to celebrate, I mean? Taking that girl of yours somewhere?'

'Actually, Crispin and Nikki have invited us over for a meal,' he said. Crispin had, in fact, only just rung with the offer and he hadn't yet had a chance to put it to Josie. After last night, he wasn't sure how she'd react, and the thought was deeply unsettling. How had things become such a mess?

'That'll be nice. Young Nikki's a pretty good cook. But we'll have a proper family dinner party when I get back. I'd like to see Josie again.'

'Sure,' Linc agreed. He hadn't told his father about Abby's accusations and the present sensitive nature of his relationship with Josie. Time enough if anything came of it, God forbid.

Crispin and Nikki's dinner party was a great success. When Linc rang Josie to relay the invitation she accepted instantly, showing none of the previous night's indecision, but scolded him unmercifully for not warning her of his birthday in advance.

'What the hell am I going to get you?' she wanted to know.

'You don't have to get me anything,' he said in the age-old and totally unrealistic way that people have in such situations. 'Anyway, how was I supposed to warn you? I could hardly just come out with it in conversation. "Oh, by the way, I think you should know it's my birthday next week." It's not exactly subtle!'

'Well, *I* would have found a way,' she maintained, 'if it was *my* birthday – which, while we're on the subject, is on December the twenty-eighth.'

In spite of her complaints, she turned up at North Lodge Cottage at the appointed time with a large, square silver-papered box under her arm. Crispin sent her through to the sitting room, where Linc was already drinking a beer and playing with the laptop computer which had been his brother's and Nikki's present to him, and went to fetch her a glass of wine.

Putting aside his new toy, Linc got up to meet her, said 'Hi', and kissed her on the cheek.

She responded in kind and then held out the package. 'This is for you. Many happies, and don't you dare say "you shouldn't have"!'

'Thank you.' He took it meekly, but his eyes returned to her face, asking softly, 'Are we all right? Last night, I wasn't sure . . .'

She nodded. 'We're fine. It's just, all this stuff going on . . . I feel like I'm being pulled in all directions. But I lay awake a long time last night, thinking, and I know now that whatever happens I'm with you. Nothing else feels right. So,' she added briskly, 'you're stuck with me, buster! Now open the bloody present, will you!'

The box, when he finally fought his way through the paper and sticky tape, contained a new crash hat.

'I thought you might need that if you're riding Hobo tomorrow,' Josie told him. 'Since your old one is completely shattered!'

'God! I hadn't thought of that. Yes, thank you very much.' Not having ridden Noddy all week, Linc had forgotten that – designed to absorb and disperse the shock from a fall such as he had suffered – his helmet would almost certainly need replacing.

'It's the same size and make as your old one, so it should fit. Sorry it's not more exciting but I knew you'd need one.'

'No, it's brilliant. I'd completely forgotten. Thanks.'

After an initial protest for form's sake, Nikki gladly accepted Josie's offer of help in the kitchen, and it was decided by mutual consent that Linc and Crispin would go for a walk while the girls put the finishing touches to the meal.

Although the day had been fine and fairly bright, a chilly east wind had sprung up as the sun started to sink and now the sky threatened rain. Crispin hesitated at the door, looking at his brother's canvas jacket.

'That might be the height of fashion, Bro, but it doesn't look very weatherproof. Do you want to borrow a proper coat?' He indicated a miscellaneous collection of garments that hung on a row of hooks in the porch.

'Well, I didn't know I was going to be trudging round the countryside in the dark, did I?' Linc pointed out. 'Thanks. I will borrow something, if I may. Actually, that's the downside of going out with a model. You've got a lot to live up to.'

'You know Josie's not like that,' Crispin said, holding out an old and much-worn waxed jacket. 'Here, take this, we call it our utility coat. It's nobody's in particular and available for the use of the community – well, within reason anyway!'

They walked for the best part of an hour through the gathering dusk, Linc enjoying the company of his younger brother more than he could ever remember. He supposed it was because they were both more mature and shedding all the hang-ups of sibling rivalry, but whatever the reason they returned to the cottage in light-hearted mood. The wind had become unseasonably cold as darkness fell and Linc slid his hands into the pockets of the borrowed coat amongst the jumble of bits and pieces they already contained. He tried not to analyse these, but the left pocket was being weighed down by what felt like a plastic tub, and by the time they got back to the house curiosity had got the better of him and in the light of the porch he investigated it.

It turned out to be a pot of Vaseline, exactly like the one he'd bought to stop the pink skin around Noddy's mouth chapping. In fact, judging by the horse hairs stuck to a smear of grease on the outside of the pot, it *was* his. By the weight of it, there was a fair amount left, so he showed Crispin.

'Somebody's pilfered my Vaseline,' he joked. 'I'd better have it back because I'm riding Nina's horse tomorrow, and she has been known to forget the odd item of kit!'

Crispin nodded. 'Yeah, take it. I can't remember who was wearing that coat last Saturday. Must have been either Beverley or Niks. Let's blame Beverley, shall we?'

'So, where is Mother-in-law this evening?' Linc asked. 'Have you sent her out for the evening, or is she gagged and bound in one of the rooms upstairs?'

'Don't tempt me,' Crispin said, laughing. 'Actually, she's gone back to Surrey because her house-sitter couldn't stay another week. But,' he said, holding up a hand, 'before you cheer, she's coming back in time for the fair.'

The inner door opened and Nikki peered round it.

'Oh, there you are! When I said go for a walk, I didn't mean to Shaftesbury and back! You've got two minutes flat to go to the loo, wash your hands and be sitting at the table.'

They made it, in due course, with just seconds to spare, arriving at the table almost at the same time as the prawn cocktails that formed the first course.

Josie and Nikki followed them in, bearing two of these apiece and laughing about something that one of them had said. They were both flushed from the heat of the kitchen and appeared to have struck up a friendship.

'Well, no need to feel guilty about leaving you two to do all the work,' Crispin commented. 'You've obviously been having a ball out there.'

'Just as if you were feeling guilty anyway!' Nikki scoffed, putting a cocktail down in front of her husband. 'I bet you didn't even spare a thought for us. Well, as a matter of fact, we *have* had fun, talking about girl stuff. Comparing notes, you might say.' This last was said with a sideways glance and a wink at Josie, who smiled in return.

'Oh, God! Now I'm feeling really nervous!' Crispin said. 'Comparing notes? On what?'

'Oh, yes, we're really going to tell you. Get on with your starter.'

Linc raised an eyebrow at Josie, who shook her head.

'No. Absolutely not. It's girls' stuff. We don't ask what you guys talk about. By the way, have you seen the kittens? Nikki's going to let me have one when they're ready to go. I thought Abby might like it.'

'You mean, you want one and that's a convenient excuse,' Linc teased. Crispin had showed him the cardboard box that was home to their tabby cat and her six young kittens when he'd first arrived.

The meal was excellent, the conversation non-stop, and by midnight, when Linc reluctantly broke the party up by reminding the others that he had to be up early to ride Hobo at the one-day event, they decided they'd all attend the horse trials to cheer him on.

With the possible exception of Crispin, who was neither pregnant nor driving nor due to ride the following day, wine had been drunk only in moderation, and Linc had no qualms about seeing Josie set off for home in the E-type. Crispin and Nikki thoughtfully waved goodbye from the doorway of the cottage, leaving Linc to walk her to her car.

'Do you know . . .' Josie said, as they reached the gate . . . 'Nikki asked me how long I'd known you, and I realised it's only been six weeks. It feels like ages.'

'I'm not quite sure how to take that,' he remarked, stopping and turning to face her.

She laughed. 'No, it's just that so much has happened.'

'You didn't tell her about the engagement?'

'Of course not. We agreed, didn't we?'

'Mmm. Did I ever tell you – you look beautiful in the moonlight?'

'There is no moon,' Josie pointed out.

'Oh, God! Where's your sense of romance, Jo Jo? What am I supposed to say, you little wretch? You look beautiful under a cloudy sky with spits of drizzle in the wind? Come here . . .'

It was several minutes before the growl of the sports car's engine split the night air.

Hobo looked fit and ready for anything when Linc joined him on the showground the next morning. Nina's groom had saddled him and was gently warming him up under his owner's watchful eye.

'You'll soon be able to ride him again yourself,' Linc commented, noticing that her arm was no longer in plaster. He pulled on his new crash hat, wincing as it pressed on the remains of his bruises, and adjusted the strap under his chin.

'Mmm. I've ridden him at home, but this is a bit different.'

'Not that I'm anxious to lose the ride, especially with Noddy sidelined for the foreseeable, but I thought you must be itching to get back on.'

'Mmm,' she said again, looking pensive. 'Actually, I'd be quite happy for you to go on riding him, if you'd like to. I think he goes much better for you. You give him confidence.'

'Oh, I think that's just practice. Once you get into the swing of it again, you'll be all right.'

Nina bit her lip and then took a deep breath. 'No. I've been thinking about it for quite a while, and I'd like you to ride him for me. If you want to, that is. To be honest, I'm not really brave enough. I prefer the behind the scenes stuff, getting him fit and schooling him, maybe the odd local hunter trial. But with something like this, I find watching you take him round is all the excitement I need!'

'Well, I'd love to, of course. He's a super horse, but I want you to promise that if you ever change your mind, you won't hesitate to tell me – no matter what stage of his career we've reached.'

'That wouldn't be very fair!' she protested.

'Promise?' Linc was adamant.

She nodded. 'Okay, I promise. But it won't happen.'

Whether Linc's resulting high spirits lifted Hobo's performance or not it was impossible to tell, but the horse positively sparkled in his dressage test, and as they changed his tack for the showjumping it was with the knowledge that at this early stage he led the field by a comfortable margin.

With a neat clear round in the showjumping behind him and the start of the cross-country delayed by a fault in the public address system, Linc was free to wander round the trade stands with his brother and the two girls, both of whom appeared to be in high spirits. Josie was, as usual, effortlessly elegant, in denim and cashmere topped off by a linen hat that stopped her long hair whipping about in the breeze. Nikki was equally chic, and side by side, one dark and one blonde, they turned quite a few heads.

Crispin was experimenting with a new digital camera and was consequently taking pictures of anything vaguely photogenic – and quite a lot that wasn't, as far as Linc could see – and as a result, kept getting left behind. Linc and the girls browsed the stalls, collecting oddments that took their fancy and, in a charity tombola, Linc won a huge teddy bear that he presented to Josie with a flourish.

Nikki leaned close and whispered something in Josie's ear. It made her laugh, and as they moved on, Linc thought contentedly that the girls' growing friendship boded well for the future.

Crispin had crouched down, taking a picture of a small child who held the lead of a huge hairy dog, and Linc had paused to watch, leaving the girls to go on ahead, when a gust of wind lifted the brim of Josie's hat, snatching it from her head and tossing it on the rough grass between the two nearest stands. As she turned to retrieve it, three things happened almost simultaneously: the long-silent loudspeaker system whined and popped as it finally came to life, a rousing cheer went up from a group of youngsters outside the beer tent across the way and, just yards away from Josie's stooping form, the driver of an idling Land-Rover suddenly put it into reverse.

Bending over to pick up the hat, Josie's hair had fallen forward like a curtain, obscuring her vision, and with a stab of panic Linc realised she was completely unaware of the danger.

'Josie, look out!'

Linc lunged forward as, all around, people appeared rooted to the spot. Time seemed to slow as Josie, hearing his shout, looked up at him instead of at the vehicle.

He hit the back of the Land-Rover with both fists and one hip, in the same instant yelling at the driver to stop. The response was immediate. Even as he rebounded from the moving vehicle, staggering to remain upright, its driver stamped on the brakes, finally averting the tragedy.

Suddenly it seemed as though the rest of the world came back to life. There was a collective gasp, somebody screamed and several people swore out loud. There was even, as Linc turned to find Josie, a smattering of applause.

She was standing upright now, still clutching her hat and the soft toy, ashen-faced with shock as she stared at the vehicle that had almost knocked her down. Putting his hands on her shoulders, Linc gave her a gentle shake.

'Josie! Look at me, sweetheart! It's all right now,' he said with quiet urgency.

With an effort she transferred her gaze to his face. She blinked, as if to restore focus, and said, 'What happened?'

Linc heaved a sigh, pulling her into a hug, teddy bear and all. 'Nothing, thank God!' he said. 'Nothing.'

The Land-Rover's engine died away, the driver's door opened and a young man sprang out.

'What the fuck's going on?' he demanded as he came forward, fright breeding aggression. Then, seeing Linc comforting Josie, 'She all right?'

'No, she's not all right, you imbecile!' Linc responded furiously. 'What the bloody hell did you think you were doing?'

'I never saw her!' the youngster protested defensively. Twenty-ish and wearing denim jeans, a tee-shirt and a padded bodywarmer, he had a shaved head and a loveheart tattooed on his bicep.

'You didn't see her because you were on the phone,' someone from the gathering crowd called out.

Linc looked at the driver. 'Is that true?'

Something in his low-voiced inquiry seemed to put the wind up the lad, because he backed off a step or two.

'Is that true?' Linc asked again, more forcefully.

The young man took three quick steps, jumped

back behind the wheel and slammed the door.

Linc would have followed him, but Josie dragged on his arm and suddenly Crispin was there, in front of him.

'Leave it, Linc! He's not worth it.'

Uncharacteristically angry, it took a moment or two for Linc to simmer down. He watched the Land-Rover pull away then said, 'Yeah, you're right. Sorry, Bro.'

The drama over, most of the crowd began to drift away, one or two congratulating him as they passed.

Linc turned back to Josie.

Nikki was with her now. 'Are you okay?' she asked him. 'I think you dented his Land-Rover.'

'I didn't feel a thing,' he said truthfully. 'But I'd like to have dented him! Are you all right, Jo Jo?'

She nodded, her colour back to normal. 'Thanks to you. I feel so stupid, but I was looking the other way and honestly didn't hear it.'

'It was the loudspeaker,' Nikki agreed. 'I didn't either.'

'Nor me,' Crispin put in. 'Good job Linc was on hand to do his heroic bit.'

'Yeah, that's me,' he agreed. 'I'll do anything to impress a crowd.'

Above their heads the public address system crackled into life again.

'Ladies and gentlemen, once again we apologise for the delay. The cross-country phase of the competition will get underway in ten minutes. Will the first competitors please report to the stewards at the start? Thank you.'

'Looks like I'd better go and find my mount,' Linc observed.

341

Leaving the three of them to walk out on to the cross-country course to find a good vantage point, he hurried back in the direction of Nina Barclay's horsebox, only to be accosted on the way by Sandy.

'Hi. I didn't know you were here,' Linc said, not slowing but nevertheless looking round nervously for Tiger's brindle form.

'He's shut in the lorry,' Sandy informed him, rightly interpreting his actions. 'Yeah, I've got a pitch up the other end. All above board and legal, this time.'

'Glad to hear it. Look, I can't stop now. I've got to warm Hobo up for the cross-country . . .'

'Oh, okay. Well, can you come and see me at the unit sometime? Soon. You see, I think I might have found a sponsor for you.'

That stopped him.

'You what?' Linc asked, slightly breathlessly.

'I think I've found you a sponsor,' Sandy repeated, patently pleased with himself.

'Wow! Who?'

'Not now. You're in a hurry, remember? And I've left a mate looking after the stand. Can you come to the unit – say, tomorrow? About eleven?'

Linc was desperate to know more, but at that moment he was hailed from across the showground and looked round to see Nina leading Hobo towards him.

'Yes, okay. Tomorrow, eleven o'clock. And you'd better not be winding me up!' he warned.

Sandy shook his head, all injured innocence, and Linc turned away to meet Nina. Seconds later, he was on board and, when the girth had been tightened, rode away to limber the horse up.

It was difficult to keep his mind on the task in hand whilst he did so.

A sponsor!

Money to bolster his own, barely adequate input. The prospect opened up all sorts of new possibilities. More horses, a horsebox, relief from some of the most pressing horse-related bills. If it hadn't been Sandy's doing he would be happier, though. The saddler's approach to most things was just a tad too relaxed to be reliable. Would he have briefed this potential Godsend on the full nature of the commitment?

As he was called into the start box, Linc had to make a conscious effort to put the whole thing out of his mind. The responsibility he had to Nina, Hobo and himself, was too great to permit anything but his complete concentration. In what is one of the most dangerous of sports, a momentary lapse can spell serious injury or even death. After his fall the previous week, Linc had never been more aware of that fact.

As the countdown began, he shortened his reins, settled his feet firmly in the stirrups and, last of all, set his stopwatch running. On the word go, Nina called out to wish him luck, and he was away.

Hobo was sublime. In the few weeks Linc had been riding him, he had improved more than could ever have been hoped and today never felt like putting a foot wrong. Recalling that the ride was his for the foreseeable future, Linc's heart was singing as they took the last line of three fences and galloped in a good ten seconds inside the time allowed. Unless someone topped their dressage score, which so far no one had even looked like doing, there was now no way they could lose. It began to look as though Hobo had won his first one-day event.

When Linc set off for Shaftesbury the following morning he couldn't entirely suppress the glow of excitement he felt, in spite of his very real reservations about Sandy's reliability. Waking in the early hours, he had done a good job of convincing himself that the offer would turn out to be one made on spec, with no real understanding of what it entailed, but even so a glimmer of hope refused to be extinguished.

Outside Sandy's unit a familiar white BMW stood on the tarmac, and Linc glanced at it thoughtfully as he passed, remembering that the last time he'd seen its owner he'd been tearing a strip off Sandy.

'Linc, hi. Come on in.'

Sandy had come to the door and now stood back to let him enter. He looked eager, Linc thought as he returned the greeting, but there was also a touch of something that could have been apprehension.

'You okay?' he asked.

Sandy nodded. 'Yeah, sure. Listen, this could be your big chance, mate. Don't blow it.'

That was a strange choice of words, Linc reflected, as he followed the saddler into his office. If the offer were a good one, he would certainly do his best not to blow it.

Getting up from a chair by Sandy's desk as Linc came in was the BMW's owner. He stepped forward with a smile and an outstretched hand on which several chunky gold rings were displayed.

'Morning, Linc. I assume I can call you Linc, if

we're going to have a business relationship?'

'Everyone calls me Linc,' he said, effectively robbing the privilege of any importance. 'And you are?'

'Alan Judge. Judge Haulage. Everyone calls me Al,' Judge informed him. 'It's pointless waiting for Larry to introduce us.'

'Sorry, Al. I *was* about to,' Sandy said. 'Can I get anyone a coffee?'

He didn't react to Judge calling him Larry, and Linc wondered if it was his real name.

'Not now, later perhaps,' Judge replied, answering for both of them before Linc had a chance to speak. 'What we *would* like is a little space so we can get down to business.'

'Not for me either, thanks, Sandy,' Linc added quietly.

'Right. Well, I'll leave you to it, then,' the saddler said, apparently unoffended by this cavalier dismissal from his own office.

As the door closed behind him, Linc found himself a seat and sat opposite the businessman, looking at his short, thick wavy hair and well-formed, if slightly heavy features, and wondering why he was struggling to like the man. His rather autocratic manner was nothing unusual among those at the helm of large businesses, and Judge Haulage *was* a large business; Linc had seen their lorries in all parts of the country. The man plainly had a talent for making money, and was just as plainly accustomed to getting his own way. It was possible that he wasn't actually aware that he was brusque to the point of rudeness, but even more likely, in Linc's view, that he knew and didn't care.

Maybe that was what Sandy had been trying to prepare him for.

He sat back and tried to keep an open mind. After all, he hadn't got to like the man to do business with him, and offers of sponsorship hadn't exactly been flooding in so far.

Half an hour later, having discussed the proposed deal at length, as an outline and then in more detail, Linc's opinion of Judge's business acumen had been confirmed. When he'd asked what the sponsor expected to get out of the deal, bearing in mind that eventing is anything but a high-profile sport with even wins at world level rarely making it on to the national sports news, Judge had had his answer ready. His business was primarily haulage, he'd explained, but to keep his sizeable fleet of lorries on the road it had become necessary to have facilities for their maintenance and repair. The huge garage he'd set up in the Midlands had begun to branch out into lorry conversion and customising, and he was now turning an eye to the horsebox industry.

'We're just in the process of building an even bigger workshop just outside Blandford, to service the South, and what better place to advertise than at horse shows and events?' he asked. 'Where by the very fact of their being there, people obviously utilise horse transport. And what better way to advertise than sponsorship?'

Linc had nodded. The man certainly had a point.

With the offer mapped out their business was essentially over. Without asking Linc for a decision, Judge took it upon himself to go to the door of the office and summon Sandy.

'All right, Larry lad? We'll have that coffee now,' he said as the saddler came back in. 'Unless you'd like something stronger?'

'Coffee'll be fine for me,' Linc said, strongly of the opinion that it was not up to Judge to offer him Sandy's precious whisky. 'What's with the *Larry*?'

'Oh. Just a stupid nickname,' Sandy said, with a scowl in Judge's direction. 'He knows I don't like it. So, is the deal all done and dusted?' He switched the kettle on and sorted out mugs.

'Just got to draw up the contracts, haven't we, Linc?' Al Judge said confidently. 'I'll get my legal boys on to it at once.'

'It's a very generous offer,' he agreed. 'And one well worth considering.'

Some of the bonhomie slipped from the businessman's face for a fraction of a second, then he smiled again. 'Absolutely. Always look before you leap, eh? But don't consider for too long . . . you never know, I might come up with a better way to advertise!'

Leaving the unit some ten minutes later Linc got back behind the wheel of the Discovery, unable to shake off a slight feeling of disappointment. It was, he felt, akin to the way one might feel if, after being offered a Ferrari as a gift, one found out that it was only available in yellow.

In spite of Judge's warning about not taking too long, he intended taking just as long as he needed to feel happier about the offer. With this in mind, he started the engine and set off for home.

Linc was hoping to be able to talk Judge's offer over with Josie, not because he was in any doubt about its validity – the calculations seemed sound enough

– but because talking aloud might help him sort out his feelings about being tied, however loosely, to a man that he really couldn't like. He rang her on her mobile as he had taken to doing ever since Abby's accusations had made conversing with her parents uncomfortable. This time, however, it was Rebecca Hathaway who answered.

'Oh, I'm sorry. Is Josie there?'

'Linc. No, she's popped out to the shops for me and left her phone behind, as usual. Shall I get her to ring you when she comes in?'

'Please,' Linc hesitated. Rebecca's words had been civil but her voice gave away little as to how she felt about him at present. He wanted to ask her but couldn't find the words, and ended just by repeating himself. 'Yes, please.'

When Josie returned his call, he took her to task for not carrying her phone.

'Jo Jo, the whole idea was so I wouldn't have to bother your family at all . . .'

'Yes, I know. I'm sorry. You know what I'm like with the bloody thing. Hannah calls it my immobile phone because it hardly ever leaves the house. Mum's always trying to reach me on it and then it starts to ring just behind her or in my coat pocket in the hall! Was she okay?'

'Yeah, she was fine. I just felt a bit awkward, that's all.'

'Oh, I'm sorry, Linc. I really don't think she's got a problem with you but things are a bit tense today . . . Abby's coming home this afternoon, all being well, and nobody's quite sure how it's going to work.'

'That's great,' he said, wondering, even as he did

so, what it would mean for his relationship with Josie in the short term. 'The doctors must be pleased with her.'

'Mmm, they are. Physically, at least. Emotionally might take a bit longer.'

'Well, it's a good job she's got you lot to support her. I guess it might be best if I stay away for a day or two, as I can't ride Noddy anyway.'

'Do you mind dreadfully?'

'Yes,' he said flatly. 'But this isn't about me. I'll ring in a day or two. No – second thoughts – you ring me, okay?'

Robbed of the chance to talk it through at length with Josie, Linc mulled the offer over in his own mind repeatedly, always coming back to the same question: did he ignore his instincts and go with the guy for the sake of his Olympic ambition, or did he throw over what looked to be a generous deal because of personal prejudice?

The age-old conflict – head or heart.

He was still undecided when Sandy phoned him a couple of days later.

They exchanged the normal platitudes and Sandy asked if Noddy was up to being ridden yet, to which Linc returned a regretful negative, adding that he had just that morning booked the services of an equine physiotherapist.

'Are you in a hurry to offload the saddle?' he enquired. 'Because I can pay you for it, if you like, and then if we have to change it, we'll sort out the difference later.'

'No. No hurry,' Sandy assured him. 'So, have you thought any more about Al's offer?'

'Did he ask you to call?'

'No. I just wondered . . . Well, yes, actually,' he amended. 'It's just the way he is. Likes to keep things moving along. What have you been thinking? It *was* a good offer, wasn't it?'

'Very generous,' Linc agreed.

Sandy obviously picked up on the reserve in his voice. 'I know he can seem a bit full on at times. I mean, a bit pushy perhaps . . .'

'I think rude is the word you're searching for,' Linc put in.

'He's all right when you get to know him, though.'

'Is that why you let him walk all over you?'

'Oh, I've known him forever. Anyway, as I said before, he did me a big favour once, so I kind of owe him. It'd be different with you . . .'

'Hmm,' Linc said non-committally.

'He's a good businessman. Surely that's what matters?'

It had been Linc's argument with himself all along but suddenly, hearing Sandy say it, he knew it wasn't enough. If he was going to turn the offer down, though, it was only fair to tell the man himself. He changed the subject.

'Why does Judge call you Larry? Is it your real name?'

Sandy hesitated. 'No. It's rhyming slang. Larry Adler – saddler. Stupid, really, but it's stuck.'

'So what's your nickname for Judge?'

'Er . . . We haven't really got one. We just call him "the Boss".'

'We?'

350

'Sorry. Old habits die hard. I used to work for him.'

'So what's slang for boss?'

'Pitch. Pitch and toss,' Sandy said, adding hurriedly, 'Look, somebody's just come. I'll have to go now. Speak soon. And don't let the man put you off the money, eh?'

'Okay. I'll bear it in mind.'

Linc rang off and sat looking at the office wall. Had Judge used his apparent hold over Sandy to get the saddler to try and influence him? If he had, it had backfired somewhat. Through no fault of his own, Sandy's gentle prodding had finally decided Linc against the deal. He just hoped his backing out wouldn't make things awkward for his friend.

He was still deep in thought when the phone rang again.

'Linc? It's Mike. Mike Farquharson.'

'Oh, hello, Mike.' He hadn't heard from the wine merchant since he'd met him in Blandford that day.

'Look, I'm in a bit of a hurry but I'd like a word with you sometime. Can you meet me?'

'Yes, sure. Where and when?'

'Well, I shall be in Blandford this afternoon. Is that any good for you?'

'Er . . . yes, I think I can manage that.' It was a public day at Farthingscourt and his father wouldn't be pleased, but Mike sounded quite buoyed up and Linc was intrigued.

'Great! How about Hopgoods again? Three o'clock okay?'

'Half-past would be better,' Linc told him. He'd try and get Crispin to stand in for him, and the fewer hours' cover he needed, the more likely he was to be successful.

'Terrific. I think it'll be worth your while. See you later then.'

Linc was late. A last-minute telephone call from the millwright had left him with a quarter of an hour to make up, most of which he'd regained before a police speed trap put him back where he started.

He was on a roundabout just outside Blandford when a grey Judge Haulage lorry cut across his bows to change lanes. Linc leaned indignantly on the horn, at which the driver stopped his vehicle, opened the door and let loose a string of abuse before continuing on his way.

Linc recognised the man. Lean, fortyish and mean-looking: it was Marty Lucas, the man from the greyhound track. Small world.

In Blandford he parked the Morgan, bought a ticket, and then set off at a brisk pace for the coffee shop, taking with him the laptop Crispin and Nikki had given him for his birthday. He had some work to catch up on, and it *had* been his intention to use any spare time to do so. That was before his timekeeping had gone awry.

Hurrying so as not to keep Mike waiting, Linc rounded the corner into the high street and walked slap-bang into a youth who was coming the other way.

'Oh, sorry.' Linc turned sideways to let the youngster pass and saw combat trousers, a torn tee-shirt, an eyebrow ring and a stretchy hat pulled down over his hair.

Beanie! It was turning into quite a day for meeting old friends.

'Hey! Come here!' he exclaimed, grabbing for the lad with his free hand.

If he hadn't had the laptop under his left arm he might have held him, but it was debatable. The boy was just as strong as Linc remembered from the night in Shaftesbury, only this time, in a busy street, he wasn't disposed to hang around.

With a muttered obscenity, Beanie tried to pull away from Linc, and when that didn't work, struck out with his fist, catching him on the cheekbone and knocking him off-balance. With a final tug he pulled free, ripping his tee-shirt still further, and before Linc could recover, was off down the pavement at a run.

'Bugger!' Linc straightened up and watched him go. It was no earthly use trying to give chase. He was already twenty or thirty yards away and Linc doubted he could even match his speed carrying the computer, let alone overhaul him.

'Linc! Are you all right?' Mike came hurrying up breathlessly. 'I saw what happened.'

'Yeah, yeah. I'll survive,' he sighed, rubbing his face. So near and yet so far.

'He didn't get it, then. Well done!'

'Get what?'

'The laptop, man. That's what he was after, wasn't it? I saw him pulling at it.'

Linc shook his head. 'Actually, *I* was trying to hold on to *him*! It's a long story, I'll tell you about it over coffee. I just wish I could have held on to the bastard.'

'Well, if you're sure you're okay, let's go and get that coffee,' Mike suggested.

They went together to Hopgoods and ordered a cappuccino and a large Irish coffee, as they had before, and at a quiet, corner table, Linc gave the wine merchant a potted version of the attack in Shaftesbury.

'So you see why I wanted to keep hold of him,' he finished. 'If I could find out who he is and who he was working for that night, I might be a bit nearer to finding the men who put Abby in hospital.'

'But I know who he is,' Mike said, surprised. 'Most people round here do. That's Scott Phillips. Vandal, school bully and all-round thug!'

14

Because Hopgoods was a 'mobile-free zone', Linc had to go out into the street to ring Rockley, but came back in without having spoken to the man himself.

'Rockley wasn't there,' he told Mike as he slid back into his chair. 'Nor was Manston. They're out on a case.'

'Probably that security scare in Bournemouth. I heard about it on the news, lunchtime. Some crackpot sitting on the top floor of a double-decker bus in the city centre, threatening to blow it up if his demands aren't met.'

'What demands?'

'Search me. I only turned it on for the weather, and they obviously weren't going to get round to that in a hurry, so I got it on Ceefax.'

'Well, you could be right. Anyway, I left a message about young Scott. I hope Rockley gets it.'

Just in case he returned the call, Linc switched his phone from ring-tone to vibrate and put it back in his trouser pocket.

'So, what can I do for you, Mike?'

'Ah, yes. I'd almost forgotten. Well, I've had a bit of luck, or rather the company has. We've managed to land a deal with K & B Cruises – you know, they operate out of Southampton. We've been contracted to supply them with all their wines and spirits, and it's a mind-boggling total, I can tell you!'

'I'll bet it is. Well done, Mike! My congratulations. I'd drink your health but I can't really do it in coffee.'

'Thanks. But that's not what I asked you here for. The thing is, with things on the up, I started thinking again about the idea of sponsoring you. I felt awful about what happened last time.'

'But, my father . . .'

'Yes, I know. But to be honest, although the Farthingscourt account is one we're very pleased to have, it wouldn't bring the company to its knees if we lost it, especially now. And I'm not sure your father really would take his custom elsewhere, because – if you think about it – it would look a little strange if he did that when Farquharson's was seen to be supporting his son's sporting ambitions.'

'I guess so,' Linc said slowly. 'Though I wouldn't bank on it. You know how bloody-minded he can be!'

Mike shrugged. 'Oh, well. If the worst comes to the worst, we'll wear the loss. After all, come the day when you'll be Viscount Tremayne.'

The proposition he laid before Linc was well thought out and forward-thinking. It was not, perhaps, upon quite such generous lines as the Judge Haulage offer, but the excitement Linc felt as they discussed the terms was untempered by any of the doubts he'd had about doing business with Judge.

'Well, there it is. What do you say? Are we a partnership?'

'Just show me where to sign,' Linc declared happily.

'Brilliant. I'll get my solicitors to draw up the draft copies and we should be ready to roll mid- to late-July.'

Feeling that it was only fair, Linc phoned Al Judge as soon as he parted from Mike. He used the contact number he'd been given but it was a woman who answered.

'Oh, I'm sorry. Is Mr Judge there?'

'He's a bit busy at the moment. Who shall I say is calling?'

Linc gave his name and heard the woman repeating it, presumably to Judge. After a moment, the man himself came on the line, his tone warm and welcoming. Linc's hackles rose instantly.

'Ah, Linc. I was hoping I'd hear from you soon. Ready to sign on the dotted line, are you?'

'Er . . . no, as a matter of fact. I'm afraid not. It's a very generous offer but—'

Judge didn't let him finish. 'Look, Linc, we need to discuss this but I haven't time just at the moment. I think we should meet. Where are you now?'

'Well, actually, I'm in Blandford . . .'

'Good. Could you meet me later?'

'Well, yes, I suppose so, but there's really not a lot to say. I've had a better offer and—'

'Nonsense!' Judge stated briskly. 'Look, I've got

to go out to the new site in about, what . . . three-quarters of an hour. Can you meet me there? It's just off the A350. The Meadows Industrial Park, you can't miss it. Come on, you owe me that much at least!'

Linc looked at his watch. It was nearly five o'clock and he had things to do, but . . . 'I suppose I could. Okay. Quarter to six. I'll see you there.'

He rang off and sat staring at his mobile in frustration. Why had he agreed? For his part there was nothing more to say, but he had a feeling that he was in for a very uncomfortable session with Judge.

'Damn, damn, damn!' he said aloud, thumping the Morgan's steering wheel with his fist. He had some paperwork to finish and some e-mails to send, and didn't particularly want to spend all evening in the office. It was a good job he'd brought the laptop. Crispin had helpfully installed all his contact addresses on the computer's memory for him that morning, so there was nothing to stop him working from the car as long as he could get a decent signal on the mobile. Feeling that the industrial park couldn't be any noisier than the town car park, Linc decided to go straight there and work while he waited for Judge to arrive.

In spite of Judge's assurances, Linc did manage to miss the turning into The Meadows, mainly because it wasn't signposted from the main road. A large board advertised the name of the construction company but the industrial park itself was at the end of a long, wide approach road, and hidden from the highway by an environmentally conscious fringe of trees.

Linc drove between the open, metal-framed, chain-link gates, noticing CCTV cameras perched on the gate posts and, with no idea which of the plots was to be Judge Haulage's new garage-cum-workshop, he pulled in and parked on the side of the tarmac apron where he hoped he wouldn't be in the way. The industrial park was, at present, not much more than a building site. Three or four vast, cavernous concrete and metal structures had already been erected, there were a couple more partially completed. The rest existed only as piles of bricks, sand and timber, waiting to be built. A Portakabin office completed the scene.

Surprisingly for the time of day there were a number of workmen still on site but they were moving with an end-of-the-day lethargy, and even as Linc watched one of them switched off his JCB and, with a wave to his colleagues, made for his car.

Linc unzipped his laptop case and turned it on, plugging the connecting lead into his mobile phone. The noise of an approaching vehicle made him look round but instead of Al Judge it was a white mini-van which, he soon discovered, had come to pick up most of the remaining construction workers.

In due course it left again, bearing its load of dusty, sweaty men back to their outside lives. A couple of cars followed, the last being a dirty white pick-up truck which slowed up and stopped beside Linc. The window was lowered and a pleasant, weathered face appeared, regarding the Morgan with open admiration.

'Can't stay there, mate. I've gotta lock the gate,' the man said.

'I'm waiting for Mr Judge. He said he'd be along

about quarter to six,' Linc told him. 'D'you want me to wait outside?'

The man looked at the Morgan again, and then apparently deciding, with doubtful logic, that the owner of such a car wasn't about to loot the site, said, 'Nah, that's all right. He did say he was coming over. I'll leave the padlock undone and he'll lock it when he's finished.'

He drove forward a couple of feet then stopped, adding as an afterthought, 'If he doesn't come, can you do it? The boss'd flay me if he found it unlocked!'

Linc nodded. 'No problem,' he agreed, thinking that if *he* were the boss he would be less than happy with his foreman's notion of security. Still, thankfully, it wasn't his problem.

As the dust settled behind the departing pick-up, he looked at his watch. Twenty-five minutes to six. He let his gaze drift over the deserted site, where the fitful wind was making dust devils in the loose cement and lifting odd scraps of paper and plastic in a bizarre, fleeting dance. Cranes, JCBs and forklift trucks stood silently around like so many metal monsters caught in suspended animation. Strange how much lonelier such a place seemed, after hours, than did the open countryside.

Fifteen minutes later, Linc had sent two e-mails and left an electronic memo for himself, and there was still no sign of Judge. He found himself remembering his earlier conversation with Sandy, and on a whim called up a search engine and tapped in Cockney Rhyming Slang. The result startled him; there were dozens of websites. Picking one of the more promising he struck gold, coming up with a comprehensive dictionary of slang, accessible either from the plain English or Cockney route and listed by initial letter.

For several long minutes he amused himself scanning the lists, and was surprised to see how many terms in everyday usage actually originated from the slang. Some made him laugh. Apparently one might take one's cherry (cherry hog – dog) for a bowl (bowl of chalk – walk). Chuckling, Linc read on. He looked for boss and found pitch and toss, as Sandy had said. Then he looked for Judge and abruptly the smile died as shock hit him like a bucketful of cold water. There were three variations: inky smudge, chocolate fudge, and Barnaby Rudge.

Here at last was the elusive Barnaby!

All he could do for a moment was sit and stare at the screen, his mind racing. Surely it couldn't be a coincidence.

Al Judge and Barnaby, one and the same. And just that afternoon he'd seen Marty Lucas driving one of the Judge Haulage lorries; Marty, who seemed to spend a good deal of his life around greyhounds and greyhound tracks. Should that have set the alarm bells ringing?

Probably not, he decided. The link was tenuous at best, until you knew about Barnaby Rudge. No wonder Sandy had been uncomfortable with Judge drawing attention to his Cockney nickname!

Linc's heart sank. Sandy. If Judge was the king-pin, it was impossible to believe that Sandy wasn't involved . . .

First things first. Rockley had to be told. Linc disconnected the laptop and found the policeman's number in the phone's memory.

Once again he was told that the DI was busy.

'Can you please make sure he gets my message, then? It's important. Tell him *Alan Judge of Judge Haulage is Barnaby*. Have you got that?'

The voice on the other end assured him that it had and repeated the phrase to prove it to him.

As he rang off, it occurred to Linc that, in the light of what he'd just discovered, a deserted building site in the middle of nowhere really wasn't the best place to be – especially with Judge on his way. Slipping the phone into the pocket of his leather jacket, he closed the laptop and put it behind the passenger seat, then reached for the ignition key.

He was already too late.

In his rearview mirror he could see, coming up the approach road, a familiar white BMW, a pick-up, and one of Judge's lorries. His hand dropped away from the key. If he tried to make a run for it now, it would be clear to Judge that he had some-how made the connection, and Linc wouldn't like to bet money on his chances of getting past that little lot. His best chance was to stay calm and hope to bluff it out. After all, he had no reason to believe Judge meant him any harm at this juncture.

The three vehicles swept through the open gates and stopped, with the lorry, which had been bring-ing up the rear, somehow carelessly blocking the exit. It wasn't a promising start.

As Linc got out of the Morgan, trying to appear relaxed and unconcerned, Al Judge climbed out of the BMW. The other two vehicles disgorged Marty Lucas, looking lean and surly in black jeans and a leather jacket, Scott 'Beanie' Phillips, and a biggish man who Linc recognised as the site foreman he'd spoken to earlier. No wonder he'd been so casual about leaving a stranger with the run of the place.

Suddenly the construction site felt like the loneliest place on earth.

'Linc. Hi! Sorry to keep you waiting.' Judge came forward with a smile on his face, as if the presence of the other three was somehow incidental and held no significance.

Linc wasn't fooled. The fact that the businessman was openly acknowledging his alliance with Scott Phillips indicated that he suspected Linc either knew of or was close to discovering it. That was disturbing.

'That's okay. My people know where I am,' he returned coolly.

'Ah,' Judge nodded approvingly. 'You told them where you were going. Very sensible.'

'I did.' Linc wished to goodness he actually had, but at the time he hadn't thought this anything more sinister than a meeting with an over-pushy businessman. 'However,' he went on, striving to keep things as natural as possible, 'I do have rather a lot to do this evening, and as I really don't feel we have much to discuss . . .'

'Ah, yes, I understand, you're a busy man, I'm sure. But you can spare me a few minutes, surely? Come. Walk with me a little way. I'm a busy man, too, and I came here primarily to check on the progress of the building work.'

Linc hesitated, glancing at Judge's silent companions, uneasy somehow at leaving the vicinity of his car. Realistically, though, it offered no security and no real prospect of escape, with the lorry parked where it was. He was just as vulnerable here as he would be anywhere on the site.

With a shrug he gestured to Judge to lead on, stifling the impulse to warn the waiting men not to tamper with the Morgan. It would probably be all the encouragement they needed and, besides, what could he do to stop them?

After a few strides he turned his head, feeling uncomfortable, but the other three weren't following. The foreman appeared ill-at-ease and looked away when Linc caught his eye, but Marty Lucas and the youngster were laughing about something, and when he saw Linc watching, Marty provocatively perched himself on the bonnet of the Morgan.

Smothering irritation, Linc ignored him and walked on, his mind racing. What had put Judge on his guard? Even if 'Beanie' Phillips had run straight to him after Linc recognised him in Blandford that afternoon, why should Judge have felt threatened? Knowledge of the boy's name wouldn't have given Linc any clue as to whom he'd been working for. Had Judge been worried that, under pressure, Scott might give the game away? Or had Sandy called, warning him of Linc's interest in his nickname? Even though they couldn't be certain his curiosity would take him any further and lead him to Barnaby Rudge, there was always a chance it would, and Judge didn't strike Linc as a person who would leave too much to chance.

Whatever had tipped him off, the thing that was occupying Linc's mind most forcefully just at the moment was, what did Judge intend doing about it? What manner of leverage or warning did he have in mind this time?

'Now, about this sponsorship deal,' Judge interrupted his thoughts. 'Can't I persuade you to think again?'

'I *have* thought it through, and I'm not interested.' Linc spoke quietly but firmly.

'Now that's a pity. I had hoped we could come to some arrangement. It would have saved so much – what shall I say? – unpleasantness.'

Linc's pulse rate, already above normal, stepped up another notch.

'There's no need for unpleasantness,' he said, putting an element of bewildered surprise into his tone. 'I've just had a better offer, that's all. But if you're set on sponsoring someone, you'll certainly have no problem finding another candidate.'

'Ah, but we both know that's not the real issue here, don't we?' Judge countered. 'This was more in the nature of an insurance policy, wasn't it? A case of, I'll scratch your back if you don't stab me in mine.'

Linc didn't pretend to misunderstand him this time. 'You mean, you'll fund my riding if I ignore the fact that you nearly killed my girlfriend's sister!'

'Not me, Linc. I didn't touch the girl.' Judge kept his tone even. 'Besides, I hear she's doing well now. Back at home and on the mend, no lasting harm done.'

Linc could hardly speak for the fury that was rising in him. 'No harm done? She nearly died, you evil bastard!'

'Come on now. There's no need for name-calling. It was regrettable, but an accident after all. An error of judgement made under stress, you could say.'

They had been walking down a tarmac roadway between plots of building land in various stages of development. On their left, vast empty shells stood, rapidly filling with shadows as the light failed, whilst on their right, some were as yet just so many piles of building materials in designated plots. Now Judge stopped in front of one of these that had just had the hard standing laid; a vast expanse of concrete gleaming wetly in the setting sun.

'This will be my new garage,' he told Linc. 'In a month or so, this unit will be finished and full of people and vehicles, and no one will give a thought to what might be under their feet.'

Linc glanced sharply at the businessman, frowning slightly as he tried to decipher this cryptic remark. The only explanation that presented itself was almost unbelievable; it belonged in the realms of TV and films. *Didn't it?*

'Ah, I see you understand me,' Judge said, nodding. 'I knew you were a bright lad. It's a pity you're so stuffy with it. Such a waste . . .'

This casual confirmation of his fears took Linc's breath away and for a moment his brain refused to function sensibly. Then reason reasserted itself.

'You *are* joking?' he prompted.

Judge didn't look particularly amused. 'What do *you* think?'

'But, I told you, people know where I am.'

'People,' he mused. 'Oh, yes, you said you told someone where you were going – that was quick thinking, but not quite quick enough. Who's to say you ever got here?'

'The construction workers saw me, they won't forget my car in a hurry,' Linc pointed out.

Judge shook his head sadly and adopted a tone laden with regret. 'Yes, I did arrange to meet Tremayne, officer, but I'm afraid I was late and the site foreman had to ask him to leave so he could shut the gates. I don't know where he went then. He certainly wasn't around when *I* got here . . .'

'And what about the foreman? He doesn't look too happy about all this. Is he going to stand by and let you commit murder?'

'Ah, yes. The foreman. Cursed with a conscience is poor old Ray. But also, unhappily for him, cursed with a nephew who's building up quite an impressive criminal record for one so young. You've met young Scott before, I believe. If the coppers got to know about some of the stuff he's done for me there'd be no keeping him out of the slammer and that would cut Ray's sister up something rotten!'

Beanie's uncle. Not much chance of help from that quarter then, Linc thought with gathering despair.

'They've got CCTV,' he stated, remembering.

'Ah, yes. I must remind Ray to switch that on when we leave.'

Balked at every turn, it began to dawn on Linc that he might actually have to physically fight for survival and, struggling to retain a grip on reality, he backed a couple of steps away from Judge and looked round to see where the others were. He didn't have to look far. Some twenty yards behind him and closing, was the hefty figure of the foreman, with Beanie swaggering at his side, and when he looked beyond Judge, it was to see Marty strolling nonchalantly into view round the end of the closest building.

Linc swallowed, his mouth suddenly dry. He'd been hoping for a chance to get far enough away from Judge to use his mobile. Not much chance of that now. Even getting away across the site involved going towards one or other party first, unless he attempted to wade through the wet cement, and he had no idea how deep that might be.

Then, in his jacket pocket, as if in answer to a prayer, his phone began vibrating silently. Could it possibly be Rockley, returning his calls? What to do now?

Thanking providence that he hadn't activated the ringtone again after leaving Hopgood's, he put his hand up to rub the back of his neck, then casually down into his pocket, deftly flicking the flap of the phone open.

'Okay, Judge. So I'm trapped,' he said immediately, and as loudly as he dared. 'So what now? Maybe you *can* dispose of a body in a couple of feet of concrete, but the Morgan won't be so easy.' As he spoke he moved back closer to the businessman, unsure of the effective range of the phone's built-in microphone.

'Why do you suppose I had Marty bring the truck along?' Judge enquired. 'We can have that car halfway across England before anyone even realises you're missing.'

Linc hesitated; it wasn't easy, discussing arrangements for one's own death and disposal, but there was one other thing it was imperative for Rockley to know – if indeed Rockley it was. 'Got it all worked out, haven't you? One could almost think you'd done it before. Is The Meadows the first, or is there some other industrial park up North with a body buried in its foundations?'

Judge didn't answer. His eyes narrowed suspiciously. 'What are you playing at? Why all the questions? Most people would be shitting themselves by now . . .'

While he'd been talking, Linc had moved round slightly behind Judge, who now turned to keep him within view.

'Ah, but I'm not most people, am I, Al?' Linc looked away from him, to where Marty stood kicking his heels some thirty feet away. A similar distance in the other direction, Beanie and his uncle had slowed up, apparently engaged in conversation.

Linc looked back at Judge. 'My ancestors were fighting duels when yours were probably still grubbing around in the hedgerows! We don't just turn belly-up when we're threatened . . .' Mid-sentence, he took two swift steps towards the businessman and cannoned into him, shoulder-first, catching him off balance and sending him stumbling backwards. Arms windmilling, Judge tripped over the raised edge of the metal retaining sheet and sat back heavily in the liquid cement, swearing like a trooper. '. . . we bite back!' Linc finished, with exquisite satisfaction.

Without pausing to enjoy the sight of Judge, leather coat, cavalry twills and all, floundering around in the thick grey sludge, he took to his heels and ran through the open doorway into the gloomy depths of the nearest unit.

Even as he plunged into the semi-darkness he was aware that the other three were already in pursuit, but because he'd seen it in passing, he was also aware – which they might not have been – that there was a small, personnel door standing open on the far side of the structure, and it was towards this that he sprinted.

Grateful that he was wearing soft suede desert boots, he sped across the gritty concrete floor with the noise of his pursuers echoing nightmarishly around the empty interior, spurring him to extra effort. Reaching the doorway, he shot out into the comparative brightness, skidding a little as he hesitated to get his bearings.

Ahead lay a rough grassy strip some forty or fifty yards wide, on the far side of which was the ten feet or so of chain-link security fence. Although Linc was reasonably fit, he was not at all sure he could climb the fence, and was almost certain he couldn't do it before one or more of his pursuers got close enough to grab his foot and haul him back. If his sense of direction was true, the gate and the abandoned vehicles should be somewhere to his left, so he set off, as fast as his legs would carry him, in that direction.

Racing alongside the metal wall of the unit, Linc couldn't resist throwing a look back over his shoulder to see how close those following were. What he saw wasn't very reassuring. Marty and Scott were just emerging from the building, the teenager pulling ahead and possibly gaining ground on him, and there was no sign of the site foreman. As he pounded on, his breath beginning to come fast and hard, Linc wondered whether this was because the heavier man had fallen behind the others, or because he'd taken another route altogether.

Passing the first alleyway, he glanced sideways and found it clear, but thirty yards or so further on, as he reached the next opening, the missing man hurtled out just feet away and launched a flying, rugby-style tackle at Linc's running form.

Desperately, Linc veered away, spoiling his assailant's aim and instead of taking him waist high, the man's arms wrapped around his legs, just above the knees.

The immediate effect was basically the same. Linc and his pursuer hit the rough ground hard in a slither of stones and building debris, and rolled through one complete revolution, still locked together. As they finally stopped moving, the foreman made a fatal error. Rather than maintaining his perfectly adequate grip until help arrived, he tried to gain a better hold by hooking his fingers into the belt of Linc's jeans and shifting his weight higher up.

Linc wasn't in the mood to hang around. He knew that once the other two caught up, the game would be over, so as soon as he felt the man's grasp ease, he kicked out with all the force he could muster, and felt his left foot score a direct hit. With a grunt, the foreman let go, and without further ado Linc scrambled to his feet, glanced over his shoulder, stumbled and ran on.

That quick look was enough to show him that his advantage over the chasing pair had been halved and when he reached the next alleyway he turned into it in desperation.

It wasn't a good move. The passageway was perhaps six feet wide and littered with builders' debris: odd lengths of wood, bundles of dirty-looking polythene, pallets, scrap metal and a split bag of cement powder. It wasn't impassable by any means as far as it went, but unfortunately it only went about twenty feet. At this point the two buildings apparently became one and Linc's heart skipped a beat as he found himself faced with a towering, blank wall.

For an instant he paused in disbelief. What was the point of an alleyway that didn't lead anywhere? It was a waste of space. Then, about two-thirds of the way down on both sides and flush with the rippled walls he saw doors, and knowing he no longer had time to go back he ran on, hoping against hope that at least one would be unlocked.

They both were. With swift inspiration he threw the one on the right-hand side open and then slipped through the left-hand one, pulling it quietly shut behind him.

If there was someone up there looking down on him, they'd come through in grand style. A weak light filtered in through skylights, way up in the roof; just enough to show Linc, not the vast empty space that he'd been quite prepared to find, but a building stuffed to the rafters with building supplies and machinery.

Knowing his trick with the doors wouldn't mislead Marty and Beanie for long – especially if the other half of the building turned out to be empty – Linc sprinted down the length of the structure to the big double doors at the front. Here, however, his luck ran out. The doors were securely locked on the outside. To the right a personnel door linked the two buildings but when he cautiously tried it, it wouldn't budge.

Heart thudding from a mixture of exertion and fear, Linc scanned the area for the best hiding place. Suddenly, outside the front of the unit, he heard voices.

'What the fuck are you playing at?' This was unmistakably Judge, his professional veneer gone as if it had never existed. 'How the hell did you let him get away? Am I surrounded by fucking idiots?'

'He hasn't got away, he's in one of these units.' Possibly the foreman, Linc thought.

'Then what are you doing out here? Get in after him!'

The other voice muttered something by way of a reply but Linc didn't stop to try and hear more. It was obvious that to stand any chance of escaping from the building, the best place to be was as near the rear door as he could safely get. He loped, soft-footed, back the way he'd come, urgently scanning the unit's contents for somewhere to conceal himself.

'He's not in here. The tricky sod must be next-door.'

The sound of Beanie's voice spurred Linc to a swift decision. Most of the piles of bricks, breeze-blocks, wood and bags of cement were loaded on pallets, wrapped in polythene or plastic mesh and secured with tough nylon tapes. They stood around, piled one on top of another, in regular square-based towers that, at ground level, offered only the most basic of short-term refuge, and none at all from two or more searchers. Remembering childhood games of hide and seek, Linc decided his best hope was to go up and, using the wheels of a dumper-truck as a step, was soon lying spread-eagled on top of two adjoining plastic-wrapped towers of breeze-blocks.

Just in time, as it turned out. He'd barely stopped moving when the door opened and someone came in.

'Oh, shit!' Beanie again. 'There's even more stuff in 'ere. It'll take all bloody night!'

'Better get on with it, then. I've never seen old Barnaby so mad! I wouldn't like to be in Tremayne's shoes when we catch up with him!'

Marty – if Marty it was – could have been no more than ten feet away from the base of the stack on which Linc hid, and he had to suppress his impulse to shrink away from that edge of the square. Any noise at all would have been audible to the two men below. Lying on his face, Linc could feel the mobile phone in his pocket pressing against his ribs, and realised, with a sudden cold sweat, that it was presumably still switched on; could even still be connected to the last caller. What if someone spoke?

He dared not move to make it safe. All he could do was lie there, heart thudding painfully, and pray to a God he wasn't sure he believed in.

From the sound of it, one of the men was now searching further down the building, but as far as he could tell, one was still nearby. Linc wished he had something loose to hand that he could lob down the unit and perhaps draw the second man away.

Seconds ticked by and Linc began to think that maybe the second man was also at the other end of the unit after all, but then he heard a match flare and, shortly after, a wisp of cigarette smoke drifted up barely a yard away. He found he was trembling and tried to concentrate on his breathing, scared that if he shook too violently the waiting man would hear the movement.

'Scott? Any sign?' It was Marty.

'Nah. Why don't you help?'

'I'm doing this end. Gotta cover the door till the builder bloke gets round here.'

Linc heard the sound of his footsteps as Marty started to prowl, quartering the rear end of the building. At one point the noise grew fainter and he was steeling himself to risk a look when the door swung open again and someone, presumably the foreman, said, 'Is he still in here?'

'Must be. Didn't see him leave.' Marty's reply came from shockingly close to Linc's hiding place, and his whole body jerked inwardly in a nervous spasm. The tension of remaining inactive, with discovery just a whisker away, was agonising, and in spite of the unthinkable consequences, he was aware of an almost irresistible urge just to call out and surrender.

'Come on, Tremayne!' Marty again. 'There's no way out of this. Why don't you give yourself up?'

Linc screwed his eyes shut and bit hard on the mound at the base of his thumb. Marty was right. So much easier to get it over with.

'If I have to come and find you, it'll be worse for you when I do,' Marty vowed.

How much worse could it get than being buried in concrete? Link thought sardonically, and cynicism helped quell his rising panic. Stay quiet; stay still. Your moment will come.

'Fuckin' hell!' Marty spat the words, slamming his hand into the side of Linc's tower. 'Right. You've had your chance, you upper-class shit!

When I get my hands on you, you're gonna wish you'd never been born! You – whatever your name is – watch the door.'

Relief washed over Linc as he heard Marty move away. He'd come through it feeling somehow empowered. He wasn't finished. He was still in control and his actions were still capable of causing Marty grief. Linc didn't think he would ever be quite that scared again.

After a moment he heard Marty speak to Beanie, much further off, and knew the time had come to move. Getting his hands under him he lifted his head and shoulders just high enough to be able to locate the foreman, who was standing inside the door, dabbing at a cut eye with a handkerchief and looking pretty fed up with life. In the increasingly dim light, Linc couldn't see much of the far end of the building but he could hear Marty and Beanie's comments as they co-ordinated a systematic search. The logical option, Linc reflected, would have been to start their sweep at the top end of the unit, near the door, thus driving him into a corner, instead of towards his one possible avenue of escape.

Lucky for him they didn't seem too hot on logic.

Even so, the problem remained as to how to get down from his hiding place and across to the door without being seen or heard by the man who stood somewhere nearby. Unfortunately the plastic that encased his tower of breeze-blocks reacted to the slightest friction with a swishing, hissing sound, which more or less ruled out any attempt at stealth, and Linc had just resigned himself to a bull-in-a-china-shop approach when he became aware of a sporadic tapping sound.

It began very slowly but the frequency soon built up and suddenly, as the patter became an insistent drumming, and the light inside the building grew ever poorer, Linc realised what it was.

Rain.

Heavy, noisy rain, falling on to the single-skinned roof. Maybe there was a benign presence up there after all! But whether it was divine intervention or merely happy coincidence, Linc had no intention of wasting the moment. As the shower turned to a deafening downpour he slid swiftly down from his refuge and ran the twenty feet or so to the door, trying to keep out of sight behind the loaded pallets.

He needn't have bothered. When he reached the doorway, the foreman was leaning out, squinting up at the rain-filled sky.

Not at all sure that he could land the kind of punch with which movie heroes seem unfailingly to lay out their opponents, Linc opted for the safer option and picked up a stray length of broken pallet.

That did the trick. Seconds later, the unlucky foreman was stretched out cold, face down in a growing puddle of rainwater outside the door. Unwilling to have a death on his conscience, Linc paused long enough to roll the man on to his back, then dragged him a couple of feet so he could close the door and prop it shut with another length of wood from the pile outside. It would, perhaps, have been safer to leave him inside rather than out, but he dare not take the time. Instantly drenched by the cloudburst, he took off in the direction of the gate and the abandoned vehicles.

Rounding the end of the last unit, slipping and sliding on the newly wet ground, Linc was half-prepared to find that Judge had conjured up another couple of heavies from somewhere but there was no one to be seen, and he plunged on across the open ground towards the gate.

The three vehicles were exactly where he'd last seen them, and it was obvious that he would be going nowhere in the Morgan or the BMW with the lorry parked in the gateway as it was. The idea of trying to get away on foot didn't overly appeal to him, as the approach road must have been the best part of a mile long and he didn't fancy his chances if he was caught out in the open. And catch him they undoubtedly would. He was under no illusion that his makeshift prop would withstand the combined efforts of Marty and Beanie for very long, and after all, Judge was still around somewhere.

It had to be the lorry. With barely a glance for his own open-topped car, Linc headed for the huge grey liveried beast, hoping that the controls were at least similar to those of the much smaller horsebox he was accustomed to driving. Pulling the door open, he swung himself up into the cab, registering the smell of stale cigarette smoke and the mess of crisp bags and chocolate wrappers that littered the floor, before urgently scanning the dashboard and steering column for an ignition key.

It wasn't there.

It had to be. A movement on the construction site caught his eye and he glanced up to see, not only the two he'd imprisoned, but also Ray, the foreman, coming at a run. Linc swore. He clearly hadn't hit him hard enough.

His mind raced, reviewing his options. It would have to be the BMW. Out of habit, the keys to the

Morgan were safely in his pocket, so if he took off across the site in the BMW, the only possible pursuit vehicle would be the lorry and he felt confident in his ability to out-manoeuvre that. If he could draw it away from the gate, his way would then be clear, and woe betide anyone who got in his way; in his present mood, he was quite prepared to run them down and take his chance in court later.

With an eye on the approaching men he turned to climb down from the cab and found Judge sneering up at him, grey with drying cement from the waist down, and dangling the lorry keys from his forefinger.

'This what you're looking for?' he asked smugly.

Linc didn't bother to answer. In his new-found spirit of moral liberation he put his foot behind the cab door and smashed it as hard as he could at the smirking face.

Judge threw up an arm instinctively to protect his face, but the force of the impact knocked him from his feet and down on to the tarmac. Linc leaped out of the lorry and scooped the keys up from where they'd fallen, before climbing back into the cab. The BMW would still have been the better option but he couldn't be sure that Judge hadn't removed the keys from that, too, and he certainly didn't have time to search for them. The others were almost upon him, Beanie marginally ahead of Marty, and the foreman trailing some twenty yards behind. Out on the Blandford by-pass he could hear the whooping of a police siren, probably chasing a speeding motorist, Linc thought wryly. Where were they when you really needed them?

With shaking fingers he fitted the most important-looking key into the ignition and turned it, and with a hiccup and a shudder, the massive engine roared into life. As he selected first, the gearbox protested loudly and the lever almost jumped out of his hand, but on the second attempt it accepted his direction, he let the clutch in and was moving.

Not a moment too soon. With a flying leap, Marty launched himself at the cab and landed on the running board, trying to wrench the door open. Linc stamped on the accelerator, causing Judge to scramble hastily out of the way, and the cab lifted a little as the lorry leaped into the harness. From the initial sluggishness, Linc suspected that the machine was carrying a fairly full load.

Beside him, undaunted, Marty had succeeded in opening the door and Linc responded by hauling the steering wheel round hard to the left. The lorry listed sharply under this unsympathetic handling, the unfastened door swung out to the limit of its range where it stopped with a jerk, and Marty was shaken loose and flung – cursing and swearing – into a patch of rough grass and nettles.

Still accelerating, Linc dragged the wheel back the other way causing the lorry to lurch unhappily, and the cab door to slam shut again. His attempt to engage second was scarcely more fluent than the last, but he managed it and suddenly he was putting a comforting amount of space between himself and his pursuers. Unfortunately, he found as he returned his attention from the wing mirror to the rain-obscured screen in front of him, he wasn't putting very much space between the lorry and the first of the buildings, which now loomed large in front of him.

'Shit!' Linc said through clenched teeth, as he pulled the protesting machine into an even tighter curve. There wasn't time to apply the windscreen wipers, even had he known for sure where to find the controls but, after what seemed an eternity, the wall of the unit slipped away to the left and he was clear.

He'd missed it. With a sigh of relief, Linc spun the wheel the other way to get back on course, only to plough straight into a medium-sized concrete mixer.

If he'd kept his foot on the accelerator, there was a good chance that the rig might have cleared the obstruction from its path and carried on. However, Linc's immediate instinct was to brake, and having done so, the vehicle only succeeded in pushing the heavy mixer a few yards before it ground to a halt and stalled.

As the grinding, screeching cacophony ceased, Linc slammed the heel of his hand into the steering wheel in frustrated disappointment, before reaching for the key to restart the lorry.

The machine was having none of it. It sat still, with the huge orange barrel of the cement mixer reflecting in the thousands of raindrops on the screen, and stayed stubbornly silent.

Beside Linc, someone pulled the cab door open, making him jump. In desperation he snatched up a heavy-duty socket spanner that was lying amid the debris on the seat and prepared to do battle.

15

'Whoa, Linc! steady on! He's one of mine!'

Linc looked past the black-waterproof-coated man he'd been within an inch of clobbering to see the familiar and eminently welcome face of Detective Inspector Rockley. With a sigh that went way beyond relief, he lowered the spanner, closed his eyes and leaned back in the seat.

'Sorry. I thought you were one of Judge's lot. I wasn't expecting you.'

'I don't know why. You told us where to find you,' Rockley observed, breathing heavily.

Linc opened his eyes. 'So that *was* you on the phone! I hoped it was but I wasn't sure.'

Rockley nodded. 'That was quite an impressive bit of quick thinking. I took it you didn't want me to answer.'

'I prayed you wouldn't!' Linc agreed. 'What's happened with Judge? Did you catch him?'

'Oh, yes,' Rockley said, with great satisfaction. 'And his partners in crime except for Scott. But he won't get far, we've got a helicopter up there. Look, call me picky if you like, but I'm not a great fan of standing around in the rain, and it's just starting to run down my neck. Shall we go somewhere dry?'

'Sorry,' Linc said again, noticing for the first time that both Rockley and the black-jacketed man were looking like drowned rats in the unremitting downpour. He slid out of the cab and followed them across the rough grass to the Portakabin where another officer had switched a light on and was attempting to ignite a Calor gas heater. The cabin, which was probably the foreman's office, was furnished with an untidy desk, two or three chairs, a filing cabinet, kettle and microwave, and the obligatory page three-style calendar.

Linc dropped into a semi-comfortable chair, feeling emotionally and physically wrung-out. The rain pounding on the roof was, if anything, getting harder, or maybe it just sounded that way on the thin skin of the cabin. Either way, he thought, the open-topped Morgan, with his new laptop behind the seat, was going to be absolutely soaked.

Rockley spoke in a low voice to the man in the black waterproof, who turned with resignation and made his way back out into the rain.

Linc felt in his pocket for the life-saving mobile phone and flipped the top shut. Almost immediately it chirruped, probably to advise him of messages left, but he ignored it. He supposed he should really let someone at Farthingscourt know where he was but just at the moment he lacked the energy for explanations.

He watched as Rockley took off his buff-coloured mackintosh and hung it on the back of the door. It was of the type beloved by TV detectives and

Linc wondered whimsically if they were standard issue to the senior ranks. The DI's radio crackled into life and he answered it while the second policeman turned away from the glowing heater and busied himself with a kettle and some mugs.

The door opened and a paramedic peered round it. 'All okay in here?'

'Could do with some blankets,' Rockley replied, breaking off from his conversation. 'And maybe a dressing for our friend over there. Everyone else all right?'

'Just cuts and bruises,' the paramedic said, nodding, and disappeared, presumably to fetch the blankets.

Linc had frowned at the mention of a dressing and in doing so became aware of a tightness on his forehead. An exploratory hand found a cut on the hairline, though he had no idea how it had come about, unless it was the result of the collision with the cement mixer.

'So.' Radio communication over, Rockley came across and pulled a stool up to sit facing Linc. 'Tell me what's been going on. The *whole* story, please. I got your message about Scott Phillips, who is of course known to us, but with everything else that's been going on, I didn't have a lot of time to follow it up. I thought it would keep. I wasn't aware of any connection with Alan Judge, and even if I had been, I wouldn't have expected you to plunge straight into battle with him. What the hell were you playing at? After all my warnings! You're a persistent bugger, I'll give you that!'

'I didn't know about Judge until it was too late,'

Linc protested wearily. 'I certainly wouldn't have come here if I had. I'm not a complete idiot! Sandy introduced us and, as far as I knew, Judge was just a businessman who fancied the idea of sponsoring my riding.'

'Hmm. We'll come to Sandy in a minute. Well, then I got your message about Judge and rang your home number, only to be told that you weren't there and no one was quite sure where you were. You really should keep your staff better informed, you know.'

'Yeah, well, it wasn't estate business.'

'Anyway, I tried your mobile and the first thing I heard was you talking to Judge, saying – well, you know what you were saying. Suffice to say it made me sit up and listen. I was just hoping you wouldn't forget to tell us where you were. So what happened then?'

Accepting a blanket from the returning paramedic, Linc gave Rockley a brief description of events while the cut on his head was patched up. 'I didn't know for sure that anyone was actually on their way,' he finished. 'Or I might have tried to stay hidden for a bit longer. As it was, I had some idea of using the lorry to bust out through the fence but my driving skills let me down a bit!'

'When we arrived it looked like something out of a James Bond film,' Rockley said. 'You at the wheel of the juggernaut, fighting off all-comers and scattering bodies in all directions. Roger Moore's got nothing on you!'

Linc smiled tiredly. 'Pierce Brosnan.'

'What?'

'Pierce Brosnan,' the other officer put in helpfully, handing them both mugs of tea. 'Roger Moore was years ago.'

'You can tell how long it was since I went to the pictures,' Rockley said, unabashed. 'Anyway it was very impressive.'

'Till I crashed.' Linc took a sip of his brew and wrinkled his nose as he found it loaded with sugar.

'Yes, until then.'

The paramedic finished up and left, followed by the tea-making policeman, and the DI looked at Linc critically.

'How d'you feel now?'

'Shattered but okay, I guess.'

'You're a resilient bugger, too!' Rockley said with a smile.

Linc's mobile began to vibrate once more and he fished it out. 'Hello.'

'Where the hell have you been?' Crispin's voice demanded. 'That Inspector bloke was looking for you earlier, but nobody knew for sure where you were and we couldn't get through on your mobile.'

'Yeah, sorry. Anyway, I've seen Rockley now.'

'So where've you been?'

'I . . . er . . . had a couple of meetings and they went on longer than I expected,' Linc said with selective veracity. 'Did you want me for anything in particular?'

'No, not really. It's just . . . well, with everything that's been going on lately, we were worried about you, that's all.'

'*Ah*, that's so sweet,' Linc teased, and was rewarded with a pithy description of his character.

He disconnected and found Rockley regarding him with a raised eyebrow.

'A couple of meetings? I suppose that's one way of putting it. But it makes me wonder what you're not telling *me* . . .'

Linc shrugged and pursed his lips. 'Nothing important.'

'But . . .? Come on, Linc. I can see you've got something on your mind.'

He looked down at his hands, frowning; not sure whether he wanted to talk about it. It seemed incomprehensible, looking back on it.

'I almost gave myself up, back there in the unit,' he said finally. 'Marty was so close I was breathing his cigarette smoke, but I was well hidden, he couldn't have found me without climbing up. I knew what they'd do if they caught me – Judge made that perfectly clear – but suddenly I just wanted it all to be over, as if anything was better than waiting for it to happen. I can't explain it . . .'

He looked up at Rockley, not knowing what to expect, but the policeman was nodding, apparently unsurprised. 'It's actually not that unusual. It's a known phenomenon – probably got some high-faluting name, if we did but know it. It happens even under war conditions when people know they'll be shot on sight. The tension becomes too much to bear and they just stand up in front of the guns. It seems daft but it happens. Try not to worry about it.' He paused, looking thoughtful. 'I hate to do this, but I need to ask you a favour . . .'

'Just as long as it doesn't involve vigorous physical activity,' Linc stipulated. 'I haven't done that much running since I hung up my rugby boots, and that was longer ago than I care to admit.'

'No running,' Rockley assured him. 'And no

stunt driving either. No, I'm afraid this has to do with your friend Sandy Wilkes.'

'Ah,' Linc said heavily.

'I know he's your mate, Linc, but it's too much to suppose that being in the business he is *and* being associated with Alan Judge, he had nothing to do with the tack theft ring. That would be one hell of a coincidence, and in my line of work those kind of coincidences almost always turn out to be something else altogether.'

'He saved my life . . .'

'Yes, I know. And I wouldn't mind betting he got a rocketing from his boss because of it, if Judge ever found out.'

'But . . .' Linc paused, remembering the day he'd gone to Sandy's premises, bottle of Scotch in hand, to thank the saddler. Judge had been there then and he'd been patently unhappy about something. He forced his mind back. '*If you'd used your head there wouldn't still be a problem,*' Judge had said. '*. . . you had a chance to put things right and you didn't . . .*' Had he been talking about the night Sandy had found Linc unconscious in his car? Was he suggesting that Sandy could have finished what someone else had started?

'He needn't have done it at all,' Linc persisted, but even to his own ears he sounded less sure. 'He could have just left me there in my car but he took me to the Vicarage . . .'

'I'm not saying he's a murderer, or even that he had anything to do with the attack on Abby Hathaway, but I *am* saying that I'm pretty sure he's guilty by association, if nothing else. I'd stake my reputation on it.'

'Who do you think did attack Abby? Have you any idea?'

'An idea, yes; the proof may take a little longer. I think it lies in the concept that people, to a large extent, see what they expect to see. I think Abby was convinced it was you because she went down to the yard expecting it to be you, saw someone – perhaps from behind – who was enough like you not to raise any suspicions, and was struck down before she was fully aware that it wasn't you.' Rockley paused. 'And who do we know – not a million miles from here – about your height, dark-haired and wearing a leather jacket very much like one I've seen you wear?'

'Marty Lucas!' Linc said on a note of discovery. 'Of course. So what now? Do you think he'll confess?'

The detective shrugged. 'I'm afraid it's not very likely. It's not the first time we've had occasion to question Mr Lucas, and he's notoriously silent under interrogation. No, this is where we need a favour from you—'

He broke off, looking up enquiringly as the officer in the black waterproof stuck his head round the door.

'We've got the lad, Guv.'

'Good. You'd better get them all back to the station, then. Any injuries to speak of?'

'Nothing much. I'll be off then,' the policeman said, suiting his actions to the words.

'What'll happen to Scott?' Linc asked. 'A slap on the wrist and a caution?'

Rockley shook his head. 'Not this time. He's got an ASBO on him. Anti-social behaviour order. He must have breached that a dozen times this afternoon. It'll be a custodial sentence this time. He's run out of chances.'

'Well, that's something at least. So, what is it you want me to do?' Linc said, reverting to their previous conversation, and afraid he already knew the answer.

'Well, as I was saying, I don't anticipate getting much joy from Marty Lucas. Naturally we can charge him in connection with what's gone on here today, but unless Judge is forthcoming we don't have any evidence against him or anyone else for the attack on Abby, and that's what I'd really like to pin on them.'

'But Judge more or less admitted responsibility to me, I told you.'

'Yes, but I'm afraid "more or less" via a third party – however respectable – would be torn to shreds in court by a good lawyer,' Rockley told him. 'I want the case against them to be absolutely concrete. Sorry – bad choice of word, considering what you've been through!'

'I don't know whether Judge really meant that, about the concrete. I mean, the stuff he showed me – the base for his new garage – wasn't deep enough. When I pushed him and he sat down in it, it only came up to his waist.'

'Plenty of other places on a building site. With the site foreman on side, they could have put a body under the rubble in one of the foundation trenches and the lads would have topped it off with cement the following day, none the wiser.'

'I guess so.' It was a deeply sobering thought. 'So what are you saying? That you want me to get

Sandy to talk, is that it? What if he doesn't know anything? He could just be the . . . what do you call it . . .?'

'The fence?' Rockley supplied. 'No, I don't think so. If this was a small-scale operation then maybe. But we're almost certain that the saddles were shipped out to Ireland – which is of course where Judge Haulage would come in very useful. And besides, it was obvious that they had inside information. Where the stables were; whether they had security; even knowledge as to when the owners were going to be away. I think Sandy Wilkes was well aware what was going on, and who was involved. All we need is for him to agree to testify, and that's where you come in.'

Linc looked long and hard at Rockley, then sighed.

'Okay, I'll give it a go. When?'

'ASAP. Now, preferably. Before he finds out what's happened from someone else.'

Linc ran a hand through his wet hair.

'Oh, God! What a day!'

'I know. I'm sorry to have to ask you . . .'

He didn't look particularly sorry, Linc thought. What he did look was grey and exhausted. All at once he remembered what Farquharson had told him, earlier that afternoon.

'It's all right. I guess you've had a pig of a day, too. I gather there was a bit of bother in Bournemouth. Someone with a bomb?'

'Said he had one in a shoebox. Waved it at us through the window. We cordoned the whole area off, evacuated the buildings, the works.'

'But it wasn't a bomb?'

'No. It was a pair of shoes.' Rockley rubbed his eyes. 'And, yes, I have had a pig of a day. I haven't been home for thirty-six hours and I'm running on caffeine. So what do you say? Will you do it?'

Linc nodded, shedding the blanket and getting to his feet. 'Lead on, MacDuff.'

It was generally agreed that Linc should drive the Morgan to Shaftesbury, to present an appearance of normality, but in spite of a vigorous mopping up and towelling down, the leather seats still felt decidedly damp, as, consequently, did Linc's trousers by the time he arrived at Sandy's unit.

Parking next to the saddler's lorry, Linc could see a light through the high, narrow window of the office, and was forced to relinquish the faint hope that Sandy might be out. Outside the building, a man in overalls was halfway up a ladder, apparently doing something to the telephone wires. Linc greeted him briefly and went on in.

It wasn't possible to be sure whether Judge had kept Sandy advised of his plans regarding Linc, but the saddler's reaction, when Linc knocked and entered the office, seemed to suggest that he hadn't.

'Linc. You look a bit soggy! D'you fancy a cuppa?' he asked, showing no particular surprise at seeing him. Tiger bustled forward, his stumpy tail wagging ecstatically.

'Thanks. Yes, I got caught in a cloudburst with the soft-top down. The Morgan's going to take ages to dry out.'

'Oh, bad luck! Pull up a pew.' Sandy busied himself with the kettle and mugs.

'Got trouble with your telephone?' Linc asked, waving a hand towards the window.

'Well, I didn't think so, but apparently there's a fault on one of the lines and the guy said he needed to check all of them to locate it. I told him I didn't mind what he did as long as he didn't charge me for it. So . . . have you spoken to Al yet?'

Even though it was what Linc had come to talk about, the swift change of direction caught him napping. He ducked his head, making a fuss of the dog.

'Al?'

Sandy turned, eyebrows raised, with a jar of coffee in one hand and a teaspoon in the other.

'Yeah, Al Judge. About the sponsorship?'

'As a matter of fact, yes, I have. I turned his offer down.'

Sandy became very still.

'Why would you do that? I thought you were desperate for a sponsor.'

'Not *that* desperate,' Linc replied. 'Sandy, I know who Barnaby is.'

'Barnaby? Oh, the Barnaby you were looking for. So, who is it?'

'Come on, Sandy. Don't pretend you don't know. Barnaby Rudge – Judge. You almost told me yourself.'

'Ah.' The saddler sighed, looking disappointed but not noticeably shamefaced. 'I told Al it wouldn't work. He had some stupid idea that once he had you on the payroll, so to speak, he could talk you round even if you found out. I told him he was wrong but he wouldn't listen.' He turned back to his coffee-making. 'So what're you going to do about it?'

'I was hoping *you'd* have the answer to that one,' Linc said. 'I don't have any proof, only supposition. You, on the other hand, could give the police all the information they need.'

Rockley had agreed that in this situation it might be best to keep Sandy in ignorance of the day's events and encourage him to come forward of his own free will, but at first it didn't look as though the plan was going to work.

'Me?' he exclaimed, swinging round. 'Why me? I admit I guessed that Judge was the Barnaby you were looking for, but surely you don't believe I was involved in the rest of it?'

Linc said nothing, merely stared at the saddler, deeply disappointed.

Sandy turned away, pouring boiling water and then milk in a silence that fairly buzzed with tension. Finally, he put a mug of coffee on the desk in front of Linc, sat down opposite him and said in a low, slightly unsteady voice, 'He'd kill me if I talked!'

'With your testimony, he'd be put away,' Linc coaxed. 'He wouldn't be able to get at you.'

Sandy shook his head. 'I can't.'

'I don't think you have a choice, Sandy. If you knew what Judge was up to, you're already involved, whether you like it or not. Don't you see that this is your only way out? If you agree to testify, it'll count in your favour. We can't let Judge get away with this. Think of Abby . . .'

Sandy looked directly at him, his good-natured, freckled face intensely troubled. 'That's just it though, Linc. Abby. I was there. I *am* involved!'

Linc felt as though someone had kicked him in the stomach.

'You were there?' he repeated stupidly.

'I didn't hit her! That was Marty,' Sandy declared, caution thrown to the winds now in his desperation that Linc should believe him. 'I wouldn't have hit her. I was putting stuff in the van, I didn't even see her go by. I would never have hurt her, you've got to believe me!'

'You left her there,' Linc stated flatly. 'On the floor of the tackroom.'

'I wanted to ring for an ambulance but Marty said they'd trace the call. Linc, for God's sake, you know me. You know I'd never hurt anyone.'

'I thought I did. But when I think how you sat in the kitchen at the Vicarage, just three days later, having lunch with her family . . . How could you do that? Little Toby was crying,' Linc remembered, shaking his head in disgust. 'And how could you lead Ruth on like that? Take her out, make her fall for you, after all you'd done? You're a complete bastard, do you know that?'

Sandy flinched. 'I'm sorry. What can I say? I never meant for any of this to happen. I owed Al big-time for some stuff way back, and he called in the favour. At first he just wanted a bit of information; you know, who had stables away from the house, who'd got new tack, and what the security was like. I chat to people all the time, and get to know when they're going away or going to be out for an evening. Sometimes I'd get invited to parties or to bring my gear along to riding demos, and I'd see who was there and then give Al a ring and let him know.'

Linc could hardly believe what he was hearing. 'So, while you were out socialising with these people, Marty was clearing out their tackrooms!'

Sandy looked uncomfortable. 'The stuff's all insured. They just replace it. The only people who lose out are the insurance companies, and they can afford it.'

'Oh, yeah, the old excuse,' Linc said, nodding. 'And who has to fork out for the higher premiums, huh? You can't justify it, mate, so don't even try. Besides, it's not just the money. It really messes up people's lives, being burgled. Makes them feel they're not safe in their own homes.'

Sandy offered no response to this, merely sat staring into his coffee, and after a moment Linc went on. 'I guess you did a nice trade, replacing their lost tack. Playing the Good Samaritan, generously delaying payment until the insurance money came through. Didn't you ever feel just the slightest bit hypocritical?'

Sandy still had nothing to offer.

'So when did you start helping Marty at the sharp end? Was it all getting a bit tame? Did you fancy a bit of an adrenalin rush?'

'No, it wasn't like that! That night at the Vicarage – that was the first time. There was another bloke used to help Marty, but that night he couldn't make it and Al said I should go.' Sandy met Linc's contemptuous gaze at last. 'I didn't want to, but you don't know Al Judge. He's a real bastard – you don't cross him! I've seen him break a man's kneecaps with a cricket bat. I can still hear his screams. Nobody crosses old Barnaby and gets away with it.'

Having had recent experience of the man, Linc

could well believe that, but knowledge of Sandy's subsequent deception of the Hathaways effectively suppressed any sympathy he might have felt.

'What happened to the tack that was stolen? The police didn't find anything here last time, but you must have kept some of it because you had my snaffle.'

'Judge took care of that. Most of the saddles went to Ireland, hidden in his lorries, and then he'd bring stuff back, too. Some of it would end up here, some in other areas. But the smaller stuff, I got to keep. It was my cut. I'm always buying old tack from people, and from auctions. Quite often it's just a box of stuff, so it's easy to keep my books straight. I dismantle the bridles and sell the bits separately. Nobody recognises the smaller stuff – or at least they didn't until you turned up with that bit.'

'Did you know that was mine when you sold it to me?' Linc was curious.

'Yeah. I guessed it was 'cos it's a fairly unusual one. I wouldn't normally sell back to the same person but I didn't have another one, and how was I to know you'd recognise it? Sod's law, that was!'

'A chance in a million,' Linc agreed. 'And like a fool, I didn't believe you could have had any knowledge of it. I trusted you, like everyone else did. You know, you had such a good thing going here . . . loyal customers, a terrific reputation. You're a bloody fool to throw that away.'

'It was hard slog, and I was making peanuts,' Sandy complained. 'It's all right for people like you. You've never had to go without.'

'Oh, yeah. I'm rolling in it. That's why I'm looking for a sponsor. And, of course, while I was away my father sent me a big fat cheque every week – I don't think! Get real, Sandy! You can't make those kinds of generalisations. Sure, some people have money to burn, but did it ever occur to you that they might have worked bloody hard to get it? The world doesn't owe you a living, you know.'

Sandy went back to staring at his mug.

'So what now? Are you going to tell the coppers?'

'They already know,' Linc told him, and felt no compunction at seeing the look of despair that settled on the saddler's face. 'They've already picked up Judge and Marty Lucas. I talked Rockley into giving you a chance to do the right thing and turn yourself in, but that was before I realised what a gutless sod you are.'

He got wearily to his feet. 'Oh, and by the way, don't bother trying to change your story now. There's a guy up a ladder out there who's had an extremely sensitive microphone and recording equipment pointed this way for the last twenty minutes. Thanks for the coffee.'

He left the office and at the outer door of the unit, passed Rockley and one of his men coming the other way.

'Did you get that?'

'Yes. That should wrap that little business up nicely,' the detective observed with satisfaction. 'Thanks for your help.'

Linc was sitting in the Morgan a couple of minutes later when Rockley brought Sandy out, trailed by the other officer with, on the end of a rope lead, the jaunty figure of Tiger. The little procession halted level with the car and Linc looked up at them enquiringly.

It was, surprisingly, Sandy who spoke.

'Linc, I'm sorry, I know what you think of me, but I need a really big favour. It's Tiger. I can't leave him here and I don't know who else to ask . . .'

Linc groaned. 'Oh, God! I don't want him. What normally happens to dogs when you take their owners in?' he asked Rockley.

'It depends. If there are no relatives, we get them signed over to the dogs' home.'

Linc looked reluctantly at the dog who wagged his stumpy tail and grinned back trustingly. He liked dogs, but between his father's two wolfhounds and Geoff Sykes's labradors he didn't go short of canine company and, just at the moment, having one of his own wasn't high on his wish-list. Even if it had been, he reflected, eyeing Tiger's ugly-attractive brindle face with some distaste, this definitely wouldn't be the dog he would choose.

'Please, Linc . . .' Sandy pleaded. 'Whatever else I've done, I did save your life that night, remember?'

Linc looked away, then back at Tiger, who looked a little uncertain, as if sensing the enormity of the moment.

'Oh, give the bugger here!' he said suddenly, opening the car door. With very little encouragement, Tiger climbed in and Linc looped the end of the rope round the handbrake, which caused Rockley to frown.

'I shall pretend I didn't see that,' he decided.

'Well, it was that or the gear lever,' Linc joked. Then as Sandy was about to be led away, 'Tell me. That night – do you know who doctored my drink?'

Sandy shook his head. 'No. I honestly knew nothing about it.'

'So it wasn't Judge's doing?'

'No, he said not. But when he found out that I'd helped you, he went ballistic! You should thank your lucky stars it wasn't Marty or Scott who found you!'

'Oh, I do,' Linc assured him.

It was well into the evening before Linc finally made it home, and Farthingscourt was quiet. Nobody appeared, demanding to know where he'd been, for which he was grateful – he'd had quite enough of answering questions for one day. It was strange to think, though, that his life-or-death drama had been played out in such a relatively short time that no one who wasn't directly involved had any inkling that anything out of the ordinary had happened.

Still unsure as to what he was going to do with Tiger, and unwilling to imbue him with any delusions of permanency, Linc installed him in the office for the night. He was a dog who stubbornly resisted any form of reasoning and Linc had a feeling that once admitted to his flat, Tiger would quickly make himself at home and be extremely difficult to evict. With this in mind, he piled a couple of old horse blankets in the corner of the office, put down a bowl of water, and left him crunching happily on a double handful of the wolfhounds' dry mix.

Mentally and physically exhausted, Linc slept long and deeply, waking to find his room flooded with daylight, and wishing, as he did every morning, that Josie were beside him. This time, however, as he recalled the events of the previous day, he could allow himself to hope that the longing would soon be reality.

A more complete recall of the previous day brought another, more immediately pressing matter to mind.

Tiger.

Glancing at his watch, Linc discovered that it was past nine, and realised that the poor dog had been shut in the office for the best part of eleven hours. Hoping that the mongrel was blessed with adequate bladder control, he leaped out of bed, dressed and ran down the back stairs, through the old kitchen and out into the yard, unsure whether the probability that Mary had got there first was a good thing or a bad.

The office door was unlocked and Linc opened it cautiously, half-expecting a brindle torpedo to hurtle out, but the room was empty; the pile of blankets dented but abandoned. Had Mary been taken unawares and allowed Tiger to escape? Surely if that had been so she would have woken him up to tell him. Muttering curses under his breath, Linc left the office and went across to rap on the door of her cottage.

After a brief pause, Mary answered his knock.

'Good morning, Linc. Have you lost someone, by any chance?'

He sighed. 'Ah, you've found him.'

'He's been having breakfast with me.' She stood back to afford Linc a view of her kitchen, where Tiger lay curled up next to her Rayburn stove. The dog raised an eyebrow and twitched his apology for a tail but made no move to get up. 'He's very agreeable company, aren't you, lad?'

The pairing of neat, orderly Mary Poe with Sandy's in-your-face, streetwise dog was not one that would have suggested itself to Linc in a thousand years, but such was the odd nature of friendships. And Tiger was the sort of dog who would always be quick to recognise a good thing when he saw it.

'His name's Tiger,' Linc told her. 'He belongs to a friend of mine who's had to go away for a while.'

Even as he heard himself terming Sandy a friend, he knew it was no longer true. He could have forgiven the saddler for being weak, and even for his lack of morals, but didn't think he would ever be able to forgive the way he'd left Abby unconscious on the night of the raid and then unashamedly accepted the friendship and warmth extended by the Hathaway family, and Ruth in particular.

'Well, you can't leave him in the office, poor little mite,' Mary said.

'I didn't know where else to put him. It was rather a last-minute thing.'

'Well, he's welcome to come in with me when I'm here, but I draw the line at taking him for walks,' she warned.

Linc thanked her, relieved to find such an easy solution to the problem, and returned to the office to see to the first business of the morning, ahead of a succession of planned meetings with Reagan, Geoff Sykes, and Saul the millwright. It looked like being another busy day.

The day progressed much in the manner of many Thursdays. Having taken the dressing off what was no more than a superficial cut on his hairline, there was nothing about Linc to show that the previous day's adventure had ever happened. As a result, no one showed any curiosity and, even though his head was full of it, appropriate opportunities to introduce the subject into the conversation seemed few and far between. He had intended telling Crispin, but when he met him briefly at lunchtime his brother was in a hurry and full of the news that Nikki's mother had returned unexpectedly that morning.

'Just when we'd got used to having the house to ourselves again,' he complained. 'I wouldn't mind but the fair's not for days yet.'

Linc commiserated.

'By the way,' Crispin went on, 'hope you didn't mind me ringing you yesterday. It's just – you told me you just had to nip out for an hour or so and you'd written "Mike, three-thirty" on your jotter and underlined it. By half-past six I was starting to wonder.'

'That was Mike Farquharson, the wine merchant,' Linc told him. 'He's offered to sponsor my riding.' Incredibly, he'd almost forgotten that, with what came after, and now the memory of it gave him a frisson of pleasure.

'That's brilliant!' Crispin exclaimed. 'So you were out celebrating.'

'Well, something like that,' Linc hedged. Somehow it didn't seem to be the moment to say, 'No, actually, after that I went on to meet someone else and narrowly escaped being killed and buried in concrete'.

'So what did Rockley want?' Crispin was on his way to the door.

'It was about the attack on Abby. They think they've caught the man who did it.'

'Oh, good, so that's over. That's a relief. Having a private detective in the family's a bit of a worry.' He glanced at his watch. 'Look, I must go, I've got to pick Nikki up from the gym because her car's at the garage. Tell me about it later.'

As he disappeared, Linc sighed. Next stop the mill for the meeting with Saul. He collected the keys to the Discovery from the office and made his way out to the yard where Tiger greeted him joyfully and accompanied him to the vehicle. Linc looked round in vain for Mary, then gave in and opened the tailgate to let him jump up.

Halfway to the mill his phone rang.

'Linc, it's Rebecca.'

'Oh. Hi, Rebecca. Is everything okay?'

'Yes, fine. At last I can say that! We saw Inspector Rockley this morning and he told us the good news – but then, I gather you know all about it?'

'I spoke to him yesterday,' Linc agreed, wondering just how much he'd told them.

'Yes, *and* the rest!' she said wryly. 'According to him, it was you who tracked them down.'

'More by luck than judgement.' It appeared that Rockley had spared Rebecca the details, for which Linc was extremely grateful.

'Well, thank you anyway. It's such a relief. Maybe now Abby can begin to move on.' She paused. 'I wouldn't blame you if you said no, but we'd very much like you to come over for a meal tonight . . . ?' The rising note of uncertainty in her voice turned the invitation into a question.

Linc hesitated. 'What about Abby? Is she okay with it?'

'It was her idea. I mean, we all want you to come – of course we do – but we wouldn't have pushed her. Then, this morning, after the Inspector had left, she was a bit tearful and said she supposed you'd never want to speak to her again. I said I was sure you would . . .'

'Of course I do.'

'So she wanted me to ask you. Please come, Linc. I know it's been rough on you and Josie these past few days, and I'm sorry, but we only wanted to protect Abby. She's been through so much . . .'

'Rebecca, you don't have to apologise,' he cut in. 'And yes, I'd love to come.'

He arranged to be at the Vicarage around eight o'clock and slipped the phone back in his pocket, feeling that finally things were beginning to look up.

Saul was waiting at the mill and together they did the rounds, inspecting the ongoing work, discussing the timetable for the following week, and standing for a long time watching the water that was now flowing back into the millpond, creeping imperceptibly up the newly rendered sides. The pump, piping the water away to the bypass stream, had been turned off thirty-six hours ago and Saul thought it would take the best part of a week to bring the pond up to its original depth but still the process held a fascination for Linc. When the millpond was full, water would start to pour over the weir, where – if it was found to be necessary to build up the level preparatory to milling – the old sluice-gates might one day be replaced.

Now the end of the renovation was in sight, Linc

was looking forward with increasing impatience to the day when the old waterwheel would come back to life.

They left the mill site by way of the new pedestrian gate into the car park, wincing as its hinges screamed a dry protest.

'You would think the workmen would have oiled that when they put it on, wouldn't you?' Linc remarked.

'I imagine there's some oil around somewhere,' Saul said. 'If I'd come in my van there'd be some in the back, but I haven't.'

'Well, as a matter of fact, I've got a pot of Vaseline in the glove compartment,' Linc remembered. It was the one he'd found in the coat he'd borrowed at Crispin's, and subsequently forgotten about.

He retrieved it and liberally smeared the offending hinge, working the gate to and fro until the squeak was silenced. Saul picked the tub off the gatepost where Linc had rested it, and made to put the lid back on.

'Is this some special mix?' he asked, pausing in the act.

'No. Just bog standard. I use it to stop my horse's mouth getting sore when I'm eventing. It acts as a barrier to all his slobber.'

'But it's got bits in it,' Saul observed. 'Looks like rust but it shouldn't be 'cos those hinges are new.'

Linc held out his hand, frowning. Sure enough, the clear grease *was* liberally speckled with tiny dark-coloured particles. He sniffed it but it seemed to have no smell so he replaced the lid, shrugging.

Perhaps it hadn't been his own tub, after all, but then there were the horse hairs . . .

It was with a mixture of eagerness and apprehension that Linc presented himself at the Vicarage that evening. In the past it had been his custom to let himself in at the back door and call a greeting as he made his way to the kitchen, but this evening he hesitated on the doorstep and then knocked instead.

A few seconds passed and then he heard footsteps approaching on the tiled floor.

'Linc! Gosh, I thought it must be someone collecting for a charity or something,' Ruth exclaimed as she opened the door. 'What are you doing out here?'

'I didn't like to barge in,' he explained. 'After everything that's happened, it just didn't feel right.'

Before Ruth could reply, Tiger, who'd insisted on coming with Linc, in spite of bribes offered by Mary, slipped between the two of them and disappeared up the passage towards the kitchen.

She looked after him in surprise.

'Well, there's someone who doesn't mind barging in! Is that . . .? It looked like . . .'

'It was,' Linc said apologetically. 'I'm sorry, Ruth. I tried to leave him behind but he's a little bugger for getting his own way.'

'No. That's all right, Linc. I didn't realise you'd got him, that's all. It's not his fault his owner turned out to be a bastard. Come on in.'

Linc put his hand on her arm.

'Ruth, are you all right? About Sandy, I mean.'

'Oh, sure,' she declared, perhaps a little too airily. 'He's no loss.'

Linc wasn't fooled. He watched her with silent sympathy.

'Okay, I'll admit it,' she amended. 'I'm not all right. I feel wretched, betrayed, angry – but mostly I feel such a fool for having been taken in like that.'

'We were all taken in. He fooled us all, but if it helps, I don't believe he set out to do it. I think, for all his happy-go-lucky bluster, he's really a pretty lonely bloke who fell under the spell of your lovely family. I should know – it happened to me.'

Ruth shrugged. 'I don't know whether it helps or not. Maybe it will in time. But it was a nice thing to say, thank you. Now, come on in before you have me in tears again.'

The meeting with Abby, which Linc had been viewing with a certain amount of apprehension, went better than he had dared hope. The whole family, with the exception of her father, was gathered around the kitchen table when he went in, as on so many of his visits in the past. He could hear them chattering as he followed Ruth down the passageway and Rebecca immediately drew him into the conversation, allowing no time for awkwardness.

'Ah, Linc, we were just discussing possible names for this kitten Josie's foisting on us in a week or two. I still think if it's ginger it should be Marmalade, but Hannah and Abby don't agree.'

'But that's so boring!' Hannah protested. 'It's like calling a white one Snowy, or a black one Sooty. My friend Katy's got a cat called Einstein and a dog called Shakespeare. They're cool names!'

'And everything has to be *cool* at the moment, doesn't it, Hannah?' her mother said tolerantly.

'But all the same, I'm not sure I could live with a literary cat, and Einstein is giving the poor thing a lot to live up to!'

'It's no good asking me to suggest a name,' Linc said, going round the table to greet both Rebecca and Josie with a kiss on the cheek before slipping into a vacant chair next to them. 'I can never think of anything. So what's your suggestion, Abby?'

He glanced across at her and saw a faint pinkness stain her still too-pale skin. Her hands and face looked painfully thin, but her hair had been washed and brushed into a shining dark curtain. This, in itself, took a bit of getting used to, as Linc couldn't recall ever having seen it loose before. Watching the way it fell forward as she now dipped her head, he realised that it was indicative of her present, vulnerable state of mind.

With an obvious effort she looked up under her lashes to meet his eyes.

'I like Toffee,' she said.

'Toffee?' Hannah repeated, scornfully. 'You always go for food names. Syrup, Treacle, now Toffee!'

'What about Fudge?' Toby put in, with the air of one not expecting to be considered. He had one hand under the table and Linc guessed that was where Tiger had got to.

'Actually, I think Fudge is a good name,' Linc said approvingly. 'Especially when you see what I've got here.' He opened a brown paper bag he'd been carrying and took out a large box of dairy fudge, amused to see Toby's eyes instantly light up.

'Wow! That's huge!'

409

'Linc, you shouldn't . . .' Rebecca began, but Hannah cut in with a sneer.

'I hope you didn't bring that for Abby because she's not eating at the moment. It would be a real waste.'

'It's for all of you,' Linc assured her.

'I *am* eating, you little cow!' Abby said, stung into childish retort. 'Just because I don't want to end up stocky, like you!'

'I'm not stocky!'

'That's enough!' their mother interposed, but Linc could see she was pleased to see some of Abby's old spark resurfacing.

'Right. Time to lay the table,' Josie said, getting to her feet. 'Hannah – tablecloth.'

David Hathaway, who appeared just before the meal was served, took Linc aside and offered a gracious apology for the scene at the hospital.

'The silly thing is, as soon as I stopped to think, I knew you couldn't have done it, but for a moment there I just saw red. I couldn't see anything beyond the fact that somehow your presence was upsetting my little girl, and after everything she'd been through, I couldn't bear it. It wasn't very Christian, but I think in that moment I'd have turned on the Archbishop of Canterbury himself!'

Linc accepted his apology without hesitation, and his relationship with the family slipped back on to more or less the same footing as it had been prior to the trouble. The exception, unsurprisingly, was Abby, who picked at her food and was noticeably withdrawn, and although Linc found her watching him on a number of occasions, she always looked away when their eyes met.

After the meal he joined in a boisterous game of Monopoly, and it wasn't until he was on the point of leaving that he finally had a chance to speak to Abby alone. Hannah and Toby had been sent up to bed, and somehow, as the coffee cups were cleared away, Linc found that the rest of the family had disappeared, on one pretext or another, leaving Abby sleepy-eyed at one end of the kitchen sofa and him at the other.

'I think we've been set up,' he remarked, smiling at her.

Abby bit her lip and looked down at her hands.

To Linc's horror, a tear welled up and spilled over to run down her thin cheek.

'You don't have to say anything, you know,' he said gently, feeling intensely sorry for her. 'I know what happened, and I understand.'

'But I *have* to say something!' she insisted. 'The things I said – I can't believe I ever thought it was you! I must have been out of my head!'

Linc moved across and took her thin hands in his. She made as if to pull them away, then stopped herself but still wouldn't look at him.

'Abby, you were ill. Drugged up to the eyeballs. You weren't thinking straight. You have to put it behind you; to move on. And you've got to eat.' In a private moment, earlier, Josie had told him that Abby was existing on almost nothing. 'You'll have to put on a bit of weight if you're going to groom for me on Hilary Lang's training course in August. It's not long now.'

The girl's eyes lit with sudden interest.

'Hilary Lang? It *is* true then? I thought I'd dreamed that. I had some seriously weird dreams.'

'Yes, it's true. So you'd better concentrate on getting fit.'

'Wouldn't you rather take Josie?'

'Josie? No, she's not such a good groom as you.'

'But I thought . . . Um, she told me about you and her . . .' Abby looked sideways at him through her glossy fall of hair.

'And you don't mind?'

'Of course not. I know I was a bit silly before but . . . well, I suppose I always knew nothing would come of it. Besides, you're way too old!'

Linc nodded wryly. 'I'm afraid so. Positively prehistoric!'

Linc left the Vicarage on his own to make his way back to Farthingscourt. The kisses he'd shared with Josie when she'd walked him out to his car had left him filled with a frustrated longing, and she'd obviously felt the same because as they drew apart, she murmured, 'I know, I know, but it won't be long now, I promise. Soon they won't need me.'

Bugger them! I need you! Linc's inner self cried, but he kept the selfish words in his head, knowing that when she did come to him, it must be wholeheartedly.

Home once more, he installed Tiger in the office, switching on the light briefly to check that he had water and to give him his biscuits. There, laying on his desk was a brown envelope with *LINC TREMAYNE – BY HAND* printed in capital letters on the front.

With casual interest, he slit the top and drew out the paper it contained, but felt a jolt of shock when he realised it was a folded sheet of newsprint.

Surely that was all in the past. Al Judge was locked away in the police cells, as was – presumably – Sandy. The scare-tactics were done with. *Weren't they?*

He unfolded the paper carefully, holding it by the outer edges with deference to Rockley and his forensic team, and read it with deepening dismay.

It was identical in form to the previous three and this time the highlighted words stated:

> *You were warned but you took no notice.*
> *Now you and the bitch will pay the price.*

16

Linc wasn't sure afterwards just how long he stood there with the sheet of newspaper in his hand. In the end it was Tiger who recalled him to the here and now, by bringing it to his attention, with a prodding paw, that he still hadn't received his biscuits.

'Sorry, lad.' Linc tossed the treats on to the dog's bed absent-mindedly, and then sat heavily in the chair at his desk, trying to make sense of the situation.

Why had the note arrived now, when the investigation into Abby's attack was over and done with? Was there someone else involved who'd slipped through the net? But if so, he'd be stupid to draw attention to himself now. Unless, Linc thought, his heart thumping, it was warning him of a revenge attack.

. . . *you and the bitch* . . .

Oh, God, not Josie! *Please*, not Josie!

He forced himself to think rationally.

If the note had been delivered by hand, who had brought it? And where had they left it? Presumably not in the actual office, although apart from public days it wasn't always locked. Had they, perhaps, been seen by someone at Farthingscourt?

Linc's best hope was that Judge had sent it before his arrest and it had taken a day or two to get to him. That was possible and, he decided, the most likely answer. His pulse rate slowing to the low hundreds, he stowed the paper in his own private drawer, gave Tiger a pat and headed for bed.

Halfway across the yard he remembered that, until Wednesday afternoon, Judge had presumably believed Linc was going along with the sponsorship deal, and so would have had no reason to send him a threatening note.

The first thing he did the following morning, was to ring Josie. He had no wish to alarm her unduly, but on the other hand couldn't bear the thought of something happening to her because he'd failed to warn her.

'If it wasn't Judge, then who on earth did send it?' she wanted to know.

Linc had no idea. The mystery had kept him awake for a substantial part of the night. Apart from anything else, he hadn't asked any questions or done any snooping around since the last warning; unless one counted talking to Sandy about the rhyming slang. Why go to the trouble of warning someone not to do something they weren't actively doing in the first place?

Could it have been Sandy who was behind the notes all along?

'None of it makes much sense,' he told Josie. 'But I thought you should know, that's all. Don't go wandering down any dark alleys or accepting lifts from shifty-looking strangers.'

'Oh, well! That's ruined my plans for the day, then!' she observed.

'Yeah, well, you know what I mean. Just be careful.'

'So what did the message actually say?'

Linc hesitated. He'd been, somewhat unrealistic-ally, hoping to avoid that one.

'It said something about my having been warned and not having taken any notice,' he said.

'And? What about me?'

'And, er . . . it said, "Now you and the bitch will pay the price",' he recited, finally biting the bullet.

Josie was quiet for a moment, then said lightly, 'I see. And you just naturally thought of me!'

'Well . . . Tiger's a dog.'

'*You sod!*' she exclaimed, laughing. 'Okay, I'll be careful. And you, presumably, will take the paper to Rockley.'

'Yeah, I guess so. Another one for his collection.'

Both Rockley and DS Manston were unavailable, he was told, so Linc left the offending sheet of newsprint in its envelope at reception, with a covering note for the inspector. Stowing it in the glovebox for the journey, he'd rediscovered the pot of Vaseline, and on impulse left that at the station for the attention of Rockley's forensics team, too.

Feeling the need for some quality time, away from the craziness that his life had become, Linc dropped in to see Barney and the greyhounds, and spent a happy hour or so helping out around the kennels and getting to know his chosen dog.

Back at Farthingscourt he decided that someone in the family should know what was going on, and to that end spoke to Crispin and Nikki, giving them the gist of the business with Judge and telling them about the threatening message.

'I don't want to worry Dad with it,' he finished. 'It may be no more than a stupid hoax, or it may be that now Judge and his crew are out of the way, there's no longer a threat anyway. I don't suppose either of you knows how it ended up on my desk?'

'Yes, I put it there,' Crispin confessed instantly. 'It was in our mailbox at the cottage.'

'That's right, I remember because you were complaining about having to run round delivering Linc's post,' Nikki corroborated.

'I was joking.'

'Well, that explains how it got there anyway,' Linc said. 'Now all I've got to do is discover who sent it and why.'

With the Georgian Fair just over a week away preparations were in full swing and much of Linc's time that day was taken up with sorting out the endless stream of minor problems it inevitably threw up. He'd given Jack Reagan the job of over-seeing the car-parking arrangements and, waking to heavy rain with no change forecast for the next few days, this in itself was proving to be a headache.

Liaising with the forester on the issue, Linc was aware of a change for the better in his behaviour. Perhaps, he thought, giving him the benefit of the doubt over the affair of Jim Pepper and the crowbar had won Reagan's trust where all Linc's previous friendly overtures had failed. The authorship of that

417

particular note was another mystery yet to be solved. Incredible to think that the incident had only been a week ago; so much had happened in those seven days that he felt a good ten years older.

In fact, the rain continued on and off for several days, finally clearing away the following Wednesday night when the wind sharpened and moved round to the southeast. It had been touch and go as to whether, even at this late stage, the fair should be called off, but an inspection of the site went in favour of continuing and preparations forged ahead.

From Linc's point of view, the only plus resulting from the inclement weather was that the millpond filled far faster than anyone had anticipated, and by the Thursday morning the millstream was in spate, with the excess water pouring over the weir in a spectacular display.

He visited the mill in the afternoon, when he knew Saul would be there, and found him engaged in the skilful task of dressing the stones. This involved chipping a particular pattern of grooves into the milling surfaces with an implement known as a mill-bill, to facilitate the efficient grinding of the grain.

Linc watched in fascination for a while, and then together they inspected the final stages of the renovation work. With the roof, floors and windows done, and the overhaul of the mill machinery nearly complete, the restoration of the building was tantalisingly close to completion. The next phase would be the conversion of the various outbuildings into bakery, shop, and tearooms. After that, most of what remained to be done was concerned with making the area safe for the public to visit – namely, railings to keep them from falling on to, or being pulled into, the many moving parts.

'I wish we'd arranged for Peter Neville to move into the cottage this week,' Linc said, watching the water cascading over the weir into the stream beyond. Neville was to be the mill manager. 'Now we're so close to starting her up, and with this weather we've been having, I'd feel happier with someone on site.'

'Yeah, but Peter doesn't finish his other job until Sunday,' Saul reminded him. 'I expect it'll be all right. He'll be here on Monday. You don't get a lot of trouble with trespassers down here, do you?'

'Not usually, but we've got this fair on Saturday and Geoff says you always get a few wanderers when the estate's open for a public event.'

Saul shrugged. 'As long as the door's locked you should be okay. You've still got the signs everywhere so you shouldn't be liable.'

'I guess so. It doesn't look as though it's going to be the sort of weather that will encourage people to strip off and dive into the millpond!'

In addition to the warning signs placed around the site by the company doing the renovation work, Linc had added on the gate a notice that pronounced, *No Swimming. No Diving. No Fishing.* To which someone had tacked a smaller, makeshift one that said, *No Water-skiing. No Bungee-jumping. No Fun Whatsoever!*

As it turned out, the mill wasn't destined to be deserted for the whole day anyway because Josie had arranged with a photographer friend to meet there at lunchtime on the Saturday, with a view to assessing its suitability as a fashion shoot location. She okayed it with Linc on Thursday evening when he invited her, Crispin and Nikki to his flat for a meal.

He'd told his guests eight o'clock, but just after seven, when he was still wrapped in a towel after a quick shower, there came a knock at the door of his apartment. He opened it to find Josie standing on the landing, clutching a bottle of wine and a bunch of flowers in cellophane.

'Please say you're early and I'm not an hour out,' he pleaded, kissing her nevertheless.

'I thought you could probably do with a hand. I know how late you've been working these last few days,' she said, holding out her offerings. 'These are for the table and this is for the icebox.'

'Well, thank you. But it was supposed to be my treat, Jo Jo.'

'I like cooking,' Josie replied. 'So it'll still be a treat.'

'Okay. Well, make yourself at home while I go and make myself decent. Help yourself to coffee or tea or whatever. I won't be a minute.'

By the time he'd pulled on some trousers and a clean shirt, and run a comb through his damp hair, he could hear voices and returned to the living room to find that Nikki and Crispin had also arrived, having had the same idea as Josie. The result of this was that eight o'clock found four people in Linc's not over-large kitchen, trying to prepare a pasta dish that mutated several times over the course of its creation as first one, then another of them, added a new ingredient.

The mood was buoyant, bordering on juvenile at

times, and by half-past eight, armed with bottles of wine, glasses, and plates piled high with what Crispin had christened Fusilli Chameleon, they made their way back into the living room to eat.

'Hey, you don't seem to have got as much as the rest of us,' Crispin told Josie as they sat down to eat. 'I've got enough here to keep a small platoon marching for a week. You're not doing your share!'

'No, this is really all I want,' she protested.

'Jo Jo's been feeling a bit under the weather lately, haven't you, Josie?' Linc explained. He knew she'd seen the doctor about it and been diagnosed with some unspecified bug that was doing the rounds.

'A bit,' she confessed. 'I just don't have much appetite at the moment.'

'It should be Nikki that's off her food, but she's fit as a fiddle, aren't you, Niks?' Crispin declared.

'Not everybody gets morning sickness,' Nikki pointed out. 'Mum says *she* didn't.'

'My mum did, but only when she had Toby,' Josie remembered. 'She always swore it was because he was a boy. But, honestly, I'm okay really. It's just some bug I've picked up.'

The meal was surprisingly good but extremely filling, and afterwards they sprawled on the leather sofas, drinking wine, chatting about anything and everything, and laughing a lot more than was strictly necessary.

It was gone one o'clock and two rounds of sobering coffee had been made and drunk when Crispin and Nikki finally left.

'It's a good job you haven't got to drive on the public highway,' Linc observed as he let them out. 'Go carefully, won't you?'

Finally shutting the door behind them, he turned to Josie, who was sitting on the arm of the sofa, watching him.

'So what about you, Missus?' he said, pulling her to her feet and into an embrace. 'Do you want me to call you a taxi? I suppose you'd better not drive, although I don't think you drank as much as the rest of us, did you? Are you sure you're okay? You do look a bit pale.'

'I'm fine. Much better than I was. Whatever it is, I think we're all having it in rotation. Ruth started it, then me, and now Dad's got it. The doctor thinks we're probably all a bit stressed, but I guess that's not surprising, is it?'

'No, I suppose not,' Linc murmured into her sweet-smelling hair.

'I know *I* am. What with the worry about Abby . . .'

'Well, at least she's on the mend now.'

'And you trying to kill yourself every five minutes . . .'

'Sorry about that. I'll try not to let it happen again.'

'And, of course, receiving death threats doesn't help one's peace of mind . . .'

'I'm sorry, are you really worrying about that?' Linc asked, remembering the latest note for the first time in days. He pulled back to look at her. 'I'd almost forgotten about it. I should think it was most likely something to do with Judge, and with him safely gathered in, that'll be the end of it. So you're not to worry, you hear?'

She bowed. 'Your wish is my command. By the way, have you said anything to Nikki and Crispin

422

about us? I mean, about the engagement?'

'No. I thought we said we wouldn't, for now.'

'I know we did. It was just something Nikki said when we were out in the kitchen making coffee. Nothing specific, but I got the feeling that she might have guessed.'

'Well, if she has, it wasn't from anything I've said. So, do you want me to call that taxi or . . . what?'

She pursed her lips, primly. 'Well, I have got my reputation to think of, you know.'

Linc stepped forward and swept her up off her feet.

'What reputation?' he asked, heading for the bedroom. 'You little hussy!'

The morning of the Farthingscourt Georgian Fair dawned bright and blustery, with towering white clouds in a deep blue sky. It was the kind of weather that could turn either way, Linc thought, casting a wary eye upwards. Nevertheless, with the fair starting at ten o'clock, it promised to hold fine long enough to tempt people out of their homes and through the gates.

The festivities were to take place on the gentle green slopes in front of the house, and for security the building itself would have all doors locked except for the one into the yard, which would be monitored constantly by two of the regular house guides.

The close-mown turf had, in the last few days, sprouted half a dozen white marquees, and by eight o'clock that morning several dozen trade stands, charity stalls and snack bars had joined them. Bunting and balloons abounded, but Linc had held out against the ubiquitous bouncy castle, on the undeniable grounds that it would be a horrendous anachronism. A group of village mums had set up a Pets Corner, and the local riding school had brought two ponies and a hefty skewbald cob to give rides and, presumably, try and bump up a bit of extra business in the process. With very few exceptions, everyone involved had dressed to follow the Georgian theme, although, it had to be said, with widely varying degrees of accuracy.

Bearing in mind the strength of the early-summer sun, and the amount of running around he was likely to have to do, Linc had decided against wearing the richly ornate dress costume of the day, and wore instead the full-skirted brown coat, breeches, boots and tricorne that constituted the riding garb of a country squire.

Crispin and Nikki made an odd pair, for although Crispin was resplendent in pale blue satin, knee stockings and a grey wig, Nikki had followed Linc's example and gone for the rustic look. With a full linen skirt, a daringly low-cut cotton blouse and a riot of golden curls cascading over her shoulders, Linc thought she looked like the cover illustration from a lusty historical romance. Which was, he had no doubt, the very effect she had intended. When she saw him, she put her hands on her hips, pulling her shoulders back, and with a sparkle in her eye said, 'How do, Master. Be there anythin' I can do for'ee?'

'Oi! Do you mind?' Crispin demanded. 'There's no need to offer your favours around!'

Linc laughed. Whatever her faults, Nikki was great fun.

As a matter of fact, he would have been hard put to it to have got the whole thing off the ground without his sister-in-law's excellent organisational skills. As the crowds began to trickle in, it became clear that one of her ideas was definitely bearing fruit. In an attempt to encourage people to turn up in costume, she had advertised that a voucher for a free hot-dog would be given to each and every person who did so, and also that a prize would be awarded to the best family group. As the day progressed, it was seen that a good ninety per cent of those attending qualified to claim their free snack.

Josie had arrived early to help Linc with the last-minute preparations, looking gorgeous in rose satin, her hair piled high with two or three ringlets loose on one shoulder.

'I would have done the pale make-up, too, but I've got to meet Pierre at the mill at one o'clock. I'll do all the gubbins for the dance tonight.'

'You look fantastic!' Linc told her, greeting her with a kiss.

'And you look like Dick Turpin or somebody. Is it my imagination, or has your hair grown since I saw you last?'

'It's rather clever,' Linc said, fingering the long black-ribboned ponytail. 'It comes off with the hat.'

'You look more than ever like poor old St John,' Josie declared. 'I rather like it.'

'Mmm. The trouble is, dressed like this, I'm not sure I should be talking to "Quality", like you.'

'Oh, that's all right,' she replied airily, sweeping past him with her head held high. 'I like a bit of rough.'

Linc's response was to slap her elegant rump as she passed.

'You look very nice, Josie.' Nikki's mother had arrived on the scene, wearing a late-Georgian high-waisted gown and lace cap, and resembling no one so much as Mrs Bennet from *Pride and Prejudice*, though Linc wouldn't have dared say so. 'I wish I could say the same for my daughter. A wonderful chance to dress as befits her station and she looks like a gypsy!' She bent a critical eye on Linc. 'And you're just as bad! At least your brother has made an effort.'

She moved on, leaving Linc and Josie to exchange amused glances.

'Poor Beverley!' Linc commented, leaning close to Josie's ear. 'It's really sad when your snobbery extends as far as fancy-dress!'

'Poor Nikki!' Josie said. 'Imagine having a mother like that!'

'So, what about *your* mother? And the others? Are they coming?'

'This afternoon.'

'Abby too?' Josie had told him that her sister was as yet very nervous about leaving the house.

'Yes. She's going to try.'

'She's a brave girl. Good Lord, look! My father in costume! That must be Mary's doing.'

Sylvester and Mary approached across the gravel looking splendid in full Georgian dress, she with a parasol and he with a silver-topped walking cane.

'My Lord. My Lady,' Linc said, bowing low as they drew level. 'Mary, you're a miracle worker – and you look amazing!'

She smiled and thanked him prettily, whilst at her

426

side Lord Tremayne looked his son up and down with an expression of disdain.

'Good God, Lincoln! You look like a bloody footpad!'

By eleven o'clock the crowds were arriving in a steady stream, a testament to Nikki's efforts in securing advertising space on local radio and in the regional press.

Among the attractions, a toffee-apple seller and the World's Strongest Man were cheek by jowl with a bearded lady and a gypsy fortune-teller. There was a coconut shy, a chance to guess the weight of the piglet, and a colourfully dressed tinker extolling the virtues of his patent elixir. In a roped-off arena, terriers were being raced, to the noisy delight of the crowd, and over and through it all, a fairground organ added its cheerful melody.

Linc recognised many familiar faces behind their period disguise, including DS Manston and his young family, Mike Farquharson, and Nina Barclay.

Coming up with Linc during a rare quiet moment, Manston introduced his wife and children and then begged a word in private.

'Er . . .' Linc consulted his watch. 'Okay.'

'It won't take a moment,' the sergeant said. 'It's just that the guvnor's a bit busy and he asked me to pass on a message. It's about the last warning you received. We've matched it to a page from Thursday's *Daily Mail* – Thursday before last, that is – so it matches the third one in that respect. The envelope is from W.H. Smith. Two sets of unidentified fingerprints on the outside, none on the inner.'

'So it wasn't Judge or Sandy – at least, not in person, because you'd arrested them the day before. That makes the timing a bit strange, doesn't it?'

'Yes, and that's not all that's strange. What's the story with the pot of Vaseline?'

'I'm not sure there is one,' Linc said hedging. 'Why?'

'Well, you must have had some reason for wanting forensics to look at it.'

'And they found . . .?'

Sighing, Manston gave up. 'They found that someone had scooped out the contents, doctored them liberally with strong chilli powder and then put them back in.' He watched Linc's face for reaction. '*Now* are you going to tell me?'

'Um . . . Chilli powder would be rather nasty if it got in your eyes, wouldn't it?'

'I should imagine so. Whose eyes exactly?'

'Well, I'm not sure, but possibly my horse's eyes, three weeks ago.'

Manston's expression sharpened. 'That could have caused a nasty accident if you'd happened to be riding at the time.'

'I was. And it did,' Linc confirmed.

'So how come we didn't hear about this?'

'Because I thought it *was* an accident. I don't come running to you lot every time I fall off my horse!'

'And now? Have you any idea who might have done it?'

'Ideas, maybe. But I need to think about it. Anyway, you're off duty. You're here to enjoy yourself.'

'A policeman is never off duty,' Manston countered. 'So when you've done thinking, let me know.'

The way Linc felt for the next couple of hours, he didn't think he would ever be 'done thinking'. His mind was buzzing with thoughts and none of them very pleasant. The main thrust was that, given Noddy's completely uncharacteristic behaviour at Coopers Down, his weeping, sore eyes, and the subsequent discovery of the doctored Vaseline, there was no getting away from the conclusion that the horse had been got at, with the intention of causing a very nasty accident.

True, it had been by no means inevitable that Noddy would fall; it was quite possible that, realising he was uncomfortable, Linc might have pulled out before he even started the cross-country, or pulled him up part way round. Which was, of course, what nearly happened.

What was equally inescapable was that the two people who'd had the best opportunity to ad-minister the doctored grease were Nikki and her mother. For a long time Linc shied away from this conclusion. It was one thing to come to terms with the fact that somebody wished him harm – the business with Judge had already given him some experience of that – but it was quite another to accept that the somebody in question might be a member of his own extended family.

He racked his brains for some other explanation but could think of none. Although it was just conceivable that the doctored Vaseline could have been exchanged for the original one without anyone noticing, the fact that he'd found the evidence in the pocket of a coat belonging to Crispin and Nikki made this rather a forlorn hope.

If opportunity was taken care of, that left motive.

Ambition.

The word crept unbidden into his consciousness. But for oneself or another? He found himself remembering Beverley at the dinner party. She'd exhibited a ghoulish interest in his encounter with Beanie and his thugs. Had his narrow squeak on that occasion fired her imagination? She'd never really forgiven him for dashing her hopes of seeing her daughter become a viscountess, and if anything happened to him, Crispin would step into the title.

Crispin. He'd been at the Coopers Down event . . .

No. Linc gave himself a mental shaking. He wouldn't go down that road, it was unthinkable.

What then of Nikki? She'd been bitter when they split, but afterwards had seemed very content with her new life, and surely now, with the baby on the way . . .

'Linc. There you are!' Josie interrupted his thoughts. 'I've been looking all over for you. I shall have to go in a minute.' She gave him a searching look. 'Are you okay?'

'Yeah, fine,' he lied, summoning a smile. He briefly considered sharing Manston's revelations with her, but it wasn't really the time or the place.

'Well, I'll just go and get out of this clobber, and then I'll be off.' She leaned forward and kissed his cheek. 'See you later.'

'Yeah, okay. Take care, won't you?'

'I'll try not to fall in the millpond,' she promised, laughing as she turned away.

Linc didn't feel much like laughing. He felt a little panicky. There was something important here that he was missing, but the more he searched his muddled thoughts, the further away it seemed to be slipping.

'Jo Jo?'

'Yes?' Josie turned, clearly surprised by the urgency in his voice, and he forced himself to calm down. After all, the threat wasn't a new one, and whoever was behind it couldn't know he'd discovered the doctored Vaseline.

'Nothing,' Linc said, lamely. 'No problem.'

Josie looked at him oddly. 'Are you sure you're okay?'

'Yeah. Look, do you want me to come with you?'

'No. Whatever for? Anyway, you can't just walk off and leave this.' She glanced at her watch, hidden discreetly under a long sleeve. 'Linc, I must go. I mustn't keep Pierre waiting – he's on his lunch break. 'Bye.'

With another kiss she was gone, weaving her way through the crowds towards the house, and Linc's attention was almost immediately claimed by Geoff Sykes, dressed for the Georgian period but somewhat incongruously refusing to abandon his flat tweed cap.

By the time the Hathaway family arrived, some twenty minutes later, the clouds had given up the unequal battle with the early-summer sun and gone off to dampen someone else's day.

Running hither and thither, Linc had become far too hot in the heavy brown coat and joined the many others who had stripped down to shirt-sleeves. He persevered with the tricorne and its attached hairpiece because, without it, it looked almost as though he hadn't bothered to dress up at all.

He didn't know the Hathaways were there until he felt a hand on his shoulder and turned to find Rebecca at his side, smiling at him from under a lace cap. They greeted each other with a kiss on the cheek and Rebecca congratulated him on the success of the day.

'I was looking for Josie,' she continued. 'Pierre asked me to get her to call him back and – of course – she left her phone at home. I've got it with me but I haven't seen her yet.'

'I'm sorry?' Linc was confused. 'Why should Pierre want her to call? She's with him now, at the mill.'

'Oh. Well, she shouldn't be. He rang earlier, a couple of hours ago. He's had to cancel and he'd been trying to get her on her mobile but couldn't – obviously – so I told him I'd pass the message on, but then I couldn't get *you* either.'

'No, we're using the radios today,' he said, indicating the device on his belt. There were six of them in all; he had one, as did his father, Reagan, Sykes, Nikki and the guide who was on duty at the house door.

'Yes, that's what your sister-in-law said when I rang.'

'You spoke to Nikki? When?' The question came out more sharply than he'd intended, but Rebecca didn't appear to have noticed.

'Earlier this morning. When I couldn't get hold of you on your mobile, I tried the office and Nikki answered. She offered to pass the message on to

Josie so I left it at that.' She looked closely at Linc. 'Is something wrong?'

He shook his head, trying to think clearly through the mounting unease that was gripping him. 'No. I'm afraid she didn't get the message, though. I expect Nikki just forgot. She's been very busy.'

'Oh, well, never mind,' Rebecca said. 'I expect Josie'll soon give up and come back when Pierre doesn't turn up. If you see her before I do, tell her I've got her phone.'

'Sure.' Linc produced a smile. He hated to deceive her but on the other hand he could hardly say, 'Well, actually, I think someone in my family may be trying to murder your daughter because I've asked her to marry me.'

The act of putting his fears into words, even if only in his own mind, effectively crystallised them, and abruptly he knew he couldn't just wait and hope for Josie's safe return. At the same time, he couldn't justify causing untold damage to family relations over something that was, as yet, mere supposition.

He didn't like just to walk out on the afternoon's festivities. God willing, he would be no more than a few minutes, but nevertheless somebody would have to be told that he was going and be asked to deputise in his absence.

Crispin.

Linc set off to find his brother, for the first time cursing the numbers of people who had turned up to the fair. When he found Crispin he was, predictably, taking photographs. Still gallantly wearing his costume and wig, despite the temperature, he'd lined up a group of costumed youngsters of primary school age and was managing to keep them amused while he took shots of them in various poses, presumably for the benefit of their doting parents who looked on indulgently.

Crispin was clearly as popular with children as he seemed to be with everyone else, Linc thought admiringly as he approached, and would no doubt take to fatherhood like a duck to water when the baby arrived.

The baby.

Nikki.

The reason for his errand came back to Linc with a jolt and he slowed to a halt in an agony of indecision.

'Sir?' Reagan had appeared beside him. 'What do you want to do abou—'

'Jack,' Linc cut in, seizing on the forester as the answer to his dilemma. 'I've just got to nip down to the mill for something. Can you take over for a minute? Crispin's busy. I'll have my radio, if there's a problem.'

'I . . . yes, I suppose so. Is something wrong?'

'No, not really. Just something I left there the other day. I shouldn't be long.'

Reagan looked surprised, probably wondering why he didn't send someone else to fetch whatever it was, Linc thought, as he hurried towards the house, returning a mechanical smile and polite answer to one or two people who spoke to him on the way.

In the yard, he made for the office and his car keys. It was almost unbelievable that, in spite of everything, he'd felt more able to trust Jack Reagan than his own brother. Nothing less than his worry

434

for Josie would have been strong enough to drown his wretchedness at the thought.

Car keys in hand, he sprinted across to the Morgan, which was the easiest to remove from the gridlock in the yard, only to find that in his haste he'd let Tiger out and he was now sitting on the back seat with an expression that indicated his determination to stay there. Linc had no time to waste in dragging a recalcitrant dog out of the car and back to the office, so contented himself with swearing at him as he slipped into the driving seat. Putting the car into gear, he caught sight of himself in the rear-view mirror and realised that he was still wearing the tricorne with its attached ponytail. Within moments it had joined the astonished dog on the back seat.

He had no wish to draw undue attention to himself by accelerating down the drive at high speed, and so kept his impatience in check until he was clear of the house and entering Mill Lane. Once there, however, he floored the pedal, and within a couple of minutes was turning down the slope into the mill car park.

Stopping in a spray of asphalt beside Josie's E-type and another car he didn't recognise, Linc leaped out, leaving the car door open, vaulted the gate and raced for the mill building, almost tripping over Tiger, who was not about to be left behind.

'Jo Jo?' She was nowhere to be seen. 'Josie!'

He heard the panic in his own voice and thought briefly how daft he'd look if Josie came round the corner just now, having been for a walk round the millpond while she waited, as she thought, for Pierre the photographer.

Just at the moment he'd gladly look foolish.

The mill itself was kept locked when the workmen weren't there, but Linc paused to try the handle, just to be certain. He'd given Josie a key so she could show her colleague around.

It turned, and the door swung in.

'Josie?' He peered into the gloomy interior. 'Josie? Are you there?'

His voice sounded dead; as though the wood of the old building had somehow soaked up the noise and stifled any resonance.

Linc's heart was thudding heavily.

Inside or out? Where should he search first? Where lay the greatest danger?

The answer had to be the millpond.

Leaving the door swinging, he ran on along the front of the mill to its corner and over the footbridge that spanned the tailrace. Following the path left-handed, he passed the massive wheel where it hung, greased and ready for milling to start the following week. Ahead, the millpond stretched away from him, the light breeze raising only the slightest of ripples to disturb the sky-blue reflection on its surface. To his right the overflow pounded down the steps of the weir and into the bypass stream.

No sign of Josie.

He shouted again, the pitch of his voice rising as his anxiety did, and suddenly he heard it: a thin reply, barely audible over the rushing of the weir.

'Linc?'

'Josie? Where are you?'

'Linc? Help me!'

He looked down to his left where water lapped lazily at the sluice at the end of the millrace. At first, half-blinded by the bright reflections on the mill-pond, he could make out nothing in the comparative gloom beside the building, but as his eyes adjusted he saw Josie at last.

With one arm hooked over the woodwork of the sluice gate, her face was white and there was desperation in her dark eyes.

'Josie! Hold on!' Linc's mind was racing. What to do? His first impulse, that of jumping in beside her, was not necessarily the best course of action. What if *he* couldn't get out either? A rope or a ladder would be a sensible precaution. The builders would have used ladders and ropes. Somewhere there would be one or the other. There had to be.

'Hold on!' he repeated.

Josie's head tipped back, her beautiful long hair floating round her shoulders in the greenish water, and she looked imploringly up at him.

'I can't,' she moaned, weakly. 'You have to help me.'

'I will,' he promised. 'But first I have to leave you for a moment . . .'

Even as Linc said the words he saw her eyes widen with panic. He opened his mouth to reassure her, then realised that her gaze had shifted beyond him, and whirled round to locate the threat.

He was only halfway round when the threat located *him*. He caught the briefest of glimpses of a powerfully built man in a white tee-shirt, before a chopping punch caught him on the side of his face and sent him reeling backwards. His second stumbling step missed the edge of the millrace and he fell, without a hope of saving himself, into the cold dark water below.

17

Linc went into the millrace backwards and head first.

After the warmth of the day, the water felt icy and the shock as he went under made him gasp and inhale a quantity of it. A cacophony of bubbles surrounded him as he plunged downward, finally slowing as his body's natural buoyancy asserted itself and began to return him to the surface.

Momentarily stunned by the force of the punch, Linc was at first disorientated and unable to help himself, but after what seemed an age of drifting weightlessly, his head cleared and he kicked hard for the light. He rose through shoals of silvery bubbles and broke the surface, coughing and spluttering as he struggled to get air into his lungs.

Someone was calling his name in a high, hysterical voice, and as he rubbed his eyes to expel the water, a pale blur resolved itself into Josie's terrified face, barely five feet away. On his right the stone wall of the mill rose a sheer forty feet or so, its lowest window some six feet above his head; on his left, more stonework, only three feet high this time but that was three too many. Newly pointed, when the pond was drained, it offered no hand or toehold whatsoever, and had the added disadvantage of being patrolled by the man in the tee-shirt, although at present he was nowhere to be seen.

Linc was furious with himself. How could he have been such an unwary fool? He'd raced to the mill because he was afraid Josie might be in trouble, but the horror of finding her in the water had temporarily driven everything from his mind except the problem of how to rescue her as quickly as possible.

Still cursing his own stupidity, he kicked towards Josie, who remained clinging to the sluice gate at the end of the channel. Beyond her, even more darkly impressive from this angle, the buckets of the mill wheel arched away, five feet wide and towering to some five or six feet above her head. The wash from his undignified entry was still lapping heavily at the perimeters as Linc reached Josie, and she was worryingly low in the water.

'Josie love – are you all right?' Linc had to speak up to make himself heard over the rushing water of the weir.

She didn't look all right. She was shivering violently and, close to, he read the strain in her eyes. He caught hold of the wooden sluice with one hand and slipped the other under her arm to support her, but she winced at his touch.

'You're hurt. Where does it hurt?'

'My arm,' she cried. 'I tried to swim out, but I couldn't . . .'

'Did you see who it was?'

'No. I've never seen him before. He just came at me out of nowhere . . .'

Her voice broke on a sob and Linc soothed her.

'Shhh . . . Josie, look at me. We'll go together. I'll hold you up. All you have to do is kick your legs, if you can. We'll head for the jetty, okay?'

She nodded mutely and Linc pushed away from the sluice gate to swim round behind her. Sliding his forearm under her armpit and around her body, he told her to let go and lean back against him, and after a fractional hesitation, she did.

Their only hope of getting out of the water was to swim out of the millrace and along the back of the mill building to the jetty and the metal ladder set in the retaining wall of the pond. If they turned the other way, they would be drawn inexorably to, and over, the pounding waterfall of the weir, the result of which Linc didn't care to contemplate. Why, oh why, he thought, hadn't he had another ladder set into the wall of the millrace?

Kicking with both legs and sculling with his free arm, Linc began to swim backwards towards the millpond, wondering as he did so where the tee-shirted man had got to. Could it be that he'd done his worst and decided to cut his losses and leave?

Linc didn't have long to wonder.

They had barely started their swim when he became aware of a change in the water around him. Almost insignificant at first, but gathering in strength, a current was beginning to develop, pulling them back towards the sluice. Initially he couldn't think what was happening, and then he saw the great buckets of the waterwheel start to slide downwards.

Someone inside the mill had opened the sluice gate, and the wheel, so long redundant, had begun to turn.

As the tug of the millrace increased, Linc swore and redoubled his efforts, urging Josie to do the same. He wasn't sure whether the gate would open far enough to allow a body to be pulled through and on to the wheel, but he wasn't especially anxious to find out. His loose-fitting Georgian costume dragged heavily, slowing him down, but after a brief, panic-inducing hiatus their combined strength won the day and they made slow but steady progress towards the millpond once again. Linc was just thankful that Josie had changed out of her long, cumbersome dress before coming to the mill.

But their tormentor hadn't finished with them.

Josie gave a cry and Linc looked up to see the man's burly figure cross the footbridge and come towards them at a run. Wearing a blue cotton scarf tied gypsy-style round his semi-shaven head, the man had a ring in one ear and tattoos on his forearms, and even though Linc was not exactly at leisure to observe him carefully, he felt there was something familiar about him. What concerned him more at that moment, however, was just what he intended to do with the length of four by two timber he was carrying. Linc had an unhappy feeling he knew, and kicked even harder, feeling Josie do the same, but there was never going to be any contest.

Coming alongside, the man leaned out and started to jab the piece of wood energetically in their direction. Mercifully, it was too long to be easily wielded and his first attempt fell short, but the second landed with uncomfortable force on Linc's shoulder and the next cracked painfully into his elbow, sending pins and needles shooting up his arm, and causing his grip on Josie to falter.

At this point, a welcome interruption occurred in the shape of a furiously angry brindle tornado which appeared seemingly from nowhere and attached itself gamely and, no doubt, painfully to the calf of the burly man, growling ferociously all the while.

If he'd had the breath to do so, Linc could have cheered, as with a curse the man stopped stabbing at him and Josie and tried, with little success, to detach Tiger's steel-sprung jaws from his lower anatomy. Fortunately, the wooden rail was too long to be used at such close quarters and it consequently took him quite a time to disengage the enthusiastic dog. He finally managed it by dint of a series of vicious kicks with his other foot.

Tiger gave a high-pitched yelp and then backed off, still barking, leaving the man free to get back to business with the length of timber. However, the dog had bought Linc and Josie valuable time and they were now only a couple of feet from where the channel opened out into the vastness of the mill-pond.

Linc forced his weary limbs to extra effort and, perhaps seeing this, their attacker changed his tactics. Coming to the very edge of the millrace, he held the rail high and pushed the end of it into the angle of Linc's neck and shoulder. Before he had time to try and dislodge it, the pressure increased and he found himself going under, dragging Josie, whom he was still holding, down with him.

For a panic-stricken moment, Linc held her even tighter as she began to struggle but somehow he managed to override his instincts, loosen his grip and push her towards the surface. Being forced away from the man on the bank and ever deeper, Linc fetched up against the wall of the mill building.

He was trapped.

Drowning.

He thrashed his arms and legs in a frenzied attempt to free himself, his ears buzzing and his lungs and throat bursting under the strain.

The pressure on his shoulder slackened, and then increased sharply, and Linc hit the wall with a thud that forced most of the pent-up breath from his body in a rush of bubbles and caused him to gulp in a quantity of water. Strangely, all at once his panic left him, and in the calm that followed the answer became clear. He couldn't get to the surface or away from the wall, so he hooked his fingers in the stonework and pulled himself deeper still, hoping to take himself beyond the reach of the man with the rail.

The tactics were successful. As he went down, the pressure eased and Linc was able to slide sideways and free himself. Looking up towards the light, he could make out the blue jeans and white tee-shirt of the man above him, and as he kicked for the surface, he angled away from him towards the millpond. By the time his head broke clear of the water, the buzzing in his ears had increased to a roar and his chest and lungs were cramping with air starvation.

Coughing and choking, Linc could do nothing except tread water at first, while at the top of the wall, the burly man lined up his wooden rail for a fresh onslaught.

All at once it came to Linc where he'd seen the

man before. Weeks ago, when he'd visited the doctor after his encounter with Beanie and his gang, he'd seen this man outside the health and fitness club with Nikki. Given that, he thought grimly, there seemed little doubt that this was her personal trainer; the man she'd known in London and for whom she'd subsequently provided a reference. The name Terry flashed into his mind: Terry Fagan.

Damn her! Linc thought. Damn Nikki!

In order to get within range, Fagan was forced to move forward to stand on the edge of the footpath; on the *very* edge, Linc noticed, an idea rapidly forming in his mind. Still wheezing, he concentrated on the end of the timber as it lanced out and, as it came within reach, caught it in both hands, twisted to one side and tugged it sharply down towards the water.

It worked, at least partially. Overstretched as he was, Fagan was pulled off-balance, let go of the wood and teetered on the brink of the millpond, arms swinging wildly. When he finally won his fight to stay on the bank, Linc wasn't sure whether to be glad or sorry. He'd love to have dragged Fagan into the pond, but on the other hand, the idea of having the big man next to him in the water wasn't quite so appealing.

One problem dealt with, at least temporarily, Linc looked round desperately for Josie but couldn't immediately see her. With only one good arm, she surely couldn't have got far.

Still treading water, he turned, sweeping his gaze over the surface of the pond, and then he saw her. Not, as he'd hoped, making for the jetty and ladder at the other end of the mill, but swimming slowly in the direction of the boathouse, and with each stroke being pulled ever nearer to the deafening white water of the weir.

With no further hesitation, Linc struck out strongly on a course that he hoped would intercept Josie's drifting one. Although he was a good swimmer, he soon found he'd underestimated the power of the current above the stone steps. Because the surface was glassy smooth, it was easy to forget that, aside from the narrow millrace, this was the only exit point for the substantial flow that was pouring in from the valley above. Glancing to his right as he swam, Linc could see where the water slid over the sill to cascade down the four curving steps into the frothy confusion below.

He didn't even want to imagine how it would feel to be carried over that.

By the time he was halfway across the width of the weir he knew it would be touch and go whether he made it to the other side, let alone with enough strength to help Josie. He could see her, off to his left, still bravely fighting her losing battle with the pull of the water, and wanted to shout some encouragement but he knew, even if he'd had the breath, it would be futile with the constant noise of the cascade in their ears.

Ducking his head into the flow, he ploughed on, coming up for air only every fourth stroke, and inch by painful inch he began to gain, finally pulling through the funnelling current at the side of the weir and catching hold of the corroded metal post that was part of the original sluice gear.

His body was swept sideways as soon as he

stopped swimming but his hold was good, and looking round for Josie he found that, for once, luck was with them both. Patently exhausted, she was barely going through the motions of swimming now as she was drawn backwards at an ever-increasing speed, but Linc could see that she would pass within a couple of feet of where he waited.

Retaining his hold on the sluice gearing with his right hand and timing his lunge carefully, he surged through the current, wrapped his left arm round Josie's waist, and hung on grimly as the pull of the water on their combined body-mass threatened to dislocate his right shoulder.

He had her again – but for how long? Seeming only semi-conscious, she was a dead-weight, her head lolling against his shoulder, and he knew it was vital to get her back to his anchorage pretty damned quickly, while he still could.

If he still could . . .

As Linc struggled desperately to keep Josie away from the lip of the weir, a shadow fell across them, but he didn't even look up.

What did it matter if Fagan had returned? There was nothing Linc could do about it. His most immediate battle was with the water, and as the seconds ground torturously past it became clear that he was losing it. With his back to dry land, stretched between the metal post and the drag of the current on Josie's body, he was forced to come to terms with the shattering realisation that he simply wasn't strong enough to win through. Sometime soon his burning muscles would give out, and he and Josie would be swept helplessly away.

Linc alternately groaned and swore as the water

surged against and over them both, making breathing a hit-and-miss affair, and the whole of his upper body began shuddering under the strain.

'Linc! Let go, man! Let go!'

A voice, shouting over the roar of the cascading water, finally penetrated his despair and he tipped back his head to see.

It was Crispin.

Standing just off the end of the bridge that spanned the weir, he had one hand clamped on the wooden upright while the other reached down to hold Josie's wrist.

'Let go, Linc! I've got her. I won't let her go. Trust me.'

For a fraction of a second, Linc hesitated. Could he? Where did Crispin fit into all this?

Searching his brother's face for an answer, all he could see was anxiety and earnest entreaty. He had always considered Cris easy to read. Praying that he was right, Linc slowly uncurled the cold, cramped muscles of his left arm and let Josie go.

In the heart-stopping seconds before Crispin took up the strain, her weakly struggling body was swept to the brink of the weir. Then in one long smooth pull Crispin hauled her on to the bank and out of danger, her legs scrambling for a foothold and water running off her clothes in silvery rivulets.

Even relieved of his burden, Linc found he could do nothing to help himself. His right hand remained locked to the metal post whilst a spell of black dizziness came and went, then suddenly Crispin was close behind him and a hand closed on Linc's right wrist.

'Linc! Grab my hand!' he shouted urgently.

He lifted his left arm obediently, Crispin grasped it, and all at once he was slithering up and over the retaining wall to lie on the gravel path, shivering in the sunshine and being enthusiastically washed by an ecstatic Tiger.

'Are you all right?' Crispin was bending over him.

Linc nodded, gulping in air. 'I will be . . . Just give me a minute.'

'What the hell's going on?' As he spoke, Crispin was peeling his ruffled white shirt off over his head.

'It's a long story.' With an effort, Linc sat up, pushing the dog away. 'That's enough. Good lad.'

'He *is* a good lad. He was standing here barking like a maniac. He showed me exactly where you were.' Crispin moved across to where Josie sat leaning back against the bridge support, cradling her left arm with her right. Her long dark hair straggled over her shoulders and her face was pale with pain and exhaustion.

'Has he gone?' she asked, looking anxiously from one to the other. 'He won't come back, will he?'

Abruptly, Linc remembered that the cause of their present troubles was still at large.

'Where's Fagan?' he asked Crispin sharply. 'Did you see him?'

'Who?' Crispin was clearly nonplussed. Using the cotton shirt, he began to fashion a crude sling to support Josie's damaged arm, tying the sleeves carefully behind her neck.

'Fagan. Big bloke, white tee-shirt, blue head-scarf . . .' Linc prompted. 'Did you see anyone at all when you got here?'

Crispin shook his head. 'No. I yelled into the mill for you, then heard Tiger barking and came on

448

round. Didn't see a soul. Is that better?' he inquired of Josie.

She nodded, her teeth chattering. 'Yes, thanks, much better. It's painful . . . but I can still move my fingers . . . so I don't think it's broken.'

Linc got shakily to his feet and looked away down the path to the boathouse. The area appeared deserted.

'He's either still here somewhere or he's trying to make a run for it up the valley. He'll have his work cut out if he is. It's boggy at the best of times, and after all that rain . . .'

'Who will?' Crispin still hadn't quite caught up.

'Fagan!' Linc snapped, anxiety and fatigue taking their toll on his temper. 'The bastard who did all this! If you didn't pass him, he must have gone up the valley.'

'I didn't see anyone,' Crispin repeated. 'Who is this Fagan?'

'Terry Fagan. Nikki's fitness trainer,' Linc told him, dreading the inevitable questions that must follow. How was he supposed to tell his brother that he was pretty sure his wife had conspired with the man to kill both Josie and himself?

'Nikki's trainer? I've never met him. How do *you* know him?'

'I don't, I just saw them together once.'

'But why on earth would he be here? I don't understand . . .'

'No. I'm not sure I do completely,' Linc admitted. 'But it looks as though he's gone anyway. Come on. We'd better get Josie to a doctor. We can talk about this later.'

Crispin understandably looked as though he

wanted at least *some* answers straightaway but he acknowledged Josie's need, and helped Linc draw her to her feet.

'Oh God, my legs feel like jelly!' she groaned, and Crispin invited her to put an arm round his shoulders.

'I think I'm a better bet than Linc, just at the moment,' he suggested.

With Linc and Tiger following behind, they made their way slowly back over the wooden footbridge towards the mill, Linc's clothes stiffening as they began to dry in the warm breeze.

'But *I* don't understand either,' Josie said after a moment. 'Where's Pierre? And why on earth did that man attack me? I've never seen him before in my life. Is he mad?'

'Pierre couldn't make it,' Linc told her. 'He did send a message but it never reached you. You left your phone at home.'

They had turned along the path at the end of the mill, where the waterwheel was still rhythmically turning. God only knew what damage it was doing to the stones with no grain to mill, Linc thought, gloomily. Somewhere in the back of his mind he remembered Saul talking about such friction causing fires.

'What's that ringing noise?' Crispin asked. From inside the building they could hear the constant, if muffled, ting-ting-ting of a bell.

'It's the alarm – to say that there's no grain in the hopper and the stones are running dry. We ought to stop that wheel,' Linc commented, cravenly glad to be able to avoid the question of Fagan's involvement for a few minutes more.

Crispin looked over his shoulder. 'I would offer but I don't know how.'

'It's all right, I'll do it,' Linc said as they crossed the second bridge. 'It won't take a moment.'

He'd reached the open door and was just about to go in when Tiger shot past them all, raced along to the far corner of the building and disappeared round it, barking furiously.

Linc and Crispin exchanged glances and Linc hurried forward to peer round the end of the mill, keeping well out from the stonework in case Fagan should be waiting to pounce.

There was no one in sight, just a gravel path and beyond it the pond with its striven-for jetty. He was, however, just in time to see the door near the back of the building slam shut in Tiger's indignant face. It seemed that Fagan had managed to cross the millstream further up the valley and had come back round the lane side of the millpond, perhaps hoping to make it to his car and away before anyone saw him. It might have worked, too, if he'd been just a bit quicker.

'I think he's in the mill,' Linc told the others as they caught up. 'The side door was unlocked.'

'Yes, I opened it while I was waiting,' Josie admitted.

'The question is, what do we do now? I don't much fancy going in after him.'

'Well, Josie can't drive, obviously, but can't one of us go for help while the other one stays here to keep an eye on this Fagan character?'

Linc shook his head. 'You haven't seen this guy! He's big. He'd just walk straight through either one of us. Damn! It's so frustrating that Manston's just up the road and we can't get word to him. Your mobile won't be any good down here but my radio would've been, if it wasn't absolutely saturated.'

'It's no good locking him in, he'd just climb out the window,' Crispin stated.

'Well, can't we disable his car?' Josie suggested. 'Take off the distributor cap or whatever modern cars have.'

'She's not just a pretty face, is she?' Crispin declared. 'It would certainly slow him down.'

'Okay. I guess it's the best we can do. But I still need to do something about that wheel. I'll be damned if I'm going to stand by and see the place burn down after all the work we've done on it!'

'Linc, can't you leave it? Please?' Josie looked uneasy.

'I'll be all right. The sluice control is just inside. I'll be in and out before he knows I'm there. Besides, I don't think he'll try anything now. He'll just want to get away.' Linc gave her a bright, reassuring smile and moved off before she could say anything more.

The interior of the stone building struck cool after the warmth of the sun, and Linc, in his wet clothes, shivered. Or at least, he blamed it on the cold. The bell on the stone floor sounded much louder in here, even over the rumbling of the mill machinery, insisting that someone do something, fast, before the stones were ruined. Pausing for an instant to let his eyes adjust to the reduced light, Linc moved on into the mill. Fagan was nowhere to be seen; quite possibly he had gone up to one of the other floors.

He made his way cautiously across to the

business end of the structure, where the huge axle-tree passed through the wall from the wheel outside, hoping that Fagan wasn't lurking in the shadows or behind one of the massive supporting timbers. In spite of his brave words to Josie, he was by no means sure the man wouldn't take the chance to attack him again if it presented itself.

Passing the huge wooden gear wheels, Linc located the smaller metal wheel that operated the sluice and began to turn it, becoming aware of a number of sore muscles as he did so. Gradually the rushing of the water on the other side of the wall lessened and the whole mechanism slowed as the waterwheel was robbed of its power source.

Finally, thankfully, the frantic ringing of the bell died away into silence, and as it did so Linc heard the sound of a vehicle drawing up on the asphalt of the car park.

His spirits lifted. He wondered who'd come. Given the circumstances, Manston would be the most welcome, but almost anyone would be a plus because they could be sent for help.

Linc started back towards the door. Somewhere above him a board creaked and there was the sound of a foot scuffing on the wooden planking.

Fagan. Up on the stone floor.

A shadow showed in the square of light on the flags as Crispin appeared in the doorway ahead.

'Nikki's come,' he announced.

'Nikki! What's *she* doing here?' Linc's brain raced through all the possibilities and couldn't find any particularly comforting ones. He fervently wished he'd had time to share his suspicions about Nikki with Josie.

'I don't know. I expect she wondered what was going on. Anyway it's great because we can send her for help while we tackle this Fagan character.'

'Yeah, well, he's gone upstairs so there's not much we *can* do about him other than keep an eye on the stairs until help arrives. He can't go anywhere from up there.'

Crispin looked disappointed. 'I suppose so, but it seems a bit tame after everything that's happened.'

'Believe me, tame is good where this guy's concerned!' Linc assured him, as he emerged thankfully into the sunlight. 'You really don't want to be tangling with him!'

Following, Crispin shrugged, resignedly. 'Okay. If you say so.'

Nikki was coming through the gate from the car park. 'What's going on? I was wondering where you guys had got to. Oh my God, Josie! Are you okay? What happened?'

Josie didn't have a chance to answer because a window was flung open on the upper floor of the mill, and Fagan bellowed, 'Nikki! I need to talk to you. Now!'

Linc was watching his sister-in-law and could virtually see the blood drain from her face. Fagan's car was still there for all to see, but maybe she'd assumed he was lying low until the coast was clear. She recovered her composure with impressive speed, though, and by the time the others had transferred their attention from the window above, she was wearing an expression of total bewilderment.

'*Terry?* What on earth are you doing here?' Her tone held a perfectly judged mixture of surprise and disbelief, and Linc felt she almost deserved a round of applause. It was a virtuoso performance.

Fagan was nowhere near as impressed. 'Cut the crap, you little bitch! You know damn' well why I'm here.'

At Linc's feet, Tiger began a low, rumbling growl.

'Nikki?' It was Crispin this time, and the puzzlement in *his* face wasn't simulated. 'What's going on? Who is this man?'

She turned to him, her eyes wide and anxious. 'Terry Fagan. He's my fitness coach from the leisure centre but . . .'

At this point, she was interrupted by Tiger who, apparently finding the sight of his enemy leaning out of the casement too much to bear, got to his feet and shot into the mill building at top speed, emitting a throaty snarl as he went.

With an oath, Fagan instantly disappeared from view, and seconds later those below could hear all hell let loose as the foolhardy dog launched his attack.

'Shit!' Crispin exclaimed, and tore after him.

'Crispin! No!' Linc paused just long enough to tell the girls to stay where they were, then – spurred on by fear for his brother – he charged through the doorway, across the flagstone floor and up the wooden stairs, taking them three at a time and cursing all the way.

When Crispin reached the top he paused. Peering past him, Linc could see why. Fagan had snatched up one of Saul's mill-bills and was standing no more than six feet away, wielding it with more energy than accuracy in an attempt to keep the dog at bay.

Tiger, snarling his hatred with unflagging

vehemence, was dodging the swinging implement without too much trouble but was, nevertheless, confined by this activity to the corner at the top of the stairs.

It was something of a stand-off, Crispin and Linc being unable to proceed for the same reason as Tiger. The mill-bill consisted of eighteen inches of polished ash handle culminating in an eleven-inch, double-ended chisel, made of high-carbon steel. Weighing in at some three and a half pounds, it was designed to chip stone and consequently capable of inflicting horrific injuries if turned against flesh and bone.

'What do we do now?' In the heat of the moment, Crispin reverted to the habit of childhood and instinctively looked to his older brother for guidance.

Which was all very well, Linc thought wryly, if his older brother had had any ideas at all.

But he hadn't.

'Call your fucking dog off!' Fagan shouted, sweating freely as he continued his frenzied defence.

Linc was by no means sure that Tiger would consent to being called off, and he had no intention of trying just at that moment because he had little confidence that either he or his brother would be as successful at dodging Fagan's swipes.

'Call him off!'

'Only if you put that thing down,' he yelled back.

'Not fuckin' likely!'

Linc looked thoughtfully past Fagan to the business end of the mill, then touched Crispin on the shoulder.

'Stay here and keep him busy,' he said into his

ear, and ran lightly back down the wooden stairs to the ground floor. At the base of the steps he almost ran into Nikki, who was on her way up.

'Stay out of it!' he advised, but moved on without waiting to see if she did as he suggested.

His first port of call was past the gearing to the end of the building where the sluice control was. Ignoring the aching weariness of his arm muscles, he released the hook that kept the small wheel securely anchored, and began to turn it as fast as he could. He was rewarded after a few revolutions by the sound of water beginning to pour on to the waterwheel from the millrace.

Gradually at first, then swiftly gaining speed, the oaken axle-tree began to rotate, setting in motion the pit wheel, the great spur wheel and stone nut and, out of sight on the floor above, the crown wheel and the runner stone. Instantly the alarm bell was reactivated, but Linc hoped that even if Fagan noticed this, he would be too busy fending off Tiger to wonder what it portended. From the sound of it, the dog was still enthusiastically harrying him. Sandy's unwanted bequest had certainly earned his keep ten times over during the course of the afternoon.

With a silent apology to the absent millwright for causing yet more damage to his freshly dressed stones, Linc moved across to where the rope end of the sack hoist trailed on the floor. Looking up, he could see the double trapdoors through which thousands of sacks had disappeared over the years, on their way to the bin floor and the start of the milling process. Hoping he could hang centrally enough to pass through the opening without hitting the sides, Linc wound his left arm round the rope and tugged on the cord that tightened the belt on the pulley two floors above. With no further ado, the sack hoist was operational and he began his unorthodox journey up through the mill.

It took only a second or two to reach the low ceiling and, as he approached, Linc curled his right arm up over his head to take the brunt of the impact with the double trapdoors. The wooden edges slid past his shoulders, waist and legs, before dropping back into place with a thud. As soon as they did so, Linc relinquished his hold and dropped down on top of them. The moving rope briefly snagged his loose sleeve and then he was free and standing less than ten feet behind Fagan.

The manoeuvre was one hundred per cent successful, as far as it went, but Linc was now faced with the problem of how to put his momentary advantage to the best use. There had been nothing on the ground floor that had instantly suggested itself to him as a weapon – at least, nothing that he had felt confident of transporting by way of the sack hoist – and now he had arrived on the stone floor, he found a similar dearth. True, there were two or three other mill-bills on the floor by the wall but he would have had to pass Fagan to reach them and that was inviting disaster.

Fagan knew he was there. The noise of the trapdoors closing had made him turn his head for a fraction of a second, and now he edged sideways to keep Linc in his peripheral vision whilst he continued to swing at the dog.

As he looked round for inspiration, Linc caught sight of a cluster of paint pots, brushes, rags and bottles of turpentine that the workmen had left against the wall. Three smaller paintbrushes had been left standing in a jam jar of cloudy liquid, presumably for someone else to clean, and moving swiftly Linc scooped it up, tossing the brushes aside. Stepping forward, he shouted Fagan's name and as the big man turned, threw the turpentine in his face.

Not all the liquid left the jam jar but what did slosh out could not have been better aimed, hitting Fagan across the bridge of his nose. Immediately, the arm wielding the mill-bill dropped and his other hand clutched at his face as the spirit stung his eyes.

Tiger took advantage of the moment by leaping forward and fastening his teeth on the haft of the weapon, which was slipping from Fagan's fingers, and Crispin moved from the stairwell to Linc's side.

'That was brilliant!' he exclaimed. 'What now?'

Swearing blue murder, Fagan had backed up to the wooden tun, under which the millstones ground dryly on and the little bouncing bell jingled its rhythmic warning. Here he stood hunched over, rubbing at his painful eyes with the heels of both palms.

Tiger, deciding that an unmanned mill-bill wasn't worthy of his attentions, dropped it and turned to seek out enemy number one, at which point Linc took a firm hold of his collar and commanded him to sit. To his surprise, the dog did as he was told, contenting himself with addressing a low, menacing growl to Fagan. Linc picked up the mill-bill and rested it on a ledge.

'Now I think we should hear what Mr Fagan has to say for himself,' he suggested.

In response to this, Fagan directed a stream of obscenity in his direction, and Linc shook his head, sighing.

'Oh, well. I suppose we'll have to leave it to the police, unless . . .' He winked at Crispin. 'Have you got your cigarette lighter on you?'

Crispin had never smoked, but he caught on, instantly.

'Mmm, somewhere,' he said making a pretence of searching his pockets.

Fagan straightened up and squinted through watering eyes.

'You wouldn't . . .' he said thickly, but his tone was tinged with doubt. His shirtfront was soaked in turps.

'You can't believe anything he says, he's a criminal!' Nikki stepped forward from the stairwell, where she'd been standing half-hidden. 'He'll try and blame me. The police are after him in London for assault. He'd say anything to cover himself.'

Linc turned to his sister-in-law with raised eyebrows.

'Oh? Is that what you put in the reference you gave him for his job at the Silver Pine?'

'Reference?' Nikki hedged unconvincingly, recognising too late the trap she'd made for herself.

'Oh, come on, Nikki, you told me yourself. An old friend, up from London, looking for a job . . . You know, if you're going to lie, it pays to remember what you've said before. So what is he to you? Friend, lover, or just a tool to use in your vicious schemes and then discard?'

'Linc, that's enough!' Crispin protested, stepping forward. 'How dare you speak to her like that? Have you lost your mind? Nikki's got nothing to do with this.'

'I wish that were true, Cris, I really do,' Linc said sadly. 'But I'm afraid she may well have everything to do with it. Ask her why she didn't pass on the message to Josie about Pierre cancelling the meeting.'

Crispin frowned. 'Well, I expect she forgot. It's not surprising, she's been incredibly busy.'

'Of course I forgot. Why else wouldn't I tell her?' Nikki put in.

'Because you saw your chance to arrange another of your little *accidents*,' Linc countered. 'Like the one at Coopers Down when Noddy fell with me. That was very clever. I'd probably never have found out if you hadn't left the pot of Vaseline in the pocket of your coat.'

'What are you talking about?' Crispin demanded.

'Nikki knows, don't you, Nikki? About the chilli powder that half-blinded Noddy, so he couldn't see the jumps.'

'You're mad! Why would I want to harm you?'

'Because I'm in line for the one thing you want more than any other: a title. And if I were not around to succeed to it, it would be Crispin's and yours. You've always been fascinated by the story of St John and how the title passed to his brother when he died young. Was that what gave you the idea? Or was it when I was attacked, and you realised how easily the title could have been yours?'

'That's ridiculous!' Crispin exclaimed. 'You can't really think Nikki's trying to – kill you?' He hesitated over the word, as if it was awkward to enunciate. 'Besides, I told you, I can't even remember for sure

461

who was wearing that coat at Coopers Down. It could have been me or Beverley. It's not much to base an accusation on, is it?'

'No,' Linc agreed. 'Not on its own. But, you see, that's not all, by a long way.'

At this point Fagan, who was still troubled with his eyes, apparently lost patience with the maddening tinkle of the alarm bell and, with a curse, ripped it from its position and threw it across the mill.

Tiger stood up and voiced his displeasure.

'Oi, you! Stand still!' Linc told Fagan, who held up one hand and squinted at him through red-rimmed and weeping eyes.

'What else then?' Crispin asked, ignoring this outburst.

'Okay. What about the business with Jim Pepper? *Someone* sent that note and I'm pretty sure it wasn't Reagan, so who was it?'

'Oh, and you'd sooner believe that arsey forester than one of your own family?' Crispin was really bitter now and, remembering his own feelings earlier in the day, Linc couldn't blame him. 'Any number of people could have found out about the meeting – you said so yourself. Anyone who had access to the office. Anyway, you're forgetting, it was Nikki who turned up to help you out.'

'Only after I'd got hold of Pepper,' Linc said relentlessly. He hated what he was having to do to his brother but it was too late to turn back now. 'And of course she'd somehow managed to walk off with my mobile that morning, leaving me without any means of calling for help . . .'

'No. You're twisting everything! So she picked up

your mobile by mistake . . . so what? It's easily done. She took the trouble of finding you to give it back, didn't she? That's why she happened to be there when you got hold of Pepper. Reagan was the one who didn't turn up on time, as I remember. This is all supposition. None of it proves someone was actually trying to kill you. I mean, a scuffle with a middle-aged ex-employee is hardly the same as setting a hitman on somebody. Pepper was never likely to have killed you, was he?'

'He had a crowbar,' Linc pointed out. 'And what about the party? *Somebody* drugged me. And no one had a better opportunity than Nikki.'

Crispin looked helplessly from Linc to his wife, and back again.

'Cris, you don't believe him, do you?' Nikki asked softly, and with reluctant admiration, Linc could see that she'd managed to produce real tears to plead her cause.

There was a moment's pause, where the only sound was the monotonous rumble of the mill-stones.

'Of course not.' Crispin had no defence against those beseeching eyes, and her case was helped by his eagerness to trust her. 'But I still don't understand what's going on, Niks. Why did Fagan attack Linc and Josie? And why should Linc lie about all this? I thought you were friends . . .'

Nikki bit her lip, lowering her eyes. 'I – I think it's because I wouldn't sleep with him,' she announced.

18

Nikki's words produced a moment's stunned silence.

'What?' Crispin and Linc spoke simultaneously, outraged and incredulous.

'When?' Crispin added.

'He came on to me several times,' she said, avoiding eye contact with him. 'But the first time was in the hall, after the dinner party. As soon as you and Josie went out he was all over me.'

'Oh, no, you don't, my girl!' Linc cut in. 'It was the other way round, as I remember. And you were half-cut anyway.'

'I didn't know what I was doing. You knew I'd had too much to drink and you took advantage of me. I'm nowhere near as strong as you.'

The cunningly added inference that Linc had used his superior strength to force his attentions on her fired Crispin up. He turned and blazed a look of pure scorn at his brother. 'You bastard . . .' he began.

Linc had had enough. 'Oh, spare me the drama. Can't you see the woman's playing you for a fool?

Why don't you ask yourself where Fagan comes into the equation? Personal trainer, my arse! If I was you, I'd want to get that baby paternity-tested when it arrives!' It was cruel, he knew, but his brother's stubborn refusal to accept any slur on Nikki's integrity was as exasperating as it was commendable.

His words stopped Crispin in his tracks. Brows drawn together, he scanned Linc's face intently, as if searching for some sign that he hadn't meant what he'd said, then turned to his wife and intercepted a look of pure poison directed at Linc.

'Nikki?'

'Crispin . . .' she began, softening her expression, but Fagan cut in.

'You're having a baby?'

'Shut up, Terry! It's got nothing to do with you,' Nikki said, moving closer to Crispin.

'How do you know that?' Fagan asked, clearly no longer content merely to look on. 'How can you possibly know?'

The significance of his question was not lost on Crispin.

'He's your lover.' He said each word slowly and deliberately, his face reflecting more disgust than pain. 'How long?'

'Crispin! You don't believe him?'

'How long?' This time he addressed Fagan, who responded with a sneer.

'Since way before she met you, pretty boy,' he taunted. 'We've been laughing at you!' He took a step forward but was brought up short by a rattling snarl from Tiger. Making a conciliatory gesture, Fagan stepped back.

Linc put a steadying hand on his brother's

shoulder. Crispin was as tight as sprung steel and Linc felt him take a deep breath before saying to Nikki in carefully controlled tones, 'And the other? The things Linc said – were they true, too? Did you put the drug in his drink?'

'Cris, I told you, Linc's bitter because I rejected him. He's just trying to get back at me . . .'

'Shut up!' Crispin's self-control broke, and the raw anger in his eyes shocked her into silence. 'Linc wouldn't do that.'

Linc could see by Nikki's expression that for the first time she was realising her hold on Crispin was slipping away.

'*I'll* tell you,' Fagan offered, clearly accepting that things were over for him and determined to get every ounce of enjoyment that he could out of Nikki's fall from grace.

She glowered at him, and he grinned nastily.

'I worked for her old man, in the clubs, but I had a spot of trouble and had to leave London in a hurry. Well, I knew Nikki'd got herself a cushy number up here, and I thought, considering what we'd shared in the past, she might like to help an old friend out. She was quite pleased to see me. Very pleased, in fact!' he added with a meaningful leer. 'And after we'd got reacquainted she said she'd help me get a job – you know, give me references and the like – if I'd help her with a little problem she had.'

Nikki put her hand on Crispin's arm. 'You can't listen to him! He knows he's in the shit and he'll say anything to drag me down with him.'

Crispin shook her hand off.

'Go on,' he invited quietly, staring at Fagan with

a steady intensity that belied the torment he must have been feeling, and Linc's heart went out to him.

'Well, like I said, she'd got herself a cushy number here, but being my Niks, she wasn't satisfied. She'd set her heart on a title, and all that stood in her way was her brother-in-law here. But it seemed that he'd got on the wrong side of some rough types, so Nikki reckoned, with a little planning, we could do away with Mr Viscount-in-waiting, her adoring hubby would step into the title, and no one would be any the wiser. She said once she was Lady of the Manor she'd see I was all right.'

Through the open window, over the rumbling of the stones, they heard the swish of car tyres turning on to the asphalt surface of the car park, but Crispin and Linc were intent on what Fagan had to say, and only Nikki went to look out.

'Quick!' she said, rushing back. 'Terry, we have to get out of here!'

Fagan gave her a scornful look. 'And where do you suppose we'd go?' he asked, sniffing. 'Even supposing I still gave a shit about you, which I don't. You're not that hot as a lover, you know!'

Nikki flushed red with humiliation. 'You never complained.'

'It passed the time,' he observed.

'You bastard!' Her slap rocked him back but he countered with one of his own, which brought tears to her eyes.

'That's enough!' Crispin said sharply, instinctively stepping in to shield his wife.

By Linc's side, Tiger was leaping and straining at his collar.

'What did she get you to do?' he asked Fagan.

'Did you plant the note on my car that day in Blandford?'

'Nah, that was Nikki. She said someone was threatening you, and she wanted to keep the pressure up. It was her idea to drug you, too. The night you had that little party in the village.'

'You were in the car park!' Linc said, remembering suddenly. 'When I came out of the hall, you were sitting in one of the cars.'

Fagan nodded. 'Yeah. She slipped you the Mickey, I was supposed to finish the job. But the stupid bitch used too much, didn't she?'

'GHB.'

'Yeah, GHB. Or GBH, as they call it round the clubs. I told her I wasn't sure of the mix but she still ballsed it up. The amount she must've given you, it was touch and go whether you'd even get out of the hall.'

'I didn't know how much he'd drink,' Nikki complained, stung into betraying herself completely. She stepped out from behind her husband. 'He kept saying he couldn't stay and I was worried he wouldn't have had enough.'

'But . . .' Crispin stopped short, shaking his head and laughing humourlessly. 'Christ, listen to me! I was just going to say you could have killed him, when of course that's what you were trying to do! You see, I just can't seem to get my head round it. My own wife has been sleeping with her personal trainer and plotting to kill my brother – it's quite simple really. I can't think why I have a problem with it.'

'Cris, don't beat yourself up,' Linc said quietly. 'You couldn't have known.'

'*You* ballsed it up, too,' Nikki retorted. Absorbed

in her row with Fagan, she seemed to have forgotten her audience for the time being. 'You only had to push his car into the fucking stream, but you couldn't even do that right!'

'I told you what happened! Some bloke came along in the middle of it. What the hell was I supposed to do, push him in too?'

'You could have thought of *something*! After all my hard work in setting it up.'

'And what about the business with Pepper?' Linc said, hearing voices below, indistinct over the noise of the machinery. 'You're a devious little cow, aren't you? Trying to frame Reagan. It almost worked, too, but those initials were a mistake. It was a touch too far. And then I spoilt it all by sorting Pepper out myself. You really should choose your tools more carefully. He was mad at me, but I don't think he would have killed me.'

While he was speaking, suddenly, blessedly, the nerve-jangling drone of the machinery began to slow and within seconds had stopped completely as the stones ground to a halt.

'He didn't have to. Terry was there to finish the job,' Nikki said into the ensuing silence. 'Everybody knew the old fart had been threatening you, and then of course Reagan would have found your body. Throw in the note, and the cops would have been so busy trying to decide which of them had done it, they'd never have thought of looking for anyone else. It would have been the perfect cover if Pepper hadn't fucked up!'

'Reagan said he thought he saw someone in the trees, but I didn't really believe him,' Linc stated, thinking back.

'Terry was with me,' Nikki said. 'But you were late and then Pepper took so bloody long that Reagan turned up, so he had to hide.'

'And Noddy?' Linc prompted, aware that the voices below had quietened, presumably listening. Thank God whoever it was had had the knowledge and sense to close the sluice gate and stop the wheel.

'It was worth a try. You gave me the idea yourself. You were always so paranoid about him rubbing his legs and getting grease in his eyes. But I didn't want to hurt him. I just thought he might bolt and throw you off.'

'Nikki . . .' Crispin's tone was despairing.

'Oh, for Christ's sake, Cris!' she said scornfully. 'I was only doing what you should have done if you'd had any balls. You're the one who stayed at Farthingscourt with your old man. Why should you let Linc come waltzing back in after all that time to cheat you out of what could have been yours?'

'But I never wanted the title,' Crispin protested, shaking his head in disbelief. 'I've always known it would go to Linc. I don't want the title, and I certainly don't want the responsibility that goes with it. I'm quite happy the way things are and – fool that I am – I thought you were, too.'

'But we could have had more,' she persisted, apparently unable to accept his point of view as genuine.

'But why attack Josie?' Linc asked. 'She's no threat to you. Was it jealousy?'

'Oh, *please*! Get over yourself! You're not God's gift, you know!'

'Then why?' he persisted.

'Oh, for God's sake! Because she's pregnant, of course. There's no point getting shot of you if the little bitch is going to produce an heir.'

'Pregnant?' It was Linc's turn to be shocked. 'She's not pregnant! What gave you that idea?'

'Oh, I could tell you had some secret you were keeping to yourselves, and then the other night . . . All that "I'm not hungry. I think I must be going down with something . . ." It didn't take a genius.'

'Well, this time you got it wrong. You put two and two together and came up with five, and because of that she nearly died! You're a sick woman, Nikki.'

'I didn't want to hurt Josie,' Nikki said regretfully. 'I liked her, but she had what I wanted . . .'

'You don't give a damn about anyone, you heartless bitch!' Fagan broke in. 'You and your sodding mother! A couple of scheming bitches! No wonder your father's got ulcers!'

'She only wants what's best for me,' Nikki said defensively. 'She married beneath herself, and didn't want me to do the same.'

'Don't worry, my dear,' Fagan said with heavy emphasis. 'You couldn't!'

'I think we've heard enough,' a new voice remarked, and DS Manston climbed the last few steps to the stone floor, still wearing elements of his rustic Georgian costume.

Twisting round in Linc's grasp, Tiger lunged towards the policeman and said something very rude.

'Hey, no, Tiger! He's one of the good guys,' Linc told him severely, bringing him back to heel.

'He's been too long with Sandy,' Manston

observed, eyeing the dog with disfavour. 'Old habits die hard.'

Somewhere outside, sirens could be heard approaching.

'Ah, back-up,' the sergeant said. 'Not that there'd be much point in either of these two making a run for it after that little performance. A pretty comprehensive confession, I'd say, from what I heard.'

'Yeah, though I wouldn't call it pretty. God knows what my father will say,' Linc commented, with a sigh. 'But thank heaven you're here. Have you seen Josie? Is she okay?'

'She's fine. She's down below with her father,' Manston said. 'She found Mrs Tremayne's radio in her car and put out a Mayday call. She was worried sick about you, but she's a sensible girl and knew she couldn't do anything herself. As it happens, we would have been on our way here shortly anyway. Your collective disappearance had been noted, and the general consensus was that someone should look into it. Luckily the Hathaways had spotted me at the fair and were just enlisting my help when Josie's message came through. I made a call to the station for back-up, and then her father and I came on over, but it looks like you'd already got it all sorted.'

Linc shook his head. 'Only just. We had something of a stand-off and if it hadn't been for Sandy's anti-social hound, we probably still would have. The little bugger saved my bacon at least twice today, if not more!'

Manston laughed. 'Guardian angels come in some odd disguises.'

He glanced with interest at Fagan, who was still

472

having trouble with his eyes. 'So, who have we here, I wonder?'

'Terry Fagan. Sometime club bouncer and fitness instructor,' Linc supplied.

'His real name is Terry Fairfax,' Nikki amended, relishing the chance to get even. 'He's wanted in London for assault and possession of drugs but he's a dealer, too. I can give you names and details.'

'You fucking bitch!' Fagan spat the words. 'Don't forget, you're going down too, and I know enough people to make sure your life is hell on the inside! You'll wish you'd kept your poisonous little trap shut!'

'All right, that's enough,' Manston said evenly. 'Let's take this down to the station, shall we?'

A uniformed officer appeared at the top of the stairs, breathing hard.

'Sir?' He looked enquiringly at the DS.

'Ah, good,' Manston said. 'You can read Mr Fairfax his rights and take him in. You'll need to get the doc to look at those eyes, they look nasty.' He sniffed the air and glanced at Linc. 'What was it, paint stripper?'

Linc nodded.

'And the charge?' the newcomer asked.

Manston pursed his lips, thoughtfully. 'Take your pick, really. But attempted murder will do to be going on with, I should think. Josie Hathaway and Lincoln Tremayne.'

The PC took hold of Fagan's arm and led him towards the stairs.

'I'm arresting you for the attempted murder of Josie—'

'Yeah, yeah, I know the drill,' Fagan cut in, but the officer was not to be put off and could be heard informing him of his rights as they descended to the ground floor.

Those remaining transferred their attention to Nikki, whose face had turned ashen, and Linc thought that probably the bleakness of her foreseeable future was only just hitting home. Her next words confirmed it.

She turned to Crispin and clung to his arm, her eyes pleading. 'I can't go to jail! Cris, tell them! I'm a Tremayne! What would your father say?'

He shook his head grimly, peeling her fingers off his arm and pushing her away. 'You've made your bed, now you've got to lie on it. You're nothing to me any more. I think I have pretty good grounds for divorce.'

'Come on, Mrs Tremayne, time to go,' Manston said. 'I have to read you your rights.'

'No, wait! What about our baby?' she asked Crispin in a voice growing shrill with panic. 'You can't let your child be born in jail! Think of the scandal!'

'If there *is* a baby . . .' Linc didn't quite know why he said it, but as soon as he saw Nikki's expression he knew he'd guessed right, even though the denial came instantly.

Linc shook his head in disgust and turned away as Manston put a hand on her back in order to shepherd her towards the stairs. 'Nikki Tremayne, I'm arresting you for attempted murder . . .'

'There was a baby,' she shouted over her shoulder. 'I didn't lie about that . . . but I lost it.'

Shattered, Crispin stood and watched his wife

being led away, probably too numb for tears, Linc thought.

'Cris?' he ventured tentatively.

Crispin didn't answer. He moved past Linc to close the window and then just stood looking out. Linc went to stand close behind him and after a moment or two Manston and Nikki appeared down below, heading for the car park. Crispin gave no sign that he'd seen them; he appeared to be staring into space.

'I might have a jumper in the car,' Linc said, feeling helpless in the face of his brother's grief. After the harsh words and emotional turmoil that had gone before, he wasn't entirely sure how their relationship stood. Suddenly, the words pushed past his guard and spilled out. 'Oh, Cris, I'm so bloody sorry it had to come to this! Bloody, sodding Nikki! I wish I'd never met her! Forgive me?'

Crispin turned his head, his expression desolate and his eyes shining with tears. 'I loved her,' he said simply. 'I thought she loved me.'

Aching with sympathy, Linc instinctively stepped up to his brother's side and, because there really wasn't anything else to say, enfolded him in a huge, silent hug.

For a moment Crispin held back, then he accepted the offered comfort, buried his face in Linc's shoulder and gave way to his wretchedness.

It was some five minutes later when Josie came up to find Linc and by that time Crispin had his emotions well under control. With typical tact she affected not to see the obvious signs of his distress and addressed Linc in a very matter-of-fact tone.

'Manston's gone. He says he'll need a detailed run down of what happened, but thankfully it can wait until tomorrow. I called Mary on the radio and gave her the gist of things so she can fill your father in and let Nikki's mum know. Nikki was asking for her,' she explained.

'Thanks.' Linc was grateful to have that task taken off him. 'And you? How's your arm?' Somebody had replaced the makeshift sling that Crispin had fashioned for her with a more professional-looking one.

'It throbs a bit. Dad did this, he's got an incredible first-aid kit in the boot of his car. I should imagine he could cope with just about anything short of open-heart surgery,' she joked. 'He's a fierce exponent of the theory that God helps those who help themselves. Anyway, he reckons I *might* have cracked something, but most likely it's just badly sprained. All that cold water therapy probably did it the world of good!'

'All the same, we should get you checked out. And you must be exhausted.'

'Mmm, quite tired, but Dad'll take me to A and E. I thought you could probably do with this back,' she said, holding out Crispin's shirt.

'Thanks.' He took it and stood looking down at it. 'I'm sorry for . . . Well, for everything. I never dreamed . . .'

Josie put her good hand on one of his.

'No, Cris. Don't apologise. You've got nothing to apologise for – you've done nothing wrong. And listen, I know it's what everybody says but I really mean it. If there's anything I can do – ever – just let me know.'

'Thanks.' Crispin looked genuinely moved. 'But, hey, just keep this accident-prone brother of mine in one piece, and you'll be doing us all a favour,' he said, summoning a smile.

Josie looked heavenwards. 'Well, I know I said *anything*, but I'm not a miracle-worker!'

When they made their way downstairs, her father was waiting, grave-faced. He held out his hand.

'Crispin. This is a bad business. I'm sorry, lad.'

He nodded mutely, and shook the hand.

'Come on,' David Hathaway suggested, putting his arm round his daughter's shoulders. 'Come away. There's nothing more to do here. I'm going to take Josie to the doctor's, and I should imagine you two could do with a stiff drink and a chance to put your feet up. You must be exhausted.'

'You can say that again,' Linc agreed.

They left the mill, waiting while Linc locked the doors, and then turned towards the car park; Josie and her father leading the way, and the others trailing after.

Linc was so caught up in his own thoughts that it was a moment or two before he realised his brother wasn't following, and paused to wait.

'Cris?'

Crispin was standing gazing across the tailrace of the millstream to the trees beyond. He looked completely lost.

'I loved her, Linc,' he said forlornly. 'At least, I thought I did. But now I'm not sure I ever knew her at all. Where does that leave me?'

Linc shook his head. There was nothing he could say.

Epilogue

The stadium was a blaze of light, most of it concentrated on the oval dirt track at its centre where six slender greyhounds were being loaded into the traps for the start of the next race. In one of the boxes with a prime view, Linc Tremayne, his brother Crispin, and the entire Hathaway clan sat, the remains of a meal on a table behind them, enjoying the sport.

'This is amazing!' Abby declared. 'I feel like a movie star or something, sitting up here in a private box, being wined and dined. I mean, an hour and a half ago I was slogging round the field in the rain, taking hay to Syrup and Treacle, and now I'm here.'

'Like Cinderella,' Hannah put in, with uncharacteristic imagination. 'You *shall* go to the ball!'

Linc laughed. 'I'm glad you're enjoying it.'

'I'd never have thought of coming to a dog track,' Ruth said. 'But it's really good fun.'

The runners were all loaded now, the hare started its hopeless run and the traps snapped open, releasing their eager occupants to streak in pursuit.

Instantly bedlam broke loose in the box as six voices were raised in noisy support of their chosen favourites. Only David Hathaway and Linc remained silent; the clergyman watching the others with obvious pleasure, while Linc was absorbed in thoughts of his own.

It was fully three months since the terrifying events at the mill, and life had moved on. The case against Nikki and her personal trainer had not yet come to court, and probably wouldn't for some little while yet, the wheels of justice grinding exceedingly slow.

Sylvester Tremayne had responded to the news of his daughter-in-law's treachery by remembering several things he had never liked about her and then writing her out of his life with a finality that was typical of him.

Crispin had, understandably, found it far more difficult to adjust to the upheaval, losing his trusting, happy-go-lucky nature overnight and becoming quiet and introverted. Josie's father had offered contacts within the legal world and, in the absence of any great degree of ongoing sympathy from his own father, it was to David Hathaway that Crispin had turned, accepting help of both a practical and, to Linc's surprise, spiritual nature.

Linc had had to use a fair amount of persuasion to get him to come to the stadium tonight and, once there, he'd been a little withdrawn until a spirited dispute with Hannah had brought him out of himself. Now, sitting next to Ruth with whom he'd struck up a particular friendship during his visits to the Vicarage, Crispin looked more animated than

Linc had seen him since the exposure of Nikki's betrayal.

The race sped to an exciting conclusion and was followed by a heated discussion of the real or imagined bad luck suffered by various of the participants during which Josie looked round and smiled at Linc, before detaching herself from the group by the window and coming to sit beside him.

'A penny for 'em,' she said lightly.

He shrugged. 'I was just thinking about Crispin, actually. I'm glad I persuaded him to come. I think he's enjoying himself. Ruth's good for him. Although, to be fair, I think it was your other brat of a sister who shook him out of his mood.'

Josie laughed, unoffended. 'She's enough to get anyone going. Perhaps we should patent her as a therapy. "The Hannah Method", guaranteed to needle you out of depression!'

'Mmm. It might catch on, but I doubt it.'

Linc sighed, and Josie put her arm through his and leaned close.

'What's up?'

'Oh, I still can't shake off the feeling that I'm partly responsible for what happened with Nikki. After all, I raised her hopes in the first place, and I was never really serious about her. If I hadn't brought her home that time . . .'

'Oh, and of course you'd expect her to go off the deep end and turn psycho, wouldn't you?' Josie pointed out. 'Spare me another guilt trip! Is there anything you don't feel responsible for? What about Third World debt or global warming, are you sure you aren't to blame for those too?'

'You cheeky wench!' Linc made her squeal with a

sharp dig in the ribs. 'When we're married and you start producing the next generation of Tremaynes, I shall make sure they treat me with a little more respect! I won't have young Aloysius talking to me like that!'

'Young what . . .?' Josie spluttered.

'You know the family tradition for unusual names,' Linc reminded her, straight-faced.

'Well, in that case, it's more likely to be Ermintrude,' Josie suggested. 'Or Esmerelda. You know our family record for producing girls.'

'It wouldn't dare! Father would have a fit!'

'You can't fool me – your father's a dear.'

A few months before, Linc would have been highly amused at this description, but it had to be said that his irascible parent had mellowed significantly of late. At the 'surprise' engagement party six weeks ago, when Josie and Linc had gathered family and friends at Farthingscourt to announce their happy news, they had been upstaged on the night by a similar announcement from Sylvester and Mary.

'Linc, what do you think will win the next race?' Hannah wanted to know; she liked to keep everyone involved in the proceedings.

'Number five,' he replied promptly.

'But you didn't even look!' she protested. 'You have to look first.'

Obediently Linc moved closer to the glass and made a pretence of studying the dogs that were being paraded below. The one wearing the gold number five jacket was fawn-coloured and looked fit and handsome.

'Number five,' he repeated.

'Abby's Dream,' Ruth exclaimed, looking at her race card. 'Abby should cheer for that one, really. I prefer number three.'

'We'll cheer for it together,' Linc said, smiling at Abby.

She smiled back, looking – to any outsider – like a normal, happy, healthy teenager. Only her closest family and friends knew that beneath the teenage uniform of flared hipster jeans and clingy, camouflage tee-shirt, the legacy of the assault lived on in a deep seated insecurity and an unwillingness to mix with strangers.

In due course, runners picked or allocated by Hannah, they settled down to watch the race with varying degrees of excited anticipation. It was a race for novices, comprising just one lap of the track, and the dogs left the traps like bullets, each sporting a different-coloured jacket for easy identification.

Number five started well and went into the first bend in second place, which it maintained all the way down the back straight. Coming into the last bend, Abby's Dream began to move up on the outside of the leader and it looked as though he would come into the straight ahead, but as the runners turned for home, number six muscled through between the first two, knocking Linc's hope wide. Even then, all was not lost. Abby's Dream made a game effort to recover and they crossed the line with only millimetres between them.

As the hullabaloo in the Hathaways' box died down, Abby looked hopefully up at Linc. 'Did he win?'

Linc didn't think so, and after a few moments the action replay on the big screen confirmed it.

'Oh, what a shame!' Abby cried. 'He tried so hard!'

'With a name like that, he really should have won,' her father said.

'I know,' Linc agreed sadly. 'He obviously didn't read the script. I shall have to have a word with his trainer, he'll be up in a minute.'

'Who will?' Ruth queried.

'The trainer, Barney. He'll come up. He said he would, anyway. You see, if this had really been a fairy tale or a movie, Abby's Dream would have won. I even ordered a bottle of champagne in case.' He paused, aware that he had everyone's attention. Abby in particular was regarding him intently. 'You know what I'm going to say, don't you, Abby?'

'I think so,' she said slowly. 'But I thought it was just another of my weird dreams . . . Oh, of course! Abby's Dream! He's mine, isn't he? He really is!'

She scrambled up out of her seat and threw herself at Linc, who lifted her off her feet and swung her round, reflecting that the greyhound's considerable purchase price was quite possibly the best investment he'd ever made.

'Well, actually we're joint owners,' Linc told her. 'I promised your dad we'd share the training fees. He'll race for three or four years, all being well, then he'll need a home, but I promised Barney that if you didn't want him, then I'd have him,' Linc told her.

'Of course I'll want him!' Abby declared indignantly.

Linc laughed and winked at her father, over her head. From the delighted reactions of the rest of the family, he gathered that his surprise was approved of, the only voice of dissent coming, predictably, from Hannah.

'Well, that's all very well,' she announced. 'But I hope nobody expects *me* to walk it!'

Lyndon Stacey's exciting new thriller

OUTSIDE CHANCE

will be published by Hutchinson
in August 2005.

Read on for an exclusive extract . . .

Prologue

The smart, maroon and gold liveried horse-transporter negotiated the roundabout at the bottom of the hill with obvious care and moved out onto the dual carriageway, attacking the gradient with carefully controlled power. In the cab the wiry, weather-beaten, fifty-something driver settled back in his seat and prepared for the long haul, listening tolerantly to his two younger companions arguing in the seating area behind the cab about the outcome of a private bet.

In a lay-by at the top of the hill, three men with peaked caps and fluorescent green tabards over their uniforms lounged against a white Transit van. A row of cones stood waiting beside them, presumably to funnel reluctant motorists into the checkpoint, but at present the men appeared more interested in the contents of the mugs they cradled in their hands. It was February, late afternoon and bitterly cold; the clouds low, grey, and inclined to drizzle. A stream of vehicles swished by on the wet road, their lights reflecting off the surface and their occupants noting the disinterest of the officials with relief.

A phone trilled and one of the men reached into the cab of the van and withdrew a handset. He spoke briefly, nodded, replaced the phone and turned to say something to the others. Their relaxed attitude disappeared in an instant. Mugs were emptied, caps straightened and soon all three were moving to take up new positions: one at the roadside near the end of the lay-by, the other two nearer to the van. One of these picked up a clipboard and his companion held what could have been a torch. They were, it seemed, ready for business.

As the horsebox reached the top of the rise, the driver spotted the waiting men and groaned.

'Not me, *please*,' he begged as he drew closer. 'Not me. Not me . . . Ahh, shite!'

The unsmiling official stood back and waved him through the cones, pointing towards his waiting colleagues, and the driver nodded, 'Yeah, yeah. I know.'

'What's happening?' The two lads in the back, barely more than teenagers, had broken off their argument and one of them appeared between the seats.

'Checkpoint. Probably Department of friggin' Transport,' the driver growled. 'If we've got a light out, I'll kill that bloody Nigel!'

The lorry rolled to a halt just inches from the man with the clipboard, who had planted himself directly in front of it. He didn't so much as twitch a muscle.

'Cold blooded as a fish!' The driver muttered, robbed of even that satisfaction. He pressed a button and the window dropped smoothly. 'Yes, officer?'

'Immigration,' the man with the clipboard announced, briefly flashing some documentation. 'Turn the engine off, please.'

Resignedly he complied, and as the sound of the engine died away, the man with the torch moved to the passenger side where he kept his head averted, apparently inspecting the tyre.

'What are you carrying?' The clipboard man had glasses and a dark moustache, which, in combination with the peaked cap, seemed to hide a good deal of his face.

'Er . . . *Racehorses*, maybe?' the driver suggested, shaking his head in disbelief and indicating the panel of the cab door. It displayed – as did the body of the lorry – the words *Castle Ridge Racing* in large gold letters.

It seemed that they were the last unlucky travellers of the day. In the mirror the third uniformed man could be seen already gathering up the cones.

'Come on, mate. We don't particularly want to be here either. Let's keep this civilised, shall we?' The man stepped up onto the footplate and peered inside the cab, where the second lad had now joined his colleagues. 'Can I have your names?' His hand, on the framework, was encased in a thin plastic glove.

The driver sighed. 'Ian Rice; Davy Jackson; Les Curtis,' he said, indicating himself and the other two in turn. 'Look, you don't want to open the back, do you? Only, the horses get upset and . . .'

He never finished the sentence.

In one fluid movement, the clipboard man dropped down to the ground, opened the door, and stepped up again.

'Move across,' he ordered, and suddenly he had a gun in his hand, the muzzle applying pressure to Rice's neck, just up under his jaw.

For a moment he appeared uncomprehending, and then he gulped and a sheen of sweat formed on his brow.

'Please . . . Don't . . .'

On the other side of the cab, the second man had moved with perfect synchronicity and now held a similar weapon to one of the lads' heads.

'Just move,' the first man repeated and, as Rice did so, slipped into the seat beside him and pulled the door shut.

'Now, into the back. All of you. Slowly; no sudden moves.'

'All right, lads. Do as he says.' White-faced and trembling, Rice had nevertheless pulled himself together now.

The lads scrambled across the seat and back through the central doorway, the younger of the two whimpering faintly with fear. Rice followed and the two bogus officials brought up the rear; the one who'd held the clipboard kept his gun on the three, while the other produced lengths of fine nylon cord from his pocket and swiftly and efficiently tied them hand and foot. He then tied their ankles to their wrists, behind them, leaving them as helpless as calves at a branding. A strip of silver duct tape across their mouths ensured silence and, stripping off their tabards and caps, the two men returned to the cab.

Wasting no time, the clipboard man slid into Rice's vacated seat. Starting the engine he checked the mirror, indicated right, and the lorry moved ponderously forward and out into the traffic, its new driver waving a hand in thanks to a helpful motorist.

The whole incident had taken less than five minutes. Behind them, the remaining man bundled the cones into the back of the white transit and set off after the horsebox.

In the deserted lay-by, an empty crisp packet tumbled end over end in the wake of the van and then lay still.

Chapter One

The white horse was galloping wildly, mane and tail flying and hooves throwing up chunks of peaty earth. The saddle had slipped right over to one side and it didn't seem possible that the man who clung desperately to the underside of the animal's outstretched neck could retain his grip for many moments more.

Those watching held their collective breath. He *had* to hang on. Those pounding, steel-shod hooves made the alternative too horrific. But a further disaster loomed: the horse was running out of space. Ahead, two concrete walls converged to form a corner from which there was no escape, but the horse's breakneck pace didn't slacken. Just strides away now, it appeared oblivious to the danger.

Somewhere someone screamed and, almost in the same instant, tragedy was averted. The man, so apparently helpless until now, pulled himself up and over the horse's withers in one fluid movement, gathered his flapping reins and guided the animal into a perfectly controlled turn.

To the accompaniment of relieved cheers and applause from the thousand or more onlookers, he then proceeded to unstrap the useless saddle and hold it aloft, whilst bringing the beautiful white horse to a flamboyant, plunging halt. The clapping turned into an ovation as the crowd rose to its feet, almost as one, and the rider responded with a wide grin, his teeth, flashing impossibly white in the spotlight as he acknowledged the admiration.

'Ladies and gentlemen; Nicolae Bardu!' the announcer cried with a flourish.

From his position six rows up, near the entrance to the indoor arena, Ben Copperfield relaxed and joined in the general appreciation. No matter that he'd watched all the rehearsals for the show; he still couldn't help holding his breath and gripping his seat. He could have sworn that Nico left his recovery until later and later every time.

The music struck up once more, signalling the beginning of the finale. The horse and rider made their jaunty exit and Ben slipped out of his seat and found his way up the tiers to the doorway at the back. The strains of Tchaikovsky's *Marche Slav* faded as he pulled the door to behind him, and he descended the steps to the warm-up area where the performers were gathering to make their final triumphant entrance.

Nico was there, still full of the arrogant confidence he exhibited throughout his performances. Ben knew that some people found such rampant egotism objectionable, but he had observed it before in other high achievers: dancers, sportsmen, and athletes. They seemed to feed off their audience. They worked ceaselessly behind the scenes to hone their skills but somehow it was as if the very presence of those watching inspired them to reach the peak of their abilities. He had witnessed just a few of the countless hours of practice that went into producing those brief moments of glory and, personally, he felt that a little arrogance was perfectly excusable.

Someone Ben knew only by sight was replacing the saddle on the magnificent white stallion, which stood like a rock, only its proudly arched neck and frothily champing jaws telling of the hyped-up eagerness within. Nico was standing to one side, brushing real or imaginary specks of dust from the short, gold-braided black jacket he had just put on.

'That was a bit close to the knuckle, you mad bugger!' Ben approached to within a few feet, taking care not to get in anybody's way. The horse swung its head to look at him, its big dark eye rimmed with white, and the rich warm smell of it filled Ben's nostrils. Almost involuntarily, he took a step back.

Nico turned, his fine, arching brows drawn down momentarily, then he broke into a smile as he recognised the speaker.

'Tomorrow I go closer!' he promised extravagantly. He seemed in particularly high spirits this evening.

'Well, I hope you're insured against causing heart attacks in the audience,' Ben observed. 'Mine was going like the clappers, and *I* knew it was all part of the act! You ought to put a health warning on the tickets!'

Nico laughed delightedly. 'You ain't seen nothing yet!' he declared, the Americanism sounding strange in his slightly stilted English. He was, as were all of the troupe, of Hungarian gypsy origin – which no doubt accounted for his smouldering good looks – and Ben suspected that his grasp of the English language was attributable to a combination of questionable sources, including contact with European tourists and a multitude of American films.

'Ladies and gentlemen, I give you . . . The Hungarian Csikós!'

The trio of riders immediately before him in the parade moved forward and, with a wave of his hand, Nico vaulted on to his horse.

'Later, my friend,' he called and turned towards the arena, his back straightening and his expression settling once more into one of macho hauteur as he faced the bright lights.

Ben stepped back and watched him go. He'd been following the troupe on and off ever since they had docked, en masse, at Dover three days ago. His job, as a freelance journalist specialising in all things equine, had brought him into the sphere of a number of fascinating people, but he couldn't remember any who had so instantly captivated him in the way these Gypsy horsemen had done. He had never been a fan of circuses and had accepted the assignment with a measure of reserve. His prejudice, however, melted away within minutes of seeing their first performance, and he was now happily devoting a large proportion of his time to the in-depth article he'd been commissioned to write.

In his pocket, his mobile began ringing with the particular call-tone reserved for family members. He dug it out. The display told him it was his half-brother, Mikey, and he pressed a button to accept the call.

'Mikey. How ya doin'? Sorry I couldn't get over to see you this afternoon.' Just seventeen, Mikey was a conditional jockey – jump racing's equivalent of an apprentice – and Ben knew he'd been due to ride in a novice hurdle at Sandown Park.

'I'm at the hospital.' Never relaxed on the phone, Mikey cut straight to the chase.

The shock jolted Ben.

'What happened? Did you fall off? Are you all right?'

'No, I didn't fall off. It was on the way home, but I'm not supposed to talk about it.'

'What do you mean? Were you in a road accident or what? Why can't you talk about it?'

'The Guvnor said not to. But I just wanted to let you know I'm all right.'

'But Mikey . . .' Ben paused in amused frustration. 'If you hadn't rung, I wouldn't have known anything was wrong anyway.'

'No . . . I know . . .'

Ben was picking up a strong thread of anxiety in Mikey's voice. Something had clearly upset him. Fifteen years separated them and sometimes he felt more like Mikey's father than his half-brother; the more so because Mikey had grown up with certain learning difficulties, resulting in an overall lack of confidence and a childish need for reassurance. It was nearly always to Ben that he turned rather than to their mutual father, bloodstock agent John Copperfield, who, although he had many virtues, could not count patience as one of them.

'Why did Mr Truman tell you not to ring?'

'He said not to tell anyone, but I shouldn't think he meant you, did he?'

Ben's lips twitched. He most assuredly *did* mean him. If Eddie Truman had something to hide, the very last person he'd want Mikey to tell was his journalist brother.

'Which hospital are you in? Would you like me to come over?' he asked, avoiding the question.

'We're going home in a minute. They just checked us over. But we've got to wait for Les. He has asthma and the shock made him bad.'

'So you *did* have an accident.'

'No. It was these men . . . Look, I can't tell you. I'll get into trouble.'

Frustrated, Ben made an instant decision. 'Listen, Mikey; I'll come to the cottage, okay? But I'm in Kent so I'll be a couple of hours at least. And perhaps it would be best if you didn't tell Mr Truman you've spoken to me. Just to be on the safe side. All right?'

'Yeah. Maybe. See you later, then.'

Ben switched off, feeling thoughtful, and in due course he excused himself from the post-performance get-together and set off for the Castle Ridge Racing Stables on the Wiltshire–Dorset border. The Csikós were touring and due to move on. When he caught up with them again, it would be in Sussex.

Eddie Truman's yard stood in an enviable position on the edge of a stretch of chalk downland, which formed beautiful natural gallops for racehorses. Because of the large number of horses he had in training – ninety-five, the last Ben had heard –

Truman had a fair number of staff. These included two PAs, a farrier, an odd-job man, an assistant trainer, two head lads, a travelling head lad, a box driver and a fluctuating total of somewhere between twenty-five and thirty stable lads and lasses. Some of these had digs in the nearby village of Lower Castleton but a number of the lads occupied two former farm-workers cottages. Mikey and four others, one of whom was the head lad, occupied a cottage just a stone's throw from the yard itself.

It was in front of this that Ben parked his four-wheel-drive Mitsubishi, just before midnight. He had hesitated outside the high wooden gates at the end of the back drive, wondering if perhaps he was too late and Mikey might have given up on him and gone to bed. Something in his voice, though, had suggested a crisis that would not be solved merely by getting a good night's rest, so he'd carried on; now the well-lit cottage windows showed that nobody seemed to have sleep on their minds just at the moment. Across the intervening field, a blaze of light at the main house seemed to tell the same story. Ben began to be very interested indeed.

The Mitsubishi's wheels had barely stopped turning when the door of the lads' cottage opened and he could see Mikey looking out.

'You were watching for me.' Ben crunched across the frosty gravel to meet him. The afternoon's clouds had disappeared and it was a clear, starlit night.

'Actually there's a buzzer that goes off when the gate's opened at night. Ricey says it's better than having it locked because people will always find a way in if they're determined, and this way we know they're coming.'

'That makes sense,' Ben agreed. 'Where do you want to talk, in or out?'

'You can come in. There's only me and Davy here. They kept Les in for the night 'cos he was still wheezing. Ricey and Bess are over at the house and Caterpillar's on holiday.'

'Caterpillar?' Ben queried, momentarily distracted. He followed Mikey into the kitchen; a blue-and-white tiled room with pine units, a large pine table, and a state of tolerable tidiness that Ben suspected was entirely due to Bess's presence in the cottage.

'Yeah, he's new. You haven't met him yet. We call him Caterpillar 'cos he's got this huge moustache. Ricey says it's a relic from the seventies.'

'Oh, I see. You're not making coffee are you? I could murder a cup. It was a long drive. Talking of which . . .?'

'Yeah . . . look, I'm really not supposed to say anything.' Mikey busied himself with filling the kettle and finding mugs, his golden blond fringe flopping into his eyes as it habitually did. At five foot seven he was fully six inches shorter than Ben, taking after his mother rather than the Copperfield side of the family. He had inherited his colouring from her, too, and had dark-lashed, brilliant-blue eyes that had the girls in raptures; the shame of it was that he was far too shy to appreciate his luck. Ben was a true Copperfield, tall and fairly lean, with mid-brown hair – at present short and a little spiky – that curled if it was allowed to grow, and eyes that couldn't make up their mind if they were green or grey.

'But you already *have* said something. You can't

just expect me to forget it,' Ben pointed out reasonably. 'Come on, you know you can trust me. I won't tell anyone if it would get you into trouble.'

'I know, but . . .'

'Mikey. I've just driven over a hundred miles to get here because I was worried about you. I'm not about to turn round and go away without finding out what's going on. Why all the lights everywhere? I could see the main house was all lit up as I came over the hill. And why are Ian and Bess over there now? You can't tell me *that's* normal at midnight. *You've* been to hospital; Les is still there. So who were these men you were talking about? Come on. You're not being very fair. Something happened on the way home, didn't it? Was there an accident? Has one of the horses been hurt? What?'

'Not *hurt*, exactly,' Mikey responded reluctantly.

'Then what?' Ben was trying very hard to keep his frustration under control.

Mikey was stirring the coffee, his lower lip caught between his teeth and his brow creased with the agony of his indecision.

Ben tried again. 'Okay, if not hurt, then . . . did you lose one somehow?' He read Mikey's stricken expression. 'That's it, isn't it? No! My God, you've had one stolen! Which one? Not Cajun King?'

Mikey didn't try to deny it. 'Yes. But you mustn't tell anyone. The Guvnor would kill me.'

'No, of course I won't.' Ben's mind was buzzing with this new development. Cajun King: strong ante-post favourite for the Cheltenham Gold Cup. Castle Ridge's great hope for National Hunt glory. Stolen. Or kidnapped, perhaps? He instantly thought of Shergar. 'Where and how did they do it?' he asked.

'It was a checkpoint. They pretended to be immigration officials.'

'And then what?'

'They had guns. They threatened Ricey and the others, then tied them up.' Mikey handed Ben a mug of exceedingly milky coffee and they both sat down at the table.

'So where were you? In the back?'

'Yeah, I was in the luton, asleep. Nigel – our other driver – has got a bed up there, over the cab. I went up there after racing and I'd been there ever since. I didn't even wake up when we set off for home.'

That didn't surprise Ben. Mikey had a remarkable propensity for taking catnaps as and when he felt like it, regardless of where he was or what was going on.

'So where was this?'

'About twenty minutes after we'd left the racecourse, in a lay-by on the side of a dual carriageway, Ricey says.'

'But . . . you'd have thought someone would've seen what was going on and called the police.'

'Ricey says it was all over in a minute or two, and then they drove the box away. They took it to some private land where they could transfer the horse to another lorry.'

'And you slept through it all.'

'Yes. I didn't know anything about it until they drove down this bumpy track and I woke up.' Now he'd started, Mikey seemed eager to tell the whole story. 'We stopped, and then I could hear these men's voices calling to one another, and someone opened the back. I knew it wasn't Ricey 'cos he always thumps on the roof of the cab first, when we stop, to wake me up – and anyway, their voices sounded . . . different. Not from round here.'

'Well, you weren't 'round here' when it happened,' Ben reminded him. 'But you mean they had some kind of accent?' He knew it wasn't any earthly good asking Mikey what kind of accent it had been. The boy was hopeless in that department. He could recognise an accent again, once he'd heard it, but he couldn't tell South African from Geordie, or Indian from Scots, and if he didn't know he had a tendency to guess, to try and please you.

'Yeah. Could have been Welsh, maybe.'

'So what happened next?'

'Well, I could hear these men in with the horses, so I stayed hidden.' Mikey looked down at his coffee, shamefaced.

'I don't blame you,' Ben said, adding without irony, 'Best thing to do.'

Mikey looked unhappy. 'Davy says I should have done something.'

'Well, Davy's a moron,' Ben observed. 'What the hell could you have done on your own? Nothing; and there was no point at all in getting yourself hurt, or tied up like the others. You did the right thing.'

'Is that what you'd have done?'

'Oh, absolutely.'

'Yeah, well, I thought it was the best thing,' Mikey stated, growing in confidence now that Ben had approved his actions.

'So what happened then? Could you hear what they were saying?'

'Well, there were two of them in the back of the

lorry but they didn't say a lot, really. Just talking to the horses as they got them out. And then the other lorry turned up.'

'They got *all* the horses out?'

'Yes. They took them all out of the box and let them go. I heard them chasing the others away.'

'Playing for time, I suppose,' Ben said. 'So they transferred Cajun King to the other lorry and drove off. What then? Did you call the police?'

'Well, I was going to, but as soon as I got down from the luton I found Ricey and the others all tied up, so I got some scissors from the grooming kit and cut them free. Then we found a note stuck to the dashboard. It said that nobody was to call the police or King would be killed.'

'And what did Ian – er, Ricey do then?'

He said he was going to call The Guvnor but we were in a valley and he couldn't get a signal on his mobile, so we decided to try and catch the horses first.'

'And you found them all right?'

Mikey nodded. 'One of them was hanging round the lorry and the other two weren't far away.'

'And then you came home.'

'Well, we were going to, but on the way Les started to have an asthma attack, so we had to take him to hospital.'

'So when did you ring Truman?'

'When we got back to the main road. Ricey told him . . .' Hearing the sound of the outside door opening, Mikey broke off and looked anxiously at Ben.

Before Ben could say anything voices were heard, one of which announced, 'They're in here,' and then the kitchen door swung inwards to reveal a thin-faced, mousey-haired youngster, full of self-importance. 'Mikey and his journalist brother. I told you.'

'Yes, thank you Davy. You can go now. We'll call you if we need you.' The second speaker was a diminutive man in his late fifties, with thinning grey hair and pronounced crow's-feet at the corners of his shrewd grey eyes.

Ian Rice – Ricey – was Castle Ridge's travelling head lad, responsible for the well being of the horses when they left the yard to go racing. Ben had met him several times before, on visits to see Mikey, and liked him a lot. He was quiet – both with animals and people, efficient, and very patient with Mikey.

'Hello, Ian.' Ben could see two much bulkier figures looming behind him, and it only took a glance to recognise them as policemen, even though they wore plain clothes. His work had brought him into contact with the police on numerous occasions and he had developed an unerring eye for members of the constabulary, in whatever guise they chose to appear.

'Ben; The Guvnor – that is, Mr Truman – would like to see you over at the house, if you've got a minute,' Rice told him.

'Is it in the nature of a summons?'

'It is, rather,' he said apologetically. 'As I'm sure Mikey's told you, we've got a bit of a crisis on our hands.'

'Yeah, Mikey's told me, but don't be too hard on him,' Ben said, getting to his feet. 'He didn't want to tell me. I'm afraid I prised it out of him.'

'I'm not in trouble, am I?' Mikey glanced from Ben to Rice, and back.

'No, no, you're not in trouble, Mikey.' One of the police officers stepped into the room. 'We just need to ask you a few questions, that's all.'

'I'll stay with him,' Rice told Ben quietly, as he moved towards the door.

In the narrow hall, the second policeman blocked his way. 'You wouldn't be thinking of using your mobile phone between here and the house, would you?' he enquired.

Ben looked down at the hand that was preventing his forward movement, and after a moment it was removed.

'I hadn't been,' he said.

'All the same, perhaps I'll just come with you.'

Ben sighed. 'I've got a better idea.' He reached into his inside pocket and withdrew the tiny, metal-cased phone. 'You look after this for me, and I'll find my own way over. I think I can manage.'

Following the cinder path that led from the cottage to the main house, Ben thought over what he'd learned, and reflected wryly that it was typical that when the scoop of a lifetime fell into his lap, he should be honour-bound to keep it to himself.

Castle Ridge House – home of racehorse owner, trainer and self-made millionaire Eddie Truman – was an imposing edifice, built less than five years previously in red brick, with concrete pillars flanking its glossy, white double doors. It sat on a natural plateau, on the site of the far smaller manor house it had replaced, and was everything a rags to riches businessman could have wished for: including an indoor swimming pool, garaging for eight cars, an adjoining tennis court, and a conservatory that could have housed a modest bungalow.

Ben had seen it several times in the daylight and, privately, he thought it vulgar.

Crossing the pea shingle drive, he counted six cars drawn up in front of the mock Georgian façade. None of them were obviously police vehicles but, under the blaze of the halogen lights, Ben could see only one that bore the personalised number plates with which all Eddie Truman's cars were fitted.

A door at the side of the house stood ajar, a thin sliver of light escaping to lay a line down the path; at his approach it opened fully and a feminine figure stood silhouetted in the aperture.

'Ben?'

'That's right.'

'Good. Come on in. Mr Truman's waiting for you in the study.'

Ben stepped into the hall where the speaker was revealed as a pretty female in her late twenties, with big, dark eyes and glossy, shoulder-length, brown hair. Bess Wainwright, one of two secretaries at Castle Ridge, and the one who shared Mikey's cottage. Mikey had pointed her out once. Ben followed her through the quarry-tiled back hall, along a corridor and across an inner hall to a white panelled door with brass fittings. There, after knocking briefly, she leaned in to announce Ben's presence before ushering him through.

There were three men in the room that Ben entered: two standing, unknown to him but almost certainly policemen, and one seated at the desk, whom he recognised from newspaper photographs and TV racing coverage as Eddie Truman.

Even when he was seated you could tell he was a big man, and Ben knew, from the way he dwarfed interviewers, that he must be well over six foot tall. Square shoulders and a square-jawed, freckled face added to the impression of bulk, and the fingers that tapped impatiently on the desk were short and spatulate. Hair that had once been bright ginger was fading, now that he was in his fifties, greying at the temples and decidedly thin on top, but it was still easy to see why the trainer had picked up the nickname of 'Red' Truman.

'Ah, come in, Mr Copperfield. Take a seat.' Truman's voice held a rich Yorkshire burr, apparently the one part of his background that he had not tried to hide. 'Gentlemen, this is Ben Copperfield – Michael's brother; Ben, this is DI Ford and DS Hancock. Doubtless you already know why they're here.'

Ben inclined his head, sat in a buttoned leather wing-chair, and waited, taking in the overstated opulence of his surroundings with an interested glance. Chairs, desk, footstool and window seat were all finished in red leather; all fittings were of burnished bronze, including the fireplace surround; and several art deco maidens held glass lampshades aloft at strategic points in the room. One wall supported shelves of expensive, leather-bound books from floor to ceiling, but none of the spines bore any signs of use. Tassels were very much in favour on cushions, gold velvet curtains and a bell pull, and there was enough mahogany in evidence to have laid waste to a small rainforest. Ben had no doubt that it was real. For someone who had spent a sizeable number of his student days protesting against various environmental crimes, it was a sad sight.

'I'm not going to mince my words, Ben – may I call you that?' Truman began. 'I was deeply disturbed to find that you were here and talking to Mikey. I suppose he contacted you and asked you to come – it would be too much to suppose your appearance was a coincidence.'

'Yes, he called me. He was, understandably, very upset, but he didn't tell me why. It was my decision to come and see him. I was worried.'

DS Hancock cleared his throat. 'Mr Copperfield, we understand you're a journalist. Is that correct?'

'Yes, that's right.'

'What paper do you work for?'

'I'm freelance.'

'May I ask you what you're working on at the moment?'

'You can *ask* . . .' Hancock's attitude was putting Ben's back up.

'Obviously your brother has already told you what's going on.'

'Obviously.'

'And I suppose you're thinking this is the scoop of the century . . .'

Hancock had two millimetres of dark hair and the eyes of a cynic. Plain clothes for him were black jeans, a black turtleneck and a tailored black leather jacket. Ben felt that, had he not been a police officer, he would have worn an earring.

'I could more or less name my price,' he agreed.

Hancock glared at him, plainly squaring up for a confrontation, but his superior stepped into the breach.

'But you won't, will you, Mr Copperfield? You're intelligent enough to understand that this is a delicate situation in which inappropriate publicity could be disastrous, and you have conscience enough to put moral duty before monetary gain.'

'Do I indeed?' Ben regarded the DI through narrowed eyes. 'That's pretty analytical. Are you always that quick to form an opinion, or have we met before?'

'Neither. I just remembered a certain journalist called Ben Copperfield who was instrumental in exposing the Goodwood betting scandal a couple of years ago.' He smiled. 'That was good work.'

Somewhere in his forties, Ford could not have been many years older than his colleague, but nature had taken the controlling hand in his hair loss, leaving him with a thick brown fringe circling a completely bald pate. Slightly overweight, he presented an avuncular air, but his rank alone would suggest that there was a sharp mind behind the genial appearance.

Ben acknowledged the praise with a slight inclination of his head. The Goodwood affair had started out as a simple reporting assignment, but he had caught the whiff of corruption and, anticipating a diversion from what was becoming a fairly monotonous string of jobs, he'd jumped into the investigation with what, in hindsight, could be described as rather foolhardy zeal.

'A journo is a journo, as far as I'm concerned,' Hancock persisted.

'Oh, I think Ben will toe the line,' Truman interjected confidently. 'After all, he wouldn't want to do anything that might jeopardise Mikey's career.'

Ben frowned at the trainer. 'I'm sure you didn't *intend* that to sound like a threat,' he remarked softly.

'Of course he didn't,' Ford cut in. 'Look, let me propose a deal. For better or worse, Ben already has part of the picture, so I suggest we fill him in on what we know so far. Ben will undertake not to breathe a word of it to any outside party, in return for which we grant him exclusive rights to the story, as and when it's safe to print it. What do you say?' He looked hopefully from Ben to Truman.

Ben nodded, keeping his eagerness hidden. 'That seems fair.'

'Truman?'

'Well, if you say he's to be trusted, I'll go along with that. But if the whole story is splashed over the morning papers tomorrow, I'll hold you personally accountable,' Truman promised, the expression on his heavy featured face giving weight to the warning.

Ford was not noticeably intimidated. 'Good. Now, gentlemen, given that we've established that we're all on the same side, can we shelve the attitude and move on? Ben, you know that this afternoon, at approximately five-fifteen, the horse-box bringing four of Mr Truman's horses back from Sandown racecourse was hijacked, near Guildford, by three men, driven to an out of the way location, and one horse, er . . .' he consulted his pocketbook. 'Cajun King, was then removed while the others were set free.'

Ben nodded.

'It would seem to have been a well-planned and executed operation,' Ford continued. 'Mr Rice says they came through Guildford and over the Hogs

510

Back to avoid the M25, but the hijackers obviously knew which route the horsebox would be taking and had posted a lookout to call ahead to the men who were waiting to pull the vehicle over.'

'Mikey says they posed as immigration officials,' Ben commented.

'Yes, after a manner of speaking. According to the driver they had a white van with an orange flashing light on top, a quantity of cones, fluorescent green jackets, a clipboard and some kind of laminated ID card. All fairly easily sourced. Nothing to challenge the ingenuity of anyone with reasonable intelligence. Rice is kicking himself for being so easily taken in, but the fact is that almost anyone would have been. People see what they expect to see, to a great extent. If you set the scene well enough, people will fill in the gaps for you, it's been proven time and time again. He's not to blame.'

'Mikey says the men had some kind of accent but he couldn't say which.'

'That's interesting. Rice only heard one of them speak but he remembers the man as being quite well spoken. He describes him as of average height with a moustache and glasses, and a rather sallow complexion.'

'So, what did he say?' Ben asked.

'Not a great deal.' Ford consulted his notes again. 'Asked him to turn the engine off; said he was an immigration officer and wanted to know what they were carrying, and all their names. Then, before Rice had even finished talking, the hijackers jumped them.'

'Mikey said they had guns.'

511

'Yes, they did,' Ford said grimly. 'Of course, we can't be sure that they'd have used them, but we have to assume they would. It makes the whole business extremely serious.'

'Lucky that Mikey wasn't found,' Ben commented. 'Or rather, that they didn't look for anyone else. He wouldn't have been hard to find if they'd bothered to look. Presumably Rice didn't tell them he was there.'

'No. He said, in the heat of the moment, he completely forgot the lad was there, which was lucky, because then Mikey was able to set them free when the hijackers had gone.'

'So, are you treating it as kidnap?'

'Well, there's been no ransom demand, as yet, but it seems most likely. There's not a lot you can do with a stolen racehorse, and especially not one who's as well known as Cajun King. You certainly can't race it.'

'And I suppose he's gelded – being a steeple-chaser?'

'Yes, and microchipped,' Truman interposed. 'Easily identifiable if we *do* find him. I just wish – if they do want money – that they'd get on with it.'

'They'll leave you to stew for a bit,' Hancock told him. 'Softens you up. Makes you more ready to part with your money.'

'Is the horse actually yours?'

The trainer nodded.

'So . . . will you pay, if that's what this is all about?' Ben asked.

'Oh, yes. DI Ford says we more or less have to, and I agree. I want that horse back where he belongs as soon as possible. Cheltenham's only three weeks away, and every hour he spends away from here screws his chances even more.'

'Paying's the only real option,' Ford explained to Ben. 'We can stall for time and try to set up a dialogue, because of course the more contact we have with them, the greater the chance that they'll give something away. But realistically, the best chance we have of catching them is at the handover. That's potentially the weak point in any kidnapper's plan.'

'But if they do manage the pick-up, what then?'

Ford shrugged. 'We have to hope that they keep their word. A horse can't give us any information about where he's been – except forensically, I suppose. And, after all, setting him free somewhere has got to be a whole lot easier than digging.'

Truman groaned. 'It never occurred to me that there'd be any security risk with King. One of the colts, maybe. I mean, two years ago when Pod Pea won the Guineas, I was quite paranoid about security. That horse was worth millions in potential stud fees, but King? Sure he's worth a few grand, and quite a few more if he does win the Gold Cup, but nothing in comparison with a dozen or so others I've got here.'

'But Mikey says it would be your first Cheltenham Gold Cup,' Ben pointed out. 'It's the prestige at stake here. It comes down to how much you're willing to pay for the chance of running the favourite in one of the biggest steeplechases in the world.'

'Damn them to hell!' Truman slammed his fist on the desktop and stood up, pushing his chair back so violently that it rocked and nearly fell over. He stepped round it and went to the window, pulling the edge of the curtain aside so he could look out into the darkness. 'I've worked so damn hard to get that horse fit for the race, and now he's spot on. Or was. God knows what state he'll be in when we get him back.'

'*If* you get him back.' Hancock voiced the fear that was in each of their minds. 'The precedent isn't good. Think of Shergar.'

'I don't want to think of bloody Shergar!' Truman responded, with what Ben thought an entirely pardonable flash of temper.

'Hancock. Can you go and get an update from forensics?' Ford asked quietly. 'They're working on the lorry and the note,' he told Ben as his colleague left the room. 'We're not expecting fingerprints, because Rice told us the one he spoke to was wearing plastic gloves, but there may be something else – a hair, perhaps, or clothing fibres. It's unfortunate that the cab has been occupied by upwards of two dozen different people in the last fortnight alone, but all we can do is look for something unusual, something that doesn't fit.'

'What about the hijack site? Nothing there, I suppose.'

'It's a popular overnight stop. Rice says it was empty when he drove up – the bogus checkpoint saw to that – but by the time we got someone there the burger van had arrived and half a dozen lorries and commercial travellers had gathered. It was hopeless.'

'Weren't they taking a bit of a chance? I mean, what if one of your lot had driven by?'

Ford shook his head. 'They'd probably just have

514

raised a hand. We don't get involved unless we're asked to.'

Ben digested this. 'And the note?'

'The usual format: "We will contact you. Do not call the police or you will never see your horse alive again." '

'Damn them!' Truman said again. 'If this is those bloody animal liberation people, I'll see every one of them strung up!'

'I'll pretend I didn't hear that,' the DI stated quietly.

'Is there any reason to think it is animal lib?' Ben enquired.

'Mr Truman has been having a bit of trouble from a local splinter group, calling themselves ALSA, which, I'm reliably informed, stands for Action for the Liberation of Sport Animals. They're a fairly small group but well organised. They spend their time protesting about racehorses, greyhounds, animals in circuses, dog shows – you name it. If they had their way, all animals would be returned to the wild. They make a lot of noise but so far that's pretty much all they have done. I have my doubts as to whether they would take on something like this.'

'They stole those greyhounds a couple of months ago.' Truman was pacing the room now.

'Yes, but that was a publicity stunt. They handed them in to the RSPCA two days later. There were no threats.'

'They've sent *me* threatening letters,' the trainer persisted. 'I lost a horse in the King George on Boxing Day and had a flood of abusive letters. They sent a load more to the owner. It was the last straw for him; said he'd had enough, sold his other horse and quit racing altogether. They wrote to all the papers, even organised a petition. They can't seem to understand that losing a horse upsets us just as much as it does them – more, really, because they're personal friends to us. Some of the lads are depressed for days, for God's sake. It's not just about the money.'

'Didn't you lose another one a week or two ago?' Ben remembered. 'Mikey said something about it.'

'Yeah, on the gallops. Stress fracture. Just suddenly went, mid-stride. Promising two-year-old, too. Bloody tragedy.'

Taken at face value the words were almost casual, and Ben could see how the man's attitude could be misconstrued by someone on the watch for evidence of brutality.

'I suppose they picked up on that too?'

'Oh yes. They don't miss a bloody thing. And Sod's Law made it happen on the gallops nearest the road. I think they're up there most days; they seem to be on a personal crusade against me at the moment. Thing is, even if you could chase them away, you can't tell them from the bloody journalists.'

'It's a public highway,' Ford reminded him.

'Yeah. Don't I bloody know it? If it wasn't such a perfect slope I'd shift the gallops somewhere else. It doesn't seem right that you lot can't do something about them.'

'Well, in future we should be able to do a bit more. New proposals are being put forward to deal with animal rights activists but I can't promise the problem will go away entirely. It's still got to be policed, and staffing numbers aren't – as you well know – as high as they might be.'

'Bloody ridiculous, if you ask me! Don't know what we pay our taxes for.'

There was a tentative knock at the door; at Truman's terse invitation it opened and Bess came in. She was carrying a tray holding a kettle, teabags, a jar of instant coffee, sugar, milk, mugs and spoons, and – especially welcome from Ben's point of view – a large packet of digestive biscuits. Aside from a bag of crisps bought at a petrol station, he hadn't eaten since six o'clock that evening.

'Thought you could probably do with a drink but I wasn't sure how many were in here, so I brought the makings,' she announced, putting the tray down on the end of Truman's desk. 'Any news?'

Truman shook his head, coming to sit down. 'Not yet.'

Bess started to dispense coffee and tea, according to preference. Ben eyed her thoughtfully before saying to Truman, 'You've got, what, forty-odd staff? How do you propose to keep this thing a secret, with countless journalists eager for any snippet of news about the horses?'

'I don't suppose we shall be able to in the long run, but for now we're going to tell the lads that King's picked up a slight muscle strain and has been sent straight from the racecourse to have some intensive physio. If Mikey and Davy Jackson can hold their tongues for a few days we might just carry it off.'

'Mikey's pretty good with secrets,' Ben commented, accepting coffee and biscuits from Bess with a grateful smile. She twinkled back at him in a mildly flirtatious manner, which he knew from previous encounters to be standard issue in her case. It was, however, common knowledge that she was seeing a lot of Rollo Gallagher, Castle Ridge's regular and highly successful jockey.

As if drawn by the lure of a hot drink, Hancock reappeared.

Ford raised his eyebrows hopefully but was rewarded by a shake of the head.

'No. Nothing yet,' he reported. Then to Bess, 'Tea, please love.'

'Where did they take the horsebox to unload the horse?' Ben asked. 'Mikey said it was private land. Do we know who the land belonged to?'

'Yes, it's up for sale at the moment. Disused brickworks just outside Guildford. Big, locked-up factory building with a huge concrete apron where they used to stack the bricks. Tucked away in the woods it is, down a private back road. Not much chance that they were seen, especially on a wet day like today. It seems everything went their way.'

'Except for Mikey being there to let the others go,' Ben suggested.

'Yes, but even so, I should think they were well away by the time Ian Rice telephoned Mr Truman to let him know what had happened.'

'And he immediately phoned you.'

'Yes, but unfortunately by that time the horsebox was on its way home. If we'd known sooner we'd have stipulated that it should remain at the transfer point until CSI could get there. Still, it couldn't be helped. Rice says he couldn't get a signal.'

'They seem to have thought of everything,' Ben observed.

'Mm. As I said, we've located the brickworks but as yet that's yielded no clues, and we found no trace of them *or* the lorry they transferred the horse into; no cigarette butts, no soft ground for tyre tracks; the place looks clean. But if there *is* anything, forensics will find it. It was rather late in the day for roadblocks, but we did cover the major routes for an hour or two. Meantime, we've got people watching ports and airports but, to be honest, without much hope. If that's their game, I should imagine they'll have organised a flight from a private airfield. So there you have it, Mr Copperfield. You know as much as us. Possibly even more, as I haven't had a chance to speak to Mikey myself yet. Talking of which . . .' he drained his coffee mug and slid forward on his seat, preparing to stand up.

'Thought you were going to put a tracer on my phone,' Truman said.

'We are.' He looked at his watch. 'It should be on by now.'

'Oh. I thought . . .'

Ford smiled and shook his head. 'No, there's nothing to see. No gadget with dials and tape spools. It's all arranged through the telephone company. All it takes is the proper authorisation.' Ford got to his feet. 'Come on, Hancock.'

'But I've only just got my tea,' Hancock protested, pausing in the act of taking a biscuit.

'Well, swallow it down or bring it with you. I don't mind which, just as long as you come.' He turned to Ben. 'Here's my number. If you have any further thoughts on any of this, I'd be glad to hear them.' At the door, with a surly Hancock on his heels, he turned again. 'I've taken a chance, trusting you. Please don't let me down.' With a wave of the hand he was gone.

519

In the silence that followed, Ben finished his coffee, studying the card in his hand and wishing all of a sudden that he didn't have to move. The leather chair was comfortable, the room warmed by a top-of-the-range, coal-effect gas fire, and he'd had the sort of day that made the morning seem like a distant memory.

Bess took his empty mug from him, adding it to those already on the tray.

'Anything else I can do for you, Mr Truman?'

'No, Bess; thanks. I should get to bed.' Truman had been sat at his desk, chin on hands, staring into space, but as the door closed behind his secretary, he straightened and looked directly at Ben.

'DI Ford seems pretty impressed with you,' he stated. 'Is he right to be, I wonder?'

It wasn't really a question to which he could give an answer, even if Truman expected one, and Ben wasn't sure he did.

'I wonder,' the trainer repeated, almost to himself, 'Just how straight *are* you, Ben Copperfield?'